THE HIDDEN GROVE

THE HIDDEN GROVE

BROOKWOOD MYSTERIES
BOOK 5

JORDAN JACE

DEDICATION

To Alice—my partner in love, words, and wonder.

Thank you for believing in every story, and for sharing this beautiful journey of writing together.

CONTENTS

FOREWORD

The Brookwood Mysteries have always been more than tales of secrets and shadows—they are stories of legacy, love, and the ways the past whispers into the present. Now, in the breathtaking conclusion to this bestselling series, readers are invited back to Brookwood for its most haunting and luminous chapter yet.

After seasons of unraveling hidden vows and unspoken histories, Marley Taylor and Damien Hawthorne stand at the threshold of a new beginning. Their engagement promises joy, yet the town's most mysterious inheritance demands their attention: the grove above Brookwood, a place of moss-covered stones, forgotten rituals, and a spiral path that seems to breathe with memory itself.

It begins with discovery—a ring of stones revealed after a late frost, a bloom that no botanist can identify, a wax-sealed box with maps drawn in cipher and initials tied to healers long erased. Each clue leads Marley and Damien deeper into the story of a secret society—the Order of the Grove—whose rituals once bound the community in balance. Yet the ledger of its members reveals not only devotion, but betrayal.

Visions overtake Marley: dreams of women robed in green, flames rising in the clearing, a sacred seed stolen under a blood moon. Her waking hours carry their marks—soot on her palms, soil beneath her nails—as if the veil between past and present has thinned beyond repair. Damien, torn between honoring his late wife's unfinished notes and building a new legacy with Marley, must decide whether love can carry more than one inheritance. Together, they confront the possibility that Brookwood's grove is not merely history to be studied, but a living archive demanding restoration.

The circle begins to reform. Seven women step forward, each bearing a gift—herb, stone, silence, light—each risking not only tradition but themselves. Candles flicker in the night, compasses spin wildly, and the grove itself begins to respond. Yet with Claire, a young botanist with a contested legacy, pressing ever closer to claim what her grandmother once betrayed, Marley must determine whether healing is possible without trust—and whether redemption can root itself in tainted soil.

At the heart of this sweeping final volume lies a question that resonates far beyond Brookwood: what does it mean to inherit mystery not as secrecy, but as promise? As unseasonal blooms flood the grove, as a spring opens where none has flowed for generations, as children press seeds into soil with whispered vows, Marley learns the answer. Legacy is not possession. Legacy is circle.

Rich with lyrical atmosphere, gothic tension, and profound romantic depth, The Hidden Grove brings together every thread of the Brookwood Mysteries—The Bookshop Secret, The Bridge of Echoes, The Lighthouse

Prophecy, and The Winter Bell—into a finale that will leave readers breathless, weeping, and inspired. It is a story of broken vows and restored circles, of flame and seed, of love rooted so deeply that it can carry both the living and the dead.

Step into the spiral. Listen to the trees. The grove is waiting. And once you hear its call, you will never leave Brookwood the same.

PROLOGUE

The last snows had melted into the thirsty earth, leaving Brookwood's streets slick with rain and the sharp smell of moss rising from stone walls. Spring did not announce itself with trumpets here—it seeped in quietly, as though testing whether the town was ready to bear renewal. Marley Taylor stood at the threshold of her bookshop, inhaling the scent of wet soil and lilacs. She should have felt only relief that the long, haunted winter had passed, but a pulse beneath her feet told her the story was far from finished.

She had carried that pulse with her ever since the bell had tolled twice. The sound had been both promise and warning, echoing through her bones like a vow inherited, not chosen. Some nights she still woke, sure she heard it again, though no bell stirred in the tower. It was Damien who steadied her in those moments, pressing his hand to hers, whispering, *We already carry it together.* And she believed him. Yet belief did not dissolve the weight of a mystery still rooted in the town's soil.

On this morning, Damien came to her side with a map

tucked beneath his arm. The parchment, brittle and smudged with ink that had nearly faded into time, bore a symbol she had not been able to forget: two entwined branches forming a circle. He had found it weeks earlier in the archives, but its meaning had eluded them—until their walk beyond the mills, where the river bent and the ground sank into shadow. There, brambles had parted just enough to reveal a ring of stones, weathered and half-swallowed by earth. A grove. A circle. A place once known, now hidden.

Marley brushed her fingers across the edge of the map. "It doesn't feel abandoned," she murmured. "It feels like it's been waiting."

Damien's eyes, weary from years of study and loss, searched hers. "Waiting, yes. But for what—or for whom?"

They set out toward the bend, boots soft in mud, the air thick with birdsong. The farther they walked from the town's square, the more Marley felt the rhythm beneath her skin—like a heartbeat not her own, steady, insistent. The river grew louder until it drowned conversation, a rushing hymn that seemed to guard the path ahead. When they reached the clearing, the grove appeared exactly as before: a faint circle marked by stones, brambles choking its edges, tree roots twisting like knotted veins around its perimeter. But in the pale light, Marley saw something more. The stones shimmered faintly with moss that glowed emerald, brighter than nature alone could account for.

She stepped between them, breath catching as the air shifted. The damp heaviness of spring vanished; instead, she felt a cool stillness, as if the grove itself exhaled around her. Damien watched carefully, his scholar's gaze sharp with both fascination and caution.

"Do you feel that?" she asked, her voice low.

"I do," he admitted. "As though the earth remembers us."

Marley crouched, pressing her hand against the soil. It pulsed faintly, not with warmth but with resonance, like the final reverberation of a struck bell. She thought of Amelia, of the vow passed forward, and wondered whether this grove had been part of that inheritance all along.

Damien unfolded the map, laying it across a fallen log. "The founders marked this place, but they left it unnamed. Only the emblem remains. And in Aurelia Ward's letters, I found a phrase—'the breathing cathedral.' I dismissed it once as poetic metaphor. Now..." He gestured around them. "Now I'm not so sure."

Marley traced the spiral inked faintly across the map's center. "If this is a cathedral, then it's alive. Not stone, not mortar—roots, branches, soil."

Her words settled between them, and silence returned—until a sudden rustling drew Marley's gaze to the edge of the clearing. A deer stood there, slender and trembling, its coat patchy from winter. Its eyes locked on hers with uncanny steadiness, unblinking. Then, with a startled leap, it vanished into the brush, leaving only the echo of its presence.

Marley's pulse raced. "It was watching us."

Damien folded the map, lips pressed thin. "Or guarding."

They left reluctantly, the air heavy with questions that felt too large for words. Back in the square, life carried on as though no hidden grove waited beyond the mills. Children skipped across puddles, the baker pulled steaming loaves from his oven, and neighbors traded gossip over market stalls. To them, winter's silence had broken; the season of fear was over. Marley almost envied them, the ease with which they returned to ordinary life. But she and Damien had crossed a threshold that could not be uncrossed. They had seen the stones, felt the pulse. And deep down, Marley knew: the town's harmony rested on soil not yet fully turned.

That night, she lit a single candle in the bookshop window, letting its glow spill across the darkened street. The Book of Wishes rested beneath it, pages heavy with the townsfolk's hopes, their handwriting mingled like roots in shared ground. Marley opened it to the page she had written after finding the grove: *May what is buried rise again in peace, not conflict. May we have the courage to keep what was once kept, and the wisdom to let it root where it belongs.* The words steadied her, but they also carried weight. To write them was one thing; to live them would demand more than she yet understood.

Damien entered quietly, shrugging off his coat. "You're still awake."

"I couldn't sleep," Marley confessed. She gestured to the book. "It feels like the wishes are listening. Like they're waiting for us to answer."

He came to stand beside her, gaze moving from the book to the candle's flame. "Then we'll answer," he said softly. "Together."

But when he took her hand, Marley noticed the tremor in his grip, the shadow of hesitation he tried to hide. Love bound them, yes—but the grove had asked for something beyond love. A legacy. A charge. A test of whether their roots could hold beneath the weight of buried truth.

Outside, rain began again, tapping against the shop's windows like a whisper. Marley closed the Book of Wishes, snuffed the candle, and leaned into Damien's steadiness. The night carried them into silence, but the grove's memory lingered—alive, patient, waiting.

· · ·

THE RAIN PERSISTED FOR DAYS, washing Brookwood in a kind of restless clarity. Gutters overflowed, the river swelled, and the air carried the metallic tang of storm. Marley spent her mornings in the shop, cataloging new arrivals and repairing the spines of beloved volumes, but her mind strayed again and again to the circle of stones beyond the mills. The memory of its pulse lingered in her hands, as though the soil itself had marked her.

One afternoon, when the clouds finally broke and light fractured through in pale gold, Damien arrived with a leather satchel slung over his shoulder. He laid its contents across the counter: his late wife's journals, brittle from years of careful handling. Marley had seen them once before, but only in passing. Today, Damien's expression carried a weight that suggested he had read something he could not ignore.

"She wrote of the grove," he said quietly, opening to a page inked in flowing script. "'A place where roots remember more than men, where silence speaks, and the air carries breath older than prayer.' She called it a breathing cathedral."

Marley traced the words, feeling the way they echoed Aurelia Ward's fragments. The connections tightened around them like vines, pulling them toward something larger than either of their individual legacies.

"What did she mean by silence that speaks?" Marley asked.

Damien hesitated. "I think she meant the kind of silence that isn't empty. The kind that holds memory. Like the bell before it tolled."

Marley shivered. "Or like the grove before it's found."

They closed the journals together, but neither could close the unease they stirred.

That evening, they returned to the river bend, this time carrying lanterns and a notebook to sketch the layout of the stones. Twilight cast long shadows across the clearing, and the circle seemed to breathe with an awareness that unnerved even Damien, who rarely admitted to superstition. They paced the perimeter, counting seven stones clearly shaped and positioned, while fragments of others jutted half-buried, suggesting the circle had once been complete.

Marley stepped into the center, her boots sinking slightly into softened soil. She closed her eyes. At first there was nothing but the drone of insects, the distant rush of the river, the faint swaying of branches. But then, like a low hum beneath it all, she felt rhythm. Not sound exactly, not touch either—something in between. A steady cadence rising through her soles and into her chest.

When she opened her eyes, Damien stood at the edge, studying her with both fascination and fear. "You felt it, didn't you?"

She nodded, breath unsteady. "It's alive. Not just memory—present. Waiting."

They marked the stones on their sketch, noting cracks etched in odd angles and moss patterns that seemed almost deliberate, curling in spirals rather than spreading randomly. Damien's historian's mind sought rational explanation, but each detail tugged at something irrational within him. His late wife's words echoed in his thoughts: *a breathing cathedral.*

Before leaving, Marley knelt to press her palm against the center again. This time, when she rose, her skin bore faint smudges, not of dirt but of ash-like soot. She rubbed at them, unsettled, but they clung stubbornly until the lanternlight itself seemed to burn them away.

That night, sleep eluded her. When it came at last, it carried dream. She saw women in green robes, seven of them, standing in the same grove, holding branches tipped with flame. They sang—not in words she knew, but in a cadence that made the air ripple. As the fire spread around them, the robes did not burn; instead, the flames rooted into the soil, leaving glowing veins across the ground. The circle pulsed, then dimmed, then pulsed again, as though keeping breath with the women themselves.

Marley awoke in the small hours, her palms tingling with phantom heat. The air in her room smelled faintly of pine smoke, though the hearth was cold.

She sat upright, the dream still pressing against her chest, and found Damien already awake at her desk, scribbling in his notebook. He had sensed her stirring. "Tell me," he said simply.

So she did—every detail, every flame, every note of song. He listened intently, then cross-referenced her vision with fragments of Aurelia Ward's journal he had copied. "The Circle of Seven," he whispered. "It wasn't just symbolic. It was real."

"Then this grove..."

"...was their sanctuary," he finished.

Morning brought no comfort, only confirmation. When Marley descended into the shop, she found a small parcel waiting at the doorstep, unmarked and unsent by any known hand. Inside lay a wooden box, its surface carved with spirals and leaf motifs. Within, pressed herbs and petals, a small brass compass, and a folded map—one nearly identical to Damien's but annotated with moon cycles and initials she half recognized.

Marley's breath caught. The initials read: A.W., M.C., H.G.

"Aurelia Ward," Damien said at once. "And the others—Mirabel Colvin, maybe? Hannah Gearhart?"

Names from history, tied to families still rooted in Brookwood.

The map outlined not just the grove but a spiral path leading inward, as though the stones themselves were only the perimeter of something deeper. At the center, the shape of a seven-petal flower was drawn, its ink faint but purposeful. Beside it, a phrase: *Only in circle shall the breath of balance return.*

Marley traced the words, her throat dry. "It's a restoration guide."

Damien looked at her, jaw set. "Or a warning."

They stored the box carefully in the bookshop's back room, but its presence seemed to radiate, humming faintly like the bell had before it tolled. Marley found herself drawn to it often, lifting the compass, watching as its needle spun erratically whenever she faced the direction of the grove.

By evening, townsfolk began to murmur. A local historian, grey-haired and soft-spoken, stopped Marley outside the café. "If you plan to stay rooted here, child," he said, lowering his voice, "you'll need the grove's blessing. Brookwood doesn't belong fully to any who ignore its roots."

She carried his words with her long after, feeling them echo from weeks earlier: *The vow is not kept by one ringing, child. It is kept in every season, in every root that grows and every stone that is turned.*

The cycle pressed forward, both in her dreams and in the waking soil. What had been hidden was stirring, and Marley and Damien had stepped directly into its charge.

. . .

THE DAYS that followed brought a restlessness Marley could not shake. The Book of Wishes, once a comfort, now felt like a mirror—every inscription from the townsfolk whispered back at her, reflecting both their hopes and their fears. She traced their handwriting at night, sensing that even the simplest wishes—health for a child, rain for the fields, reconciliation between old friends—were all threads tied to deeper roots. The grove had become the silent loom where those threads would either weave harmony or unravel entirely.

One evening, as twilight blurred into night, she and Damien returned once more to the circle. Lanterns in hand, they crossed the muddy slope and entered the grove's hush. Tonight the air felt different—charged, almost metallic, as though a storm brewed beneath the soil rather than in the clouds above. The compass spun in Marley's palm, whirring until it stopped abruptly, needle pointing toward the circle's center.

She followed its pull, kneeling beside a stone half-swallowed by earth. Scraping back moss, she found a shallow carving: a spiral etched so finely it could only have been placed with intention. Damien crouched beside her, brushing the dirt away to reveal more markings—sigils, faint and weathered but distinct.

"They're directional," he said, voice low. "Markers guiding inward."

Marley ran her fingertips over the spiral, feeling its grooves as if they carried memory. "Toward the flower," she whispered. "The one on the map."

The lanternlight flickered, shadows lengthening across the clearing. Suddenly, a rustle broke from the thicket. A deer stumbled into the circle—the same one, Marley thought, though thinner now, its coat ragged. Its eyes glistened strangely, reflecting more than light. It staggered, antlers tangled with leaves, and collapsed at the circle's edge.

Damien rushed forward, but Marley caught his arm. "Wait."

The animal's chest heaved, then slowed. As its last breath left, the air shifted. Marley swore she heard the faintest tone—a low, bell-like resonance—not from above, but from the ground itself. The stones hummed, barely audible, before settling back into silence.

Damien's face was pale. "It mirrored the spiral."

Marley swallowed hard. "A warning. Or a call."

They buried the deer at the grove's edge, covering it with brambles. When Damien pressed a stone over the mound, he whispered something Marley couldn't quite catch. She didn't ask—his grief was private, tied as much to the grove's awakening as to the memory of his wife.

Back in town, word had already begun to spread. Whispers moved through the café, across the market stalls, down the church steps. Some said Marley had found sacred ground. Others muttered about superstition, about stirring what was better left buried. The town, still healing from the bell's silence and toll, now faced the unease of another mystery.

One night, Councilor Miriam Merrick visited the bookshop. Marley poured her tea, but the elder waved it aside, leaning forward with the weight of urgency.

"You've stepped where most fear to tread," Miriam said. "The grove isn't forgotten. It's waiting. But waiting is not the same as welcoming."

Marley felt her throat tighten. "What do we do?"

"You listen. Not with your ears—those will deceive you. With your roots. The vow you carry was Amelia's, but the grove's vow is older. If you mean to keep it, you must be willing to carry both."

Marley nodded, though the words pressed heavy against her chest. "And if we fail?"

Miriam's eyes glistened with something like sorrow. "Then Brookwood will fail too. For the grove was planted not just in soil, but in soul."

After Miriam left, Marley sat long into the night, the compass turning slowly on the counter beside her. Damien joined her, his notebook filled with sketches of the stones, the spirals, the map. He placed it between them.

"I used to think history was about preserving the past," he said. "Now I wonder if it's about carrying it forward. Choosing which roots to tend and which to prune."

Marley touched his hand. "Maybe it's both. Maybe it's about trust—that the roots know more than we do."

They were silent, the air heavy with what lay ahead. Outside, rain softened against the windows, carrying the scent of earth into the shop.

The following week, the café hosted an informal gathering to celebrate their engagement. Friends and neighbors filled the space with warmth, laughter, and clinking teacups. Yet beneath the smiles, Marley felt the tension—the watchful glances, the whispered questions about the grove.

At one point, a local historian leaned close, his voice just for her. "The blessing matters," he murmured. "Without it, the town will never root you here."

As if to seal the words, an elder pressed a small gift into Marley's hand: an old brass compass, heavier than the one from the box, its glass cracked but intact. "Used by the ones who planted healing into soil," she explained.

Marley accepted it with reverence. Two compasses now —one erratic, one steady. A choice, or a balance, she could not yet tell.

Later that evening, when the crowd had thinned, Damien slipped outside with her. They walked beneath the lamplight, the night cool and damp. He took her hand, pressing it against his chest.

"Marley," he said softly, "this town has tested us from the moment you arrived. But I don't think the grove is testing us separately. It's testing us together. Whether we're strong enough to carry both legacies—yours and mine, Amelia's and Aurelia's, Brookwood's and the Circle's."

She leaned into him, her heart both heavy and fierce. "Then we'll carry them. Not because they're easy, but because they're ours now."

The compass in her pocket turned faintly, as though agreeing.

When they reached the edge of the square, Marley paused, looking toward the mills and the river bend beyond. Somewhere in the darkness, the grove waited, roots deep, stones silent, soil remembering. She felt its pull in her very bones—not threatening, not welcoming, but insistent.

"We're keepers now," she whispered.

Damien's hand tightened around hers. "Then let us keep well."

And together they walked on, their steps carrying them not just toward home, but toward the hidden grove that would soon test what it meant to belong—not just to each other, but to Brookwood itself.

1

THE GROVE AWAKENS

The frost had come late that year, a final sweep of winter unwilling to release its grip on Brookwood. For three nights, the hillsides shone with silver, each blade of grass rimed in white, each rooftop glittering as though dusted with crushed glass. The townsfolk grumbled at the delay of spring, muttering about lost planting days and stubborn skies. Yet for Marley Taylor, the frost carried something else—an omen, a hesitation in the season's breath, as though the earth itself were pausing before it spoke again.

On the morning the frost lifted, Marley woke to a light that felt sharper than usual. The bookshop window shone with clarity, and the air carried the damp richness of thaw. She pulled on her boots and coat, restless, and walked beyond the square, past the mills where the river bent, and up the slope that overlooked Brookwood. It was the same hillside she and Damien had walked before, when they'd first stumbled across the circle of stones. Yet today something new pressed against her awareness, urging her onward.

The bramble that had once choked the slope seemed to have retreated overnight. The frost had stripped away its brittle thorns, leaving the ground bare enough for her to see the faint impression of a circle etched into the hillside. Stones, moss-covered and hunched, jutted from the earth in a ring. Some leaned, as though weary from centuries of keeping their place; others stood more upright, their surfaces carved with the patient green of lichen. She stopped at the edge of the ring, her breath misting in the cool air.

The sight unsettled her. She had expected the circle to remain hidden, stubborn as secrets often are. Instead, the frost had unveiled it, as though nature itself had chosen to reveal what had been waiting. Marley felt her chest tighten. It was not simply the discovery of old stones—it was the sensation that she had been expected, that the ground had been holding its breath for her arrival.

She stepped forward, boots crunching softly against thawing soil. As she crossed the ring's boundary, a sudden shift coursed through her. It was not wind, not sound, not touch exactly. It was a pulse—subtle, insistent, rising through the soles of her feet into her calves, her chest, her throat. She froze, hand instinctively clutching the fabric of her coat. It was as though the earth itself had exhaled beneath her, and she was standing in the center of its breath.

The feeling unsettled and steadied her all at once. She crouched, brushing moss from one of the stones, revealing the faint spiral of growth patterns etched in lichen. A memory stirred in her mind—of her dreams, of the women in green robes singing as flame rooted into soil, of her palms marked with soot when she awoke. She pressed her hand to the stone and whispered without thinking, "What do you remember?"

Behind her, the crunch of footsteps. Damien approached, his scarf loose around his neck, his satchel heavy with books and notes. He had risen early too, unable to ignore the restless air. He stopped at the circle's edge, brow furrowing as he studied the stones.

"So it's true," he murmured. "The frost uncovered it."

Marley turned to him, her expression taut. "It feels alive."

He hesitated before stepping forward, as though crossing the threshold were more than a simple act. When his boots touched the soil inside the ring, he let out a breath that trembled slightly. "Yes," he admitted. "I feel it too."

They walked the perimeter together, counting each stone, noting gaps where others might have once stood. Damien crouched to examine the moss, tracing his fingers across grooves worn deep into the surfaces. He pulled a sketch from his satchel, one of his late wife's unfinished drawings. It was faint, lines trailing off as though she had been interrupted mid-thought. Yet the image was clear enough: a spiral path leading inward, ending in a circle marked by a flower with seven petals.

Marley's heart jolted. "She drew this?"

He nodded slowly, his eyes clouded. "Years ago. She was working on a restoration project. At the time, I thought it was simply artistic fancy. But look—" He gestured to the stones around them, then back to the sketch. "The spiral. The circle. It's almost identical."

Marley held the paper carefully, her fingers brushing the faded lines. She could feel the weight in Damien's voice, the grief threaded into memory. His late wife, Jackie, had carried this image before them, and now it had been passed forward, unfinished, waiting for their steps. Marley touched his arm gently. "It wasn't just fancy. She saw it. The same way we do now."

Damien's jaw tightened. He stared at the stones for a long time before speaking again. "Then perhaps Jackie knew more than she ever told me."

Silence stretched between them, filled by the steady hum of the earth beneath their feet. Marley moved to the center of the circle, the compass from the carved box tucked into her pocket. She pulled it free, watching as the needle spun wildly before stilling at last, pointing not north but toward the stone where Damien's sketch had aligned. She swallowed hard. "It's responding. As if it knows."

Damien's eyes sharpened. "Compasses don't do that. Unless..." His voice trailed off, the logic of science colliding with the weight of legacy. He closed his satchel with deliberate care. "Unless we're dealing with something more than stone."

Marley felt her pulse quicken, the hum in her chest growing louder. She remembered Councilor Miriam's words, the historian's warning, the inscription on the map: *Only in circle shall the breath of balance return.* She pressed the compass to her palm until it left a mark on her skin, as though anchoring her. "Then it's not just history," she whispered. "It's alive. And it's waiting."

Damien's gaze met hers, steady and conflicted. "Alive, yes. But for what?"

Marley glanced around the stones, the air thick with possibility. She thought of the deer that had collapsed in the circle, the bell's toll, the vow carried forward. She thought of the town's fragile harmony, its roots both tangled and deep. And though she did not have the answer, she felt the truth settle into her bones: whatever the grove was, it had chosen not to stay hidden. It had awakened. And in its awakening, it had chosen them.

THE LIGHT SHIFTED as the morning sun angled higher, spilling across the stones like liquid gold. The frost that had bared the circle was nearly gone now, seeping into soil that exhaled a damp, mineral scent. Marley stood in the center, the compass warm in her palm, her heart thrumming in rhythm with the hum she felt rising through her boots. The longer she stayed within the ring, the more the sensation grew—not violent, not overwhelming, but steady. Like the way a body recognizes another heartbeat in close embrace.

She closed her eyes, letting the sound of the river blur into background. What remained was a cadence beneath her, a pulse that seemed older than language. It was not asking her to decipher it; it was asking her to listen.

Breath, she thought suddenly. *The earth is breathing.*

Her chest rose unconsciously in time with it, until she found herself exhaling with the rhythm, as though her body had always known this forgotten song. The sensation carried memory she couldn't place—hands planting seeds in circles, voices rising against fire, roots gripping soil to steady what might otherwise have been lost. The air thickened with the sense of presence, though she stood alone within the stones.

Damien cleared his throat behind her. The sound was sharp, human, and it cut through her trance. She opened her eyes. He was watching her, his arms crossed, the sketch of his late wife still clutched in one hand. His expression was torn—half awe, half unease.

"You look as though the ground itself is speaking to you," he said carefully.

Marley steadied her breath. "It is." She gestured toward him. "Step here. In the center."

He hesitated, but her insistence carried weight. He crossed the soil slowly, each step deliberate, as if afraid the ground might collapse beneath him. When he reached her side, he stilled. For a long moment, his face betrayed nothing. Then his shoulders slumped slightly, his eyes softening.

"I feel it," he admitted. "Faint, but there. Like...like when you stand near a church organ and sense the vibration more than you hear it."

Marley nodded. "Exactly that. It's not sound, but presence."

He looked down at the sketch, tracing the spiral path with his thumb. "She saw this. She must have. I remember her sketching late at night, candle burning low. She said she was trying to remember a pattern she'd once walked in a dream. A spiral path, a circle of seven." His voice caught, and he swallowed hard. "I thought it was just grief drawing itself out. She'd lost her sister that year. I thought she was looking for order in chaos."

Marley touched his arm gently. "Maybe she was looking for truth. Maybe she found part of it."

His jaw tightened. "And left the rest to me." He folded the sketch as though its lines were fragile bones that might break. "But I don't know if I can carry both her memory and this place's legacy. It feels...disloyal. As though one love eclipses the other."

Marley's heart ached. She had known Damien's late wife only through stories, but her presence lingered in subtle ways—the journals, the sketches, the pauses in Damien's voice. Marley stepped closer, her hand resting lightly against his chest. "Love doesn't erase, Damien. It expands. Roots don't strangle each other; they grow together, shaping the soil. Maybe her memory isn't a burden—it's part of the grove itself. Part of what we're meant to continue."

His eyes glistened briefly before he blinked the moisture away. "I want to believe that."

"Then let's try," she whispered.

A sudden breeze shivered through the trees, rustling branches like whispered approval. The compass needle in Marley's palm jerked once, then spun and stilled again, pointing toward the eastern edge of the ring. She glanced at Damien. "It's pulling again."

They followed its direction, brushing through damp undergrowth until they found a stone nearly swallowed by earth. Its surface bore shallow grooves—sigils unlike anything Marley recognized. Damien knelt, tracing them with reverent fingers.

"These aren't decorative," he murmured. "They're markers. Directional symbols. She drew something similar in her notes—arrows that curved rather than pointed, as though guiding a path rather than leading to an end."

Marley crouched beside him, brushing moss away. "The spiral."

"Yes." He looked up at her, conviction brightening his features. "This grove wasn't meant to be seen all at once. It's meant to be walked, step by step, in a pattern that draws you inward. A path of remembering."

The words settled deep inside Marley. *A path of remembering.* That was what she had felt: not discovery, but memory stirring. She pressed her palm against the sigils, and once again the hum rose faintly, a rhythm that answered the pressure of her touch. Her skin tingled as if the stone itself had recognized her.

When she withdrew her hand, faint ash-like dust clung

to her palm. She stared at it, unease prickling her spine. "It's the same as before. Soot."

Damien frowned. "But there's no fire."

"Not here," Marley said softly. "But maybe once."

They remained crouched in silence, the grove holding its breath around them. Finally, Damien stood, folding the sketch carefully and slipping it into his satchel. "If this is truly what she began, then I have to choose whether to finish it. Or whether to let it rest with her."

Marley rose too, brushing soil from her coat. She looked at him steadily. "What do you feel when you stand here, Damien? Not what you fear. What you feel."

He closed his eyes, inhaling deeply. When he spoke, his voice was low, almost reverent. "I feel her. Not as memory, but as presence. And I feel you. Both woven into the same soil."

Marley reached for his hand, threading her fingers through his. "Then maybe the choice isn't between her and me. Maybe it's between silence and voice. Between letting the grove stay buried and letting it awaken."

He held her gaze, the struggle in his features softening into quiet acceptance. "Then I choose voice."

The moment carried them into stillness, the air around them tinged with something like promise. Marley exhaled, feeling the pulse beneath her feet steady, as though acknowledging his words. The grove did not demand resolution—it demanded honesty. And in Damien's confession, some balance had shifted.

They left the grove reluctantly, the compass needle still trembling faintly in Marley's pocket. As they descended the hillside, the town spread before them—Brookwood's rooftops glistening from melted frost, the square bustling with morning life. Ordinary, unknowing. Yet Marley felt the line between ordinary and extraordinary had thinned to a thread. The grove's pulse followed her down the slope, a reminder that the earth's breath was no longer hidden. It was awake. And it was waiting.

THAT NIGHT, the frost returned. It crept silently over Brookwood, sheathing branches in silver, hardening the river's edge, drawing breath into clouds that curled above chimneys. Marley woke before dawn, a chill heavy in the room though the fire still glowed faintly in the hearth. She felt it instantly—not simply cold, but the same pulse she had carried since stepping into the circle. Only stronger. Insistent. As if the earth itself had chosen the night to speak.

She dressed quickly, wrapping her shawl tight, and found Damien already waiting by the door. He carried a lantern in one hand, the sketch in his coat pocket, his expression tense with recognition.

"You feel it too," he said.

Marley nodded. "It won't let me sleep."

Together, they climbed the hillside again, boots crunching through frost so crisp it echoed like broken glass. The moon still lingered, pale against the dim horizon, casting the grove in spectral light. When they reached the ring of stones, Marley felt her breath catch. The frost had not merely dusted them; it had traced each stone with perfect spirals, etched as though by unseen hands. The marks glowed faintly, crystalline veins threading across moss and lichen.

Damien knelt, his breath fogging. "This isn't natural," he whispered. "It's the same spiral she drew."

Marley stepped into the ring, the compass warm in her pocket. The pulse surged instantly, stronger than before, rising in waves that made her skin prickle. She pressed her hands to her chest, steadying her breath, letting it align with the rhythm. The stones shimmered faintly, frost refracting moonlight into threads of silver that wove between them like a net.

"Do you see it?" she asked.

Damien rose slowly, eyes wide. "The frost itself is forming the path."

The compass needle jerked violently, then steadied, pointing toward the center. Marley followed, each step echoing as though the ground carried memory of her tread. At the center, the soil shimmered beneath the thin layer of frost, a seven-petal flower pattern faintly visible—just as the map had shown. Marley crouched, brushing the frost with her glove until the outline became clear.

A wave of energy swept through her, not violent but commanding. It pressed against her chest, demanding acknowledgment. She gasped, tears springing to her eyes from the sheer weight of presence.

Damien was at her side in an instant, gripping her shoulder. "What is it?"

"It's...testing me," she whispered. "No—not me. Us."

As if in answer, the frost crackled. Spirals spread outward from the flower, connecting stone to stone, until the entire circle was bound in luminous threads. The hum grew louder, no longer subtle but resonant, vibrating through the ground beneath them.

Marley stood, her breath visible in rapid bursts. "It's asking if we will keep it. If we're strong enough."

Damien's jaw clenched. His hand found hers, steady despite the tremor in his voice. "Then answer."

Marley closed her eyes, focusing inward. She thought of Amelia's vow, of the bell's toll, of Miriam's warning that roots remember more than men. She thought of Damien's late wife, of sketches left unfinished, of love that had not died but changed form. She thought of her own place in Brookwood—outsider and yet chosen, skeptic and yet believer.

We will keep it, she whispered in her mind. *Not alone, but together. Not as owners, but as keepers.*

The hum deepened, then softened, wrapping around her like a mantle. When she opened her eyes, the frost had dimmed, the spirals fading slowly into soil. Only the flower pattern at the center remained, glowing faintly before it too dissolved.

Damien exhaled, his shoulders sagging with relief. "It accepted you."

"No," Marley corrected softly. "It accepted us."

They stood in silence, the grove breathing around them, the frost melting faster now as dawn began to streak the horizon. Marley felt both drained and renewed, as though part of her had been claimed by the earth while another part had been given back, stronger.

But Damien's expression carried shadows. He held the folded sketch tightly, his knuckles white. "It asked for us both," he murmured. "But I can't stop thinking—what if it would have accepted her? What if she was meant to finish what she began, and I've stolen her place?"

Marley touched his cheek gently, drawing his gaze back to hers. "She began it, Damien. But you're here now. That doesn't erase her. It honors her. Roots don't choose which seed belongs—they hold them all, side by side."

He searched her face for a long moment before nodding, the struggle softening into weary acceptance. "Then this is my vow. To keep it with you. And to let her memory guide us, not haunt us."

Marley pressed her forehead to his, the frost around

them dissolving into steam as the sun rose. "Then we keep it. Together."

The first light of morning broke across the hillside, and the circle of stones returned to quiet. But Marley knew the silence was no longer absence—it was presence, a promise sealed in frost and soil. The grove had awakened. And with it, so had they.

As they descended back toward town, the rooftops gleamed in dawn's light, ordinary life resuming as though nothing extraordinary had stirred. Yet Marley carried the hum in her chest, the compass steady at her side, the memory of frost spirals burned into her sight. Brookwood had not yet seen what had been revealed, but soon it would.

And when it did, she and Damien would be ready—or tested again.

For now, though, as their steps traced the path back home, Marley felt the vow settle in her bones like roots gripping earth: they were keepers, chosen not by chance, but by the breath of the grove itself.

2

———

THE ENGAGEMENT TEA

The café had the kind of light that makes even ordinary mornings look celebratory. Sun threaded through lace curtains, pooling in bright patches on the scrubbed wood floors. From the ceiling, mismatched teacups—chipped and cherished—hung upside down like a whimsical chandelier. Someone had tied twine around sprigs of rosemary and lavender and tucked them along the windowsills, so the air smelled like bread and gardens and something faintly evergreen. It might have felt innocent, uncomplicated, if not for the whisper of frost still clinging to Brookwood's rooftops and the memory of spirals cardiganed in ice.

Marley paused outside with her hand on the café door, feeling the compass in her coat pocket give a soft, inexplicable twitch. She glanced at Damien. His jaw was set, his eyes gentle. In daylight he looked less haunted by the grove and more like the man she had first fallen toward in a town that believed in bells and vows. She exhaled, pressed the door open, and stepped into warmth that was almost loud.

"Look who's late to their own party," called Evelyn from

behind the counter, three aprons layered over her dress like armor. "Forgiven only because you're beautiful, and he looks like he's remembered how to smile."

Laughter rose from the tables—the easy kind, not yet complicated by questions. The town had gathered the way small towns do: without invitation, as if belonging were a right and duty. There were crocks of lemon curd and bowls of sugared berries, platters of shortbread stamped with little seven-petal flowers, a detail that made Marley's chest pull tight. Evelyn had written "Congratulations" in chalk along the floorboards, the letters even and cheerful. Even Mayor Richard Connelly had shown up, tie loosened, balancing a saucer with the careful reverence of a man who knew porcelain could be as temperamental as people.

Damien's hand settled lightly at the small of Marley's back. "We can do this," he said, and the softness in his voice was a gift.

They were immediately claimed. People she had met only once or twice greeted her like a relative. Hands clasped her forearms. Children peeked around skirts and pant legs. Councilor Miriam Merrick, wrapped in her shawl like a queen in winter, sat near the window with a cup of something dark and bitter balanced on her palm, watching the room with an expression that made Marley think of stones keeping counsel.

"Tell us about the ring," Evelyn urged, shoving a tray of scones toward them. "Or is it not a ring? I saw you're not wearing one. Doesn't matter. Love is love, it doesn't need metal to certify it." She pushed her glasses up her nose and added, "But if you want a ring, I know a jeweler in who does magic with old gold."

Damien grinned and toasts began, uncoordinated and overlapping. A mechanic spoke about loyalty. A teacher spoke of books changing a life. The mayor cleared his throat and offered a few lines about the way love anchored towns through hard weather, as if affection were a civil project like paving the west road. Often the speeches wrapped back to the same observation—Marley, the newcomer, somehow feeling like someone who had always been here.

Yet beneath the sweetness ran something taut. Marley heard it in the pauses after jokes. She saw it in the sideways glances and the way conversations drifted like boats away from the same shoal: the grove, the stones, the pulse that had made the air itself feel sentient. Brookwood was a place unembarrassed by mystery, but it remembered how quickly the past could divide the present.

"Raise your cup," Evelyn called, "to the ones who feed us with words and patience." Cups lifted, china clinked like warm rain. "To Damien and Marley, who somehow made winter a little less long."

When the laughter softened, Professor Edmund Ashcroft found Marley. He moved with the deliberate care of a man used to deciphering brittle paper; it felt as though the café shifted slightly to accommodate his gravity. Professor Ashcroft was recently voted chair of the Brookwood historical society and wore tweed like a uniform. His hair, unruly in a way that suggested he'd fought it and lost, silvered at the temples. His tie was crooked, which made the correctness of his posture seem a kindness rather than a rule.

"Miss Taylor," he said, as if introducing himself anew, though they had met a dozen times. "May I borrow a minute of your celebration?"

"Of course." Marley glanced back to Damien, who was cornered into a good-natured debate about whether scone size could be a metaphor for civic virtue. He lifted a palm to her—go on—and she followed Professor Ashcroft past the pastry case to the short hallway by the restroom door, where the scent of yeast and soap was oddly comforting.

Professor Ashcroft looked at her with the solemnity of a doctor delivering news he hoped the body already knew. "I'll be brief," he said. "You and Mr. Hawthorne—Damien— you've given this town something to gather around again. But Brookwood has two ways of accepting people. One is paper—the deeds, the licenses, the public toasts and the baked goods. The other is root. The old way. The way this place keeps its own books."

Marley was careful with her breath. "You're talking about the grove."

"I'm talking about what the grove represents." He folded his hands, fingers interlaced not like a prayer but like a puzzle. "If you plan to stay rooted here, you'll need the grove's blessing."

He didn't dramatize it; he didn't need to. The sentence settled like silt. Not a threat, but a law spoken in a language that preceded ordinances. "How does one get a blessing from a place?" Marley asked.

"By standing where it can see you," Professor Ashcroft said gently. "And by letting others see you stand there." He glanced toward the café, toward the laughter that had a little too much brightness. "Some people here prefer their history framed behind glass—kept but inert. Others remember it was grown in dirt and sung over. They're the ones watching you now."

Marley kept her voice even. "Do you think the grove remembers us?"

"I think it remembers everything," he said. "And I think it's been forgetting the town, because the town forgot to ask its leave." He dipped his head, as if that admission were an apology. "Eat your cake, accept your toasts. Then take your love somewhere the trees can hear it."

When Professor Ashcroft returned to the room he did not look back to gauge whether his counsel had landed. He trusted it had. Marley stood a moment longer, palm against the cool plaster, steadying the quickened beat in her wrist. She was not afraid, exactly. It felt more like the sensation of being correctly named.

By the time she reached Damien again, Councilor Miriam had climbed from her chair. She stood better than most people sat—dignity learned from a lifetime of making meaning where no one had taught her how. Beside her on the table lay a small cloth-wrapped parcel, tied with plain twine. "For the bride," Miriam said, though there were no rings and no dates, just an agreement drawn in frost and breath.

Marley took the package. The cloth felt like a shirt that had been washed a hundred times and hung in winter light. When she untied the knot and pulled back the fabric, the café seemed to hush, not fully but enough for the scrape of a chair to sound like punctuation. Inside lay a brass compass and a length of leather cord, the glass face spidered with a hairline crack, the casing mottled with a patina the color of old coins.

Miriam's voice didn't rise, but it carried. "Used by the ones who planted healing into soil," she said. "Before the ledger said who belonged, the land knew who kept it."

Marley's throat tightened. The compass felt heavy in her palm in a way that had nothing to do with metal. She held it up and the needle flicked, then steadied—not north, not any direction the café recognized, but aligning with a line only she and a handful of others felt. She looked at Damien. He had gone still, the kind of stillness a man adopts when he realizes coincidence has begun to behave like intention.

"Do we deserve this?" Marley asked, and immediately wished she'd asked something sturdier.

Miriam's mouth curved. "Deserving isn't in it. Work is. Notice is. Courage is. The blessing can't be bought, but it can be answered. Wear it." She lifted the leather cord between thumb and forefinger. "Not as decoration. As declaration."

Marley slipped the cord through the compass ring and let it hang against the hollow of her throat. Slightly too cold. Perfectly heavy. The needle quivered, then calmed. A murmur moved across the room in the way air moves ahead of rain. In the same moment, Evelyn clapped once and declared, "Cake," with the insistence of a woman who refused to let mysticism steal dessert.

They cut into a lemon layer cake that tasted like memory and sunlight. Children dragged chairs closer to see. Someone began a story about the bridge being haunted and was shushed by a grandmother who believed even stories had to ask the town's permission to be told. Between slices, hands found Marley's shoulders, her palm, the crook of her elbow. Blessings disguised as touch. Caution disguised as politeness. It was all there.

Damien leaned toward her, his breath a question against her ear. "You're all right?"

"I'm...exactly where I'm supposed to be," she said, and knew it was true even as her heart stumbled at the size of what she had just agreed to carry.

It should have been simple after that—eat, laugh, nod at the speeches, stand for the awkward photographs Evelyn insisted on taking with her ancient Polaroid—but the day had developed a second current, and Marley found herself moving in it as much as in the celebration. She was approaching the table where some boys had built a tower out of teacups and napkin dispensers when an older woman stepped into her path. Mrs. Keene, who had run the post office longer than anyone in town had been alive if you believed her stories, wore a cardigan the color of moss and a brooch that looked like a flattened coin.

"May I?" Mrs. Keene asked before permission could be granted. She lifted the compass gently and peered at the cracked face. "Miriam never could let go of a good thing," she said, not unkindly. "This was my grandmother's, then Miriam's sister's, then Miriam's. And now yours, I suppose, until the grove decides otherwise."

"The grove decides?" Marley repeated.

At the counter, Professor Ashcroft was arguing softly with Councilor Price, whose haircut was as precise as her sense of order. "I'm not saying ban," Price insisted, his smile all diplomacy. "I'm saying guidelines. If people start treating that hillside like a carnival, we'll have erosion, litter, fires. History requires caretaking."

"History requires courage," Professor Ashcroft said without raising his voice. "And it requires that we stop calling living things exhibits."

Marley drifted past them with her cake, pretending to be too happy to listen, and Damien slid in beside her, the practiced tango of two people learning to move through rooms as a unit. He could feel the change in the air the way sailors feel weather. "We can leave," he offered.

"We shouldn't," she answered. "We should be seen." She tapped the compass with one finger. The needle gave a sympathetic tremor. "Miriam is right. This can't just be something that happens to us. It has to be something we do."

They were interrupted by a cheer: Evelyn had popped a cork from a bottle of ginger ale with exuberance normally reserved for ships leaving port. Foam geysered onto the floor and was met with applause. For a moment the day reset to merriment. It didn't last. People will always find the seam where joy gives way to worry, and Brookwood had a knack for finding seams.

When the first wave of guests drifted toward the door—work to return to, babysitters to relieve, garden beds to worry over—Marley slipped into the kitchen with a tray of empty plates. The room smelled like vanilla and steam. Evelyn was elbow-deep in suds, humming something that might have been a children's song or a hymn, depending on how you believed. "Well?" she asked without turning. "Is your heart racing with happiness or with doom?"

"Yes," Marley said, leaning against the doorjamb.

Evelyn snorted. "You'll be fine. Towns are like sourdough—fussy if you don't feed them, forgiving if you keep showing up. Has anyone told you that you'll need the grove's blessing yet?"

Marley blinked. "In those exact words."

"Good," Evelyn said. "Means they're still saying the quiet parts out loud. It's when they stop that you'll have to worry." She flicked water off her hands and looked up. "Do you feel it, when you're on that hill?"

"I do," Marley said. The ease of the confession surprised her. Perhaps this was what Evelyn meant by feeding the sourdough. "It feels like breath. Not mine."

Evelyn nodded as if she'd expected nothing less. "Some of us feel it, some of us don't. The ones who don't will follow the ones who do, if the ones who do remember not to be smug about it."

"Smugness is not my temptation."

"No," Evelyn agreed, then grinned. "Yours is martyrdom. Try to avoid both."

Back in the dining room, Damien was waiting with Miriam, Mrs. Keene, Professor Ashcroft, and a few others whose families had lived in town since before deeds were written in ink. It was not a quorum, not formal, but it had the feel of a moment when order tips into ritual. Professor Ashcroft cleared his throat. "We're not making proclamations," he said mildly. "We're making requests."

Miriam glanced at Marley's throat, then at Damien's hands, steady and open at his sides. "Take your love to the hillside," she said. "Not to flaunt it at the wind, but to place it where roots can find it. Walk the perimeter. Speak no words you don't intend to keep. If you hear anything, you keep it until it's ready to be spoken, then you share it as if it didn't belong to you, because it won't. If you hear nothing, you keep walking until the silence becomes instruction."

Damien's fingers brushed Marley's. The gesture said, *We can do this. I want to do this.* She felt relief so sharp it almost hurt. It wasn't only her vow any longer. It was theirs.

"Will you come?" Marley asked.

Miriam shook her head. "You don't bring a crowd to ask a blessing. You bring truth. If the grove wants us, it will call us after. If it wants only you two, it will keep its reply between the stones and your ribs. I'll count either answer as a yes."

The councilwoman watched from across the room with an expression that was not unkind, but precise. Marley wondered if she would become an adversary or a steward. Perhaps both. In a town like Brookwood, most people were both things in turn, depending on which day they met you and what weather was moving in.

Damien squeezed her hand once and let go. "We should go before the afternoon grows noisy," he said softly. "Before all this"—he gestured to cakes and laughter—"drowns out what we owe."

They thanked Evelyn until she swatted them out with a tea towel. At the door, Mrs. Keene caught Marley's sleeve. "Remember," she said, "the grove wants keepers, not heroes." She tapped the compass with one knuckle. "And it prefers questions to speeches."

"Then I'm ready," Marley said, and realized as she spoke that she truly was.

They stepped into the bright, thin light of early afternoon. Brookwood shimmered with the particular clarity that follows a chill. The mills hummed. The river shouldered sunlight. Somewhere a dog barked in a pattern that sounded like the riddle of a song. Marley's shoulders dropped, and she felt the day tilt toward its next task.

THEY DID NOT SPEAK on the walk up the hill. It was not prescription; it was instinct. Words would have been too eager, a way of trying to prove they belonged by narrating how they belonged. Instead they let the rhythm of their steps do the talking. Mud slicked their boots; birds stitched the sky to the field; a wind came off the river smelling like stone and something wild. The compass against Marley's sternum tugged now and then, as if a small hand were reminding her where to look.

When the brambles thinned and the circle of stones appeared, the change in the air was immediate. It always was. Sound fell a shade lower, as if someone had dimmed the room. The skin along Marley's forearms prickled. She stepped to the ring and waited. The compass needle quivered and swung, not north, but toward the stone she had touched that first day, the one with the spiral that seemed etched by patience itself.

Damien didn't enter the circle until the needle steadied. Then he stepped beside her, and the pulse rose through the ground—not aggressive, not demanding, but unmistakable. Marley thought of Professor Ashcroft's counsel, of Miriam's instructions, of Mrs. Keene's distinction between heroes and keepers. She thought of the café's warmth, the way joy and caution had braided like two threads that refused to be separated. She thought of the bell that had tolled twice and of the frost that had written a question in silver over stone. Then she let all those thoughts fall away, like twigs dropping into a stream, and stood with her ribs open to the next thing.

They walked the perimeter slowly. Once counterclockwise, once clockwise, the way you smooth a bed sheet before lying down so the fabric knows the shape of you. At each stone they paused. Marley let her palm rest against lichen and cold. Damien laid his fingers beside hers and, when he steadied, traced symbols she could no longer pretend were accidents of weather. The hum in the ground found her heartbeat and, for a handful of breaths, they were the same thing.

At the seventh stone, Damien spoke first. "I carried a love here that I thought was completed by loss," he said, voice low enough that the words felt placed rather than thrown. "I see now it was unfinished in a way that asks me to live larger, not smaller. I won't let grief make me stingy."

Marley closed her eyes. It was not a fancy speech; it was better. It was ordinary language hung where the air could do something with it. "I came a stranger," she said, "thinking belonging was an invitation other people could give me. I see now it's a vow you make with the place itself. I ask the grove to teach me how to keep what I've asked for."

They stood in the center. The soil held the faint memory of the seven-petal flower, seen in frost and in dreams, and now felt in the soles of their feet. Marley lifted the compass and held it out with both hands. The needle jittered, then settled—first toward Damien, then toward her, then toward the east where the river wore the hillside thin. It didn't choose. It named.

"Do we kneel?" Damien asked, a half-smile at the edge of his mouth.

"This isn't a church," she said, though reverence tugged at her anyway.

"It's a cathedral," he answered, recalling his late wife's phrase, and the word passed between them like a kind of absolution.

They waited. The wind shifted and brought the metallic scent that often comes before rain, but the sky remained high and clean. Far below, a truck backfired, and the sound arrived small and ridiculous in the sanctity. The pulse in the ground—breath, song, the memory of women in robes, whatever it was—gathered itself. Marley felt it thicken at her ankles, climb her calves, occupy her sternum, pause at her throat. She swallowed. "We're here," she whispered, and that was as close to a ritual phrase as she allowed herself.

The answer did not come as a voice. It came as a sensation of widening: the edge of the circle sliding outward, the air making room, her sense of herself dilating until it included soil and stone and the idea of a town trying to remember how to live with what had grown it. Tears came quickly and without heat. Damien's hand found hers, and the widening encompassed that too.

A sound like a bell, but not a bell, trembled through the trees. It could have been the river on rock. It could have been a bird's wing cutting the air just so. It felt like a reply.

Damien's breath left him. He nodded once, a man accepting a commission he'd hoped would go elsewhere and is relieved to discover it won't. "We'll keep it," he said. "Not as possession. As promise."

The pulse softened. The soil let them go. The needle on the compass steadied in the one direction the instrument had not shown all day: home.

On the walk back to town, they met no one, though there were signs of having just missed people: boot prints, the sweet rot of apple cores tossed toward the ditch, a square of cloth that had snagged on a thorn. The silence didn't feel secretive. It felt respectful. Marley imagined the town itself closing its eyes while they asked—so as not to make the answer performative.

In the square, the café door stood open. Evelyn had moved on to wiping chalk dust from the boards; children had been allowed one last riotous session with colored sticks and had written the word "LOVE" so many times it had ceased to look like a word. Professor Ashcroft, sitting alone at a corner table with a ledger and a pot of tea, glanced up and saw their faces. He did not ask. He nodded. Miriam, who seemed to appear and disappear like weather, stepped out from the smell of yeast with a dish towel over her shoulder and the kind of smile that suggests God had taken the morning off to watch two people keep their appointment with the ground.

"Well?" she asked anyway.

"We were heard," Marley said.

"Then be careful with what you speak next," Miriam answered, pleased and grave in the same breath. She handed them a small packet wrapped in waxed paper. "Shortbread for the walk home. You can't keep anything on an empty stomach."

Mrs. Keene intercepted them on the sidewalk and pinched Marley's chin just enough to be affectionate and annoying. "Good," she said, which might have meant a dozen things. "Now get some rest before you start collecting other people's dreams like party favors."

At the corner, Councilwoman Lorraine Gearhart offered a measured congratulations that contained no barbed wire —only the suggestion that she would be watching and, perhaps, learning. Damien surprised them both by asking if she would consider serving on a stewardship committee if such a thing were to exist. Something like respect passed between them like a new coin. "Perhaps," she said, and meant it.

When they reached the bookshop, Marley paused before the window where the Book of Wishes lay open to the page her hand had written weeks ago. The compass touched the glass. The needle steadied. It did not tremble toward the hill. It did not yearn away. It pointed to the space between her ribs where vows seat themselves when they're serious about staying.

Inside, the shop smelled like paper and the faint, sweet signature of midnight tea. Damien closed the door behind them, and the bell above it gave a small, decisive chime. Not the town bell. Their bell. Their threshold. Marley leaned her forehead against his chest and felt the day rearrange itself into a pattern she recognized—work laid beside wonder, root laid beside branch, love braided through both so finely you couldn't tell where anything began.

"We did one thing," she said, not letting triumph get ahead of humility.

"We did the right first thing," he answered.

Outside, spring remembered itself and went on with the business of thaw. In the hill's shadow, a circle of stones kept counsel. In the café, dishes dried in orderly stacks. In the square, chalk words softened under the feet of children who would forget they'd written them until, years later, they found the same words in their mouths without knowing where they'd learned them.

The engagement tea would be remembered for laughter and lemon cake, for the way the town's smiles stretched around a question, and for the old compass flashing once at a certain angle as if catching sun that hadn't been there. It would also be remembered—by the few who felt such things—for a shift that had nothing to do with pastry or speeches. Something had been asked and answered. Not a wedding vow; a place vow. Not a signature; a song, sung without notes, written in steps along a spiral path.

When night came, Marley placed the compass on the table beside the Book of Wishes, the leather cord coiled like a root waiting for rain. She propped Miriam's note against it —four words in tidy script: *Keep it by keeping.* It read like instruction and blessing at once.

Damien turned off the lamp. Darkness held a moment and then resolved into the familiar silhouettes of shelves and windows and each other. The day's noise, even the quiet noise of love, finally fell away. In the breathing that followed —two bodies, one room, a town at rest, a grove awake— Marley felt the work ahead rise like a tide that did not intend to recede.

They would not be heroes. They would be keepers. And beginning tomorrow, the keeping would begin in earnest.

A MYSTERIOUS BLOOM

The morning after the engagement, Brookwood wore the kind of light that makes everything look newly washed. The alley behind the bookshop held a small square of garden Marley had coaxed from stubborn soil—a rectangle of loam fenced by cedar slats and a row of river stones that held the day's warmth after sunset. Mint tangled with lavender, rosemary kept watch like a small sentinel, and a few brave foxgloves had pushed up through last year's leaf litter. She came out with a broom and a stubborn urge to set things right: sweep the stoop, empty the saucers, deadhead the faded pansies. Ordinary work felt like a prayer she could do with her hands.

The compass Miriam had given her lay cool against her sternum on its leather cord. It had been quiet since the hillside. Not mute—merely content, the way a good animal settles under a calm hand. Marley knelt to loosen the soil around a thyme plant and stopped before the motion completed. Something—no, a scent—rose from the far corner of the bed. Not mint, not wet cedar, not the bread-soft perfume of roses in June. It was green in a way she didn't have words for, green the way the grove had been green in the dark: breath and sap and a hint of smoke, as if someone had sung to a fire until it decided to be a forest again.

She moved along the stones and saw it, small as a child's palm and unapologetically itself—a bloom she had not planted and had never seen. Six—no, seven—petals arched from a calyx stippled like river pebbles, each petal thin enough to take the light and make it glow. The color couldn't be named outright; it shifted depending on where you stood, tilting from milk-white to a faint lunar green with veins like silver thread. The stamens were short, tight to the center, dusted with a fine pollen that caught the light as if the air itself were jeweled. The leaves beneath were narrow and glossy, arranged in a spiral that felt deliberate rather than accidental, the way handwriting sometimes tells you more than words.

Marley crouched, the hem of her sweater gathering damp from the path. She inhaled again. It wasn't just familiar; it was the scent that had haunted her sleep since the first dream of the circle—the smoke that didn't hurt, the pine that didn't crowd, the sweetness like honey letting go of its own shape. She reached out and stopped an inch above the petal. The compass warmed against her chest in a sudden, silent acknowledgment.

"Damien," she called through the back door, voice low as if the plant were a skittish animal. "Come here, please."

He appeared with a pen clipped to his shirt and a mug he forgot to set down, eyes already searching her face for whether this was wonder or worry. She pointed and said nothing else. He leaned, then blinked, then shifted angle, as if the flower might resolve differently from a new perspective. "I don't know it," he said at last, and the admission came with something like humility. "It's...new."

"Or very old," Marley said. She let her hand hover again. The pulse she had felt in the grove eased up through the soil and into her palm, the echo of a heartbeat where no human body lay. The bloom's stem held firm against a breeze that didn't seem to touch it. "I dreamed this scent," she said, and didn't have to explain. He had learned the grammar of her sentences when they bent toward the grove.

He set the mug on the stone edging and crouched beside her. "Let's not name it before it names itself," he said. Practical. Tender. He pulled his phone and took half a dozen photographs—close, distant, with his hand for scale, with a coin beside it, the way he would document an artifact at a dig site. "We should press one petal for the shop ledger," he added, then hesitated. "But only if the plant agrees."

She smiled despite the prickle along her arms. "Ask it."

"I'm not mocking," he said.

"I know," she answered. "I wasn't."

They waited the way people wait at the edge of a sanctuary—even those who don't believe in sanctuaries tend to lower their voices there. A honeybee drowsed past, hovered as if surprised, then drifted on as if recalling an errand that had nothing to do with wonder. Marley slid a finger under a fallen maple leaf and used it to shade the bloom. "May I take a petal?" she asked, not aloud exactly. The question felt like something she placed in the air rather than spoke into it.

The compass clicked—no sound, but a tactile answer against her sternum. She pinched the edge of the outermost petal and felt the smallest give. The knife Damien handed her glinted, then caught itself, as if reluctant to make the cut. She sliced clean and set the petal on white paper. The scent intensified for a breath, then settled. The plant did not wilt, did not recoil. If anything, the stem stood taller, as if relieved to have been noticed.

They brought the petal inside and set it between two sheets of paper and a flat volume of Whitman's poems—a press of words to hold a wordless thing. Marley glanced back at the garden through the screen. The bloom seemed to glow a fraction more in shade than in sun. "It found us," she said.

"Or we made room for it," Damien answered, but his voice held the same hush.

He fetched their field kit—once a romantic joke between them, now a drawer that held envelopes, labels, a hand lens, a ruler, cotton gloves, the kind of discipline that lets reverence do work. Marley wrote a note for the shop ledger: *Unidentified bloom, appeared in southwest corner, bed three. Scent familiar from dreams.* She didn't write *from the women's singing* or *from the fire that did not burn.* The page would feel it anyway.

When she returned to the garden, she found a second bud she had not seen before, tight as a fist and the color of late afternoon. It held still, then shivered, the shiver moving through it like breath. She thought of Professor Ashcroft's words about the grove's blessing and Mrs. Keene's steady gaze and Miriam's equal parts warning and blessing: *keep it by keeping.* The day widened around the nameless bloom as if to make room for what it would ask next.

By MIDMORNING, their small kitchen had become a field station. The pressed petal lay under weight, and Marley had managed to collect a single pollen grain onto a slide with a piece of tape and an old hobby microscope that Damien insisted was better than nothing. He peered through it and frowned. "Triaperturate," he murmured—three pores—but the grain's shape wasn't quite like any he remembered. "I can't tell if we're looking at a family we know with an unfamiliar face or something that's never introduced itself."

"What do we do?" Marley asked, already pulling an index card and an envelope from the drawer.

"We share," he said. "With caution."

He drafted an email to a regional botanist he'd worked with when cataloging plant dyes from a settler's trunk—a woman at the university research herbarium with a mind like flint and a heart she kept hidden under sensible sweaters: Dr. Sarah Hoffman. He attached photos: the bloom, the leaf arrangement, the bed with a ruler for scale. He described the scent—aware that science bristles at adjectives—and the petal's thin translucence, the stamens' modesty, the spiral of leaves. He did not share coordinates. He did not mention the compass. He signed with the tone of a colleague asking for help rather than the tone of a supplicant.

"Should we send a specimen?" Marley said.

"Half a petal," he answered. "Pressed. The rest stays here."

They worked with gentle economy. Marley cut a sliver from the pressed petal, slid it into a glassine envelope, and labeled it in her careful hand. Damien wrote a cover letter that sounded like a bridge between worlds—polite to the discipline, loyal to the mystery. He sealed the packet and drove it to the post office himself, returning with the particular posture of a man who has sent something precious into the indifferent machinery of the world.

They waited the way people wait for test results, making tea they didn't drink and reading the same paragraph three times. Marley cleaned the back room and arranged a display of local history pamphlets and a basket of rosemary sprigs tied with twine, some impulse in her insisting that a space shows gratitude by being tidy. Every so often she slipped into the garden to stand with the plant. By noon the second bud had opened, smaller than the first, its petals scalloped as if the edge of the world had left a fingerprint there. The scent lifted and settled, lifted and settled, in the rhythm of someone asleep.

A ping from Damien's worn laptop. He glanced at the screen, then tilted it toward Marley so the words belonged to both of them.

From: Sarah Hoffman

Subject: Re: Unidentified bloom

Damien,

I've gone through our reference images and a few external floras. At first pass: no match. Leaf phyllotaxy and petal venation are unusual—seven is rare in the families you've sampled from—but not unknown. However, the calyx patterning and sepal adhesion are...well, I don't have another image like it. This could be a garden hybrid, or a cultivar out of place. It could also be undocumented.

Before I say the word 'new,' I want better data. Can you send me a full specimen (flower, leaf, a short length of stem), pressed and a small fresh portion in silica gel for DNA barcoding? If you prefer not to share location, I will respect that. But if it is indeed undocumented, there will be questions. If you're worried about poaching—good. You should be. The world has less gentle hands than yours.

Also: for what it's worth, the photos are...beautiful. Sometimes that's a data point too.

S.H.

Marley read the email twice, then a third time slowly,

measuring each sentence. "Undocumented," she said, the word careful in her mouth.

"Cautious," Damien corrected, but the corner of his mouth had lifted. He typed a reply: yes to the pressed specimen; no to the fresh tissue—not yet; yes to confidentiality; a promise to send more images and to keep the plant undisturbed. He attached a note about one pollen grain and his flawed microscope and received, within minutes, a single-line reply from Sarah that read: *You two break my heart in the best ways. Be careful.*

After lunch, Marley found herself unable to stay indoors. She took a stool into the garden and set it a polite distance from the plant, as one would from a stranger's hospital bed. A sparrow dropped to the path, hopped, cocked its head, and left. The bloom's shadow made a small coin of shade on the soil. Marley closed her eyes and let the scent sit at the base of her throat until it stopped being a sensation and became a place. The grove and the garden layered over each other like transparencies: the ring of stones and the row of river rocks, the hum underfoot and the throb in her pulse, the women's singing and the drip of thaw from the eaves.

She spoke softly, not words so much as intention: *You're safe here. We'll keep you by keeping this place. We won't let wonder turn into spectacle.*

From the alley came the grumbling poetry of a delivery truck. Evelyn's youngest shouted that the world's biggest earthworm had been found by the trash bins. Mrs. Keene, measuring envelopes by weight in her mind as she walked, raised a hand without slowing. The ordinary moved alongside the impossible, neither offended by the other.

By late afternoon, the light went thin in the way early spring light does. The plant closed—if that's the right verb

—petals loosening then drawing inward like a fist deciding to keep its secret for night. Marley felt an odd protectiveness rise in her chest. She leaned the little bamboo cloche she used for tender herbs against the bed. "Sleep," she said, and laughed at herself, and did not take the word back.

Inside, Damien logged the day in his journal in neat script: date, weather, first bloom time, second bloom time, scent notes, bee visitation. He paused at the entry for "location" and wrote only "bookshop garden, bed three." He did not add coordinates. He did not add "center of something that feels wider than town." He didn't need to. The page had a way of learning what wasn't written when he placed it near Marley's ledger.

At dusk, they ate soup in the back room and left the door ajar so the scent could find them if it wanted to. It did, a faint line of green in the air like a ribbon someone had tugged across the threshold and tied to the table leg. When they climbed the stairs to the apartment, Marley looked back once. The dark had not swallowed the bloom entirely. It held a pale suggestion of itself, the way a word lingers after a page is turned.

NIGHT DREW the edges of the town together. The mills idled; the river spoke more audibly; the square exhaled. Marley woke not because she had been sleeping badly but because the room itself seemed to change temperature and weight, like a body settling into a different position. She knew before her mind offered reasons: a dream had arrived and was waiting at the edge of her bed like a messenger without the rudeness to shake her.

She closed her eyes and let it take her.

Hands, so many hands, moving the way hands move

when they know more than the mouth—the first image. Soil made a hollow sound as if it were a drum. The air held the hush of a room where a baby has not yet cried but is about to. The hands cupped small plugs of earth and the not-yet-flowering plants that would become what had bloomed that day in her garden. The hands belonged to women whose faces she could not fully see and did not need to: one wore a ring of braided willow, one had a scar across her wrist pale as thread, one hummed without melody. They were standing in a circle, and that circle was not metaphor but instruction. At the center lay a newborn child, not swaddled tightly but covered lightly with a woven cloth that let light through, the kind of cloth that says: this one belongs to breath, not to weight.

Marley wanted to move closer and did not. The women pressed the soil around each plant and did not tamp too hard. Every third planting—she noticed this without deciding to—one woman pressed her palm to the ground and whispered a phrase she almost heard and then did, but the words didn't remain after she woke. The scent rose as the circle closed, the same scent but younger, like learning a song by standing beside someone who already knows it. The child did not cry. A few flakes of ash drifted down that did not burn the cloth, and one woman caught a flake on her finger and placed it on her own tongue and nodded as if to say: yes, this is good.

The dream moved the way rivers move when they fork and then rejoin. One stream showed the plants taller, their petals open, the women older. The other showed a young man—was that Damien?—carrying a map he could not read until he set it on the ground and let the plants write their shapes over it. The map changed to a face and back to a map and then to the seven-petel flower drawn in frost on the hillside. Marley felt the press of the compass against her sternum even within the dream and understood it as both tool and vow, like a wedding band worn inside the skin.

When she woke, she did not start. She lay with her eyes open in the dark and smelled the scent before she sat up. It had slipped under the door and into the room like a polite guest who knows the house well. Damien's breath lifted and fell beside her, steady and human and beloved. She put her hand against his ribs and felt, for two or three long seconds, his heartbeat line up exactly with the rhythm she had learned in the grove and in the garden. The alignment broke and returned and broke again, and she realized the point wasn't to make them identical. The point was to learn how to listen when two rhythms speak at once.

She slid from bed, bare feet on the cool floor, and put on the sweater hanging from the chair. Down the stairs, past the shelf where Damien kept the field notebooks, past the table where the Book of Wishes lay like a small, sleeping animal. The back door gave a sigh when it opened. The alley was ink-blue, the garden a paler shade. The bloom—both, now; the second had opened at dusk—held a glow that was not light so much as refusal to become dark. Dew made the soil look like wet velvet.

Marley crossed to the bed and knelt, aware of the way the earth always accepted the weight of a kneeling person without complaint. Around the two plants, seven tiny points pricked the soil, as if the night had practiced punctuation and left its marks. She touched one—and felt the smallest resistance, the soft push-back of something sprouting. She had not planted these. She had not watered them. And yet the ring was there, exactly the distance a hand would place when measuring between plants without a ruler. She didn't think of theft or replication or any of the words the wider world uses for miracle. She thought of keeping.

"Thank you," she said to the air, to the soil, to the women in the dream whose faces she hadn't seen and didn't need to, to the baby in the center, to Miriam, to the frost that had written spirals on stone, to the bell that had learned to speak again. Gratitude was the only language that made sense at that hour.

The compass warmed. The needle did not swing to the hillside; it did not swing to the shop or the street. It aligned with the tiny circle of emerging lives and then turned, slowly, toward the door of the bookshop as if to say: *Keep both. The big circle and the small. The public vow and the private tending.*

Behind her, the door brushed open and Damien stood in frame, hair a wreck of sleep, eyes soft with the particular relief of finding a person you love still in the place you hoped they would be. "You dreamed," he said, not a question.

She nodded. "The hands planted these. Around a child. Not to hide him. To teach him to breathe with the world that would hold him." She gestured to the pricks of green. "They're here."

He crouched, careful not to put a knee in the bed. "Undocumented species," he murmured, half smiling, echoing the email that would alter their week and the way they stood in town. "Documented now by dream and dirt."

"By vow," she said.

He slid an arm around her shoulders and they knelt together for a while, not asking for instruction, not offering interpretation, simply keeping company with what had chosen to arrive. The air got colder. A thin strand of mist tugged along the alley. Somewhere a cat knocked over a bucket and swore in cat. The world did what the world does when miracles happen: it kept happening.

Inside, Marley wrote the dream in the ledger. She did not attempt poetry. She noted details like a good archivist and let the part of the story that wasn't hers to own float above the ink like a second text only the page could read. Damien found an old ceramic dish and set it near the window with a folded cloth for humidity, not for the blooms —those belonged to the bed—but for the petal they had pressed and the sliver they had surrendered. He labeled a new envelope for Sarah: *Second bloom, 21:13. No disturbance. New seedlings (7). Dream corroboration (subjective).* He chuckled at his own parenthetical. "We'll see how science receives that."

"Science," Marley said, tightening the cord of the compass at the nape of her neck, "is just one of the ways a place makes itself legible."

She placed the ledger beside the Book of Wishes and, in a new column she'd drawn for this season of the town's life, she wrote: *Garden asks for guardians, not gardeners.* Then, below the line, she added a wish in her own hand, the script steady now: *May what grows here teach us not to hoard wonder, but to steward it. May those planted circles become breathing rooms for the living. May our keeping keep us honest.*

They climbed the stairs again. At the landing, Marley paused, turned, and listened. The scent had followed them, softer now, like a lullaby crossing a hallway. In their room, she lay on her side and looked at Damien until he had to smile to make the looking bearable. "It will get louder," she said.

"That's all right," he answered. "We learned how to listen."

When sleep came, it came without argument. In the

garden below, dew condensed on leaves that had not been named yet, and the tiny points of green thickened a fraction in the dark. In the alley, the air remembered a circle no ordinance had ever drawn. In the ledger, ink dried on words that would outlast their hands. In the town, a rumor woke that began, as the best rumors do, with wonder and not with fear: *There's something new in the bookshop garden, and it smells like the edge of a forest after it stops burning.*

And above all of it, the vow that had started with a bell and moved into soil kept time—not with clocks, but with breath.

4

——————

BROOKWOOD TALES REVISITED

The road to Brookwood wore its history in the way it curved—avoiding a boulder that no longer stood, veering around a stand of firs that had been logged fifty years ago. Marley drove with the windows cracked an inch to catch the morning's damp breath, the compass cool against her sternum, the petal-pressed envelope tucked into the glove box as if paper could bless a car. Damien rode shotgun, a thermos between his knees, his notebook already open, ready to turn a conversation into a map.

Brookwood's oldest resident lived in a saltbox cottage that had been painted the same shade of blue for so long the color felt like a family trait. On the porch, wind chimes crafted from old spoons chimed in the key of afternoon tea. A row of jars on the sill held dried plants—yarrow, cedar tips, something pale and curled that might have been wild rose petals in a colder season. The door opened before Marley could knock.

"Nancy Averill," the woman said, saving Marley from the embarrassment of wondering whether to try "Ms." or "Mrs."

"You look like your questions are heavier than your coats. Come in and don't drip gravel on the runner. It's the runner's day to be clean."

Inside smelled like violets and old paper. Afghans layered over chairs as if the furniture were aging modestly. A photograph on the mantel showed a young woman with a braid as thick as a rope standing at the edge of a field with seven small bundles at her feet and a smile that said she had just been given a secret. Nancy's hands were knuckled and steady; she poured tea without looking and passed cups as if she had done so at a hundred kitchen tables with a hundred stories that wanted speaking.

Marley glanced at Damien—ready?—and he gave a small nod that meant: listen more than you ask. She began with the ordinary: how are you feeling this spring? how long have you lived here? Nancy parried with wit, as old story-tellers do to measure the worth of new listeners. Then Marley placed her question like a smooth stone on the table between them.

"Mrs. Averill," she said, "when we spoke on the phone, you said your grandmother used to walk 'with the women of the grove.' You meant Brookwood's grove?"

Nancy's smile thinned into something like memory's ache. "I meant the grove that doesn't care which town thinks it owns it," she said mildly. "But yes. Those women crossed the hills the way rain does—unimpressed by boundaries on paper."

"Your great grandmother—"

"Ruth Averill," Nancy supplied, eyes warming. "Ruth mended sleeves so well men swore the cloth healed rather than the thread. She kept a basket by the door with seven things in it—always seven—and if you asked why, she'd tell you you were missing the lesson. She walked at night sometimes. Not sneaking. Walking the way a person walks when they've been asked to stand somewhere. Lantern, shawl, sometimes a bundle that smelled like cedar and something a little sweet. My mother said she had a way of listening with her whole spine."

Damien's pen moved like a second pulse. "Did she ever say what they did there?"

"Not in nouns." Nancy's earrings were small blue stones that had learned how to catch light shyly. "She told me verbs. Keep. Watch. Breathe. Sing. Plant. Sometimes *root*, like it was something a body could do with more than hands."

Marley held the warmth of her cup, grateful for something to anchor her fingers. "And you? Did you ever go?"

"Once," Nancy said, her gaze drifting to the photograph. "I was ten and had lost a dog and two baby teeth, and my father, if you count the kind of losing where a train takes a man and gives a family back an envelope. There was a dry summer, and the hill on Brookwood's edge had burned in a way that made the town feel like a throat that can't swallow. Folks said lightning. Others said someone's carelessness. Ruth said whatever the cause, a fire doesn't know it's a story —it just is what it is until you teach it another verb."

Nancy shifted, the tea cooling but not unwanted. "That night the women went, seven of them, Ruth among them. I watched from the edge because I had learned how to be still. They stood in a circle that wasn't painted and yet was there, right as chairs. They had branches—cedar, I think; one had yarrow braided in—and small bowls that smoked in a way that smelled like church if church trusted the wind. They sang. Not a song with verses and little choruses you can clap to. A song with a spine." She paused and smiled at the memory for the first time. "I know the name you're going to ask me to use. They called it *Flame Rooted in Rain*."

The phrase landed like a key turned left. Marley felt the garden's scent rise in her mouth as if she'd said it aloud. "And it...worked?"

Nancy took her time. "The fire came toward them, sure as a horse that hasn't learned kindness. They didn't tell it to stop; that would have been a fight. They taught it to remember. The smoke rose in a braid and the song found the place the fire had forgotten. And in a way I can't be helpful about, the flames lowered themselves, like a person kneeling because it feels right. It didn't go out. It went *down*, into the soil, the way a root goes down. And then the rain came. Not a lot. Enough to tell the fire the truth about its proper size."

Damien was still writing, but he was writing slowly now, letting the sentences find their own weight. "Your great grandmother ever speak the names of the women?"

"Some," Nancy said. "Aurelia Ward, of course. Hannah Gearhart—she had a scar that meant she'd been brave in a way not many people would sign up for. M. Colvin—Mirabel, I think, but she was...complicated. People are polite until they decide which version of complicated you are. And there were others who knew enough not to leave names in rooms where names could be stolen."

Marley thought of the initials on the folded grove map— A.W., M.C., H.G.—and felt the clean click that happens when two parts of a story find each other. "Mrs. Averill," she said, "may I record you?"

"If you promise to let me lie if telling the truth would invite thieves," Nancy said, the gentleness back.

"I promise."

The little red light on the recorder glowed like a berry, and Nancy told the tale again, this time as if speaking to the part of the future that truly listens. When she finished, she sat very straight. "The grove doesn't belong to us," she said. "We belong to the grove as much as we are good at belonging to anything. The women knew that. They weren't heroes. They were keepers."

Marley felt the phrase seat itself in her ribs—the relief of hearing the word she had already learned on the hillside handed back from a mouth that had tasted it decades earlier. She glanced at Damien; he had his notebook open to a copied line from Aurelia Ward's fragments, and his eyes had gone thoughtful in the way that meant he had just found a rhyme across time.

Outside, a wind moved the spoon chimes to a new key. Inside, the story settled, old oxygen reentering a room that needed it. Marley sipped her tea and did not pretend to be unmoved. She wasn't interviewing to collect a relic. She was kneeling to take a vow.

She looked at Nancy. "Thank you," she said simply.

"Don't thank me," Nancy replied. "Bring me back news that you treated the story like a seed, not a souvenir."

They drove out to the edge of Brookwood where the fire had once put its mouth to the hillside. Time had done what time does to scorched earth: softened it, greened it, let alder push up where fir had fallen. But there were still marks in the way the ground rose and the way a line of black ran like thread through the root ball of an ancient stump. Damien parked at a turnout that pretended to be a view and turned off the engine. The day was cloud-bright. Somewhere nearer to town a hammer kept time for someone else's project.

Marley walked to the charred line and knelt. The soil

smelled like iron and leaf and the ghost of coal. She pressed her palm to the ground and felt—not the grove's deep hum, not the garden's tender pulse, but a faint, residual echo, like a note struck long ago still quivering in sympathetic strings. She did not chase it. She set her hand there and let it find her as much as it wanted to.

Damien crouched with his pen and his patience. "Aurelia wrote a line I couldn't place," he said. "I copied it because I liked it, not because I understood it. 'Teach the flame its root, and it will kneel to water's true name.'" He looked up the hill to where the wind traced the grass into ripples. "I think Nancy just taught me what the line means."

Marley kept her palm on the earth because it had begun to feel almost impolite to remove it. "Say it again," she murmured.

He did, slower. And she heard how the sentence contained instruction rather than superstition, how it sought balance, not spectacle. "It's not domination," she said. "It's memory. The song doesn't boss the fire. It reminds it."

Damien stood, stretching his knees, and scanned the slope with the careful gaze of a man who has learned to see without assuming. "Look—there." He pointed to a shallow depression near the old stump. In it lay a shard of blackened ceramic no bigger than a walnut. He knelt and brushed away soil until a thumb-sized bowl resolved—cracked, fire-kissed, the lip smudged with something that might still have remembered resin. He did not pick it up. He looked to Marley with a question.

She shook her head. "Not today. We don't collect from what's still keeping. We can draw it." She pulled her own notebook and sketched the curve of it, the break line that cut across the bowl like a deliberate mark. Damien took a photograph, and the shutter's gentle click sounded respectful.

They walked the slope slowly, not to hunt, but to let their feet memorize the way the ground carried story. Damaged bark healed over. Sword ferns put forth scrolls of new green exactly where the burn had once stolen the light. As they reached the turn of the hill where the river's voice grew, a band of air moved across them cooler than the rest. Marley stopped. "Do you feel that?"

He did. "As if we walked through the tail end of a rain that fell somewhere else."

They stood without speaking for a minute. A hawk wrote a cursive they couldn't read above them. The breeze changed and the cool spot faded. It would have been easy to call it coincidence. It would have been small-minded to call it less than grace.

On the drive back, Damien kept Aurelia's line open in his lap as if the sentence were a compass of its own. "Aurelia, Hannah Gearhart, Mirabel Colvin," he said. "Nancy named them without prompting. The same initials that showed on the map." He looked at Marley. "It's not only a ledger. It's a lineage."

"At the café, Professor Ashcroft said the blessing had to be public," Marley replied. "This feels like the part that must stay private. The techniques. The bowls. The song."

"The ethics," Damien said. "The center holds if the intentions are honest."

In the bookshop garden, the two blooms were closed to the afternoon in the way some flowers choose to keep their secrets for evenings. Marley stood beside the bed and told them what Nancy had told her, names left out, verbs honored. "We'll keep this," she said. "We'll keep it by not trying to own it. We'll keep it by asking questions the way

Mrs. Keene told us to." A flicker of movement drew her eye. Seven green tips showed clearer than they had the night before, tiny spears that seemed to have drawn strength from being told a story that belonged to them.

Inside, Damien spread their notes on the back table. He pulled a battered folder labeled "A.W. fragments" and set Nancy's tale beside Aurelia's copied line. "I wish," he said carefully, "that I could write to her and tell her she was understood. That the line she left someone will carry it forward cleanly."

Marley set her hand on the folder's worn edge. "You are telling her," she said. "Her line survived long enough to meet its echo. That's a yes in any language."

He breathed out and nodded. When he smiled, it was not the flash of surprise he used to save tension in a room; it was the quiet one he kept only for when something true had happened and did not need his wit to frame it.

Before dinner, they returned to Nancy's with a jar of Evelyn's lemon curd and a small posy from the rosemary bush. Nancy opened the door with a look that suggested she had been expecting precisely this cadence of gratitude. "Did you stand where it was?" she asked.

"We did," Marley said. "We found a small bowl. We left it."

"Good," Nancy answered, approving and a little fierce. "You don't take bones from a body still learning how to stand."

They sat again, and Marley, who had learned to ask for more when the storyteller was ready, said, "Would you tell me the rest, if there's a rest? The child, the planting..." She faltered and decided not to hide the dream. "We've seen a circle of plants around a newborn."

Nancy's eyes didn't widen. They warmed. "Of course you

did," she said, as if Marley had finally described a room everyone beautiful passes through. "That's the oldest piece. When a child meant to keep is born in a year that forgets rain, you ask the world to remember with you. You plant what some of us were taught to call rain-keepers. You sing until your voice stops wanting to be yours. You let smoke carry your kindness where your hands can't go."

"The rain comes?" Damien asked.

"The rain comes enough," Nancy said. "Not because you commanded it. Because you asked properly."

Marley felt the ledger calling like a friend she hadn't written to in a month. She would give this story a page with a margin wider than usual and a title that had earned its capital letters. She would leave blanks where names wanted quiet. "Thank you," she said again, and now the words were a form of keeping.

"Go on home," Nancy replied. "And if anyone tells you that singing to a fire is superstition, ask them if they've ever seen what conversation can do to a stubborn man. Same principle. Different element."

When they left, the spoon chimes moved like soft applause. A fine mist began—not rain, not fog, the polite beginning of both. Marley raised her face into it and tasted a hint of iron. On the drive back, the mist didn't follow them. It waited where it had a job, and they left it to work.

At the shop, she wrote: *Flame Rooted in Rain—told by Nancy Averill (Ruth's great granddaughter). Verbs, not nouns. Teach flame its root. Ask water by its true name.* She placed Aurelia's line beneath it and let the ledger decide what ink existed between the sentences. Damien set the recorder on the shelf as if returning an heirloom to its place. They worked quietly, grateful for nouns now that the verbs had been spoken.

. . .

NIGHT TOOK ITS TIME ARRIVING, the way it does when a town has earned good light. Marley brewed mint and carried two cups to the table where the map with A.W., M.C., and H.G. still lay like a compass that spoke in initials. She touched each letter in turn. "Aurelia Ward," she said aloud. "Mirabel Colvin. Hannah Gearhart." Saying the names felt like setting chairs, as if the room were larger when it could seat the absent rightly.

Damien opened his folder and slid out one of the few surviving pages copied from Aurelia's journal—a scrap he had not shown Marley before because it had always seemed like an orphaned sentence looking for a home. He smoothed it with the heel of his hand.

"She wrote more than the one line?" Marley asked.

"Not a lot. But yes." He pointed to a paragraph in his careful hand, the ink faded where rain had once made a claim on his field notes. "Listen."

He read: "*If you meet flame in the open, teach it to remember the way it began. Fire is not enemy; it is misplaced hunger. Show it root. Show it rain's other name, the one it answers to when it has stopped pretending it knows everything. The song is a door. Smoke is the letter you send ahead to say: we are coming as kin, not as conquerors.*"

Marley's throat tightened. "That's the story Nancy told us, in prose."

"It's the same story," Damien said, voice roughened by relief. "And if we were looking for permission to believe, I suppose that's enough."

He brought out another copied line, short and almost playful: "*A bowl that has held cedar remembers more than the hand that carried it.*" They both laughed softly, thinking of the blackened dish resting in the dirt, keeping its station. Then the laughter fell away and the room kept only the part of it that had been joy, not nervousness.

Marley folded the map and run her fingertips over the crease until the paper grew warm. "We have a responsibility," she said. "To carry this forward without making a spectacle of it. To let knowledge stay wild enough to keep itself safe."

"We also have a botanist waiting to test us," Damien replied, not unkindly. "Sarah will want a fresh specimen. She'll want coordinates eventually. She'll want to put a name on what bloomed."

Marley thought of the child in the dream and the women pressing soil around the ring of plants, of the way Nancy had said *ask properly*. "Let's give her exactly what we can without betraying what isn't ours to give," she said. "Science can borrow without stealing. If we teach it how."

He smiled that quiet smile again. "You make it sound like science is a person we're inviting to tea."

"It is," she said. "It's a person who forgets to knock sometimes."

They stepped out back with their cups to say goodnight to the garden the way you say goodnight to a room you don't want to leave messy. The two blooms had reopened in the cool—pale, veined, giving their scent with the generosity that comes from not needing to impress anyone. Around them, seven new green points had pushed a fraction higher. The circle was beginning to show itself in a way even a doubter would have to call a circle.

"Do you think this is the same plant used in the song?" Damien asked.

"I think it's kin," Marley said. "And I think kinship is sometimes the more important truth than identity."

He looked at her with the expression he used when a phrase was going into his private lexicon. *Kin over category.* He'd write it later in the margin of something and pretend he had always known it.

A small sound behind them: footsteps in the alley. They turned. Mrs. Keene stood there, cardigan pockets stuffed as if she had taken on a few extra weights to keep from blowing away. "I came to see if you listened," she said, not a question.

"We did," Marley said.

"And we will," Damien added.

Mrs. Keene stepped closer to the bed and looked down with the same appraisal she gave mail that wanted to be first class but wasn't. "You'll need to be good at saying no to people who aren't used to hearing no," she said. "That includes me. I'm practiced at no. It doesn't mean I don't need to hear it."

"We'll try to disappoint you with grace," Marley said, and Mrs. Keene's mouth twitched into what, for her, counted as a grin.

"Tell the town the story the way it can bear it," Mrs. Keene continued. "Give them the parts that make them kinder. Keep back the parts that would make them grabby. You know the difference."

"I think I do," Marley said. "Nancy gave us verbs today."

Mrs. Keene nodded once. "Then mind your nouns." She touched the compass with a knuckle as if knocking on a door that belonged to both of them. "If you need an old woman to stand in the circle with a tin pan and hit time like a bell, you know where to find me."

When she left, she left a quiet that wasn't empty. The garden breathed. The alley exhaled. A thin stripe of cloud pulled across the moon and then reconsidered.

Inside, Marley opened the ledger to a fresh page and

wrote at the top: *Brookwood interview—Nancy Averill.* Below it, she gave *Flame Rooted in Rain* three undisturbed lines of its own and copied Aurelia's sentence exactly the way Damien had. She drew a small bowl in the margin and left it unfilled. Then she wrote the line she knew she would forget if she didn't put it somewhere she trusted: *Teach science to borrow without stealing.* It looked less like a command in ink than it had sounded in her head. That was fine. The page understood. The understanding is why they chose paper over stone.

Damien leaned his hip against the table. "We should write to Sarah," he said. "Offer a pressed leaf. Tell her we're keeping location private for now. Ask for a barcoding protocol that uses the least possible tissue. Tell her this is not a race."

Marley nodded. "And ask her to keep her graduate students' hands off our town." She softened the joke with a smile. "Or at least teach them to wear gloves."

He drafted the email. He did not tell Sarah about the bowl or the precise place where the earth still ran cool. He did not tell her Nancy's name. He did include the phrase *Flame Rooted in Rain* because sometimes a scientist needs to remember that the world was singing before the lab learned to measure.

When he looked up, Marley was watching him with the attention usually reserved for vows. "I love you," she said, not in the way that wraps another person in a story, but in the way that offers one sentence to place beside another so both become truer. He rested his forehead against hers.

"Then we're dangerous," he said softly. "Because we have both love and a purpose."

Before bed, she placed the ledger beside the Book of Wishes and, almost without thinking, wrote a new wish: *May our keeping teach us to ask properly. May we remember flame's root and rain's true name. May stories not be souvenirs but seeds.* She dated it, then left the rest of the page blank, an invitation.

As they turned out the lights, a sound like a bell-but-not lingered at the edge of hearing. It might have been a truck over the bridge. It might have been the spoon chimes in Brookwood finding their key on the wind. It felt like consent.

In the morning, Marley would return to Nancy with a loaf of Evelyn's bread and the part of the story she already knew how to pass back: that they had listened, that they had not taken, that they would ask again. She would tell Nancy the line from Aurelia Ward, and Nancy would say, "Well then," as if the day had opened its hands and found what it had been holding. Damien would tag his notes with a new index card labeled *Rain-keepers; teaching fire to remember.* The town would not yet know what had been set into motion, and that was good. Ripeness comes from what a community doesn't rush.

Out back, the two blooms held their small lanterns steady. The seedlings lengthened a whisper. The bowl in the dirt watched with the concentration of an intelligent eye.

5

THE WAX-SEALED BOX

The morning mail arrived like it always did—thudding against the bookshop's front mat with the humility of envelopes that knew they were mostly bills. Marley bent to gather them, half her attention still tuned to the faint green scent drifting from the back garden where the mysterious blooms had made a small, luminous fact of themselves. Between a wholesale catalogue and a handwritten note from a school librarian sat a parcel the size of a loaf of bread, wrapped in brown paper that had long ago learned how to keep a secret.

There was no return address. The twine was knotted in a dockman's square. The wax seal was the color of dried blood.

"Damien?" she called.

He looked up from the ledger where he'd been recording timestamps for the plants' opening and closing. He came around the counter with the same careful curiosity he brought to old documents and fragile conversations. "Who's it from?"

"No sender." Marley set the parcel on the table and

lowered herself into the chair as if taking a place at a ritual rather than at breakfast. The wax seal bore an impressed emblem: a seven-petaled flower ringed by a broken circle, the break so deliberate it read as instruction. The symbol sent a shiver down her spine—not fear, not quite. Recognition's colder twin.

Damien reached for his pocketknife, then paused, palm hovering above the wax. "Do we have permission?"

"Ask properly," Marley murmured, remembering Nancy's phrasing and Mrs. Keene's admonition to mind their nouns. She set her fingers lightly against the seal. The compass at her sternum warmed a fraction. If heat can be consent, this felt like yes.

The wax snapped with a tidy sound. Inside the paper lay a carved wooden box, black walnut, smoothed by time and hands. Spirals and leafwork climbed its sides, not ornate so much as insistent. On the lid, a shallow groove traced a spiral that tightened to a small depression—thumb's width —inviting her to press there and nowhere else.

She did. The lid lifted as quietly as a breath.

Pressed herbs lay in silk compartments: cedar tips brittle but aromatic, yarrow heads pale as memory, a crescent of dried rose that had kept its color against reason. Petals from something lighter than rose—barely green, almost lunar— were nested in a folded square of paper, as if whoever sent the box had walked into their garden at night and asked for a blessing without taking too much. A brass compass, older than Miriam's but kin to it, rested in a fitted groove; its face was clear, hairline scratches like spiderwebs across the glass. And beneath a layer of tissue, tied with linen ribbon, lay a folded map.

No letter. No explanation. No name.

Marley lifted the compass first. It sat heavier in her palm

than its size suggested, a small gravity pulling her hand toward the table. The needle didn't point north. It shivered, hunted, then leaned toward a corner of the room as if the wall were a hill and the hill were calling.

Damien exhaled. "Not possible," he said, which meant: I accept that it's happening, and I need a sentence to bring me along.

Marley set the compass down and untied the ribbon. The paper had the crackle of age—rag, not pulp. She eased the map open along its old folds. Ink bled slightly where damp had once kissed it; the lines, though, remained precise: a spiral path drawn from outer ring to center, with small glyphs at intervals—a bowl, a branch, a teardrop, a small circle with seven strokes like a child's sun. The outer edge of the spiral was annotated with small moons—slivers waxing, plates going dark, a full round that someone had drawn thicker than the others, as if to weight it.

In the margin, neatly printed initials: **A.W., M.C., H.G.** The ink strokes differed—three hands, one map. Between them lay small arrows and ticks one could read as agreements. A series of dates ran along the bottom edge in pencil, smudged from being touched. Above one, faint as evaporated breath, a line of writing had been begun and left unfinished, the script angled and tight. Marley held her head just so, letting the light slide across the page. Letters rose like a bruise, not fully, not yet.

Damien crouched beside her. "Aurelia Ward," he said, tapping the **A.W.** with reverent caution. "Mirabel Colvin. Hannah Gearhart. The same trio Nancy named." He reached for his notebook, then stopped. "No. First, we see. Then we write."

Marley traced the spiral with a fingertip, not touching ink. The path wasn't symmetrical; it cut inward as if obeying terrain. In the center, a small seven-petaled flower was drawn with the unshowy confidence of someone who had drawn it many times. Around the central symbol, a ring of tiny dots—seven, then a space, then seven, again and again. She thought of the circle around the newborn in her dream. She thought of the seedlings pricking the soil behind the shop. She thought of the frost's spirals etched on stone. "It's a key," she said, and felt the certainty take root as soon as she spoke. "Not to a place we've never seen —to one we've been walking past without knowing how to open it."

"Restoration," Damien said softly, echoing, expanding. "Not discovery."

Marley lifted the layer of tissue that had hidden a second compartment. At the bottom of the box lay a small packet of ash bound in cheesecloth, a sliver of charcoal wrapped like a pen, and a short length of red thread. The charcoal smelled faintly of cedar. The ash had the particular flake of plant matter burned slow, not fast. She looked at Damien.

"Flame Rooted in Rain," he said, and though the box carried no bravado, the room itself felt as if a story had just sat down among them.

The back door chime flicked, quick punctuation— Evelyn's youngest, bringing a stack of flyers and a question about whether Marley thought a town could have a mascot that was a tree. Marley closed the box lid gently, covering map and compasses and history with the practiced motion of a person who knows when to keep something between breaths and ribs rather than between shelves and glass.

When the boy had gone and the door had stopped quivering, Damien leaned both hands on the table. "Someone trusted us."

"Or tested us," Marley said, not to dim his relief, but to call the room to attention. "Either way, we answer properly."

They carried the box into the back room where the light was patient and the table had space for documents to breathe. Marley set the compass from the box beside Miriam's compass—two needles, two hearts. Miriam's settled toward the alley, toward the hill. The new one resisted north and then quivered toward the same invisible line, a fraction to the east of it, as if hearing a harmony only it could detect.

Damien spread the map and weighted its corners with sea-smoothed river stones they kept for exactly that purpose. He placed a blank sheet beside it and wrote headings: *symbols, moons, path anomalies, initial clusters.* His neat letters calmed him; the ritual of note-making said, *We will not be swept. We will carry.* Marley set a finger over the unfinished line at the margin and let her breath slow. The faint letters wouldn't come entirely into focus, like a word on the tip of a tongue that wants context before arrival. Good. Let it keep its dignity.

"We'll catalog the contents," Damien said. "Photograph the map, but never with glass overhead. Photograph the box's joinery. Record the scents." He smiled, self-mocking and proud. "It matters. Scent is a data point too."

Marley lifted the packet of ash. Something in the weight of it put her back on the Brookwood hillside where the air had gone cool for a traveling minute. "This belongs to a bowl," she said, thinking of the blackened dish they'd left in place. "But not that bowl. A kin bowl. We can't know what the ash held without inviting it to tell us."

"We won't test it," Damien decided. "We'll conserve it. Our job is to keep the story intact long enough for the place itself to verify it."

Marley nodded. She felt the old urge to turn to the Book

of Wishes and write *Thank you for trusting us* despite not knowing who they were thanking. She stayed at the table, at her post. The map waited, not impatient, only exact. Noon came, and with it the garden's faint perfume. When she looked up from the spiral, both compasses needles lay parallel, not pointing out of the room but into it, toward the box, toward the map—toward the work.

"Restoration," she said again, and this time the word sounded less like a guess and more like a vow.

THEY SET the afternoon aside and made the back room a small conservatory for memory. Damien photographed each herb pouch and labeled it in his ledger: *cedar—old; yarrow—late harvest; rose—dried whole, petals intact; lunar petal—unknown, likely kin to garden bloom.* He drew the spiral carved into the lid and noted the way the groove thinned at the thumb-rest, as if the box had been opened by the same family for a century. From the underside of the lid he lifted a sliver of fibers—a thread of linen caught in a hinge. He placed it in a glassine envelope and wrote on the outside: *linen ribbon, undyed, likely hand-loom.*

Marley annotated the map's moons, counting phases between symbols. Every seven ticks, a small dot. At the inner ring, next to the seven-petaled flower, a circle had been shaded in, then partially erased. Erased by whom? And why? She mapped the spiral's drift against the hill they knew: here, a kink where a fallen fir had forced a path to bend; there, a gentle widening where the earth gave room. When she finally spoke, her certainty felt simple and clean.

"If we walk this," she said, "we will land where the frost wrote that flower. The map is the grove from a mind that loved it."

Damien rubbed the bridge of his nose, not in doubt, in awe. He pulled from his folder the page of Aurelia Ward's copied journal. He lay it beside the map with a care that made the paper feel honored. The handwriting wasn't the same—Aurelia's script was a little more playful, a little less schooled—but the mind behind them spoke in the same syntax: a trust in verbs, a refusal to let nouns do all the work. He read aloud the line they'd brought back to Nancy: "*If you meet flame in the open, teach it to remember the way it began.*" Then he pointed to the char-sliver. "They didn't send us a weapon. They sent us a memory."

Marley, who had learned when to move and when to still, did not rush toward conclusions. She ran a fingertip along the moon annotations and felt herself inhabit the rhythm they implied. "New to full to new again. Seven weeks, then a pause. Seven more, then a mark." She paused, letting the body of the idea ripen before the mind harvested it. "They tended the grove on a clock you could read in the dark."

They debated calling Professor Ashcroft, then decided not to—yet. The councilwoman had been precise about stewardship; Professor Ashcroft had been precise about courage. Both would need to be invited at the right moment or risk letting public spectacle eat private truth. Marley drafted a page in the ledger titled *Box, wax-sealed—received without sender.* She listed contents and left two wide margins for notes that would only show themselves when the map's instructions were obeyed. Then she added a line whose only job was to anchor their ethics: *Do not move a stone. Let the grove teach the next right step.*

Late afternoon thinned toward evening. The garden breathed; the alley stitched itself to the river's cool. Damien returned from the kitchen with bread and honey and the precise look of a man deciding how to risk exactly and no more. "Sarah," he said, meaning Dr. Hoffman. "We owe her a reply."

Marley's first impulse was protection, sharpened by Mrs. Keene's warning about hands that have forgotten how to hear no. Her second was recognition: if you ask science to borrow without stealing, you must be brave enough to hand it a cup. "Tell her we received new materials," she said. "Tell her they confirm nothing and everything. Offer a pressed leaf from our garden, not the box, and three new photographs that will look like diagrams if you squint. Say 'location withheld for protection' and mean both meanings of *protection*."

He wrote exactly that, softening the edges only where courtesy needed to keep the conversation human. Sarah's reply, when it arrived before dinner had even thought of lighting its stove, was a scientist's version of a benediction: *Keep the thing whole. Send only what no one will miss. I can help you prove it exists without teaching the world how to ruin it.* A small line followed, uncharacteristic and therefore deeply meant: *This is the best work you will ever do. Don't rush.*

Marley closed her eyes after reading, relief moving through her like warm tea. She set the phone down, then picked up the compass from the box and dangled it by its ring. The needle, free to swing, settled toward the map. Damien watched, shoulders loosening as if a choir had found its note. "It's a guide," he said. "And it wants to be used."

"Wants isn't a word I trust for objects," Marley said, and then smiled at herself. "But yes. The intention that placed it here wants us to walk."

They packed a satchel as if for a hike no tourist would register: the box wrapped in a shawl that had belonged to

Marley's aunt; a soft pencil and an eraser; a coil of red thread as if the thread could keep a path from losing its nerve; a small jar of river water because a person should never go to ask a place for anything without bringing it a drink. They left the shop lights low and the Book of Wishes open to the page where Marley had written *May what is buried rise again in peace, not conflict.* When she closed the door, the bell gave its small domestic chime and then faded, letting the larger hush of the hill take dominance in her ears.

On the climb, they did not speak. The compasses moved as if in conversation—the one from the box tugging a degree to the east of Miriam's, then aligning, then deviating again, like cousins who love each other but insist on telling the story in their own way. Twilight held steady, the river carrying the last daylight toward places neither of them needed to be.

At the edge of the bramble, Marley stopped. She did not enter the ring of stones until she had both compasses aligned on her palm and the map balanced across her forearm. "Ask properly," she said under her breath, and stepped through.

THE GROVE ACCEPTED them the way it accepted weather—without comment, with consequence. In twilight's gentle blue, the stones showed the memory of frost in their lichen, the spiral of ice now a pattern only light could unearth. Marley lay the shawl-wrapped box near the center, not in the center. She spread the map on the ground where the soil had been tamped by old feet. Damien knelt with a pencil ready and no urge to lead.

They began at the outermost mark—a small bowl drawn

beside a waxing moon. Marley reached into the box and lifted the cheesecloth packet of ash. She pinched a flake between thumb and forefinger and let it fall to the soil. It darkened the ground the way a blessing writes a second text over a first. She spoke nothing. She breathed, the way a person breathes when a room is already full of sentences and she's decided to listen instead.

They walked. The spiral demanded slowness; too quick and the ground rose where the map expected it to recede. At the second glyph—a branch—they paused. Marley laid a cedar sprig from the box across a seam between stones. The scent lifted and stood. Damien's pencil ticked a small check in the margin of his blank page. "Match," he whispered, not to aggrandize the moment, merely to acknowledge its accuracy.

At the third mark—a teardrop—Marley dipped two fingers into the jar of river water and flicked a small arc onto the soil. It shone briefly, then sank, a swift lesson in what the world does with gifts given properly. She felt no surge of music, no heat, no omen beyond the subtle shift of her own chest as reverence took the place of adrenaline. The grove's hum rose a hair's breadth, which is to say it became imperceptibly easier to stand there without feeling the need to deserve it.

They reached the kink in the spiral where, on the map, someone had drawn a tiny X and then erased it. There the path narrowed to pass between stones that had not been polished by any hand. Marley turned her body sideways and slid through. A thorn nicked her coat sleeve without finding skin. She let the fabric carry the scratch and did not take it as insult. Some places like to remind you you're soft.

At the inner ring—seven dots, a pause, seven dots— Marley set the lunar petals from the box on her open palm.

Their color shifted with the failing light, taking on the pale currency of dusk. She placed them on the ground exactly where the map drew the flower. The air's temperature changed in the way quiet rooms do when someone important sits down. Damien's breath caught—not fear, recognition's older cousin.

He unfolded Aurelia's copied line and held it near but not over the map—as one would hold a candle near another light, not to overshadow, not to compete. "*Teach the flame its root,*" he read softly, "*and it will kneel to water's true name.*"

From far down the slope, a dog barked twice and went quiet. Leaves rehearsed a wind that would arrive later. The needles of both compasses steadied and then, with the delicacy of a musician edging into tune, aligned exactly with the spiral's center. Marley felt the ground's hum step into the same rhythm as her pulse for a handful of beats and then relax back into its more ancient tempo. In that small interval, she knew—not with the certainty of an answer key, but with the conviction of a body that remembers—what the unfinished line on the map's margin wanted to be. Not the words, not yet. The shape of the sentence in the mouth.

Damien looked at her. "Do you hear it?"

"I hear *where* it will be," she said, smiling at the improbable correctness of the statement.

At the very center, the soil held a depression no wider than a saucer. Marley passed her fingertips over it and found the faintest scratch, a handmade groove worn by years of someone setting down a bowl in the same place. She did not move the blackened dish from Brookwood. The bowl in this grove had been carried away or broken or buried by time. The groove remained, the way a promise remains after the person who made it is gone.

She opened the packet of ash again and let a little more

fall, barely enough to smudge the line. The smell that lifted was cedar and something sweeter, and though the night was dry, Marley tasted rain at the back of her throat—not the storm kind, not the catastrophe kind, the kind that shows up just past midnight and explains to the ground that thirst has a limit.

"Restoration," Damien said again, steadier now, the word settling inside his voice until it felt like his.

They didn't try to finish anything. They walked the remaining curve to where the spiral rejoined itself and tied a short length of red thread to a twig at knee height—not as a flag, not as a claim, but as a reminder to themselves where to begin again next time. The thread looked almost silly in the grandness of trees and stone. That was right. Keeping is mostly small.

When they wrapped the box in the shawl, the compasses did not protest. The needles leaned toward home as if the work was to be carried into rooms where paper waited, where a ledger could memorize what voices forget. On the walk down, a fine mist stitched the air. It didn't wet them; it occupied space with the quiet authority of things that know their job.

Back in the shop, Marley set the box on the table and, after a moment's deliberation, placed the Book of Wishes beside it. She wrote a single sentence at the bottom of the page that had carried her earlier prayer: *We will not move a stone.* She dotted the period with her usual small firmness and felt the room agree.

Damien opened the ledger to a fresh page and drew the spiral freehand, not perfect, perfect enough. He copied the moon ticks and the order of the glyphs and left a blank margin where the unfinished line awaited its time. Then he wrote, as a man grateful to find his pen can hold what his chest cannot: *Box arrived without sender; contents comport with Nancy's tale and Aurelia's line; map describes path we have already been walking by mistake. We will walk it on purpose.*

Before turning out the lights, Marley carried the box to the back shelf where she kept the things that were both ordinary and unstealable by thieves who didn't know how to ask: an apron that still smelled like her aunt's soap, a bundle of dried rosemary, a photograph of a woman long dead smiling like someone who had just been given a secret. She slid the box into the space between the photo and the herb. It fit without asking the other objects to move too much. Good keeping knows how to make room.

"Someone trusted us," Damien said again, softer.

Marley rested her palm over the box for a breath. "Or the grove did," she said. "Either way, we answer properly."

They went upstairs through the kind of quiet that carries rather than isolates. In the garden below, two pale blooms held their lantern-faint glow. The seven seedlings stood like punctuation practicing their grammar. On the hill, a circle of stones kept counsel with a map laid briefly upon its skin, then folded and carried back where human hands could be taught to deserve it.

6

____

MARLEY'S DREAM OF FIRE

The dream came like a door flung open, not a gradual slipping of thought into image. Marley stood in the grove, the stones brighter than moonlight, the air charged as if a storm had chosen to arrive without rain. Around her, women in green robes moved with a solemn grace, their sleeves brushing the earth as they circled. The fabric seemed woven from leaves themselves, each robe textured with veins that glimmered faintly as though light passed through living foliage. No faces were fully visible, but the sense of presence was undeniable—elders, sisters, keepers. A lineage that did not end with her but reached forward and backward like roots through soil.

The women hummed—not words, but a tone that carried weight, a resonance that made Marley's ribs ache with its frequency. She felt herself joining without effort, her chest vibrating, her voice threading into the sound though she never opened her mouth. The compass on her sternum pulsed like another heart, its needle alive beneath the metal.

At the center of the clearing lay the map she and Damien had unfolded only days before, but here it was rendered in light rather than ink. Spirals glowed along the ground, the dots and symbols shimmering like embers that refused to cool. Marley felt a pull toward the center, her steps aligning with the path drawn in frost and paper, now revealed as energy. The women opened their circle to let her pass, their robes brushing her shoulders with a softness that carried gravity.

She reached the flower symbol, the seven-petaled shape at the heart. She knelt, placed her palms on the soil, and whispered a word she did not know until it was already leaving her lips. The hum swelled. The soil trembled.

Then fire.

It did not fall from sky or climb from match. It erupted from the center outward, tongues of flame leaping higher than the stones, consuming the spiral with a hunger that roared like a storm breaking. The women did not scream. They raised their arms, their voices shifting from hum to chant. Marley could not tell if they were summoning the fire or resisting it; both seemed true. The robes caught but did not burn, green fabric shimmering like pine needles refusing to yield. Smoke coiled into the night, thick but strangely sweet, threaded with cedar and resin. Marley coughed, tried to move, found herself bound in place—not trapped, but required to stay.

The fire closed in. Heat seared her face, singed her hair. She pressed her palms harder into the earth, desperate to hold on to something solid. Flames surged up her arms, yet she felt no pain—only a mark, as if soot itself were writing its story on her skin. She looked at her hands. Black streaks lined her palms, not ash to be wiped away but something seared into flesh, lines like runes she did not recognize. She raised them toward the women, pleading for understanding. They nodded in unison, their chant deepening, their robes still unburned, their eyes—those she could glimpse—alight with something fiercer than fear.

The ground heaved. A wind blasted through the clearing, whipping the fire into a spiral of its own, mirroring the map's path, rising into the sky as a column of flame that became, impossibly, rain. Fire turned to water in midair, crashing down as sheets that doused the clearing. Steam rose in clouds, thick enough to obscure the women until Marley stood alone, soaked and scorched, her breath ragged in the damp silence.

She woke gasping.

The bedroom was dark, but the scent was unmistakable: pine needles burned green, smoke that curled sweet instead of bitter. She sat upright, hands trembling. The lamp clicked on with a harsh glow. Damien was beside her in an instant, his hand steady on her shoulder. "Marley?"

She turned her palms upward. Black smudges streaked them, as though she had pressed them against chimney soot. Her throat tightened. "Look."

Damien's eyes widened. He took her hands gently, turning them in the light. "It's not dirt," he said after a moment. "It's on your skin. Like it's—stained."

Marley wiped them against the sheet. The marks remained. Her breath came fast, uneven. "I was there. In the grove. With them. And then...everything burned."

Damien reached for his notebook on the nightstand, the one he had begun filling since the first bloom in the garden. He wrote quickly, not to dismiss her but to honor her words. "Tell me everything. From the start."

She closed her eyes, forcing herself to steady her breath, to replay the images in order. "Women in green robes. A chant. The spiral glowing in the ground. My hands on the soil. Fire—coming from the center, not outside. It didn't hurt, but it marked me." She opened her eyes, held out her palms again. "These. And the smoke smelled like pine. Like it's here now."

Damien set the notebook aside for a moment, cupped her hands between his. His voice was calm, but his eyes carried the same awe she felt. "It's residue," he said. "Not just dream. Residue." He lifted her palms to his lips, kissed the blackened lines as though they were scripture. "We'll document everything. Dreams, weather, moon. We'll treat them as parallel texts."

Marley swallowed hard. "Damien...what if it wasn't a dream?"

"Then we were given a warning. Or a memory. Or both." He reached for the compass on her nightstand. The needle trembled, as though stirred by an invisible wind. "Whatever it was, the grove is not done speaking."

They sat in silence, the faint scent of smoke clinging to the room. Marley's palms still tingled. The fire still roared in her ears. And deep in her bones, she knew this dream was not an isolated visitation. It was the beginning of a pattern, one that would demand more than sleep to decipher.

By morning, the marks still lingered. Marley had scrubbed her palms with soap until her skin reddened, but the black lines remained faint but undeniable, as though soot had seeped beneath the skin rather than sat atop it. When she placed her hands on the kitchen table, the sunlight through the window made the stains appear darker, sharper, like runes that resisted translation.

Damien had already converted the table into a field station. His notebook lay open, a ruler across its spine, pencil sharpened to the nub. He had tacked a calendar sheet to the corkboard with thumbtacks, already marked with moon phases and small weather icons for each day. A thermometer, barometer, and the kind of hygrometer used in libraries to monitor paper sat on the counter, salvaged from his days documenting old archives.

"Let's start simple," he said. His voice carried that journalist's tone—steady, pragmatic, as if naming the facts could keep the extraordinary from slipping away. "Date: Tuesday. Moon: waning gibbous, two days past full. Weather: high clouds at dawn, wind east to west. Dream: fire in the grove, women in robes, chanting." He looked up. "Correct?"

Marley hugged her shawl around her shoulders. "You make it sound like a weather report. But yes. Correct."

He sketched her palms—quick lines, then slower detail, the dark smudges etched as carefully as a cartographer outlines coastlines. "Residue: soot-like markings, persistent despite washing. Smell of pine smoke present in bedroom, dissipated after dawn. Duration: approximately four hours."

Marley winced. "Four hours?"

"I tracked it," he said gently. "Not the dream—the scent. It lingered until sunrise."

She stared at her hands again. They tingled faintly, the sensation of warmth that clings after firewood has been stacked or sparks caught on skin. "It wasn't just vision, Damien. It *was*. The chant, the robes, the way the fire... shifted. It didn't burn, it claimed. And then it turned to rain."

Damien wrote that down, his pencil pressing deep enough to score the page beneath. "Fire turning to rain," he murmured. "Aurelia's line again."

He moved to the window, staring out at the garden where the strange blooms rested closed in the morning chill. Their pale petals seemed to pulse even in sleep, as if echoing the dream's energy. "These dreams aren't accidents. They're sequential. Like chapters."

Marley pressed her fingers to her temples. "But why me? Why my hands?"

"Because you listen," Damien said simply. He pulled a fresh notebook from the shelf, labeled the spine in his neat block letters: *Marley's Dreams—Parallel Record.* He opened to the first page and began a format, half left blank, half charted. "Left column: dream content. Right column: weather, moon, bloom activity. If patterns emerge, we'll see them. If not, we'll still keep faith by keeping record."

Marley managed a faint smile. "You sound like Mrs. Keene. Or Miriam."

"Then I'm in good company," he said, not looking up. He wrote the first entry in crisp script, dating it, noting her description, then drawing two small circles—one shaded, one open—to mark fire and rain. When he was done, he closed the notebook and rested his hand on the cover. "Now it exists in two places. In memory, and in record."

But for Marley, memory didn't end when daylight arrived. All morning she felt the fire's residue in the smallest things. When she poured tea, the steam smelled faintly of smoke, as though the water itself remembered burning. When she reached for a book on the high shelf, her palms tingled against the spine, leaving behind no mark but an impression she swore she could see in her mind's eye. Even in the town square, when Evelyn waved from the café door, Marley caught a flicker at the corner of her sight—orange light in a windowpane, gone when she turned her head.

"Are you all right?" Evelyn asked as Marley came closer. "You look like you've walked through someone else's bad weather."

Marley forced a smile. "Just didn't sleep well."

Evelyn didn't push, but her eyes lingered on Marley's hands as if she saw more than Marley wanted her to. "Keep them warm," she said finally, pressing a scone into her palm. "Some marks fade when you're not watching. Others...well. Don't let anyone else tell you which kind you've got."

Back at the shop, Damien had spread the map from the wax-sealed box again, aligning its spiral with a compass and ruler. He was layering vellum sheets atop it, marking where Marley's dream symbols matched the glyphs. "See here?" he said as she entered. "The fire came at the center. The ash packet was placed at the first glyph, but your dream took it further, into transformation. Fire becoming rain—it's not just memory. It's instruction."

Marley set the scone on the table, appetite gone. "Instruction for what?"

He looked at her with the solemnity he usually reserved for lines copied from Aurelia Ward. "For how to survive what's coming. Or how to keep others alive when fire arrives again."

Her throat tightened. She thought of Nancy's story of Flame Rooted in Rain, of women singing smoke into obedience. "Do you think the grove is warning us? That another fire will come?"

"I think," Damien said carefully, "that dreams don't waste themselves on irrelevance. If the grove is speaking, we owe it not to ignore." He tapped his pencil against the column where he'd written the date. "And I think the phases of the moon will matter. Fire, rain, growth—they follow cycles. If your dream began on a waning gibbous, then what happens at the new moon?"

Marley rubbed her palms, soot-dark marks stubborn. The scent of pine still clung faintly to her hair, though she had washed it twice. She shivered, though the fire had left heat, not cold, in her bones. "What if I can't tell the difference between dream and waking anymore?"

"Then I'll tell you," Damien said, voice firm but kind. He closed the notebook, stacked it atop the map, and set his hand on hers. "You're not carrying this alone."

She wanted to believe him. She wanted to rest. But even as she leaned into his steadiness, she felt the fire's echo coil inside her like an ember waiting for air. It was not done. And she was not free of it.

THE SOOT on Marley's palms did not fade. By the third evening, Damien suggested they take the marks to the grove —not as proof, but as offering. Marley hesitated, but the weight in her chest told her the grove was already aware. Dreams had a way of breaking their banks until waking life itself became current.

They went at dusk. The compass Damien carried quivered like a bird in a cage, its needle refusing north, straining instead toward the hillside. The path was damp from a day of mist, the soil soft enough to hold the imprint of their boots. Neither spoke; words felt brittle against the rising hum that accompanied them.

At the grove's edge, the stones stood waiting, gray with lichen but alert, like sentinels who never slept. Marley paused, hands open before her. The marks gleamed faintly even in failing light. She pressed both palms against the first stone. A faint vibration traveled up her arms, familiar now —the same pulse she had felt in dream.

"The fire begins here," she whispered.

Damien circled to her side, notebook in hand, but his pen hovered idle. "Not dream," he said. "Memory speaking through you."

They stepped into the ring. The clearing seemed brighter than the sky, though no sun remained. Marley inhaled and caught it again—the resinous scent of pine smoke, strong now, thick enough that her eyes stung. Yet the air was clear. The scent was not illusion, but neither was it flame.

The spiral path mapped in ink was alive under their feet. Marley felt each turn draw her deeper, her pulse syncing with the unseen rhythm. When she reached the center, the hum surged, and her palms flared hot. She lifted them. The soot-marks glowed red.

Damien gasped softly, awe overtaking fear. "It's... answering you."

A spark leapt from stone to stone. Then another. Soon a crown of fire circled them, rising in tongues that should have consumed grass and lichen but did not spread beyond their bounds. The grove burned without burning, alive with the same paradox she had witnessed in dream.

Marley froze. "It's happening again."

"Then speak to it," Damien urged, voice steady though his face glistened with sweat. "Ask properly."

The women's chant returned—not audible in the air, but resonant in her ribs. The syllables were waiting on her tongue. Marley let them rise. A low hum became words she could not translate, yet they belonged to her mouth as if spoken before she was born. Her hands lifted, palms open, soot-runes glowing brighter.

The fire bent inward, spiraling like a dancer turning. For an instant, fear clawed her chest—the instinct to flee flame. But the marks pulsed reassurance. This fire was not here to destroy. It was here to remember.

Damien set his notebook aside, knelt, and pressed his hand to the soil. His jaw clenched against heat, but he stayed. "I see it," he said. "The pattern—the spiral. It's not chaos. It's design."

Marley's chant deepened. The fire's roar softened into a sound like wind moving through hollow wood. Sparks lifted skyward, and she recognized the moment: this was when fire turned to rain. She thrust her palms upward. "Root," she whispered. "Rain."

And it happened. The column of fire lifted high, unraveling into threads of light that shifted, softened, condensed. Rain fell, gentle but relentless, soaking soil and stone. The flames hissed and vanished, leaving steam that wrapped the clearing like gauze. Marley fell to her knees, hands trembling, soot fading from her palms in rivulets washed clean by rain that had not touched her skin.

When the last drop vanished, silence held them. No scent of smoke remained. Only the damp perfume of moss, cedar, and earth after rain.

Damien reached her side, helped her upright. His hand on hers found clean skin where soot had marked. "Gone," he whispered. "It's gone."

Marley's throat ached. "Not gone. Answered." She touched her palms together, then spread them as if opening a book. "It gave me back what it wanted to show."

Damien exhaled a long, ragged breath. "And now we know Aurelia's line wasn't metaphor. It was instruction."

They walked the spiral back out, each turn calmer, steadier, as though exiting through a prayer's amen. At the last stone, Marley paused. A thin curl of ash lay at its base, perfectly formed, untouched by rain. She picked it up. The fragment held the scent of cedar. She tucked it into the pocket of her coat.

Back at the bookshop, Damien wrote until ink pooled and pages crammed with detail: fire crown, spiral, chant, rain. He added moon phase, wind direction, barometric pressure. He even marked his own pulse at intervals, shaky notations in the margins.

Marley, meanwhile, sat with her palms open on the table, staring at them as if they belonged to someone else. She whispered the words again—root, rain—and felt the echo vibrate through her bones. "It's not warning us of fire," she said at last. "It's teaching us how to meet it."

Damien closed his notebook and set it beside hers. "Then the next time it comes—whether dream or real— we'll be ready."

In the garden outside, the seven seedlings had stretched taller, their leaves slick with dew that had not fallen from any visible cloud. Their circle had grown more defined, as if the dream's rain had fed them too. Marley watched them through the window, heart steady now. The work was not to fear the fire. The work was to keep learning how to sing it into rain.

And so the grove's test had bound itself into her waking life—fire and rain no longer symbols, but tasks. Not warnings. Instructions. And each night to come, she knew the dream would return, deepening its lessons until they were ready to keep them in the flesh.

7

DAMIEN'S JOURNAL ENTRY

The first time she wrote it, the ink had bled through the page as if the words were trying to enter the paper's grain and live there: *a breathing cathedral.* Damien ran his thumb beneath the phrase the way a carpenter tests a sanded edge, feeling for splinters the eye can't see. His late wife had a habit of pressing harder when certainty visited her hand. On this page the pressure had carved the letters into a low relief—the sentence visible even on the sheet below as a ghost of itself.

He'd told himself he'd put these journals away after the engagement tea. He'd made a fragile private promise to let the past rest while the present learned how to walk on its new legs. But the box, the map, Marley's soot-marked palms, the rain rising out of flame—every new thing bent toward the old notes as if the paper had been salted and the present were water, drawn to it by a law older than intention. So he spread the journals across the back table, set the hygrometer on the shelf out of habit, and opened to the pages where her handwriting looked most awake.

He dated the top of his own notebook—*Damien*

Hawthorne, Field Notes, Grove / Personal—then drew a line down the middle to mark the two lives he was trying to keep: evidence on one side, confession on the other. He'd been a reporter long enough to know that the sentence *I felt* is more dangerous than the sentence *I saw*. But most of what mattered here was not going to submit easily to *saw*.

He copied the words as she had written them:

The grove is not metaphor, though metaphor clings to it like ivy. It is a breathing cathedral. We enter as lungs enter—on a rhythm not our own—and if we listen long enough, we leave steadier than we arrived.

He underlined *breathing cathedral* once, because underlining twice insists too much and he was trying, for once, not to insist. Beneath the quotation he added a reporter's reduction: *She went alone that day.* He dated the entry in her margin; the year felt both yesterday and a former life. He remembered how she had come home bringing forest with her, the way her hair had held cedar as if it were a pledge. He remembered wanting to ask whether she was safe, and asking instead whether she had eaten. That was his way of loving then—care disguised as logistics, as if sandwiches could be shields.

A thin light moved across the floorboards. In the garden, the seven green tips had grown another finger-width since morning. He made a note of that, even though it belonged in a different notebook, the one with measurements and moon phases. Then he returned to her page.

Do not mistake silence for emptiness. Some rooms must be quiet in order to introduce themselves. Some questions require elbow room. If you ask while crowding, you will think the place has no answer, when in truth it is declining to answer rudely.

He smiled despite himself. She'd always had the nerve to write instructions to the future. He traced the little nick in the paper where she'd lifted her pen too quickly. If he closed his eyes he could feel the heat of that day-fashioned sun, the resin on her fingers, the confidence that had always made him a little braver by proximity and a little ashamed by contrast.

He turned the page to find the sketch he had half remembered, then fully forgotten, then been ambushed by last week on the hillside: a spiral not perfectly symmetrical, annotated with small marks that meant something to her hands if not to his then. She had drawn it with a carpenter's pencil, then returned with ink to commit it more formally. In the bottom corner she had written *Not labyrinth—litany.* And then: *Do not confuse getting lost with being led.*

He made room in his own notebook for a concession he'd been avoiding: *I am afraid of inheriting her unfinished sentence.* The line surprised him by not hurting; it steadied, like telling the truth to a room that's going to hold you regardless.

On the shelf above, Aurelia Ward's copied fragment leaned against a tin of rubber bands like a psalm propped against a pencil jar. *Teach the flame its root...*—the sentence that had moved from beautiful nonsense to architecture in the span of one night by the stones. He set Aurelia's line beside his wife's spiral and watched the two pieces of language tilt toward each other like glasses on a table sliding together when the floor shifts. The fit wasn't perfect. It was kinship, not duplication, and he had learned to trust kinship more than category these days.

He turned to a page where his wife had switched to tiny capitals, the script she used when fear tried to outrun her focus:

Do not turn the circle into theater. Do not carry what cannot be carried in daylight. Do not name what will not be kept safe by being named. A place has a right to choose its confidants.

He wrote in his margin: *I am not the only confidant now.* Then, before his guilt could walk in wearing its house slippers and take the good chair, he added: *Good. That is safer for the place and for me.* He took his hand off the paper and looked at the door as if someone might have arrived to adjudicate the sentence. No one did. The room remained the size of two people's lives and one town's work.

From the front of the shop came the soft click of the bell —the domestic one, not the one that had once refused to speak—and he heard Marley laughing softly with a customer about whether a paperback could forgive being dropped in the bath if the reader apologized properly. The sound walked straight into the older silence and sat down without asking for permission. He felt the complicated joy of that—how the present did not erase the old music; it made harmony where there had been a solo.

He turned the page again and found, tucked at the edge, a pressed leaf from a plant he did not recognize then and recognized now with a jolt—the same delicate ribbing as the lunar petals in their box. Beneath the leaf she had written a single letter: **H.** He had assumed, back then, it stood for *leaf* or *left* or *late.* Now he thought: **Hannah. Hannah Gearhart.** He wrote the full name beneath the letter and drew a line toward the spiral. The living had reached to shake hands with the dead and the dead, being courteous, had reached back through paper.

He closed his eyes and asked himself the earnest question he'd been dodging since the night in the grove when fire became rain: *Do I carry what she began?* The answer came with two voices. The first said, *Of course you do.* The second said, *How dare you.* He was practiced with both. The first had him up at dawn with a satchel of notebooks and a lunch he would forget to eat. The second had him at midnight, palms pressed to his eyes like a penitent who can't decide which God to bother.

He wrote both answers in the right-hand column, then drew a line between them and wrote, in smaller script: *What is carried does not preclude what grows beside it.* He didn't know if the sentence was wisdom or rhetoric. He let it sit. A person doesn't have to decide immediately whether a sentence is useful to keep; sometimes it tells you later, by staying.

A shadow crossed the glass of the back door. Marley slipped in sideways, the way you enter a room that might be reading. She took in the spread of journals, the calibrated scuttle of tools, the careful posture he wore when the past sat across from him like an honored guest who might not stay for dessert. She set a small paper cup near his elbow. "Evelyn made you a mercy coffee," she said. "She said you look like a man translating weather."

He smiled without lifting his head. "Tell her the barometer has learned humility." He gestured to the chair. "Sit. Or read. Or ignore me and go make friends with the plant that insists it is a fact."

She sat. She didn't read. She watched his hands the way you watch someone navigate a narrow bridge in good shoes. "How is she today?" Marley asked, meaning his dead wife, even though the pronoun was a houseguest that sometimes overstayed.

"Present," he said, then frowned at the word and let it stand. He turned the journal so Marley could see the phrase. "I found the page. *Breathing cathedral.*"

Marley leaned in, her hair brushing the margin. She read aloud softly, tasting the sentence as if making sure it wasn't poisonous. "It sounds like a place that isn't offended by prayer," she said, which was her way of being democratic with religion. She touched the pressed leaf with a fingertip. "She knew the plant."

He nodded. "Or its kin." He told her about the **H** and his guess. He told her about the capitals where caution had moved into her hand and made itself legal. He told her the part he hadn't wanted to say out loud: that some days love felt like a zero-sum ledger, that he feared if he carried his wife's work forward, he would tilt the scale unfairly; that if he chose not to, he would be guilty of dereliction in the face of a legacy that had asked to be kept.

Marley let the confession walk around the room once before she invited it to sit. "What are you afraid of more," she asked, gentle as a midwife, "keeping too much of her, or not keeping enough?"

He blew out a breath he hadn't known he was saving. "Both. I am afraid that moving this forward makes my love for you an annex to a larger project. And I am afraid that letting this go is a betrayal not of her—death has a way of surviving betrayal—but of the town that needs what she began."

He expected an argument. Marley has kindness's version of stubbornness, which is to refuse to let a person lie about their own heart. Instead she reached for his pen and flipped his notebook to the confession column. In her neat teacher's hand she wrote: *What if love is not a container but a trellis.* She slid the notebook back so the sentence faced him and the implication had room to breathe. "It can carry more than one vine without breaking," she said. "It can guide without owning."

He stared at the words a beat too long. He could feel the defense building—the old habit that insists on scarcity because scarcity protects us from foolishness. He closed the defense like a book he'd already read. Without looking up, he wrote: *Try living as if this were true.* Then, because he was learning, he added beneath it: *And forgive yourself when you forget.*

He turned to his wife's journal again and placed his palm on the page without pressing, the way one lover places a hand on another's chest to listen. "She called it breathing," he said. "I keep trying to hold my breath to keep from breaking what's already delicate."

Marley smiled. "Then breathe," she said simply. "Let both legacies draw air through the same ribs." She rose, pressed a kiss to the top of his head—the exact place where grief sometimes collected—and left him with the coffee and the paper and the sentence she had planted like a stake the vine could find.

After she went, he wrote three words on the evidence side, a place he rarely let hope trespass: *Breathing carries both.* He underlined it once. He told himself he would probably doubt it by dusk. He told himself doubt was another name for practice. He lifted his pen and began copying, word for word, the parts of his wife's work the grove had already proven, leaving blank space where interpretation would be a theft. When he finished, the page looked less like an answer and more like a path. That felt right. Paths don't compete with each other; they intersect and teach you how to keep going.

THAT NIGHT, Damien carried the journals upstairs as if they were fragile organs in need of transplant. Marley had already drawn the curtains, leaving the room dim except for the amber pool of lamplight. She watched him arrange the books at the foot of the bed like guardians taking their station. He sat on the edge, shoulders tight, his breath audible in a way that betrayed the labor of keeping himself composed.

"You're not sleeping tonight," she said gently, not as an accusation but as a forecast.

"I need to know what she meant," Damien replied, gesturing to the journal. "She had lines I ignored when she was alive, because I thought they were metaphors, or because I didn't trust that something so old could matter anymore. And now those same lines are rising in front of us as if they were written yesterday."

Marley shifted closer, folding her legs beneath her, settling the compass cord against her chest. "Then read them to me. Don't carry it alone. Let me listen with you."

He nodded, opened one of the volumes, and began. The paper crackled in his hands. His late wife's script sprawled in loops and tight turns, expressive in ways his precise lettering never was. He read aloud:

The grove breathes differently depending on who enters it. Some people make it gasp, others help it rest. It is not passive—it reacts. If you carry grief, it gives you silence. If you carry arrogance, it blinds you with birdsong until you leave. If you carry love, it multiplies it in ways you might not be ready for.

Damien's voice caught at the last sentence. He closed his eyes. "I think she knew. About me. About the possibility of someone else after her. Maybe she wasn't writing about the grove at all."

Marley's heart clenched. She touched the page lightly, not to claim it, but to let him know she was present. "Or maybe she was writing about both," she said. "The grove and you. Both can multiply love. Both can hold more than one legacy."

He let the thought sit. He traced the loops of her letters, then turned another page. This one contained diagrams: concentric rings, symbols for water, flame, seed. At the margin she had written: *Cathedral needs choir. One voice is never enough.*

He wrote the phrase in his notebook column labeled *confession*. Beneath it, he added: *I am afraid my voice will overwrite hers. I am afraid it will be drowned out by hers. I am afraid of both at once.*

Marley leaned over and read the entry. Then she took his pen and wrote beneath: *A choir isn't about erasure. It's about harmony.* She underlined it once, then gave the pen back.

Damien swallowed, the lump in his throat stubborn. "When she died, I thought harmony meant silence. That the song ended with her." He looked at Marley, his eyes raw but unflinching. "Now you stand in the same grove, and the song changes key, and I don't know whether I'm allowed to follow."

Marley did not answer with words. She cupped his face in both hands, leaned her forehead against his. The silence between them was not absence but weight—like the pause in a hymn when everyone inhales at once. When she finally spoke, her voice was steady. "The grove doesn't demand permission slips. It just asks that we show up with honesty."

He laughed, short and broken, but genuine. "You sound like her."

"No," Marley corrected softly. "I sound like me. And you're hearing the overlap because love echoes. That doesn't mean it's repeating."

The journals lay open like testaments awaiting witnesses. Damien turned another page and found a small envelope taped inside. His heart lurched. He carefully peeled it loose. Inside lay a fragment of bark, brittle but intact, with lines scratched faintly into it. Words, he realized, in a script so small it was almost impossible to decipher. He brought it under the lamp.

"'Do not mistake inheritance for obligation,'" he read aloud. "'Choose which threads you pick up, or they will strangle you while pretending to be ropes.'"

Marley's breath left her in a hush. "She left you permission. Not command."

Damien pressed the bark fragment to his chest. Tears came—not in a torrent, but in two heavy tracks that left his face bare of defenses. He did not apologize. He let them fall.

"I wanted her legacy to be clear," he whispered. "A straight line, a directive. But she left me something harder: choice."

Marley brushed a thumb across his cheek. "Choice means freedom. And it means trust. She trusted you enough to let you decide, Damien."

He nodded, slowly, painfully. Then he wrote in his notebook: *I choose to carry what still breathes, and let the rest sleep.*

They sat in the lamplight, journals spread around them, the air heavy with the mingling of smoke-scent from Marley's dream and the cedar pressed decades ago into the bark fragment. It felt like two times leaning against each other.

Damien finally closed the journal and rested his hand atop it. "She called it a cathedral. She was right. But I think she forgot to say that cathedrals are built for more than one generation to keep. Stones get replaced. Songs shift. Windows crack and are repaired. And still, the place breathes."

Marley smiled, a quiet triumph in her eyes. "Then maybe the question isn't whether you carry her work or let it rest. Maybe the question is how to let it breathe through you without suffocating either of us."

Damien exhaled. His shoulders loosened. He wrote one more line before extinguishing the lamp: *Love is not a relic to preserve. It is breath to share. Even across time.*

The room settled into silence. Outside, the grove waited, listening, as if the cathedral itself had approved the addition of a new voice to its choir.

THE JOURNALS WENT WITH THEM, wrapped in linen, not because paper needed protection from the evening mist but because reverence asked for ceremony. Damien carried them close to his chest as if they were breathing organs rather than ink and pulp. Marley held the compass Miriam had given her and the one from the wax-sealed box, the needles trembling as if already anticipating where the night would lead.

The hillside was dark, but the stones of the grove gleamed faintly with residual frost that hadn't melted even after a warm afternoon. The path was quiet in that taut way when silence is not absence but listening. Damien hesitated at the threshold of the stones, every instinct of a widower telling him he was trespassing against his late wife's memory. Marley touched his arm, grounding him.

"Remember what she wrote," Marley whispered. "'Inheritance isn't obligation.' We're here to choose, not to chain ourselves."

Damien drew a steadying breath and stepped inside. The air changed immediately. The smell of cedar lifted, faint but undeniable, like the place recognizing him again. Marley unfolded the linen and laid the journals at the center of the spiral, their spines glinting in the dim light.

Damien knelt and opened to the page where his wife had written *a breathing cathedral.* He read the words aloud, his voice quiet but firm.

The grove responded—not with spectacle, but with a shift in the very pressure of the air. Leaves whispered though no wind moved. The stones gave off a subtle warmth. Marley knelt beside him, opening her own ledger where she had recorded her dreams, her soot-stained palms, the rain that followed fire. She set the two books side by side. Old and new. Dead and living.

"Two voices," she said. "One choir."

Damien swallowed hard. "I don't know how to do this without overwriting her."

"Then don't overwrite," Marley answered. "Overlay. Let her words breathe through yours."

He nodded and began. He read one of her entries, then added his own in response, speaking aloud so the grove could hear.

Her: "Do not mistake silence for emptiness."

Him: "Then I will let silence guide me instead of rushing to fill it."

Her: "Not labyrinth—litany."

Him: "Then let my steps be prayer, not puzzle."

Marley listened, tears pooling in her eyes, not from grief but from the beauty of witnessing him find his rhythm between the lines. When he faltered, she reached for his hand. "Keep going. She's not competing. She's answering."

The hum rose—the same subterranean pulse Marley had felt since stepping between the stones weeks ago. The ground itself seemed to approve. Damien closed the journal and placed his hand over it. "All right," he whispered. "Then here's my vow. I won't try to finish her work. I'll let it keep breathing. Through me. Through us. Through whoever comes next."

Marley leaned close, resting her head briefly against his shoulder. "And love can carry it," she said softly, "without lessening what you give to me."

The words were balm. He felt the truth of them not as argument but as release. He pressed his palm into the soil, mirroring the motion his wife had once described, and whispered: "I carry both. I will not confuse keeping with hoarding. I will not confuse honoring with imprisonment. Let the grove tell me what to do next."

A flicker of light flared at the edge of the circle—no fire, no torch, only a shimmer like frost catching starlight. It curved across the stones, spiraling inward, until it touched the journals. For an instant, ink seemed to glisten as if freshly written, and Damien swore he saw his wife's hand move across the page, not to add more but to underline what was already there. Then the shimmer faded, leaving the grove quiet again.

They remained kneeling for a long while, the night deepening around them. Finally, Marley closed her ledger, brushed the soil from her palms, and whispered, "Amen." Damien followed suit, and together they lifted the journals, careful not to disturb the ash-scented hush that remained.

On the walk back, Damien felt lighter—not empty, not relieved, but lighter in the way a person feels when they have set down a burden they weren't meant to carry alone. He looked at Marley, her face serene in the lantern glow. "Love can carry more than one legacy," he said, testing the words aloud.

She smiled, her hand finding his. "And now it does."

Back at the shop, he opened his own journal and wrote a

final line for the night, leaving the left column blank, the right column fuller than usual:

The grove accepted her words and mine together. That is enough. Breathing cathedral, breathing vow. Two voices, one song.

He underlined it once, not for emphasis but for truth. Then he closed the notebook, set it beside hers, and let the silence of the house carry the rest.

8

THE SECRET SOCIETY LEDGER

The basement had always been a place Marley preferred to ignore. It smelled of damp wood and cardboard, and the rafters leaned with the grudging weight of years. But that morning, with rain drumming overhead and the shop quiet of customers, she felt compelled to go below. Compelled wasn't the right word—it was tugged, drawn, as if the compass at her sternum had extended its pull downward instead of outward.

She carried a lantern, the kind Damien had insisted they keep for storms, its glow brushing dust motes into visibility. The steps creaked beneath her, one groaning in warning like it did every time, a reminder that not all wood forgets. She ducked beneath a low beam and moved past the stacks of shipping boxes she had promised to collapse, the spare shelving she never assembled, the crates of books whose spines had cracked in transit but whose words still deserved respect.

The pull led her to the far corner where the rafters angled strangely, as though one beam had been installed by hands too tired or too secretive to follow square lines. The lantern light flicked across a glint—metal among wood. She set the lantern on the floor and reached up. Her fingers touched something rough: cloth binding, iron tacks. She tugged. A cloud of dust fell, and she coughed, but the object came free.

It was a book. Hand-stitched leather, its spine fraying, the cover stamped faintly with gold leaf long since dulled. Across the front, in faded but legible script, were the words: **Order of the Grove – Membership, 1895–1920.**

Marley's pulse surged. She sat on the step, lantern beside her, and opened the cover. The first page held a careful preamble in ink browned with age: *For the keeping of names who pledged to walk in circle, to sing flame into root, to guard the breath of balance until it was asked again.*

Her breath hitched. Names followed, written in neat columns. She ran her finger down the list, each one carrying its own gravity. Hannah Gearhart. Mirabel Colvin. Aurelia Ward. She recognized them from the initials on the grove map, from Nancy's stories, from Aurelia's fragments. But as she turned the pages, the names kept coming, each entry followed by a date of initiation and, in many cases, a symbol drawn beside it: a leaf, a flame, a crescent moon.

And then—she froze. There, written in the careful script of someone not too far removed from her own lifetime: Miriam Merrick. The woman who had left her the compass. Marley's chest tightened. She reached out to trace the name, and the ink smudged faintly onto her fingertip as if it had never fully dried.

She turned more pages, eyes widening. The surnames matched half the businesses in Brookwood. The tailors. The bakers. Families still living, their descendants walking Main Street unaware that their ancestors had been listed here as members of something secret, something bound to the grove.

She carried the book upstairs, her hands trembling, dust still clinging to the leather. Damien looked up from his notes at the table. "What did you find?"

Marley set the ledger down with care, as if it might shatter under too much gravity. "Proof," she whispered.

He pulled it toward him, turning the pages with reverence. "Order of the Grove," he murmured. "Membership records." His finger tapped Aurelia's name. "This is...this is the missing link. This ties the stories to a structure, not just scattered voices."

Damien turned more pages. He stopped at a cluster of names marked with small crosses. "These symbols—look. Death dates. And not just any. Many of them young." He flipped through, then reached for his own satchel where he kept copies of Brookwood's old birth and death records. He began to cross-reference quickly, his pencil scratching. "Here. Jonas Whitcomb. Initiated 1902. Died 1904, age twenty-two. Hannah Gearhart—initiated 1896, died 1899, age twenty-five." He frowned deeper. "So many. Too many."

Marley leaned over. The list felt like a graveyard hiding in plain sight. "What does it mean? Were they killed?"

"Not necessarily," Damien said, but his voice carried the tension of withheld certainty. "But look—every few years, clustered. Then gaps. As if...sacrifice?" He shook his head, unwilling to leap. "Or pattern. We need to know more."

Marley felt the ledger's weight like an anchor on the table. She closed the book gently, her palms still tingling from soot that had only just faded days ago. "Then we're not the first. We're only the next."

Damien nodded, flipping back to his notes. "And maybe

not the last. Which means how we keep this matters more than anything else."

The rain outside deepened, drumming harder on the roof. The grove seemed to lean closer, listening, as if the names inside the ledger were waiting to be spoken again. And Marley knew this was no longer about curiosity or history. It was about legacy—and the cost of carrying it.

DAMIEN SPREAD the ledger open across the back table, weighting its corners with river stones. The rain had not let up outside; water drummed the shop roof with a steadiness that made the room feel more like an ark than a business. Marley paced slowly, arms wrapped around herself, as Damien layered the membership list against his folder of copied town records. His handwriting, neat to the point of severity, filled the margins with names, dates, and small arrows linking one to another.

"Look here," he murmured, pencil tapping at the page. "Jonas Whitcomb—cross by his name in the ledger. Initiated 1902. Died 1904. Buried not in Whitcomb plot, but in Colvin land."

Marley stopped pacing. "Why would the Whitcombs bury their son in another family's plot?"

"That's the question," Damien said. He moved down the list. "Now Hannah Gearhart—marked with a crescent symbol in the ledger. Died 1899. Records say she drowned in the river during a flood. But no grave marker in Whitcomb cemetery. Instead—again, buried with Colvins. This pattern repeats."

Marley leaned over his shoulder, eyes scanning. "So the Colvins became keepers not just of the living, but of the dead."

"Or custodians," Damien corrected grimly. "Holding them closer than family because of something the Order required." He flipped to another page, his voice low. "Here—three initiates from 1915. All dead within four years. All buried in the same section of the old churchyard that no one tends anymore."

Marley's skin prickled. "Clusters. Always clusters."

Damien jotted notes quickly. "Yes. Clusters, then long pauses. Almost as though the Order asked for—or expected—losses during certain years." He looked up, his eyes shadowed. "You don't think...they sacrificed?"

Marley shook her head sharply. "No. That's not what the grove feels like. It doesn't ask for blood." She pressed a hand against her chest where the compass lay warm. "It asks for balance. For listening. If people died, maybe they died keeping. Like Nancy's grandmother facing the fire."

Damien conceded with a nod, though unease lingered. "Still, the burial patterns matter. Families allowing their kin to be laid outside their own lines? That means consent, or fear, or both." He shuffled another stack of papers, old obituaries and newspaper clippings he had copied. "Listen to this—'Mirabel Colvin, keeper of many secrets, interred quietly at Brookwood ridge beside those she walked with.' It doesn't list names, but the phrasing is telling. *Those she walked with.* Not her parents. Not her children. Her circle."

Marley whispered the word: "Circle." She remembered the chant in her dream, the robes, the way fire had bowed into rain. "So even in death, they remained bound to the Order."

Damien nodded. He drew a quick diagram, dots in clusters, circles connecting them. "I think the ledger isn't just record. It's map. Not of land, but of where keepers rest." He shaded a cluster near the Whitcomb-Colvin line. "Burial as cartography. Each generation marking the ground so the next would know where to look."

Marley's throat tightened. "And Aurelia—my grandmother. Her name is here. But I've been to her grave. She's buried in our family plot."

Damien paused. "Yes. Which makes her an outlier. Maybe she was the one who began bending the rule. Maybe she believed the circle wasn't just for the dead, but for the living to carry forward." He turned to her, his expression solemn. "She left you the compass. She broke pattern to give you freedom."

Marley sank into the chair opposite, staring at the ledger. The names blurred, not from age but from weight. "These families...they're still here. Their children are our neighbors. Do they even know? Or has the knowledge thinned, like smoke dissipating until only the smell lingers?"

Damien looked at the cross symbols again. "If they don't know, it's because someone decided to bury the truth along with the bodies. But the ledger remembers. And now so do we."

The rain pounded harder, as if to punctuate. Marley reached for the ledger, turned a page, and found a final column at the back: *Withdrawn.* Only a handful of names. Next to them, faint notes: *Departed town, Refused circle, Dismissed.*

She whispered one name aloud, and it echoed strangely in the rafters. Damien wrote it down, then checked his files. "Dismissed," he said. "And her obituary mentions exile, though the word is cloaked. 'Left Brookwood under strained circumstances.'" He closed his eyes. "Claire's grandmother."

Marley's pulse spiked. "The botanist?"

Damien nodded slowly. "Which means she's not here by

accident. She's come to reclaim something. Or to finish what her family was denied."

The revelation thickened the air between them. Marley closed the ledger, pressing both hands on its worn leather. "Then this isn't just history. It's unfinished business."

Damien drew one last line in his notes: *Burials—pattern of circle. Outliers = dissent, dismissal. Present descendants = potential conflict.* He underlined it twice, then met her gaze. "Whatever this ledger meant to keep hidden, it's about to surface."

They sat in silence, the rain their only witness. Above, the shop groaned in the storm. Below, the ledger seemed to hum faintly, as if the names written within were not content to rest quietly now that someone had spoken them aloud.

Marley felt it in her bones. They hadn't uncovered a relic. They had disturbed a covenant. And the covenant was awake.

THE LEDGER WEIGHED MORE than paper should. Marley carried it wrapped in her aunt's shawl, pressed against her chest as if warmth might soften the gravity inside. Damien walked beside her, lantern in one hand, his notebook tucked beneath his arm, the compasses rattling in his coat pocket like restless bones. The path to the hillside was sodden from the storm, each step sucking at their boots. But the rain had cleared; the air smelled rinsed, sharp with cedar and moss.

When they reached the circle of stones, the grove was waiting. Marley felt it immediately—the hush, not silence but presence, as though the air itself leaned closer. She stepped between the stones with the ledger cradled in her arms. Damien followed, setting the lantern on the ground where its glow brushed lichen into green fire.

"Here?" Marley whispered.

"Here," Damien said, though his voice carried more reverence than certainty. He motioned for her to set the ledger down at the center.

Marley knelt. Her fingers hesitated on the shawl. She thought of her aunt, of the compass left like a riddle, of the silence that had protected her from knowing too much too soon. Then she unwrapped the bundle and laid the book on the soil. The leather cover gleamed faintly in the lantern light.

For a moment nothing happened. Then the air shifted, subtle but distinct: colder at her back, warmer at her palms. Damien crouched and opened the cover to the first page. The list of names seemed darker than it had in the shop, the ink thickening as though it had been freshly written. He whispered the first name aloud.

"Hannah Gearhart."

The ground answered—not with words, but with a low vibration, a hum rising through their knees. Moss at the base of the nearest stone quivered.

Marley's breath caught. "It knows her."

Damien flipped to the next. "Jonas Whitcomb."

Again, the hum. This time a faint flicker of light appeared on the stone's face, like moonlight caught in quartz. It pulsed once, then faded.

He tried another. "Mirabel Colvin."

The pulse was stronger. Marley pressed a hand to her sternum, the compass heating against her skin. "They're still...present. The ledger isn't just memory. It's invocation."

Damien nodded grimly. "Which means we need to be careful. We're not archivists here. We're participants."

Marley's gaze fell to the page where Miriam's name was

written. Her hand trembled as she touched the ink. "Do I say it?"

Damien hesitated, then nodded once. "Ask properly."

Marley drew a breath, the kind that came from deeper than lungs. "Aurelia Ward."

The hum swelled, filling the clearing. The lantern flame bent sideways though no wind moved. Marley felt her chest constrict, not with fear but with recognition. The compass against her sternum vibrated, its needle spinning. A warmth bloomed in her hands, the same warmth she'd felt in dreams when soot had marked her skin. Tears pricked her eyes. "She's here."

Damien laid a steady hand on her shoulder. "Then she knows you carry it forward."

But the ledger was not done. The pages fluttered as if a breeze stirred them, though the air was still. They stopped at the final column: *Withdrawn.* Names marked with notes of exile, refusal. Damien read one aloud before Marley could stop him.

"Eleanor Whitcomb."

The reaction was immediate. The hum fractured into a low groan. The soil beneath them shifted. The lantern guttered. A cold wind whipped across the clearing, sharp enough to sting. The stones darkened as though shadow had bled into them. Marley gasped, clutching the ledger.

"Close it," she urged. "It doesn't want those names spoken."

Damien snapped the book shut. The groan faded, though unease remained, hanging in the clearing like a reprimand.

They knelt in silence, catching their breath. Marley stroked the leather cover, whispering apologies she hoped the grove understood. Gradually the compass stilled, the lantern steadied, the air softened.

"It's not just a record," Damien said at last, his voice rough. "It's a covenant. These names don't belong to us to recite. They belong to the circle."

Marley nodded, throat tight. "We woke them. And they reminded us what's forbidden."

She rewrapped the ledger in the shawl, her hands careful, almost trembling. When she lifted it, the weight felt different—heavier, but more contained, as if the grove itself had pressed its warning back into the pages.

As they left the circle, Damien paused at the stones, looking back. "Every name has consequence," he murmured. "The dead still hold us accountable."

Marley tightened her grip on the book, the compass warm against her chest. "Then we carry it with care. And never alone."

They walked back to the shop in silence, the sound of the river carrying through the night. Behind them, the grove kept its vigil, a breathing cathedral that had tested them and found them worthy—for now.

When they returned, Damien recorded the night's events in his journal, line by line, moon phase noted, weather logged, every hum and flicker described. But Marley took the ledger upstairs and placed it beneath the Book of Wishes. She added one line in her careful script:

May we keep without prying, and remember without stealing.

Then she closed both books and let the silence of the house carry the weight.

9

THE GROVE MAP

The table in the back room had become less a piece of furniture and more a cartographer's altar. Marley spread the wax-sealed box's map across its scarred oak surface, weighting each corner with smooth stones from the river. Beside it lay the ledger, its hand-stitched spine crackling faintly each time she turned a page. On another sheet, she had drawn her own sketches—amalgamations of symbols, spirals, and notes copied from both sources. A pair of compasses rested on the margin, their needles quivering as if impatient.

Damien leaned against the doorframe, sleeves rolled to his elbows, watching her with the wary fondness of a man who knew the line between obsession and calling. "Appears you've been at this since dawn," he said.

"I know," Marley replied without lifting her eyes. Her pencil traced the spiral, following its curve inward to the seven-petal flower at the center. "But it's beginning to make sense."

She flipped to a page in the ledger where Aurelia Ward's hand had drawn a crude flower, annotated with phases of the moon. At the margin was the phrase: *Only in circle shall the breath of balance return.* Marley had copied it three times already, testing the cadence, feeling how it resonated in her own chest when she whispered it aloud.

"Balance," she murmured. "That's the key. Not fire. Not rain. Not bloom. Balance."

Damien stepped closer, curiosity edging out fatigue. "And the circle? Literal or symbolic?"

"Both." Marley tapped her sketch. "The ledger's names were always written in circles—see? Lists looping around symbols. And the map—the spiral path doesn't end, it returns. The flower in the center isn't just a marker; it's the breath point, the place where everything inhales together. Fire, rain, seed, soil. Only in circle does balance breathe again."

Damien pulled up a chair, dragging it beside hers. He took her pencil and began marking faint dots around the spiral's outer edge. "The ledger's burial patterns," he said. "Look—seven, then a space, then seven again. The same rhythm appears in the graves I charted." He glanced at her, his eyes lit with recognition. "They mirrored the grove even in death. Each burial cluster completed a petal of the flower. They weren't random. They were building a map with their bodies."

Marley shivered, half awe, half sorrow. "Then the ledger wasn't just membership. It was blueprint. They carried the grove in life and laid themselves down in its pattern when they died."

Together they leaned over the map. Damien layered transparent vellum sheets atop the parchment, tracing the spiral again and again until the lines overlapped like ghostly echoes. Marley added symbols from the ledger—leaf, flame, crescent moon—at their proper points along the path.

When they stepped back, the image was clear: a living mandala, not static but designed for movement, for ritual enacted through walking and singing.

Marley pressed her fingertips to the seven-petal flower. The paper was cool, but heat bloomed in her chest. "This is what my dreams were leading to. The fire, the chant, the rain—it all belongs here. The circle holds it. Without circle, it consumes. With circle, it balances."

Damien's hand moved across the vellum, annotating swiftly. "We should test it. Not haphazardly. At the right moment." He pointed to the moon phases inked along the spiral. "See? The inner ring marks the equinox. Equal day, equal night. That's when breath balances. That's when we should be there."

Marley's pulse quickened. "The equinox is in two weeks."

"Then two weeks is what we have." Damien leaned back, rubbing his temples. "Until then, we document, prepare, and learn what they tried to leave us. But no rushing."

Marley nodded, though anticipation thrummed in her like a second heartbeat. She looked at the phrase again: *Only in circle shall the breath of balance return.* It wasn't warning. It was instruction. And now it was theirs to follow.

THE BOOKSHOP BECAME their rehearsal hall. Marley cleared the back room of its clutter, stacking unopened boxes against the wall, pushing the table aside until there was enough space to walk in a slow, deliberate circle. The spiral map lay in the center, weighted by the river stones, its ink still glowing faintly in the lamplight. The ledger was open beside it, each page a chorus of names and symbols, ancestors leaning forward to watch.

Marley took the first step.

She moved carefully, tracing the spiral in air rather than ground, her boots clicking softly against the worn planks. Each turn demanded patience; the spiral widened then tightened, asking her body to remember that this was not a line to finish but a path to inhabit. She carried one of the compasses in her palm. The needle swung as if acknowledging her motion, settling toward the center each time she turned inward.

Damien observed, notebook in hand, his pencil scratching quick annotations. "Your pace changes at each curve," he said. "Slows when the line widens, quickens when it narrows. Write that down—it might matter."

Marley stopped at the invisible center, her chest rising with controlled breath. She felt a twinge of dizziness, the way she sometimes did in the grove itself when the hum grew stronger. She closed her eyes. "It's not just walking. It's rhythm. Breath." She inhaled through her nose, exhaled in time with her step. "The ledger called it litany. This is what they meant."

Damien set his notebook aside, pulled the second compass from his pocket, and joined her. They walked side by side, their paths weaving, testing whether two voices could follow one song without stumbling. At first it felt awkward, their strides mismatched, but as they rounded the spiral a second time their movements began to align. The compasses both quivered and stilled in unison.

Marley whispered, "Only in circle shall the breath of balance return."

Damien echoed her, voice lower, grounding. "Only in circle..."

The words filled the room, quiet but resonant. For a moment, the lamplight dimmed, as if the shop itself had exhaled. Marley felt the compass in her hand pulse once, a small vibration. She met Damien's eyes, and he nodded, his jaw tight with the recognition of something larger than rehearsal happening.

They stopped at the center. Damien bent to the ledger and flipped to a page marked with the crescent moon symbol. "Here—it describes seven offerings. Not lives, not blood. Simple things: water, ash, seed, flame, song, silence, and circle itself. Each given in turn, each binding the ritual to balance."

Marley crouched beside him, tracing the words. "Seed—we have in the garden. Ash—from the box. Water—from the river. Flame—we know how to call. Song—we've already begun." She hesitated. "Silence is harder."

"Silence means restraint," Damien said. "Knowing when not to ask. We nearly learned that the hard way with the ledger." He touched the final word. "And circle—it isn't just geometry. It's us. Walking, breathing, carrying together."

They sat back, the air in the room heavy with understanding. Marley pressed her palms against the floor, imagining the spiral etched beneath the boards. "If we do this at equinox, we'll need to prepare each offering. Not just gather them, but ready ourselves to give them without grasping."

Damien closed the ledger with a quiet thud. "Then this is more than study. It's discipline." He reached for her hand, entwined his fingers with hers. "And if we're to carry it, we carry it together. No ledger, no map, no ancestor asks us to do this alone."

Marley smiled faintly, though her eyes shimmered with unshed tears. "Together," she whispered.

The rehearsal continued late into the night. They walked the spiral again and again, refining the cadence, the shared breath, the rhythm of step and word. Damien experimented with recording their pace against a metronome, jotting numbers in his notebook, while Marley tested the feel of holding small objects—seeds, a candle stub, a vial of river water—each time she crossed a symbolic threshold. By the final round, they moved almost silently, their bodies attuned to the space as if it had grown into a shadow of the grove itself.

When at last they stopped, lantern flame guttering low, Marley leaned against the table, exhausted but steady. "We're ready for the stones," she said, more promise than declaration.

Damien closed his notebook, slid it into his satchel, and nodded. "Then equinox it is. But we'll walk it here each night until then. Practice isn't just rehearsal—it's devotion."

Marley pressed her hand to the ledger's cover, feeling its weight answer her touch. "And devotion is what keeps balance."

The room fell quiet, the kind of quiet that wasn't absence but approval. They left the spiral sketched on the floor in chalk, compasses resting at its heart, as if the grove itself had extended a small piece of its breath into the shop.

TWILIGHT DRAPED itself over Brookwood like a veil, neither day nor night but a fragile seam between. Damien carried the lantern unlit; they had agreed to let the grove's own light, whatever form it chose, guide them. Marley bore the offerings in her satchel—seed pouch from the garden, ash packet from the wax-sealed box, a vial of river water sealed with wax, and a stub of beeswax candle that had burned once on her aunt's altar. The compasses hung around their necks, needles restless, tugging against one another as if eager to find alignment.

The grove greeted them with stillness. The stones loomed gray against the dimming sky, each lichen-marked face shadowed yet alert. Marley stepped first into the ring, inhaling deeply, centering herself. The spiral she had practiced for days unfolded in her mind as naturally as breath. Damien followed, his notebook tucked beneath his coat, though tonight he had resolved to record less and experience more.

They began at the outer edge. Marley placed a cedar sprig across the threshold stone, whispering, "Circle begins." Damien echoed, "Circle holds." Their voices wove together, tentative but clear.

Step by step, they moved inward. Marley carried the seed pouch in her right hand, scattering a few kernels at the first curve. The soil accepted them silently. Damien bent and touched the ground, pressing his palm flat as if marking witness.

At the second turning, Marley lifted the vial of river water. She tilted it gently, letting three drops fall to the earth. The scent of river silt rose faintly, improbably, as though the ground remembered its cousin. Damien noted the sensation silently, but more than that—he felt the hum rise through his bones, a soft vibration that matched the rhythm of their steps.

The third offering was ash. Marley unwrapped the cheesecloth and sprinkled a pinch at the base of a stone. The wind, though still air had reigned, lifted the ash into a brief spiral before it settled. Damien caught his breath. "It remembers," he whispered.

They continued. At the narrowing of the path, Damien struck the flint and lit the beeswax stub. Flame flickered, steady against the dusk, illuminating their faces as they moved. Marley carried it carefully, her eyes reflecting its glow. The spiral guided them inward, each step measured, each breath timed.

When they reached the innermost ring, the center where the seven-petal flower was inscribed on the map, Marley stopped. She lifted the flame high, then lowered it to the soil. The candle guttered and extinguished. Smoke curled upward, fragrant, pine-sweet. Silence fell.

But it wasn't empty silence. It was charged, resonant: Damien bowed his head, closing his eyes, letting it saturate him. Marley did the same, her palms open on her knees. For a long moment, they did nothing.

Then, as if cued, both compasses swung together, needles aligning toward the exact center where they knelt. Marley opened her eyes. The seven-petal flower was not carved or painted, but she saw it nonetheless: an afterimage shimmering on the soil, faint light outlining petals made of breath itself.

She whispered the phrase. "Only in circle shall the breath of balance return."

The hum deepened. The stones around them seemed to lean closer. A breeze stirred—not sharp, but cool, brushing their faces. It circled once, twice, then settled, carrying the faint scent of pine and smoke. Damien's hand found Marley's. His voice was steady, reverent. "It's listening. And it's not done."

Marley swallowed, her throat dry. "No. This is only rehearsal. Equinox will be more."

They rose together, walking the spiral outward in silence. At each turn, they paused to acknowledge what had been given: seeds, water, ash, flame, silence. Their footsteps seemed to echo, though no other sound moved in the grove. By the time they stepped beyond the outermost stone, twilight had surrendered fully to night.

Damien finally lit the lantern, though its glow felt almost redundant. The grove itself seemed to shimmer faintly, as though the stones had absorbed their offering and now carried the light inside.

On the walk back down the hillside, Damien finally spoke. "At equinox, we return. But not just to test. To enact. The ledger, the map, the dreams—they've all been leading here."

Marley nodded, her satchel lightened of its offerings. "And when balance breathes again, we'll need to be ready for whatever it restores. Or whatever it demands."

The compasses hung still now, their needles finally at rest. The circle had answered. And in two weeks, it would speak in full.

10

THE BOTANIST ARRIVES

Claire Whitcomb introduced herself with the kind of confidence that carried a room before words did. She stood in the threshold of the bookshop, tall and composed, her dark hair pulled back in a precise knot, boots polished though the streets outside were muddy from last night's rain. In her hand she carried a leather satchel worn by use but meticulously cared for, its brass buckles gleaming.

"Marley Taylor?" she asked, voice brisk yet friendly.

Marley looked up from the counter, where she had been cataloging a delivery of poetry volumes. Something in the cadence of the woman's voice made her skin prickle—not hostile, but insistent, the way a question can feel like it already knows the answer.

"Yes," Marley said carefully. "And you are?"

"Claire Whitcomb." She extended her hand. "I'm a botanist with the Northwest Institute of Ecological Studies. I've come to Brookwood to document rare and endemic flora." Her grip was firm, her smile professional, but her eyes moved past Marley toward the windowsill where a potted cutting of the mysterious bloom rested in filtered light.

Marley followed her gaze instinctively, then placed a hand over the pot, subtle but protective. "Brookwood has its share of interesting plants, certainly. But most are ordinary enough."

Claire tilted her head, the smile sharpening. "Ordinary is often code for overlooked. I've read fragments—old notes, a few articles—mentioning unusual growth patterns in this region. Flora tied to cycles of weather and soil memory." She paused, her eyes flicking back to the bloom. "And rumors of plants not documented anywhere else."

Marley's heartbeat quickened. She forced her voice into calm neutrality. "Rumors rarely make reliable science."

"Sometimes they lead us to it," Claire countered smoothly. She stepped farther into the shop, glancing at the shelves, the corners, the air itself as though measuring the space for hidden secrets. "I'd love to know more about this town's botanical history. Especially anything tied to the old families. Colvin, Merrick, Whitcomb, or Gearhart." She looked directly at Marley then, and though her tone remained polite, her intent pressed. "Does any of that ring familiar?"

Marley felt her palms dampen. The ledger's names blazed in her memory. The compass at her sternum grew warm. She managed a small, noncommittal smile. "Names ring in small towns whether you want them to or not. But history is wide. You might find more at the library than here."

Claire accepted the deflection without visible frustration, but Marley caught the flicker in her eyes—calculation, not disappointment. Claire moved toward the counter, tapping her satchel. "I'm hoping to collect specimens during my stay. Perhaps interview locals, record stories. Sometimes oral histories point the way to forgotten habitats." She paused deliberately, letting the words land. "Particularly groves."

The word struck Marley like a spark against tinder. She schooled her expression, but unease curled through her. Too eager. Too direct.

Damien entered from the back room, brushing dust from his sleeves. He froze momentarily at the sight of Claire, then masked it with cordiality. "Hello Claire!"

Claire extended her arms in embrace. "Damien! So good to see you again"

He hugged her back, his grip firm but briefer than Marley's had been. His eyes darted to Marley, silently asking if she felt what he did.

Claire launched into her practiced rhythm. "I've been tracing lineages of plant records in this region. Brookwood came up repeatedly. Notes about a unique understory ecology—floral clusters, unexplained resilience after fires, species that don't appear elsewhere in the Cascades. I couldn't resist."

Damien leaned against the counter, arms folded, posture casual but protective. "Brookwood's always attracted stories. We have a gift for embellishment. Careful, or you'll find yourself chasing ghosts instead of plants."

Claire smiled. "Sometimes ghosts leave seeds. And seeds don't lie."

Marley shifted the bloom behind a stack of books. Claire didn't comment, but Marley knew she had noticed.

The conversation turned briefly to logistics—Claire asking about local trails, accommodations, places to set up field equipment. Marley answered cautiously, never volunteering more than necessary. Damien watched in silence, measuring Claire's tone, the precision of her questions, the quickness with which she brushed past small talk.

At last, Claire glanced at her watch. "I won't keep you. I've taken a room at the inn for the month. If you hear of anything—an unusual plant, an old story—please think of me." She handed Marley a card. Its design was elegant, embossed, her credentials impeccable. *Dr. Claire Whitcomb, PhD – Botanical Research, Northwest Institute.*

Marley took it, her fingers stiff. "Of course."

Claire gave them one last look, equal parts courtesy and scrutiny, then left, the bell chiming lightly as the door shut behind her.

For a long moment, Marley and Damien said nothing. The silence in the shop was thick, uneasy.

Finally Damien spoke. "She knew exactly which names to say."

Marley nodded slowly, her breath tight. "And exactly which word." She whispered it again, as if it could bite: "Grove."

Damien's jaw hardened. "We need to know who she really is. And why now."

Marley looked at the bloom hidden behind the books. Its petals quivered faintly, as though stirred by a wind only it could feel.

The grove had been waiting for balance. Now it had drawn another player to the circle.

THE NEXT MORNING, Claire returned. She did not pretend it was a casual visit. She carried her satchel again, her boots already damp with dew, her hair pulled into the same immaculate knot. Marley, shelving new arrivals in the front window, stiffened as soon as she heard the bell.

"Good morning," Claire said brightly, but the brightness was measured, like light angled through glass. "I thought I might trouble you with a few more questions—unless I'm in the way?"

Marley swallowed, pushing a book onto the shelf too firmly. "It's fine. We're open."

Claire stepped closer, unrolling a small sketchpad. Neatly drawn botanical illustrations filled the pages: stem cross-sections, leaf structures, floral diagrams. "I walked along the ridge trail this morning and found evidence of unusual soil pH—too alkaline for this part of the Cascades. Often that correlates with plants that adapt differently, or... persist." Her eyes flicked up, sharp with intent. "Does Brookwood have sites like that? Places where vegetation doesn't follow the usual rules?"

Marley forced herself to smile. "If you ask the locals, they'll tell you the whole town doesn't follow the usual rules."

Claire's smile was polite but unimpressed. She flipped another page. "I've read about fire events here. Yet records suggest the flora recovers faster than expected. Almost unnaturally fast. Do you know anything about that?"

The ash in Marley's memory stirred, fire turning to rain, soot on her palms. She kept her voice calm. "Wildfires move strangely in this region. The rains come quickly. Maybe that's what you've read."

Claire studied her for a long moment. "Maybe." Then she shut the sketchpad. "You're protective, I see. That's good. But secrets rot when they stay buried."

Marley's chest tightened. "And sometimes secrets keep us safe."

Before Claire could respond, Damien emerged from the back, carrying a box of old census ledgers he'd been sifting through for patterns. His eyes narrowed slightly at the sight of Claire. He set the box on the counter with deliberate calm.

"Back so soon?" he asked.

Claire offered her professional smile again. "Curiosity doesn't keep banker's hours."

Damien gave a short nod and began unpacking the ledgers. But his attention sharpened when Claire leaned casually against the counter. "I've been tracing some family names," she said. "Whitcomb, Merrick, Colvin, Gearhart. Even Nye." She held his gaze. "My grandmother lived here once. Briefly. I've never been told why she left."

Marley froze. Damien's expression didn't change, but Marley could feel the shift in him, the way his mind seized on the surname. Whitcomb. He remembered the ledger: Eleanor Whitcomb. Withdrawn. Dismissed.

Claire's tone sharpened with just a hint of steel. "Do you remember anything about her? Eleanor Whitcomb?"

Marley opened her mouth, but Damien cut in smoothly. "We've come across the name. Small towns remember everyone, one way or another." He pushed a census book toward her. "But I can't say the story's mine to tell."

Claire tilted her head. "Then whose is it?"

Damien didn't answer. Instead, he closed the box of ledgers with finality. "Perhaps the library archives will serve you better."

Claire studied him for a long beat, then nodded slowly. "Perhaps they will." She lifted her satchel. "Thank you for your time."

When the bell chimed behind her, Marley let out the breath she hadn't realized she was holding. She turned to

Damien, voice low. "It's her. The ledger—Eleanor Whitcomb. Dismissed."

Damien nodded grimly. He pulled the ledger from the drawer beneath the counter, opening to the final column. There it was: *Eleanor Whitcomb – 1917 – Dismissed*. A faint annotation read: *Trespassed sacred boundary. Refused circle.*

"She wasn't exiled from the town," Damien murmured. "She was exiled from the Order."

Marley's throat tightened. "And now her granddaughter's here, asking about the grove."

He sat heavily, flipping through his notes. "Dismissed means the circle itself rejected her. That's different from leaving by choice. If she trespassed, if she refused to keep silence..." His hand raked through his hair. "Then this family has unfinished business with the grove. Claire didn't come by chance. She came to claim what was denied."

Marley pressed her palms flat against the counter, steadying herself. "Do you think she knows the story? Or is she searching blind?"

Damien met her gaze, his eyes dark with unease. "She knows enough to say the right names. Enough to aim straight for the grove. Blind, no. But whether she knows the cost—that's the question."

The shop seemed smaller suddenly, the ledger heavier, the very air thickened by the weight of Claire's presence even after she had gone. Marley shivered. "Then the equinox isn't just about balance anymore. It's about who gets to stand in the circle."

Damien closed the ledger with a decisive snap. "And we can't let her be the one to write herself back in."

The rain outside had slowed, but the quiet that followed felt more dangerous. Marley looked at the compass on the shelf, its needle trembling faintly though no one touched it.

The grove already knew another descendant had stepped into Brookwood. And it was waiting to see who would carry the vow forward.

CLAIRE'S PRESSURE did not arrive like a storm; it accumulated like barometric change—subtle, measurable, undeniable. By midweek, she had spoken to Professor Ashcroft on the sidewalk, to Evelyn over at the café counter, to Mrs. Keene as she sorted parcels. Her questions wore civility like a lab coat: *Are there public easements near the ridge? Has anyone surveyed the understory after that twentieth-century burn? Where do you all gather for seasonal walks—near any old stones, perhaps?* She smiled when she asked. The smile never reached her eyes.

Marley's unease thickened into vigilance. Twice she found Claire's card slid under the bookshop door with a neat note on the back—*"If you decide to collaborate, my institute assumes liability and can compensate for specimens."* Twice Marley fed the card to the stove and watched the edges curl inward on themselves like petals retreating from frost. Late one evening, closing the back alley gate, she noticed a faint crescent in the damp soil near the garden bed—a half-moon heelprint from a boot not either of theirs. Beside the seven seedlings, a single petal lay bruised, as if fingers had considered taking more and then thought better of it.

"Don't jump to conclusions," Damien said, crouched by the bed with his good flashlight. He was examining without touching—the way you look at a sleeping animal's chest to make sure it rises and falls. "A delivery driver could have wandered back here. Kids cut through alleys."

"Kids don't wear field boots with laminated shanks," Marley said, more sharply than she meant. She pressed her lips together. The old habit of apology rose; she set it down. "I feel her in the room even after she leaves it."

"Then we make the room smarter," Damien answered. He straightened, wiped his hands on his jeans. "We keep without hoarding. And we keep by documenting everything." He kissed her temple and shouldered his satchel. "I'm going to the archives."

He began with the library's microfilm, the kind that casts your own face ghostly on the glass while you scroll the town backward. The machine whirred; newsprint fluttered past in a gray river—weddings, grain prices, a banner headline about a flood that had rearranged the river's opinion of its banks. He paused at 1917. The *Brookwood Sentinel* ran a column called *Town and Temper*, equal parts gossip and grievance, written by someone with a taste for euphemism.

Disruption at the Brookwood Line, the item read in December. *An itinerant researcher, a Miss E.S., disturbed a winter rite, insisting upon the freedoms due to "science." The council discourages meddling with private observances and urges outsiders to mind weather and welcome in their proper spheres.*

He copied it by hand, then circled *Miss E.W.* He knew better than to assume—Whitcomb was not the only W in the alphabet—but the ledger had already done the arithmetic. He scrolled forward two weeks. Another item, bland on the surface, savage underneath: *Eleanor Whitcomb departed with haste after a misunderstanding regarding property boundaries and night access to ridge land. The council wishes her productivity in realms better suited to her temperament.*

"Exile, wrapped in good manners," Damien muttered. He kept going.

At the archives, Damien found the council minutes from 1916–1920, churchyard plot assignments, and the map of easements near the ridge that people pretended were current.

The council minutes were inked in a tidy hand with more ellipses than truths. *On the matter of nocturnal trespass... on the matter of proprietary knowledge...on the matter of the boundary between public curiosity and private keeping...* Names rarely appeared. Motions passed. The phrase *"the circle consents"* surfaced twice and then never again.

He was about to give up on finding anything with teeth when he noticed a slim, misfiled folder wrapped in aging twine found left in a box labeled 'Church Bake Sale 1915–22,' which is either incompetence or genius."

Inside lay three items: a letter on heavy paper with an embossed crest; a page of testimony that read like minutes taken by someone with a wounded heart; and a small, brittle handbill. Damien spread them on the table under the fluorescent hum.

The letter was dated November 28, 1917, addressed to *Miss Eleanor Whitcomb, Board of Natural Inquiry,* from *Mirabel Colvin.* The script had been hurried and sure.

Miss Whitcomb—

You insist the town's grove belongs to science. I insist it belongs to balance. You speak of classification. I speak of covenant. You call secrecy superstition; I call it stewardship. Last night you crossed a boundary drawn for the safety of more than plants. You tried to lift a bowl from its groove while a circle was walking. You refused the litany and, with it, the protections litany offers. We will not lay hands on you, but we will close the circle against you. Do not come again.

—M.C.

Damien's chest tightened. He turned to the testimony, unsigned but written in a calmer hand.

At the fifth turn, Miss Whitcomb entered the stones without invitation, carrying a lantern with a white shade. She stepped to the center and reached for the bowl, insisting she needed "a complete sample, vessel and residue both." When asked to wait, she said, "Truth is not patient." She took hold of the rim. The flame in the dish rose and circled like a hawk startled. The song broke, reassembled, broke again. There was smoke and there was a wind that did not belong to weather. Lydia stepped forward singing, and the bowl calmed. No one was burned. Miss Whitcomb was escorted to the stones. She would not bow her head to leave.

The handbill was blunt: *NOTICE. Trespass upon sacred ground will not be excused by reason of scholarship. The circle protects what cannot survive exposure. By consent of elders, E. Whitcomb is dismissed. Let the boundary hold.*

Damien closed his eyes. He had spent decades translating human failure into sentences readers could bear. This felt harder: two kinds of ardor colliding—one for knowledge, one for keeping—and the blast radius measured in smoke and years. He copied the documents carefully, then asked Harriet the price of his penance for troubling the dead. "Return what you took," she said, which he had done, and not to spill his coffee, which he had also managed.

By the time he climbed the shop stairs, twilight had pressed its shoulder against the windows. Marley stood at the back table, the ledger open, fingers splayed as if to keep it from sliding into some other era. The compass at her sternum was warm enough that the metal had left a faint circle on her skin. She looked up the moment Damien entered. "Well?"

He set the copies down like offerings. "It's not rumor," he said quietly. "It's record."

She read in silence. The letter first—her eyes flinching at Mirabel's clarity. The testimony next—her breath catching at the image of the bowl rising like a startled bird. The handbill last—her jaw tightening at the word *dismissed*. When she was finished, she placed both palms flat on the table. "She tried to take the bowl."

"And refused to wait for the litany. Refused to be bound by it," Damien said. "The circle closed against her."

Marley's gaze drifted to the garden. In the dim, the two pale blooms had reopened, and the ring of seedlings looked like wet emeralds. "Then Claire didn't come for a paper," she said. "She came for absolution. Or revenge masquerading as revision."

"As writ of return," Damien said. "For her grandmother."

They didn't speak for a long moment. In that space, the house performed its familiar night rituals: the faint chirr of the old fridge, the settling creak in the wall, the shop bell's imagined patience. Finally Marley asked, "What do we do when she asks again?"

"Tell her the truth we can tell," Damien said. "That a place is not a subject. That stewardship isn't gatekeeping. That we will share what the grove permits us to share, which is not coordinates or artifacts but protocols. And then say no to the rest—cleanly."

Marley nodded, though fear tugged. It was not the fear of confrontation. It was older: fear of the circle breaking under scrutiny, of a litany interrupted by a lantern held at the wrong moment. "She was in the alley," she said quietly. "I can feel it in the soil. If she comes back..."

"Then we draw our own boundary," Damien said. "We have allies. Mrs. Keene will stand with us, and Professor Ashcroft will listen if we speak plainly. Nancy will teach us the polite language for a hard refusal." He paused. "And we keep practicing. The best answer to pressure is capacity. The stronger our circle, the less her pushing accomplishes."

As if conjured by her name, Mrs. Keene rapped on the back door with her knuckles. She stepped in without waiting for permission—elders are exempt from certain courtesies—and took in the papers with one narrowed eye. "She's chatting up the council with her five-dollar words," Mrs. Keene said by way of greeting. "Asked me at the post if there's a mailbox on the ridge." She snorted. "Told her there's a lot on that ridge, but the only thing that wants a letter is the wind."

Marley managed a smile. "We found the story of her grandmother."

"Good," Mrs. Keene said. "Stories are better than gossip. They make sharper fences." She looked at the handbill, read it through once, then laid two fingers on the word *dismissed*. "This isn't a curse," she said. "It's a boundary. Boundaries are invitations read correctly."

"Claire reads like a person who cuts to the answer key," Damien said.

Mrs. Keene's mouth twitched—her version of pity for the young. "Then give her the kind of quiz she can't cheat: time." She peered at Marley. "Equinox is close. If she goes sniffing where she shouldn't, the grove will notice. But don't rely on the place to do your scolding. Put your bodies in the way, if you must. That's what keepers are for."

After Mrs. Keene left, they locked the back door with a care that felt ritual. Marley carried the copies upstairs and slid them beneath the ledger, as if layering new paper over old wounds might teach them to heal. She stood by the window, watching the alley's strip of sky fade to ink.

Across the street, Claire cut a silhouette under the inn's lantern—jotting notes, phone tucked between shoulder and cheek, her free hand making the precise motions of a person tracing a map in air. Marley watched her hang up, watched her head tip back as if measuring stars, then watched her turn and meet Marley's gaze through the dark. Claire did not smile. She lifted a hand half an inch in the space between them—neither greeting nor threat—and then disappeared inside.

Marley backed away from the window, heartbeat tapping time against her ribs. "She'll go looking at night," she said.

"She'll try," Damien answered. He took the compass from the shelf and looped its cord twice around his wrist. "But the stones don't like arrogance. And we have more than boundaries. We have a circle."

He pulled the shawl from the chair—the one that had wrapped the wax-sealed box—and set it on the table beside the offerings: ash, seed, water, candle. "Tomorrow we tell Professor Ashcroft and Mrs. Keene exactly what we intend at equinox. We ask them to stand on the road in case Claire decides science trumps courtesy." He glanced up at Marley, a small, rueful smile. "We keep teaching science to borrow without stealing."

Marley exhaled, fear reshaping into resolve. "And if Claire still pushes?"

"Then we draw a clean no in the air, and the grove will underline it," Damien said.

Before bed, Marley added a line to the Book of Wishes, careful script carrying the weight of both petition and promise: *When pressure comes, let our keeping be firm and kind. Let refusal not be a wall but a way back when she is ready to ask properly.*

Downstairs, the shop darkened to its breathing. In the alley, a wind touched the fence and moved on. Up on the ridge, the stones kept their counsel. And in a room at the inn, a young botanist sharpened her questions until they were nearly tools.

Equinox waited, indifferent to human calendars, certain of its arrival. The circle would either hold or fail in the company it kept. Marley laid her palm over the compass and felt heat gather, not warning, not promise—a reminder. Breath in. Breath out. Only in circle shall the breath of balance return.

11

THE CANDLE OF RETURN

The metaphysical shop stood at the far end of Brookwood's main street, a narrow storefront squeezed between the seamstress's window and the hardware store with its endless bins of nails. The air inside was heavy with beeswax, lavender, and something resinous that Marley could never quite place—like the ghost of cedar smoke. Glass jars glowed in the low light, each filled with tapers or stubby votives, colors fading from soft cream to deepest indigo.

Hazel, the shop owner and candle maker, was behind the counter, pouring wax into a mold carved with spirals. Her hair was silver, her wrists wrapped in linen bands stained with herbs. She looked up when Marley entered, her smile faint but knowing. "You've been walking with fire in your hands lately," she said, as though it were greeting enough.

Marley paused, unsettled but not surprised. "Dream fire," she admitted. "And rain. The grove doesn't stop speaking."

Hazel nodded, wiping her fingers on a cloth. "Then it's

time." She turned, reaching to the top shelf where a bundle of blackened tapers had been bound with red thread. Carefully, she unwrapped one and placed it on the counter. The candle was strange—its wax mottled, flecked with herbs, the wick thick and braided as though meant to burn slow and long.

"What is it?" Marley asked, touching it lightly.

"A returning flame," Hazel said. "My grandmother called them that. They're not for light or warmth. They're for memory. When lit, they invite what was lost to step closer—sometimes a spirit, sometimes a story, sometimes only an echo. You don't command it; you only call. And you must call from a place that listens back." Her gaze fixed on Marley's. "That means the grove."

Marley's throat tightened. "And if I do?"

"Then something—or someone—will answer."

She slid the candle forward, refusing payment. "It isn't bought. It's carried. Use it carefully. Flames that return can also reveal why they left."

Marley left with the candle wrapped in linen, her heart pounding as though she carried a live coal rather than cool wax.

THEY WENT to the grove at twilight. Damien carried the compasses and his notebook, though even he seemed subdued by the weight of the object Marley held against her chest. The air was damp from earlier rain; the stones glistened as though washed.

At the circle's threshold, Marley unwrapped the linen. The candle looked older in this light, its herbs darker, the wick almost luminous. She knelt at the center stone and placed it carefully. Damien struck the flint, touched flame to wick.

The candle caught with a low, steady burn. Its smoke curled upward, smelling of resin and rain-damp leaves. Marley closed her eyes.

It happened fast, the way a dream rushes in after you've lingered on the edge of sleep. The grove around her shifted. Darkness pressed thicker, yet light bloomed—seven branches ablaze, held aloft by seven women standing in a circle around her. Their robes were green, their faces indistinct yet deeply familiar, as though her memory had conjured them from fragments she should have known all along.

They sang—not in words but in tones that layered over one another, a weaving of breath and hum. The branches flared brighter with each note, until the grove's stones themselves seemed etched in firelight.

Marley gasped. The vision felt not observed but inhabited. She raised her hands unconsciously, mirroring their gesture. Heat licked her palms, though no branch was in them.

"Marley," Damien's voice cut in, distant but urgent.

She opened her eyes briefly. The candle still burned at her feet, but the grove was doubled—real and vision both pressing against her senses. She swayed, dizzy.

Damien knelt at the edge of the spiral, gripping his compass. "Look—" He held it up. The needle spun wildly, no direction holding. "The grove's field is breaking pattern. It reacts when you move."

Marley's vision deepened. One of the women stepped forward, lifting her branch higher. The fire bent toward Marley, not to consume but to beckon. She heard a voice— not from outside but within her chest—*Keeper of Return.*

Her knees gave way. She dropped to the soil, breath harsh, tears stinging. Damien's hands were on her shoulders instantly. The vision dimmed, dissolving into smoke, into twilight, into the simple flame of one stubborn candle.

Marley pressed her palms to the ground, shaking. "Seven women," she whispered. "Branches lit. They called me—Keeper of Return."

Damien stared at the compass needle, which had finally slowed, pointing once more toward north. "The grove just tested you," he said hoarsely. "And it marked you."

The candle guttered, then steadied, its wick glowing as if satisfied. The grove was silent again, but silence no longer felt empty. It was the pause after a vow, the breath drawn before the next word.

MARLEY HADN'T SPOKEN since the words left her lips—*Keeper of Return.* She sat cross-legged in the damp soil, arms wrapped tight around herself, as if containing the echo of that voice within her chest. The candle still burned at the circle's heart, its flame unnervingly steady despite the breeze weaving through the grove.

Damien crouched a few feet away, his compass laid flat on his palm. The needle quivered like an insect's wing. He lifted another compass from his satchel, setting it beside the first, then pulled his notebook into his lap.

"It's not random," he murmured, sketching a crude clock face on the page. "Every time the wind gusts, the needles over-correct, but when you move—" He gestured for her to extend her hand into the circle.

Reluctantly, Marley did. The instant her palm hovered over the flame, both needles spun counterclockwise, fast enough to blur. Damien's pencil scratched furiously, recording angle and speed. "Again," he said.

Marley withdrew her hand. The needles stilled.

She exhaled shakily. "Damien, this isn't an experiment. It called me something. It named me."

"I know," he said gently, but his eyes were fixed on the instruments. "And if the grove names you, it leaves evidence. If I can chart it, we'll know how it manifests, maybe even how it anchors itself."

Marley shook her head. "Evidence won't soften the weight of it. Keeper of Return. Do you hear what that means? Return what? Spirits? Memories? Burdens no one wanted?"

Damien finally looked up. His face, half-shadowed by lantern glow, was lined with worry. "Return doesn't have to mean dragging the past back. It can mean restoring what was broken. Re-balancing."

Marley hugged her knees, her eyes stinging. "But why me? I didn't ask for this. I just...listened. And now the grove thinks listening is enough to bind me."

Damien set the compasses aside and came closer, kneeling across from her. "Marley, the grove has been whispering your name since the day you stepped into it. All we've done is finally hear it out loud. But listen—Keeper doesn't mean prisoner. You have agency. You can carry what returns without letting it own you."

She shook her head. "What if I'm not strong enough?"

"Then we carry it together." He touched his notebook. "That's why I keep recording. To remind us this isn't madness, it's measurable. When your heart feels like it's drowning, the data keeps us breathing."

She laughed weakly through her tears. "Always the reporter."

"Always," he said, managing a small smile.

THE CANDLE FLARED SUDDENLY, a crackle of resin in the wick. Both of them startled. The compass needles leapt again, spinning so fast the casings rattled. Damien lunged, pinning one compass with his palm as if it might fly away. "It's still responding," he muttered.

Marley leaned forward, her pulse hammering. "Then what's it answering now?"

The flame leaned eastward, bending unnaturally, as though drawn to a force outside the circle. Marley felt her chest tighten. She followed its line of tilt toward the ridge beyond the grove.

Claire.

The thought was instantaneous, unwelcome. She saw Claire's silhouette. Could the returning flame be reaching for her, too—for something her blood still claimed?

Marley's stomach turned. She pressed her palm flat to the soil, whispering aloud without thinking: "Not yet. Not through me."

The flame righted. The compasses slowed. The hush fell heavy.

Damien exhaled, eyes wide. "What did you just do?"

"I said no," Marley whispered. "And it listened."

Damien jotted the phrase immediately, his pencil racing. "Verbal refusal stabilizes compass field. Flame realigns." He looked at her, more solemn than she'd ever seen. "You're not just witness, Marley. You're interlocutor. The grove listens when you command."

She shivered. "That's not what I want."

"It's what you've been given," Damien said softly. "Keeper of Return. Maybe the role isn't about summoning, but choosing what not to summon. Deciding what to let back through, and what to hold shut."

The truth of it pressed against her, too large to carry but impossible to ignore. She stared at the candle's unwavering flame. Somewhere beyond the ridge, she imagined footsteps in the dark, a botanist with questions sharpened to blades. If the grove called her Keeper, then her first duty might be to bar the door Claire's family had once tried to pry open.

The candle burned low, pooling wax around its base. Marley wrapped her arms tighter, rocking slightly as if the motion might steady the tremor in her bones. Damien recorded every fluctuation in the compass readings, every minute the flame leaned, every phrase Marley uttered aloud.

By the time the wick collapsed into wax and the flame sputtered out, both compasses lay still. Damien snapped his notebook shut with quiet finality. "It's done for tonight."

Marley reached to lift the cooled stub. The wax clung to her fingers, warm even in its extinguished state. She wrapped it in linen again, but the weight felt altered, heavier, as though it now carried residue of what had returned.

They walked back in silence, their lantern beam cutting through damp mist. Marley clutched the bundle to her chest. She couldn't shake the image of the seven women, branches lit, voices woven in harmony. And beneath it, the single voice naming her, marking her. Keeper of Return.

The words followed her all the way down the hillside, into the town, and into the restless dark of her own thoughts.

· · ·

THE FOLLOWING night the grove was damp with fog. The air hung thick and white, muffling sound so thoroughly that even their footsteps seemed reluctant to disturb the silence. Marley clutched the linen-wrapped stub of the returning flame in her pocket, its wax hardened into a misshapen lump. She hadn't wanted to bring it back—every instinct told her the ritual was finished—but something in her chest had insisted. The grove, once it began speaking, did not end a conversation mid-sentence.

Damien carried both compasses again, his notebook tucked under one arm. "If there's lingering effect," he said, "we'll know within minutes." He set his jaw as though bracing for weather.

Marley nodded but said nothing. The phrase *Keeper of Return* still hummed in her ribs, as though etched into bone. She hadn't told Damien the part that frightened her most: that when she had refused the flame's pull toward the ridge, it had obeyed. That power did not feel like stewardship. It felt like responsibility sharpened into weapon.

They stepped between the stones. The clearing opened before them like a lung. The compasses trembled instantly, their needles vibrating though the candle remained unlit. Damien bent low, frowning. "Residual field. The flame imprinted something into the circle itself." He scribbled measurements, muttering to himself: "Deviation fifteen degrees west, stabilizing at twenty-two..."

Marley drew the candle stub from her pocket. Even cold, it seemed to radiate warmth. She placed it on the central stone, unwrapped it, and waited. No spark, no smoke. Yet the compasses spun once, a slow circle, as if acknowledging its presence.

"See?" Damien said quietly. "It still answers."

Marley stepped forward, hesitating at the spiral's threshold. Her chest tightened. "What if we've already opened too much? What if the circle's breath is pulling at others too—people who aren't supposed to return?"

Damien looked up, his expression taut. "You mean Claire."

Marley's voice broke slightly. "She's already pressing. And if the flame calls memory, what if it calls her grandmother too? Dismissed or not—she might be listening."

The fog shifted then, curling in a slow eddy across the ground. Marley froze. Damien straightened, lantern lifted high. The mist seemed to congeal into suggestion: a figure at the clearing's edge, tall and still, as though watching.

Marley's breath hitched. "Damien—"

But when the lantern's beam swept across, the shape dissolved back into fog.

He exhaled hard. "It's your fear making form."

"Or it's the grove answering a question we haven't asked," Marley whispered. She placed her palm flat on the soil. The hum returned, low, steady. Not hostile—attentive.

Damien crouched, setting both compasses side by side. Their needles jittered, then spun together in unison. He opened his notebook, recording feverishly. "Synchronized spin at Marley's contact. That didn't happen last night." He glanced at her. "The bond's strengthening."

Marley closed her eyes, steadying her breath. The phrase rose unbidden: *Keeper of Return.* She whispered back, not as prayer but as plea. "Not yet. Not through her."

The compasses slowed. The fog thinned, receding slightly from the circle. Marley opened her eyes. The candle stub flickered once—though no flame burned. A tiny curl of smoke rose, then vanished.

Damien swore softly. "Residual ignition. Without spark."

Marley swayed, dizzy. "It's testing me again."

He caught her by the shoulders, steadying her. "Then answer like you did before. Set the terms. The circle doesn't demand obedience—it responds to authority. Yours."

Marley pressed both palms to the ground, her voice firmer this time. "Return only what belongs. Leave the rest in silence."

The compasses clicked as their needles froze north, perfectly aligned. The fog lifted entirely, leaving the grove clear and still.

Marley sagged into Damien's arms, tears cutting down her cheeks. "It listens. Damien—it listens."

He wrapped her tight, pressing his cheek to her hair. "Then keep speaking. But on your terms. Not Claire's. Not anyone's but the circle's."

The candle stub cooled fully, its surface dull. Marley rewrapped it in linen, trembling. The burden felt heavier than ever—not just keeping, but choosing what returned. And somewhere beyond the ridge, she knew Claire was pressing at the same veil, trying to force it open from the other side.

As they left the grove, Damien's notebook heavy with data and Marley's pocket heavy with wax, both of them carried the same certainty: equinox would not simply balance light and dark. It would decide who the grove answered to.

12

———

THE BOTANIST'S MOTIVE

The spiral path still smelled faintly of resin and ash from the candle of return. Marley had left a small bundle at the third curve—a sachet of dried mint, cedar tips, and fern spores wrapped in linen—an offering meant to cool the fire that still smoldered in her dreams. It wasn't ritual, not entirely, but instinct: a gesture of thanks and quieting.

She and Damien returned the following morning to check whether the soil had accepted it. The sky was overcast, dew heavy on the underbrush. The grove itself was still. Too still.

Damien was the first to hear it: the faint electronic *click* of a camera shutter. He raised a hand sharply, halting Marley's step. They moved quietly through the undergrowth, keeping low.

At the curve of the spiral, Claire knelt. She had the bundle in one hand, lifted toward the light, while her other hand snapped photographs with a slim black camera. She turned the sachet slowly, studying its stitching, adjusting her lens, then taking another burst of shots.

Her expression was intent, almost reverent, though her eyes gleamed with the acquisitive shine Marley recognized from collectors in rare book auctions: the hunger to possess.

"Put it down," Damien said, his voice firm but low.

Claire startled, jerking her head up. She clutched the bundle protectively, then caught herself, smoothing her face into calm. "I was only documenting," she said quickly. "For research. It's an extraordinary piece—clearly crafted with intention. I wanted to capture detail before time or weather compromised it."

Marley stepped forward, fury rising in her throat. "That's not yours to touch, let alone photograph."

Claire rose gracefully, dusting her knees, still holding the bundle. "I didn't disturb it. I promise. I only moved it slightly to see the stitching. It's remarkable work—linen binding like this isn't common in folk herbalism of the Northwest. Whoever made this understood ritual craft."

"Whoever made it," Marley snapped, "meant for it to stay here." She snatched the bundle from Claire's hands, clutching it to her chest. The fabric felt warmer than it should, as if the grove itself had flared at the trespass.

Claire didn't bristle. She studied Marley instead, eyes narrowing slightly, as though recalibrating her approach. "I'm not here to steal. I'm here to learn. This is exactly the kind of evidence my work requires—living tradition preserved in practice, not just written archives."

Damien moved beside Marley, his presence quiet but resolute. "Which institution?" he asked.

Claire blinked. "What?"

"You said research," Damien repeated, his voice cool. "You've mentioned affiliation before. Which university? Which grant? Who signs your credentials?"

Claire hesitated. Too long. "The Northwest Institute of Ecological Studies," she said at last.

Damien's brow furrowed. "That's not an institution. It's a consortium, and it doesn't fund fieldwork like this." He took a step closer, his height and bearing suddenly imposing. "So who are you actually working for?"

Claire's lips pressed thin. "Does it matter? I'm here. I have the training. Isn't that enough?"

Marley's chest tightened. "No," she said flatly. "Not when you step into a place that isn't yours and treat it like specimen and data."

Claire's expression flickered—frustration, calculation, then a smile too quick, too thin. "You're right. I should've asked. But I'm not the first in my family to come here. You know the name Colvin?"

Damien's eyes sharpened. "Of course."

Claire nodded, a strange pride tightening her voice. "Mirabel Colvin was my grandmother. She belonged to the Order once. And she was erased. Banished. Her work dismissed as betrayal." She glanced at Marley, her gaze almost pleading. "I'm here to set that right. To restore her name."

The words landed like stones dropped into water. Marley gripped the bundle tighter, her pulse pounding in her ears. Damien's jaw clenched, and she knew he was thinking of the ledger, of the annotations in faded ink: *M.C. —withdrawn.*

Claire's smile widened, brittle but unbroken. "So you see —I'm not intruding. I'm returning."

The grove around them whispered—a hush of leaves though no wind stirred. Marley felt the compass at her chest tremble against her sternum. The returning flame had warned her. Return could heal. Return could also wound.

And now, return had a face.

CLAIRE DIDN'T FLINCH beneath their silence. If anything, she seemed to draw strength from it, as though the weight of her revelation deserved a pause, a moment of awe. The fog hung low across the grove, muting the edges of her figure, but her eyes shone clear and sharp.

"You've read the stories," she pressed. "You've seen the same names in your ledgers that I have. Mirabel Colvin was part of the circle, and then—gone. Do you think she simply stopped believing? That she just left? No. She was erased. And you both know what that means."

Marley shifted uneasily, clutching the herbal bundle tighter. Her chest still ached with the echo of last night's refusal: *Not yet. Not through her.* She could feel the compasses vibrating faintly in Damien's pocket, as though the grove itself recognized the Colvin name.

Damien's voice cut through the tension, low and precise. "Erasure isn't the same as injustice. I've read the testimony." He pulled his notebook free, thumbing through until he found the copied transcript. "Your grandmother interrupted a litany. She tried to lift a vessel mid-ceremony. She refused to leave when asked. That isn't erasure—it's breach."

Claire's jaw tightened. "That's one version. Written by those who wanted her gone. Have you ever considered that she wasn't breaking ritual—she was exposing fraud?"

"Fraud?" Marley repeated, startled.

Claire turned to her, voice softening into persuasion. "Yes. Think about it. A circle of women guarding plants and songs like secrets, refusing to share them with the wider world. My grandmother wanted to bring knowledge into light—into science, into medicine. Imagine what those herbs could have done in hospitals, in field kits, in the hands of healers outside a grove." Her eyes gleamed. "But they silenced her. They called it dismissal. I call it fear."

Marley's throat tightened. The sachet in her hands pulsed faintly warm, as though disagreeing. Yet part of her heart hesitated. She had seen the vision of seven women, branches burning. She had felt the authority of the phrase *Keeper of Return.* But who decided which returns were permitted, and which were condemned?

Damien shook his head, his voice sharpening. "No. I've read enough accounts to know this wasn't about sharing knowledge—it was about taking it. Your grandmother wanted possession, not partnership. She called truth impatient, Claire. Those were her words. She thought the circle should bend to her timeline, her ambition. That's not science. That's arrogance."

Claire's lips curved into something between a smile and a snarl. "You speak as though ambition is sin. But what has your circle's secrecy earned you? A ledger gathering dust. Graves without markers. Whispers in the woods that no one outside this valley believes." She stepped closer, her voice gaining heat. "If she had been allowed to publish, to preserve, to propagate—Brookwood wouldn't be a forgotten footnote. It would be a center of knowledge. And her name would be honored, not cursed."

Marley recoiled slightly. Claire's fervor was too sharp, too close. She remembered Mrs. Keene's words about boundaries: *Boundaries are invitations read correctly.* Claire read everything as invitation—data, specimen, even Marley's silence.

Damien stood his ground. "Your grandmother wasn't cursed. She was warned. And she refused to heed it. The Order didn't erase her—they protected the grove from her."

Claire's eyes narrowed, her tone icy. "And now you protect it in the same way. Hoarding. Deciding who is worthy and who isn't." She gestured at Marley. "But you—you've been chosen. Haven't you? I see it in the way you carry yourself. The grove speaks to you. That candle wasn't just wax—it was litany, and you heard it. Why should you decide who hears and who doesn't?"

Marley's mouth went dry. The word *Keeper* pressed against her lips, but she couldn't speak it aloud.

Damien saw her falter and stepped closer, his body a shield. "Because the grove already decided. And it didn't choose your grandmother. It dismissed her. That dismissal is part of the covenant. And if you keep pressing, Claire—if you keep crossing boundaries—it may dismiss you too."

For the first time, Claire's expression wavered. Not fear exactly, but recognition: that Damien was not speculating, but speaking with the weight of knowledge. Still, she recovered quickly, masking the crack.

"Dismissal," she said evenly. "Legacy." She let the words hang, then added: "The difference is who writes the record. And I intend to rewrite it."

She turned sharply, her boots crunching against damp soil, and strode out of the circle. Her silhouette blurred into fog, then disappeared.

The grove sighed once, a low exhalation through branches, before settling again. Marley's pulse still raced. She clutched the sachet close, whispering to the soil, "Not through her."

Damien's notebook shook faintly in his hand. He pressed it closed and looked at Marley. "Now we know," he said grimly. "Her motive isn't research. It's restitution."

Marley shivered. "And restitution can be more dangerous than theft."

The candle of return was gone, but its weight lingered. The grove had spoken once to Marley, naming her Keeper. Now another voice pressed in—bloodline demanding reentry. And the circle, whether willing or not, was already listening.

DAMIEN RETURNED to the archives because truth never sits all in one box. He began with council minutes and moved to church ledgers, then to the dusty folder of "miscellaneous town matters" where Brookwood stored anything that didn't fit a category and therefore mattered most.

A creased envelope, brittle at the folds, bore the Colvin seal in blue wax. Inside, a letter dated May 1919, written in Mirabel's steady hand but leavened by haste:

To the Council and to the Circle—

I believe we have a duty beyond our fences. The herb we've nursed won't survive if we refuse to share its language. I have arranged a trial with a Portland apothecary to prepare tinctures under my supervision. Nothing will be taken without restoration. Nothing will be named outright. We will borrow and return.

—M.C.

Beneath it, pinned by a rusted paper clip, sat the reply: unsigned, likely scribed by a clerk for elders who preferred their caution to wear plain clothes.

Miss Colvin—

The circle is not a market. You call it sharing; we call it exposure. Ritual without place becomes recipe, and recipes are easily stolen. Your plan ignores the cost of naming and the harm of half-truths. Withdraw.

Damien read the exchange twice, then a third time, letting the tone of both letters settle in his bones. He turned to a thin packet marked *Churchyard—plot amendments.* A page of assignments—Colvins, Merricks, Whitcombs, Gearharts—then a later page with a note beside **M. Colvin:** *plot designation pending; rites withheld.* The words were precise, not cruel. The effect was brutal.

"Two dismissals," he said to himself. "First Eleanor Whitcomb in '17 for trespass. Then Mirabel in '19 for commerce." He glanced up. "And they withheld rites. Not exile from town—exile from circle."

It was a slim notebook, hand-stitched in the same way as their ledger, but smaller—minutes from "quiet sessions," the meetings the council didn't enter into the public record. Damien turned pages until he found Mirabel's name again. The entry was brief, only a handful of lines:

She brought bottles in her satchel; she swore they were empty. After we walked the fifth turn, she presented a label draft —seven leaves in a circle. "For posterity," she said. "For packaging." The bowl lifted its rim and the flame leaned toward the path, as if smelling for sale. We closed the circle and sang her name into silence. She would not bend her head to leave. Two elders guided her to the stones. She did not return.

Damien closed the book with a soft thud, the sound a small amen for a grief no one had wanted to write down. He copied the passage carefully.

On his way back through town, he passed the metaphysical shop. Hazel stood in the doorway, arms folded, eyes older than the street. "You've been listening to the dead," she said, not asking.

"They speak in other people's handwriting," he answered.

She nodded once, satisfied. "Tell the living to mind their tone."

He climbed the hill with the documents sealed in a plastic sleeve against the damp. The sky had the color of pewter, and the wind made the firs sound like an organ being tuned. Marley was in the back room with the ledger open and the returning flame's linen bundle on the table, as if presence could be wrapped and made polite.

"What did you find?" she asked, without turning, as though she recognized the way he carried news.

He laid the copies down and walked her through the sequence—the letter to share, the refusal, the quiet session, the phrase *sang her name into silence*. Marley read without blinking, jaw set, a muscle in her cheek working as if chewing an unswallowable truth.

"She meant well," Marley said at last, voice low. "And meaning well broke something."

"Meaning well without consent," Damien said. "Ambition speaking the grammar of generosity."

Marley set her fingers on the phrase *rites withheld* as if warmth could soften ink. "Claire thinks she's mending her grandmother's shunning," she whispered. "But every time she pushes, the circle strains." She glanced toward the window, to where the garden's pale blooms held their constant vigil. "I can feel it. The hum's not even. The grove keeps skipping—like a song with a scratch."

"Show me," he said.

They hiked to the grove in the hour the day tries to decide whether to hold or surrender. The path at the western edge—where brush used to hide small, stubborn stones—had more of itself showing than before, as if the earth had been coaxed or pulled. Marley crouched. A strip of bright flagging tape clung to a twig, a color the hillside did not make on its own.

"Trail tape," Damien said. "Claire."

Marley eased the plastic free and wound it around her fingers so it wouldn't flap a second, louder announcement of intrusion. "She's tracing the forgotten path," she said. "Not by listening. By marking."

At the spiral's mouth, an imbalance announced itself in the body before the mind named it. The air felt choppy, the way a current turns after someone throws a heavy stone into a clear stream. Marley stepped between the stones, and the compasses in Damien's pocket juddered. He took them out. One needle swung to the center; the other stuttered, jittering at the western arc—the direction of the flagged path.

"She's pulling on that thread," Marley murmured. "And the circle feels it."

They walked three turns in silence, then stopped where the ground had always felt solid. A hairline fissure cut across the soil, no wider than a string, dark with damp, new. Marley knelt, fingertips hovering over the crack. "Not deep," she said, "but wrong."

Damien crouched beside her and traced the line with the blunt end of his pencil. "A seam," he said. "Pressure release." He looked toward the trees, toward where Claire had been earlier that day with the sachet in her hands. "She's waking fractures that were sleeping politely."

Marley closed her eyes, pressed her palm to the ground, and did what she had begun to learn how to do: speak to a place without presumption. "What do you need?" she whispered. The hum answered, faint at first, then steadier—a plea in the shape of a single word that wasn't a word: *hold.*

She nodded. "We can hold." She opened the linen bundle and set the stub of the returning flame at the fissure's edge, unlit, a presence not a spark. Then she added a pinch of ash, the smallest seed, a drop of river water. "Silence," she said, and said nothing else.

The compasses calmed. Damien watched the needles

settle and felt his chest loosen the way it does after a cough that finally clears. He looked at Marley's profile—focused, listening, tired—and loved her with a fierceness that had nothing to do with protection and everything to do with witness.

They stayed until dusk folded itself into night. The fissure did not close, but it did not widen. The hum evened. An owl took up a position above them and pronounced the hour in a language older than science. When they finally rose, Marley left the linen bundle where it was, the stub resting like a blackened tooth beside the line in the soil.

"Won't someone find it?" Damien asked.

"I hope someone does," Marley said. "Someone who knows how to read it as 'enough' instead of 'sample.'"

They took the long way home, skirting the ridge road. A camera trap winked red from a fir trunk—the kind biologists set to learn the private lives of deer and bears. Damien plucked the card from its slot, pocketed it, and left the housing dangling empty. "We'll return it," he said, deadpan. "With the pictures we choose."

In the shop, Mrs. Keene was waiting in the back room with her coat still on. "She's been at Professor Ashcroft again," she said without preamble. "Asking about 'public access' and 'historic trails.' The phrases make a racket that sounds like law and smells like trouble."

Marley poured tea and pushed a cup into Mrs. Keene's hand. "We found a seam in the grove," she said. "Small, but real. It felt like a warning."

Mrs. Keene sipped, then set the cup down with a harder click than tea requires. "Warnings are gifts that don't come wrapped." She studied their faces and softened a little. "All right. Speak your plan."

Damien laid out the papers—the letters, the quiet

session minutes, the notes he had taken as if numbers could shoulder part of the weight. "We document. We tell the council what we can prove and what we can't. We ask for a boundary affirmation before equinox. And we invite those who still carry the circle's names to stand with us on the road that night."

Mrs. Keene nodded. "And if the girl shows up anyway with her clever bag and her camera traps?"

Marley answered before Damien could: "Then the circle will dismiss her. If it must."

Mrs. Keene held Marley's gaze longer than was comfortable. "That's not a spell you cast like a lasso," she said gently. "Dismissal isn't punishment. It's protection. It costs."

"I know," Marley said. "I felt the cost just reading the record." Her throat tightened. "But the fissure costs, too."

Mrs. Keene blew out a breath that seemed to carry decades. "Then let's hope she hears *no* as a way back later, not a door slammed now." She rose, tugged her coat tighter. "You two sleep in shifts if you have to. Places breathe easier when their keepers do."

After Mrs. Keene left, Damien slid the camera card into his laptop. The first images were harmless—a fox's shadow, raccoon whiskers too close to the lens, wind-blurred ferns. Then Claire appeared, headlamp throwing a halo, hand on the flagged twig Marley had unwound, eyes bright with the terrible certainty of a person who thinks the world owes them a door if only they knock cleverly enough. In one frame, she stood at the spiral's mouth, head tipped as if listening. In the next, she had one foot inside the stones.

Marley's stomach clenched. She remembered the fog shape that dissolved beneath their lantern, the compasses stuttering, the sudden lean of the unlit stub. "She's already pulling," Marley whispered. "It's not just intention. It's action."

Damien ejected the card, set it face down on the table like a playing piece no one should touch. "Then equinox will be a decision point, not a demonstration."

Marley went to the Book of Wishes and added two lines in a hand steadier than she felt:

Let what returns be what can be kept safely.

Let what presses without consent learn to rest.

She stood at the back window and watched the alley where night made a narrow river. Across the street, the inn glowed with the warm rectangle of Claire's room light. A shadow moved once against the curtains—head bent, the gesture of someone still writing, still planning.

Marley pressed her palm to the glass, as if the pane were the circle's edge and Claire the pressure on the other side. The cold steadied her. Behind her, Damien stacked documents and blew out the lamp. Somewhere above the ridge, the owl spoke again, and the grove answered with a hush that sounded, to Marley's ear, very much like resolve learning how to breathe under tension.

"Hold," she whispered to the hillside, to the ledger, to her own chest.

The word held. The night did, too.

13

GROVE DREAM #1 – THE CEREMONY

The dream arrived like a tide, slow at first, then pulling her entirely beneath. Marley knew it was a dream even as she stepped into it, but the knowledge did nothing to blunt its reality. She stood in the grove, yet it was not the grove she knew. The brambles and moss were gone, the stones were sharper, freshly set, their surfaces clean and unweathered. The air glowed red, as though the night itself had taken on blood.

Above her, the moon hung swollen, crimson as a heart. Its light bathed the grove in hues of rust and ember, painting the women who circled the clearing in shades of fire. There were seven of them, each holding a branch stripped of leaves and tipped with flame. Their robes were long and green, moving like water against their ankles. Bare feet pressed into the soil, steady as roots.

Their voices rose in unison—not words, but a sound older than language, a layered chant that seemed to come from beneath the earth itself. The song built upon itself, note upon note, until the air vibrated. Marley felt her own chest hum with it, her ribs resonating like the hollow of a drum.

In the center of the circle lay a shallow stone pool. Its surface mirrored the red moon, rippling faintly though no breeze touched it. Each woman dipped her burning branch into the pool in turn. Fire hissed against water, yet instead of extinguishing, the flame grew brighter, taller, as though water itself fed it.

Marley's breath caught. She knew instinctively that this was no ordinary gathering. This was consecration.

One woman stepped forward from the circle. She was older, hair streaked with white, though her movements carried the grace of someone both weary and certain. She held her branch high, flame bending toward the moon. Her voice, when it broke from the chant, was clear and commanding.

"Tonight, beneath blood's witness, we anoint the Keeper of Seed and Flame. Let her carry what roots must rise and what fire must renew."

Marley's heart thundered. She looked around, expecting another figure to step forward, some chosen one to be revealed. But the women's faces were blurred in dream-light, indistinct. Except one.

At the far side of the pool, a younger woman moved forward. Her branch flared brighter, illuminating her face. Marley's breath stilled—it was her own face, gazing back, solemn and radiant.

The older woman dipped her fingers into the pool and drew wet spirals on the younger Marley's brow. Steam rose, the scent of fern and pine mingling with smoke.

"Keeper of Seed and Flame," the elder intoned, pressing her wet hand to Marley's forehead. "You will guard the planting and the burning. You will balance death's ash with life's bloom. Through you, return will find root."

Marley staggered back, though her dream-self accepted the blessing. It was as though she inhabited both bodies: the watcher trembling at the edge, and the initiate anointed at the center.

The chant rose again, louder, fierce. The flames on the branches shot high, red against red. The pool bubbled, though no heat rose from it.

Marley whispered in disbelief, her voice nearly lost in the chant. "Why me?"

The younger self turned her head, eyes meeting hers across the dream. The answer came not in words but in sensation: the weight of soil poured into her palms, the scorch of flame against her skin, the steady beat of her heart syncing with the circle's chant.

Because you already listen.

The vision surged, the chant deafening, the moon descending closer until it filled the sky. Marley felt her body unravel, her blood burning, her bones rooting.

She woke with a cry, drenched in sweat, her palms blackened faintly as though touched by soot. The room was dark, still, the only sound Damien's slow breathing beside her. She sat upright, shaking, the dream still alive in her chest.

And then she saw it.

On her pillow lay a fern leaf, damp with dew. Its edges glistened in the dim light. The windows were closed. The air was dry. But the leaf smelled of rain and earth, as though plucked that very moment from the grove.

Marley touched it with trembling fingers. The damp seeped into her skin. She pressed her palm flat against her chest, whispering into the dark.

"Keeper of Seed and Flame."

The words tasted like fire and roots all at once.

MARLEY COULDN'T BRING herself to sleep again. The fern leaf lay on the nightstand, spread open like a hand, its damp sheen stubbornly refusing to fade. She stared at it until her eyes burned, then finally eased herself from bed, careful not to wake Damien. Her body ached with the residue of the dream—the hum of chant still in her ribs, the sensation of soil in her palms. She moved to the kitchen, lit the small lamp, and set the leaf on the table as though it were a relic.

Minutes later, Damien padded in, hair mussed, eyes narrowed in sleepy concern. "You cried out," he said. His voice was low, not accusation but care.

Marley nodded mutely, gesturing to the leaf. "Dream," she whispered. "And then this."

Damien rubbed his face, then leaned over the table. He touched the edge of the fern, then pulled his fingers back sharply. "It's wet."

"I told you."

"Marley, the windows were locked. There's no draft, no condensation. This is..." He exhaled. "Residue. That's what it feels like. The dream crossing over."

Marley pressed her palms against her temples. "It wasn't just a dream. I was there—seven women, branches lit under a blood moon. They anointed a Keeper of Seed and Flame. And Damien—" her voice faltered—"it was me. Or at least it felt like it was me."

Damien sat across from her, eyes intent. "Tell me everything. Don't filter. Every word matters."

She did. She described the shallow stone pool, the chant vibrating the air, the flames that grew stronger in water. She recounted the older woman spiraling her brow with wet fingers, the younger version of herself receiving it, and the voice that pressed against her ribs: *Because you already listen.*

Damien wrote as she spoke, his shorthand quick, precise. "Keeper of Seed and Flame," he murmured, underlining it twice. "So the grove isn't just naming you—it's giving roles. Responsibilities tied to elements. Seed, flame—life and renewal."

Marley's hands trembled. "But why me? Why now? I didn't ask for this. I don't even know what I'm supposed to do."

Damien looked up from his notes. "Maybe asking isn't part of it. Maybe it chose you because you didn't ask. Because you're not grasping. You're listening."

She swallowed hard. "And if I fail? If I can't hold it?"

"Then we carry it together," Damien said firmly, echoing the words he had spoken in the grove after the candle of return. "But we need to know whether this"—he tapped the leaf with his pencil—"is just symbol, or if it holds actual energy from the grove."

Marley blinked. "Test it? How?"

He stood, already moving. "Compasses first. Then humidity sensors from the workshop. If it bends field lines, we'll know."

They set up in the back room, the one Damien had turned into his makeshift archive and laboratory. He laid the fern leaf on a flat slate tile in the center of the table. Two compasses went on either side, their needles steady north. He adjusted the lantern light, casting the leaf in pale gold.

"Watch," he said. He slid one compass closer until its rim touched the edge of the leaf. The needle jerked, spun twice, then quivered in place—not north, not any cardinal point, but fixed awkwardly toward the leaf's stem.

Marley gasped. "It's pulling."

Damien scribbled furiously. "Magnetic deviation—small but measurable. This isn't just dampness. It's carrying field memory from the grove." He leaned closer, eyes narrowing. "Almost like it's still tethered."

Marley reached out, hesitated, then laid her finger gently along the fern's rib. A jolt shot up her arm—not pain, but recognition, the way her compass had vibrated when the candle bent toward the ridge. She drew her hand back quickly, pressing it against her chest.

"It's alive," she whispered. "Even cut, it's alive."

Damien's face was grim. "Not alive. Anchored. That dream—whatever ritual you walked into—gave you something tangible. The circle crossed its threshold."

Marley's throat tightened. "Then the Keeper role isn't symbolic. It's real. The grove put its mark in my room, on my pillow."

She glanced toward the closed windows, the locked latch gleaming. The thought chilled her. "If it can place leaves, what else can it place? What else can it summon into waking?"

Damien shut the notebook with a snap. "We need to contain it. At least until we know what triggers the tether." He fetched a small glass jar, lined the bottom with dry salt, and gestured for Marley to slide the fern inside. The leaf settled gently, its dampness darkening the crystals.

Marley pressed the lid tight, her hands shaking. "It feels wrong to imprison it."

"Not prison," Damien corrected. "Context. The same way a photograph preserves an image without letting it burn."

Still, when Marley looked at the jar, her chest ached. The leaf's green seemed brighter than before, its veins faintly luminescent in the lamplight. Keeper of Seed and Flame. A vision's blessing, now locked behind glass.

THEY SAT in silence for a long while. The compasses steadied, needles drifting back toward north. Damien finally leaned back, rubbing his temples. "If the circle anointed you in dream, then this is just the first. More will come."

Marley hugged herself. "And if Claire's pushing at the same threshold? What if she dreams too?"

Damien shook his head. "The circle dismissed her grandmother. Bloodline isn't enough. What you're carrying —they wouldn't hand it to someone pressing. They gave it to you because you don't push."

Marley's eyes filled with tears. "But I'm afraid, Damien. Afraid of what it asks. Afraid of what happens if I refuse."

He reached across the table, covering her hand with his. "You already answered, Marley. You said yes the moment you listened. Refusal isn't in your nature. And that's why the circle trusts you."

The jar sat between them, the fern leaf still damp, a fragment of dream made matter. Outside, the wind rose, brushing through branches with a whisper like chant. Marley closed her eyes and heard again the voice that had pressed against her ribs: *Because you already listen.*

She whispered back, not certain whether to herself, to Damien, or to the grove: "Then teach me how."

MARLEY COULD NOT SLEEP with the fern sealed in glass. Even as she lay down beside Damien, the jar pulsed in her thoughts, the leaf's veins glowing faintly behind her closed eyes. Each time she drifted toward slumber, she saw again the circle of women, the red moon, the flame-fed pool. The words pressed harder: *Keeper of Seed and Flame.* By dawn, her decision was made.

She carried the jar in both hands as she and Damien walked the slope toward the grove. Mist clung low to the ground, veiling their steps. The world felt hushed, as though even birds chose silence. Damien walked close, his notebook tucked under his arm, but he didn't speak. He knew this wasn't about data. It was about return.

At the spiral's edge, Marley paused. Her palms sweated against the glass. The leaf looked no less vibrant than the night before—its green unmarred, its dampness still clinging as though freshly plucked.

"I don't know if it belongs back," Marley whispered. "What if the grove gave it to me to keep? What if putting it back rejects the gift?"

Damien touched her shoulder, grounding her. "Then you'll know. The grove answers in its own way."

She nodded, trembling. With careful fingers, she unscrewed the lid. The air that escaped was damp, scented faintly of loam. She tipped the jar, letting the fern slide into her palm.

The moment it touched her skin, warmth flared through her hand—gentle, not searing. She gasped, steadying herself. "It's listening," she murmured.

She walked to the central stone pool, the one long overgrown with moss but still recognizable from the dream. Kneeling, she brushed away damp leaves, revealing a shallow depression where rainwater had gathered. She laid the fern across the surface.

The water rippled outward. The leaf didn't float like

dead matter. It sank slowly, its green deepening, veins glowing faint gold. The ripples spread across the pool, spilling over the edges, sinking into soil.

Marley pressed her hand against the stone's rim. "Do you accept it?" she whispered.

The ground beneath her hand vibrated faintly, a hum not unlike the one she'd felt in dreams. The fissure she and Damien had seen days ago seemed to ease, its tension loosening. The soil sighed as if something had been set back in place.

Damien's voice, low and awed, broke the silence. "It was never yours to keep. It was proof, not possession. And you returned it."

Marley's throat tightened. Tears spilled down her cheeks. "Then I am Keeper not because I hold, but because I know when to let go."

She closed her eyes. The circle's chant returned faintly —not deafening, but gentle, like lullaby. The pool stilled. The leaf vanished into water, its glow fading.

THEY STAYED LONG AFTER, sitting in silence on the damp ground. The compasses Damien carried pointed true north, steady as stone. He wrote notes but quietly, as if wary of disturbing the peace that had settled. Marley clasped her hands together, still feeling the warmth in her palms.

"It wanted to be back," she said at last. "It never belonged on my pillow. That was only the message. The place it belongs is here."

Damien studied her face, then reached across, brushing his thumb over the soot-like marks that still lingered faintly on her skin from earlier dreams. "And you're the one who can hear the difference. That's why they chose you."

Marley leaned against him, exhausted but steadied. The fear that had consumed her the night before had shifted. The weight was still there, but it no longer crushed. It rooted. She could bear it because she understood it now—not as burden, but as balance.

When they rose to leave, Marley looked once more at the pool. It reflected the sky, pale gray through morning mist. But when she blinked, for a split second she saw the blood moon again, saw the branches aflame, saw her dream-self anointed.

She smiled faintly. *Seed and flame.* Two halves of one whole. Planting and burning. Growth and renewal. The circle had not given her power. It had given her responsibility.

And she would not refuse it.

BACK AT THE SHOP, Marley unwrapped the linen that had once bound the candle of return. She pressed it against her chest, whispering softly, "Keeper of Seed and Flame." The words no longer tasted like fire and ash alone. They carried rain, root, and soil.

Damien placed his notes beside her. "We'll track everything," he said. "Every dream, every vision, every object that crosses over. If the grove is weaving memory into matter, we'll map the threads."

Marley nodded, her hand still pressed to her chest. "But the mapping isn't enough. We have to live it. Hold, release, balance. That's what the grove asks."

Damien kissed her forehead, gentle. "Then that's what we'll do."

Marley looked out the window toward the ridge. The

trees swayed slightly in the morning wind. She thought she heard them whisper, not warning but affirmation.

Return had been tested. And for the first time, she felt ready to bear the name they had given her.

"Keeper of Seed and Flame," she whispered once more, and this time the words did not tremble.

They rooted.

14

TENSION AT THE LIGHTHOUSE

That morning, the fog clung thick along the coast.

Sophie sat at the kitchen table, her small hands clenched around a mug of cocoa she hadn't touched. Her eyes were wide, too old. Damien sat opposite her, trying not to show how her silence unnerved him. Finally, she whispered, "Can you make the trees stop whispering?"

The words hit him like a wave. He leaned forward, his voice careful. "What trees, sweetheart?"

"The ones by the ridge," she said quickly, as if speaking fast might keep fear from catching. "When the wind blows, they sound like voices. Not like normal wind. They call. They know my name." Her eyes brimmed with unshed tears. "I don't like it."

Damien's chest tightened. He wanted to tell her it was only wind, only branches rubbing. But the compass in his satchel still carried yesterday's tremor, and Marley's damp fern leaf still glowed in his memory. He reached across the table, covering Sophie's hands with his own. "You're safe here. The grove can't hurt you."

"But it wants something," she whispered. "I feel it. When I'm in bed, I hear it through the window. 'Sophie,' it says. Soft, like when you call me to come inside. But it isn't you."

Damien's throat closed. He glanced toward the window, where the lighthouse's beam had once swept. Beyond the bluff, the ridge waited, its dark silhouette thick with firs and secrets. "You don't have to go near it," he said. "Not ever. That's my choice, not yours."

Sophie nodded but her knuckles stayed white around the mug. She looked older than ten, carrying fear that didn't belong to her. Damien felt the old ache return—the one that had gnawed him since the night his wife had died. The ache of failing to protect.

Later, after Sophie had retreated to her room, he stepped outside, the ocean wind sharp against his face. He pulled the compass from his pocket. The needle wavered, as if uncertain whether to honor north or bend toward the ridge. He shoved it back into his coat and cursed under his breath.

The grove wasn't content with whispers to Marley. Now it reached for his daughter.

That evening, Marley came to the lighthouse. She found Damien on the rocks below, staring out at the horizon. The salt wind tossed his hair, but his posture was taut, shoulders rigid.

"She heard it," he said without preamble. "The trees. My daughter. She said they whispered her name."

Marley's stomach dropped. "Oh, Damien."

He turned to her, anguish in his eyes. "I can't ask her to carry this. I can't let her."

Marley stepped closer, wrapping her shawl tighter. "You didn't. The grove called me, not her."

"But it doesn't stop at you," he snapped, then softened immediately, shaking his head. "I'm sorry. I just—what if I've already dragged her too close? What if by standing with you, I've opened her to it too?"

Marley laid a hand on his arm. "You haven't dragged her anywhere. The grove whispers to all of Brookwood, Damien. It always has. But hearing isn't the same as being chosen."

He searched her face, desperate. "And if it decides otherwise?"

"Then it would have marked her already," Marley said firmly. "But it hasn't. You know it."

The tide surged, crashing hard against the rocks. Damien looked away, his jaw tight. "I don't want her to grow up with voices in the dark. I don't want her to fear sleep. I don't want her to wonder if she's next."

Marley's eyes softened. "Neither do I. And that's why I need you to choose, Damien. Not for me. Not for the grove. For yourself. I don't want you to carry this because of me. I need to know it's what you choose freely."

He turned back to her, the ocean reflected in his eyes. "And if I can't choose both? If choosing you means risking her?"

Marley's hand slipped from his arm. The ache in her chest was sharp, but her voice stayed steady. "Then choose her. Always her. Because love that protects is stronger than any legacy."

The wind howled between them, a sound like branches whispering. Damien closed his eyes, torn between blood and vow, between past and present. Marley stood beside him, silent, refusing to force him, knowing this moment would shape everything that came after.

The lighthouse loomed above, its beam long dark but its walls still bearing witness.

The grove was waiting.

DAMIEN DID NOT SLEEP that night. He sat in an old recliner chair with worn arms and a sway that creaked against the floorboards. Sophie's door was closed, her light long out, yet he kept glancing toward it as though silence itself might betray her.

On the table before him lay two objects: the leather-bound ledger Marley had entrusted to him for study, and the compass he carried everywhere now. The compass needle trembled faintly, quivering between north and something else—an invisible pull east, toward the ridge where the grove waited.

He stared at it, jaw clenched. "You don't get her," he muttered under his breath. "Not my child."

The words sounded braver than he felt. Because hadn't the grove already proved it reached where it wanted? Into Marley's dreams, onto her pillow, into their very bones? He pressed the compass closed, as if snapping a lid could silence hunger.

The ledger lay open to a page where names curved in ink, some scratched out with deliberate care. He read them again: women erased, dismissed, banished. Mirabel Colvin, Eleanor Whitcomb. He thought of Claire prowling like a shadow at the inn, the camera traps Marley had found. Legacy had teeth, and it always bit at the living.

When dawn bled into the kitchen, Marley found him still in the chair, shoulders hunched, eyes hollow. She set a mug of coffee beside him, her fingers brushing his knuckles. "You didn't sleep."

"Couldn't."

She sat opposite, folding her shawl around her. The

morning light softened her face, but her eyes carried the same exhaustion. "Sophie?"

"Quiet," Damien said. "But she'll wake with the memory. Children don't forget voices that call their names in the dark."

Marley looked down, tracing the rim of her cup. "The grove doesn't want her, Damien. It wants you."

"And that's worse," he said sharply, then winced, dragging a hand through his hair. "If it wants me, it reaches through her to get my attention. It uses what I love most. That isn't something I can forgive."

Marley's heart twisted. She wanted to protest, to insist the grove wasn't manipulative but misunderstood. Yet she had felt its pressure herself—testing her boundaries, demanding her return offerings, naming her Keeper when she hadn't asked. "Maybe it isn't about wanting," she said softly. "Maybe it's about balance. If you're near it, your family feels the echo."

Damien looked up at her, eyes dark. "That's exactly my fear. That by standing with you, I've put her in the crosshairs. I promised her mother I'd keep her safe. And safe doesn't look like this."

Marley inhaled sharply. "Then don't stay out of duty. Stay if you choose. I won't bind you with legacy. I can't. You have to be free to walk away."

He leaned forward, elbows on his knees. "But walking away doesn't erase what's already stirring. If the grove knows her name, if it's pressed its whispers into her dreams—then even leaving may not silence it."

"Then we hold the line here," Marley insisted. "We set boundaries together. Teach her that hearing isn't the same as keeping. That the grove speaks, but we decide whether to answer."

Damien studied her, seeing the tremor in her hands despite the strength of her voice. "You believe that?"

"I have to," she said simply. "Or else the fear wins. And if the Keeper of Seed and Flame is ruled by fear, the circle breaks before it's rebuilt."

Her words hung between them, fragile yet undeniable. Damien closed his eyes, exhaling slow. He wanted to believe. He wanted to trust that balance was possible—that his daughter could grow up in Brookwood without the grove claiming her piece by piece. But the image of her small hands wrapped around the cocoa mug, knuckles white, would not leave him.

He opened his eyes. "Marley, I love you. But I can't let my daughter inherit fire she never asked to touch. If I choose this, I need to know the grove won't take her."

Marley reached across the table, covering his hand. Her eyes brimmed with quiet pain. "Then we'll ask it together. Tonight. At the stones. If the grove means to press into her life, it will have to answer me first."

The resolve in her voice steadied him even as it terrified him. She was offering to stand in the breach, to use her newly given role to demand clarity from a force older than either of them. Damien's heart ached with both gratitude and dread.

"You'd do that?" he whispered.

"For her. For you. For us." Marley squeezed his hand. "Because I love you too. And love without freedom isn't love. I need you to choose, Damien—not be cornered."

The sea crashed below the lighthouse, indifferent and eternal. Damien looked at Marley and knew this was the moment that would decide not only his path, but his daughter's future. He nodded once, weary but resolved.

"Then we'll go tonight," he said. "And the grove will answer."

Marley closed her eyes, whispering the words she had carried since the blood moon dream: *Keeper of Seed and Flame.* But this time she added silently, *Protect what should not burn.*

THE NIGHT WAS CLEAR, the sky bruised purple and scattered with stars. The ridge loomed darker than usual, the grove's silhouette rising like a crown against the horizon. Marley and Damien left the lighthouse after Sophie fell asleep, a lantern swinging between them. Each step up the path carried a weight neither spoke aloud.

Damien carried his compass and notebook, though he wasn't sure either would help against what they were about to face. Marley carried only the small linen cloth that had once bound the candle of return, folded neatly in her pocket. She touched it often, as if it steadied her heartbeat.

When they reached the spiral's mouth, the stones shone faintly in starlight. The air had the stillness of something waiting.

Marley inhaled deeply. "If the grove is reaching for her, it's through me. Through you. Through us. Tonight we end that."

Damien's jaw flexed. "And if it doesn't listen?"

"Then we make it." Her voice didn't tremble.

They stepped into the spiral, following its slow curve until they reached the central stone. The clearing felt alive, the soil humming faintly under their boots. Damien set the compass down. The needle spun once, then froze pointing east—toward the lighthouse. His stomach twisted.

"It's tethered," he said hoarsely. "It's still pulling toward her."

Marley knelt at the center. She laid the linen cloth across the stone, spreading it like an altar. She placed her palms flat against it and closed her eyes.

"Keeper of Seed and Flame," she whispered. The words rang like invocation. "I speak as one chosen. Hear me."

The ground trembled faintly, a ripple of vibration through the circle. The air thickened. The firs around them stirred though no wind blew.

Damien's breath caught. "It hears you."

Marley pressed harder. "You may call me, you may test me, but you may not take what is not given. Sophie is not yours. Her name is not yours to speak. Release her."

The clearing pulsed with silence, then with sound—not voice, but the layered hum Marley had heard in dreams, the song of seven woven into one chord. It pressed into her bones, demanding attention.

She held firm. "Release her."

The compass needle quivered, then swung back north. The tremor in the soil eased. Damien's eyes widened. "It's listening—changing course."

But then the hum grew louder, more insistent. Marley staggered, vision flashing with images: Sophie's small hands clutching her cocoa mug, her frightened eyes, her name whispered by branches. The grove pressed harder, not yielding but showing. *It has already touched her.*

Marley gasped, nearly losing balance. Damien caught her shoulders, steadying her. "What is it? What do you see?"

"Her," Marley choked. "It already reached her. Not possession—attention. Like...like it was asking a question through her." She pressed her palms back down, tears stinging her eyes. "Then hear my answer now. Not her. Me. I carry the seed. I carry the flame. Take your balance from me alone."

The hum shuddered, then shifted. It softened, retreating from sharpness into something like acquiescence. The firs stilled. The soil's vibration eased into calm. The compass needle locked north, steady.

Damien exhaled a long, shaking breath. "You did it. You pulled it back."

Marley collapsed against him, exhausted, sweat cooling on her brow. "No. We did it. It heard me because you were here."

He wrapped his arms around her, holding her tight. The grove's silence deepened—not absence, but rest. A lull after a demand had been answered.

Marley pulled back, eyes fierce despite her exhaustion. "Now you choose, Damien. Not the grove, not me. You. Do you stand in this with me, knowing what it asks?"

Damien's throat worked as he swallowed. He thought of Sophie asleep at the house, her breath steady, her name safe again. He thought of his late wife, her sketches of spirals, her belief that places could breathe. And he thought of Marley, her palms still marked faintly with soot from dreams that would not leave her.

"Yes," he said, voice low but unwavering. "I choose. Not because I'm bound. Because I love you. Because I love her. And because balance only holds if someone stands in the middle. I'll stand with you."

Tears slipped down Marley's cheeks. She reached for his hand, gripping it tightly. Together they stepped from the circle.

Behind them, the grove exhaled, branches whispering once, then falling quiet. For the first time in weeks, Marley felt the silence as blessing, not threat.

As they descended toward the lighthouse, Damien looked back once at the stones, then at Marley. "If it tests us again?"

She squeezed his hand. "Then we answer again. But it will never have her. Only us."

The beamless tower rose to meet them, its walls still strong against the night. Inside, Sophie stirred but did not wake. The trees along the ridge swayed in ordinary wind, no whispers, no names.

For now, the grove had heeded. For now, balance held.

And for the first time, Damien believed they might keep it.

15

———

THE GROVE'S FIRST GUARDIAN

The donation arrived in an orange crate that still smelled faintly of citrus and old ships. Mrs. Keene lugged it through the bookshop door with a grunt and a conspiratorial glance that said, *Don't ask me to fill out a form first.* Marley hurried from behind the counter, wiping dust from her hands onto her apron.

"From whose attic?" Marley asked.

Mrs. Keene shrugged, setting the crate on the back table. "Estate clean-out on Harbor Lane. Widow said her husband never threw anything away; I believe her. There's a tangle of ledgers, pamphlets, and a few things that look like they remember being paper in another life." She patted the crate, then lowered her voice. "At the bottom, there's a journal stitched the old way." Her eyes flicked to Marley's chest, where the compass cord lay against her sternum. "It wanted to come here."

Marley felt the familiar prickle at the base of her neck—the sense that, in Brookwood, objects sometimes chose their owners. She lifted the top layer of ephemera—rail schedules, a church fête flyer, a seed catalog with watercolor radishes—and found, beneath a folded lap blanket, a slim volume tied with faded ribbon. The leather was river-stone smooth, the hand-stitching small and sure. In the corner of the cover, pressed into the leather with a heated stylus, someone had burned a tiny seven-petaled flower.

Her pulse beat once, hard. She untied the ribbon, eased the cover open, and read the first line written in a young hand that wanted to be careful and could not help being ardent.

This is the book in which I will tell the truth as I can bear it.

The name beneath was not the one she expected.

—M. Ward (not Aurelia, her daughter)

Marley looked up too quickly, the room tilting a fraction. "Mrs. Keene," she said, her voice a thread. "It's—"

"—not the mother," Mrs. Keene finished softly. "The daughter." She slid into the chair opposite and pulled the lamp closer, its amber circle pooling across the table. "I thought you'd better read with good light."

Marley's fingers trembled as she turned the next page. Ink bled a little into the old paper, but the words had the vividness of fresh speech.

Mother says a guardian's work is mostly patience and small hands. She means hands that can hold things gently and let them go again. I am still learning both.

Marley's throat tightened. She remembered her own hands over the returning flame, the way the grove had listened—how the fern leaf had pulsed on her pillow and then belonged, unmistakably, back in the pool.

She read on.

The circle sings differently depending on who begins the song. When Mother leads, the notes climb straight up; when Lydia leads, they bend like willow branches, and the fire prefers her voice. Tonight we planted secrets with petals. Mother says the ground will forget them unless we ask properly. I am trying to learn the grammar of asking.

"'Planting secrets with petals,'" Mrs. Keene repeated, tasting the line. "That's a line a town remembers even if the town thinks it forgot."

Marley copied the sentence into her own notebook before she could lose it to the rush of pages. She turned another leaf. The handwriting steadied.

We placed seven stones along the ridge—small enough to be called nothing by anyone who doesn't know what they're looking at. Each is carved with a mark that looks like a letter only because letters were born from marks like this. Mother says the stones listen to one another across distance, like cousins at opposite ends of a table catching a joke between them. She said: "When the wind runs clean through all seven, we have balance."

A sketch followed: seven small circles on a rough line of hill, each with a different directional sigil—tiny arrows bowed, spirals tipped, a notch like a crescent set inside a square. Marley's stomach tightened with recognition. The sigils matched the scratchings she and Damien had seen half-buried near the western edge, the not-quite-letters they had traced with the blunt end of a pencil. The overgrown path. The fissure in the soil. Here, a century earlier, were their beginnings.

She turned another page and found a passage that read like instruction and confession at once.

Truth must be planted where it can grow into shade. Names, when spoken too often, go brittle. So we press truth beneath trees that can hold it in root and branch. Alder keeps grief gently; cedar keeps pledges straight; maple keeps stories patient; fir keeps watch; yew keeps the door to those who stay; oak keeps strength; and birch keeps beginnings clean. Mother says this is how to make a map that refuses to be called a map.

Seven trees. Seven keepings. The ache that lived just under Marley's breastbone bloomed and then steadied. She could see, suddenly, what the diary was pointing toward without saying outright: a grid that was not lines and numbers, but living anchors. A design built to carry charge through chlorophyll and chant.

"Damien," she whispered. "He needs to see this."

"Finish the page," Mrs. Keene said, a palm raised in gentle interruption. "There's more."

Marley read.

We walked the spiral at dusk, Mother and I, with only a bowl of water and a lantern for company. There were no other women tonight; it was my naming lesson. Mother said: "Listen to where your feet do not want to go. That is the place in you that still wants to control outcome." I am twelve, and I want everything to bend. The grove does not bend. It breathes. Tonight the breath was short—like someone had been running and only just stopped. We set our hands on the stones and waited until it steadied. Mother said: "A guardian's first work is to share breath. The last is to know when to keep it for the dying." I do not yet know how to do either without tears.

The lamplight trembled. Marley reached up, found she was crying, and let the tears go without apology. Mrs. Keene's face softened, the sternness in her features smoothing into something like pride and grief mingled.

"She was a child," Mrs. Keene said. "And the place expected a grown heart from her. Brookwood has always asked much of its daughters."

Marley turned to a page where the ink had blotted from wetter weather or a steadier hand pressing too hard.

There is a man—he says the names for us are quaint and the plants are promising. Mother says promise is what a plant gives ground in exchange for patience. He says promise is what one writes on a bottle to pay for winter. I saw the flame lean away from him when he spoke. I saw it look for other mouths. We sang his name into silence after he left. Mother said: "This is guarding, too."

The air in the room shifted. Mrs. Keene exhaled. "And there," she said, "is the shadow of what came after."

Marley turned the page and found a sketch of the shallow stone pool, drawn from above—seven concentric ripples labeled with the moon phases. Around it, small notes in the margin: *ash at third turn; seed at fifth; silence at seventh.* She traced the words with her fingertip, feeling again the weight of the returns she hadn't asked for. A sentence below the pool made her heart hitch.

When fire met water, I thought the world would choose a side. It did not. It chose balance. Mother says: "This is the first lesson of any keeper."

She closed her eyes. The blood moon returned behind them, the red branches, the wet spiral drawn on her brow. *Keeper of Seed and Flame.* The dream had not been invention. It had been instruction revived.

When she opened her eyes, Mrs. Keene was watching her with that careful, assessing kindness Marley had come to lean on. "You'll need more than poetry," Mrs. Keene said softly. "You'll need proof for the ones who insist on types and measures. Show Damien the diagrams and the tree notes. Let his mind in where it can walk and not just wonder. Strengthen his faith with his own tools."

Marley nodded, already gathering what she would show him. She turned a few more pages. The entries grew sparser, then resumed, older, as if years had folded and the diary had waited.

Mother says we map what cannot be seen by walking it, singing it, and planting it. She says a grid that does not look like a grid will last longer than one you can roll up and steal. The map lives in root, not in ink.

And then, a line that felt like someone had slipped a key into Marley's palm.

When I am guardian, I will keep truth beneath trees and plant secrets with petals, not because I am hiding, but because some truths are seeds. They cannot survive exposure. They must be placed where time can make them into shade.

Marley copied that sentence down, word for word, tears blurring the loops. She turned to the inside back cover and found three names written on the leather itself, not the page: **Aurelia Ward**—and beneath it, in smaller script—**M. Ward (daughter)**—the name rang like a bell in her bones. Her grandmother. Of course. The ledger had not told everything. Her grandmother had kept a line between generations with more than a compass.

Marley closed the diary and cradled it against her chest. "I'll take care of this," she said, and did not have to explain to Mrs. Keene whether she meant the diary, the grove, or the girl who had written in the book a century ago.

"Bring Damien," Mrs. Keene said, rising with a small groan. "And when he begins drawing his lines, don't let him forget the part that doesn't fit lines." She tapped the cover with a knuckle. "Truth beneath trees."

Marley found Damien at his house in the late afternoon, Sophie painting at the table, the cottage warm with small, ordinary life. Sophie glanced up, shy smile, and Marley's heart steadied to see the fear of the night before replaced with the fierce concentration ļof choosing a blue that matched the sea. Damien's eyes met Marley's, a question already there. She lifted the diary by way of answer.

On the drive back to the shop, she summarized what she could without rushing: the directional stones, the seven trees with their keepings, the bowl that chose balance, the line about planting secrets with petals. Damien listened like a man being handed the missing center of a puzzle he had been circling for years.

"Flora as circuitry," he murmured, half to himself. "Trees as capacitors, soil as conductor, ritual as current. A grid that looks like a forest." He shook his head, a grin ghosting his mouth despite the worry that had become his first language. "Of course."

"What?" Marley asked, stunned by the sudden light in him.

"Maps that refuse to be called maps," he said, tapping his temple. "We've been trying to overlay the ledger's burial clusters and the spiral's ritual path on our modern topographic. No wonder it wouldn't clean up. We were looking for lines in space when we should have been looking for species in place." He turned the diary in his hands like a delicate machine. "If the daughter's right, the grove is a spiritual grid. The elders drew it with roots, not ink."

Marley's hand found the compass against her chest. The needle quivered, then steadied. "Then we can read it if we learn its language."

Damien's eyes lit with the old ardor that had drawn her to him before grief muted his edges. "We can try. We can test for microclimate anomalies along the seven-tree arc. We can chart pH and moisture at those stone markers. We can listen for the hum when you stand in the right place." He caught himself, softened. "And we can hold all that science inside the circle's consent."

Marley exhaled, something in her loosening at his last sentence. "Yes," she said. "Consent first. Always."

Back at the shop, she set the diary on the table and opened to the pages she had marked with thin strips of torn ribbon. Damien bent over the sketches, jaw working, mind on fire. He began laying translucent vellum over the drawings, roughing in the ridge line, then overlaying a town plat he'd memorized, then the trail map Mrs. Keene had once insisted was only "mostly accurate because a man drew it."

"Here," he murmured, pencil moving sure and quick. "If alder keeps grief and there's a grove of alder at the river bend, and cedar keeps pledges and the oldest covenant tree stands beside the churchyard, then the line between them—"

"—is not a line," Marley finished, smiling despite herself. "It's a path of stories."

He looked up at her. "And stories conduct as well as copper if told often enough."

She touched the diary again, feeling the warmth of fingers long gone. "Then let's begin telling this one properly," she said. "With root and with tongue."

Night leaned against the window as if to eavesdrop. The lighthouse lamp would be dark again, but in this room the lamplight pooled kindly, and in the grove the hum, for once, felt even. Marley traced the seven-petaled flower pressed into the leather and whispered to the girl who had written in it, to the mother who had taught her, to the aunt who had taken up their keeping for a time and then quietly passed the compass forward.

Planting secrets with petals. Truth beneath trees.

"Yes," she said aloud, to Damien, to Mrs. Keene, to the listening air. "We're ready to learn the grid you left us."

He nodded, already sketching the first of seven arcs, careful to leave space where the page wanted breath.

· · ·

DAMIEN SPREAD the vellum across the long oak table in Marley's shop, pinning its corners with stray books. The diary lay open beside it, the daughter's looping script glinting in lamplight. He leaned over, pencil in hand, eyes narrowed in concentration. Marley watched him sketch sigils in quick strokes, each one laid carefully over the map's contour lines. He looked both like the architect he had been before grief slowed him and like a man rediscovering his voice through lines and arcs.

"Look here," he murmured, tracing between two of the seven-tree points. "Alder at the river bend, cedar by the churchyard—you could plot them as a diagonal. Now add oak on the ridge and birch at the eastern slope. The geometry doesn't resolve into a shape we'd call Euclidean, but..." He stepped back, brow furrowed. "It's an energy grid. You can see the symmetry even if it refuses clean lines."

Marley came to stand beside him. The overlay was rough, but the pattern was unmistakable: a constellation, not a blueprint. Roots for stars, stone markers for compass points.

"Mother says this is how to make a map that refuses to be called a map," Marley quoted softly, remembering the diary's words.

Damien smiled faintly, but his eyes were serious. "Exactly. If the elders wanted a pattern no one could plunder, they designed one that hides in plain sight. You'd only see it if you cared about grief and pledges, patience and silence. And who, outside of the circle, would bother?"

Marley leaned closer, inhaling the faint graphite scent. "So you're saying they designed the grove to hum like a circuit. A spiritual grid."

"Yes." His voice sharpened. "And grids have flow. If one point weakens, the whole system staggers. That fissure we saw—the seam? That could be imbalance along the arc. Pressure building where one anchor isn't tended."

Marley's hand tightened around the edge of the table. "And the grove called me Keeper to tend it. Seed and Flame. Plant and burn. Balance."

Damien looked at her, eyes flicking briefly to the compass that rested against her chest. "The role isn't metaphor. It's function. Without someone stepping into it, the grid falters. You saw it in your dream, and now we see it on paper."

Her breath trembled. "But if I'm function, not just witness—then I'm not free, Damien. I'm tethered. Every choice I make echoes through that grid."

He set down the pencil and reached for her hand. "You're tethered because you listen. That's not a chain. It's a thread."

She looked into his eyes, feeling the steadiness there, the way his architect's mind loved form but respected emptiness. "Then you're part of it too," she said. "Because you see the pattern. You read what I can't put into words."

He didn't answer right away. Instead, he returned to the vellum, scribbling quick notes in the margin. "We'll need to walk it," he said at last. "Tree to tree, stone to stone. Document soil composition, water presence, light angles. If the grid is alive, it'll show itself through changes we can measure."

Marley smiled faintly. "Science beside chant."

"Why not?" he said with quiet conviction. "Faith needs data as much as data needs faith. Otherwise, it's just one half limping without the other."

. . .

THE NEXT AFTERNOON, they began. The western path was first—alder grove at the bend where the river slowed to a dark, steady pool. Marley crouched at the tree's base, brushing her fingers against roots thick as ropes. She felt it instantly: the low thrum of grief, not despair but weight, the kind that bends the back but does not break it.

Damien set a sensor probe in the soil, noting moisture and pH. "High acidity," he murmured. "Consistent with alder. But look—the reading is stronger than expected. It's not just the tree; it's the soil around it amplifying."

Marley laid her ear against the trunk. "It holds sorrow gently. Like a mother's lap. This is where they planted grief, Damien."

He recorded her words beside the numbers, refusing to treat them as separate.

At cedar, near the churchyard, the air sharpened, resin sweet. Marley inhaled, chest clearing. "Pledges here," she whispered. "I can feel them binding."

Damien ran his compass along the bark. The needle quivered, then steadied. "It's magnetic," he said. "Slight, but measurable. This tree is an anchor."

Maple on the southern slope sang slower, patient. Fir at the ridge watched like sentries. Yew stood heavy, its shadow deep, the air colder within its reach. Oak towered strong on the rise, its roots sprawling like arms. Birch, white and clean, gleamed even in shadow, its bark peeling in soft curls like new pages waiting for script.

At each point, Marley spoke what she felt. Damien wrote and measured, sketched and compared. Together, they walked a pattern that revealed itself more fully with every step.

By the time they returned to the spiral clearing, twilight had fallen. The stars above mirrored the arc they had traced below. Marley set her palms on the central stone, feeling the hum settle into her chest.

"It is a grid," Damien said softly, standing beside her. "But not one we can own. Only one we can keep balanced. That's why Aurelia's daughter wrote what she did—planting secrets with petals, truth beneath trees. She knew the map would only survive if hidden in living things."

Marley closed her eyes, whispering into the soil. "Then I will keep it."

The ground exhaled. The compass in Damien's pocket steadied north. For the first time, balance felt possible.

THE TWILIGHT AIR thickened as Marley and Damien stood again in the spiral clearing. The journal rested in Marley's satchel, its presence like a pulse at her side. Damien's vellum overlays were tucked in his notebook, fragile but clear—a pattern waiting to be tested not as ink but as lived path.

"Let's walk it," Damien said, his voice quiet but certain. "Not scattered points, not half a circle. The full arc, in sequence. See if it responds."

Marley's heart thudded. The dream of the circle, the chant, the blood moon—all of it swelled inside her chest. This felt like stepping across the line from vision into covenant. "Together," she said.

"Always," Damien answered.

THEY BEGAN at alder by the river bend. Twilight painted the water black, its surface holding a faint sheen of dying light. Marley knelt, pressing her palm to the root. A wave of grief brushed her chest, not heavy this time but solemn, steadying. Damien scribbled quickly, then ran his compass across the root line. The needle bent, pointing not north but to cedar.

"It's aligning," he whispered.

They followed.

At cedar near the churchyard, the resinous air thickened. Marley's breath deepened. "Pledges," she whispered. "I feel them binding me even as I speak."

Damien's compass needle trembled, then swung, pointing toward maple.

They exchanged a glance—half fear, half awe—and walked on.

Maple greeted them with patience. Its branches swayed slowly though no wind moved. The soil at its base was warm despite the cooling night. Marley touched the trunk and felt years unfold in rings beneath her fingertips—memory held in wood.

"Silence, then story," she murmured. "Waiting made holy."

Damien's compass shifted again, tugged toward fir. He checked his watch, then jotted down the change in angle. "It's not random. The sequence matters."

At fir, the air sharpened, bracing. The tree seemed to look down at them, needles whispering faint approval. Damien set his compass at the base; the needle swung quickly toward yew.

"Guardianship," Marley whispered. "Watchers in green."

At yew, shadow deepened. The air turned cold, almost damp. Marley felt the brush of endings here, not cruel but inevitable—the door of passage. She shivered, but laid her hand on the trunk. "Death kept with dignity."

Damien's compass pointed on—oak at the ridge.

Oak towered over them, vast and commanding. Marley pressed both palms against its bark. Strength surged up her arms, fierce and grounding. She inhaled sharply. "Power doesn't belong to us—it passes through."

The compass needle jerked north-east—birch.

They hurried as night bled fully into the ridge. Birch glowed pale in moonlight, luminous against the dark. Its bark curled gently, like paper waiting for words. Marley touched it and felt freshness, beginnings, a breath after sorrow. She whispered, "Birth after death. The cycle whole."

Damien's compass spun once, then stilled, pointing directly back toward the spiral clearing.

Marley met his gaze. "It wants us to return."

They ran.

When they stepped again into the spiral, the stones vibrated beneath their boots. The air thickened until breathing felt like standing inside song. The center stone pulsed faintly with light—no flame, no reflection, but a glow rising from within.

Marley moved forward, heart pounding. She placed the diary on the stone, then set both hands upon it. "We've walked it," she said aloud. "Every anchor, every tree, every grief and pledge. We've kept your map."

The hum surged, filling her chest, filling her bones. Images flooded her: Aurelia's daughter pressing secrets into soil with petals, the circle chanting, the pool of fire-fed water. And then—herself, standing not in dream but here, Keeper of Seed and Flame, chosen not only in vision but in test.

Damien stepped beside her, setting his compass on the stone. The needle spun wildly, then stopped, pointing straight up into the sky. He looked at Marley, awe in his eyes. "It recognizes us."

The ground steadied. The hum softened into a rhythm that felt like breath. Marley inhaled, exhaled, and realized the grove was breathing with them.

"Balance restored," she whispered.

She turned to Damien, tears brimming. "It knows we're together in this. It chose both of us, even if in different ways."

He reached for her hand, gripping it tightly. "Then let's keep it together. Every step. Every breath."

The clearing pulsed once more, then quieted. The stars overhead blazed brighter, as if affirming.

For the first time since the grove had stirred, Marley felt not hunted but welcomed. Not burdened but held.

She closed her eyes, pressed her forehead to the diary, and whispered into the night, "We are ready."

The grove exhaled in answer, and the night held them steady.

16

THE FORGOTTEN PATH

The western edge of the grove had always felt less alive to Marley, as though the trees there were holding their breath. Brambles tangled in thick mats, hawthorn and blackberry choking out any clear line of sight. Even the birds seemed reluctant to sing in the tangle.

On a cool morning streaked with pale light, Marley and Damien armed themselves with clippers, a hand saw, and patience. They began hacking through the brush, vines snapping back at their arms, burrs clinging to their sleeves.

"This looks like it hasn't been touched in decades," Damien muttered, sweat beading on his brow.

"Maybe longer," Marley said, pulling another thorned branch aside. "If Aurelia's daughter wrote that the stones were placed to hold a line, then neglect might have hidden one of them here."

Her words proved prophetic. Half an hour in, Marley's clippers struck stone with a dull *clink*. She knelt, brushed away moss and dirt, and revealed the flat edge of a carved block. Her breath caught.

"Damien."

He was beside her in an instant, crouching low. Together they scraped at the surface until a sigil emerged—spiral tipped with a crescent, deeply etched though softened by lichen.

"Directional," Damien murmured. He traced it with one finger, reverent. "This matches the ones sketched in the diary. West point."

Marley's pulse quickened. "So the forgotten path begins here."

They pushed further, following the undergrowth. Soon, another stone appeared—this one leaning against a fallen log, its sigil arrow-like, pointing northeast. They cleared more brush, following the direction it indicated.

The path began to emerge, reluctant but undeniable: stones staggered like crumbs through the thicket, each carved with its own sigil. Some were half buried, others toppled, but all aligned in a clear sequence.

"It's like walking through an equation," Damien said quietly, jotting notes in his book as they moved. "Each symbol carrying us to the next variable."

Marley felt it differently. With each stone uncovered, the soil beneath her feet vibrated faintly, as though recognizing a long-forgotten rhythm. She closed her eyes at one marker and whispered, "Yes, we're listening." The hum deepened, almost approving.

By the time they had cleared a hundred yards, the brambles thinned, the air shifted, and the path opened onto a thicket unlike any they had seen before.

Seven trees, each distinct, circled the small clearing. Alder, cedar, maple, fir, yew, oak, birch. Their trunks leaned inward slightly, as though bowing toward the center.

Marley stepped forward, awestruck. "The daughter's map. The seven keepings. It's all here."

Damien walked the circumference slowly, running his hand along each trunk. "They're arranged deliberately," he said, voice hushed. "A circle of species, each carrying its role. This is no accident of growth. Someone planted them, centuries ago, as the living arc of the grid."

Marley moved toward the center, her compass warm against her chest. The soil there looked disturbed, a mound where roots met earth. She knelt, brushed away leaves, and found wood.

A long shaft, half buried. She pulled at the soil, fingers trembling. Grain and curve emerged—a wooden staff, weathered but intact, its length carved with the healer's spiral, etched deep enough to survive decades of burial.

Her heart stopped.

"Damien," she whispered, barely able to breathe. "It's here."

He dropped to his knees beside her, brushing earth away with careful hands. The spiral gleamed faintly even in twilight, as though oil still clung to its grooves.

"The staff of the healer's circle," he murmured. "Buried in the heart of the seven."

Marley closed her eyes, pressing her palm against the spiral. A warmth surged into her hand—not heat, but a steady pulse, a rhythm like heartbeat. For an instant she heard voices layered together, the hum of Aurelia's circle, the chant of those who had stood here before.

"Keeper of Seed and Flame," the echo whispered.

Tears spilled down her cheeks. She clutched the staff, feeling both called and tested.

Damien touched her shoulder, his own eyes wet. "We

found it, Marley. Not just proof. Legacy. The forgotten path led us here."

The trees rustled once, though no breeze stirred. The circle of seven seemed to lean closer, bearing witness.

And at the heart of them, Marley held the staff, feeling the grove's memory breathe again.

THE SOIL CLUNG stubbornly to the staff, as though reluctant to surrender what had been entrusted to it. Marley dug with her bare hands, pulling clumps of damp earth aside, while Damien used a small trowel from his pack to loosen the roots entwined around the wood. The deeper they went, the stronger the sense of pressure became—a hum beneath their knees, a thrumming that pressed into their bones.

"Almost there," Damien said, voice hushed as though afraid to disturb a sleeping elder. His hands shook slightly as he scraped the last of the soil away.

Marley's fingers closed around the shaft, cool and surprisingly smooth despite its age. With Damien steadying the other end, they lifted together. The earth released it with a sighing sound, roots snapping free like taut strings loosed from a bow.

The staff rose from the ground, taller than Marley by a head, its grain polished by time and touch. The spiral engraving ran its full length, deep grooves curling upward in perfect rhythm. In some places, the carving still held traces of a resinous substance, faintly aromatic, as though pine sap or cedar oil had been rubbed into it long ago.

As Marley stood with the staff upright in her hands, the circle of seven trees stirred. Alder rustled first, then cedar, then each in sequence until the birch leaves shimmered pale in the last of the twilight.

Damien whispered, "It recognizes its keeper."

Marley's pulse thundered in her ears. She pressed the staff's butt into the soil of the clearing. The hum surged instantly, rippling through the ground, resonating up her arms until her teeth vibrated. She gasped but held firm.

Images flared in her mind: Aurelia Ward's daughter kneeling in the same circle, the staff in her small hands; women chanting by torchlight; the spiral carved anew by careful blades; roots entwining the staff as it was laid down to rest. She saw not only ritual, but cost—exhaustion in their eyes, grief heavy on their shoulders, the understanding that what they were guarding required sacrifice.

She staggered back, Damien catching her elbow. "What is it?" he asked.

"The staff—it carries memory. Every time they used it, it absorbed what they gave. Songs, oaths, grief. It's heavy with them all." Marley looked down at the spiral, tears welling. "And now it wants more."

Damien frowned. "More?"

"Keeper of Seed and Flame," she murmured. "It's calling me to give something of myself. That's the cost of unearthing what was meant to stay buried."

Damien's jaw tightened. "Then maybe we shouldn't have lifted it."

Marley shook her head, though her body trembled. "No. It wanted to be found. But finding isn't free."

She lifted the staff again, steadying it against her shoulder. The trees leaned closer, their shadows long and strange in the deepening twilight. A wind rose suddenly, circling the thicket though the sky above remained still. The spiral in her hands warmed, then glowed faintly—lines of gold threading through the carved grooves.

Damien stared, notebook forgotten in his pocket. "Marley, it's alive."

"It's listening," she corrected, breathless. She lowered the staff so its tip brushed the soil again. The glow spread outward in a ring, faint but visible, tracing the roots of each tree in sequence. Alder to cedar, maple to fir, yew to oak, oak to birch—until the circle closed. The hum deepened, no longer mere vibration but song, low and resonant, as though the ground itself were chanting.

Marley closed her eyes, tears streaking her cheeks. "They planted truth with petals, Damien. This staff was the vessel. Without it, the grid couldn't breathe."

Damien looked at her with both awe and fear. "And now?"

"Now it breathes through me."

She raised the staff high. The trees shuddered in unison. The spiral's glow flared once, then dimmed, sinking back into the wood. The hum quieted, settling into a steady pulse like a heartbeat beneath their feet.

For a long moment, neither spoke. Then Damien said softly, "You said it wants something from you. What kind of something?"

Marley lowered the staff, leaning on it like a walking stick. Her voice was hoarse. "It wants presence. Attention. A keeper who doesn't just hold, but gives. Every time I use it, it will take something from me. Strength. Breath. Maybe more." She looked at him, eyes luminous in the dim. "That's why they buried it. Not to hide it—but to rest it, to let it sleep until another was ready."

Damien reached out, covering her hand where it gripped the spiral. "Then you're not carrying it alone. Whatever it takes, it takes from us both."

Marley's chest ached at his words. She nodded, though a

part of her feared the staff would not honor shared vows. It seemed to know the difference between one heart and two. Still, she pressed her cheek briefly to the spiral and whispered, "Keeper of Seed and Flame accepts."

The staff cooled in her hand, its glow fading completely. The clearing stilled, the seven trees once again only trees.

Yet Marley knew the cost had only just begun to show itself.

They carried the staff back toward the spiral clearing, each step weighted not only by wood but by the inheritance it carried. And in the silence between them, Marley wondered how much of herself she could give before the grove asked too much.

THE STAFF WAS HEAVIER in motion than it had been in the thicket. Marley felt its weight not only in her arms but in her chest, as though every step she took with it pressed her deeper into the soil's memory. Damien carried their lantern, its flame jittering with each stride, throwing the staff's spiral into alternating shadow and light.

The spiral clearing opened before them, the stones gleaming with dew. The air here had always hummed, but tonight it carried an edge—anticipation, almost impatience. Marley's grip tightened on the staff.

"Are you sure?" Damien asked, his voice low. "We could wait. Study. Ease into this. If we rush—"

Marley shook her head. "The grove won't wait. It called us here with the staff in our hands. That's its answer."

He frowned but did not argue. He knew as well as she did that the grove's summons was rarely gentle.

They stepped into the spiral, walking slowly until they reached the center. Marley planted the staff upright in the soil, the spiral aligned with the stone beneath it. The hum surged instantly, rattling through the clearing. The compass at Damien's belt swung wildly, its needle a blur.

Marley pressed her palms to the staff. The grooves of the spiral warmed beneath her touch. "Keeper of Seed and Flame," she whispered.

The clearing erupted with resonance. The stones around them trembled, moss shaking loose in thin clouds. A ring of pale light bled upward from the soil, tracing the spiral path outward. Marley staggered but held firm.

Images flooded her: the seven trees bending inward, roots glowing; Aurelia's daughter pressing her forehead to this very staff; the chant of women long dead yet alive in vibration. She felt them surge into her—memory, expectation, demand.

Damien's hand clamped on her shoulder. "Marley, it's pulling too much. You're shaking."

Her voice trembled but held. "It wants balance. It's trying to align the grid through me."

"Then it's too soon," he said sharply. "You've barely held the staff a night. If you give it everything now—"

"I can't stop it," Marley gasped. Her fingers fused to the spiral as though bound. "It knows I'm here. It won't let go."

The spiral's glow intensified, threads of gold lacing outward into the soil. Damien dropped his notebook and gripped the staff with her, adding his strength. A shock jolted him backward, throwing him to his knees.

"Not me," he choked, clutching his chest. "It doesn't want me."

Marley's tears streaked down her face. "Then I carry it alone."

She pressed harder into the spiral. The resonance peaked, a keening sound rising that made the air itself shiver. The stones around them lit faintly, etched sigils glowing in rhythm with the staff. For a heartbeat, everything aligned: the spiral, the stones, the seven trees far beyond the clearing. A perfect circuit of breath.

Then the staff flared too bright, the resonance cracking like overstretched glass. Marley cried out, pain shooting down her arms. The alignment faltered, the stones flickering.

Damien scrambled forward, grabbing her waist. "Marley, stop! You'll break it—and yourself!"

Her vision blurred. She saw fissures opening beneath her feet, soil splitting. In her mind's eye, she saw the blood moon ceremony fractured, flames guttering, the circle scattering. She realized with a bolt of terror: *if I keep pressing, I'll shatter the grid.*

Summoning every ounce of will, she tore her hands from the staff. The glow collapsed instantly. The hum cut off, leaving silence so sudden it rang. Marley fell forward into Damien's arms, gasping, the staff tipping but not falling.

For a long moment, neither moved. The clearing held its breath.

Finally, Damien whispered, "You stopped it in time."

Marley's body shook with exhaustion. "No. It stopped itself. It showed me what would happen if I pushed too far. Fracture. Collapse. The grid isn't ready."

Damien's grip tightened around her. "Neither are you."

She leaned her forehead against his chest, sobs breaking loose. "It wanted to test me. To see if I'd yield before pride shattered everything."

"And you did," Damien said firmly. He pressed his cheek to her hair. "You yielded. That's strength too."

The staff stood in the soil, quiet now, its spiral dark once more. Yet Marley felt its pulse, faint but steady, as though reminding her: *not now, but soon.*

She wiped her eyes, breathing slowly. "The cost is real, Damien. Every use takes something. Tonight it nearly took everything."

He looked at her, eyes fierce. "Then we decide when to use it. Not the grove. Not memory. Us."

Marley reached out, resting her hand lightly on the staff's spiral. The wood was cool again, almost ordinary. But she knew better. It was never ordinary.

The stones around them glistened with dew, silent witnesses. Above, the stars wheeled on, indifferent yet watchful.

Marley whispered into the clearing, voice raw but steady. "I am Keeper of Seed and Flame. But I will not break the balance by rushing. You'll wait until we are ready."

The soil vibrated faintly, a quiet hum, as though acknowledging her boundary.

Damien rose, helping her to her feet. Together they lifted the staff, carrying it carefully back toward the light-house. Behind them, the spiral clearing fell into silence— not defeated, but patient.

The forgotten path had been uncovered. The staff had been awakened. And the grove had issued its warning: power carried too quickly becomes fracture.

As they disappeared into the trees, Marley held the staff close, her heart heavy with fear and fierce with resolve. She would learn patience. She would learn balance. Or the grove would unmake her.

And she would not let that happen.

17

THE GROVE'S WARNING

The knock came not from knuckles but from hooves. Marley woke to the dull, uneven thud of something striking her porch. The clock on the nightstand read 3:14 a.m., its glow dim.

Another thud answered, followed by a scrape and a muffled cry that chilled the marrow in her bones. She rose, pulling on a sweater, and stepped into the hall. The boards groaned under her feet, the house carrying their tension to every corner.

Marley opened the front door and froze.

A deer stood on the porch, its flank heaving, one leg bent wrong beneath it. Its eyes were glazed, clouded not with pain alone but with something unnatural, a trance that looked borrowed from dream. Leaves tangled in its antlers, not random forest litter but sprigs of cedar, birch, and alder —seven species woven together as though by unseen hands.

"Oh God," Marley whispered, pressing a hand to her mouth.

The deer staggered forward, hooves clattering against the porch boards. It collapsed on its knees, head bowing low. Its breath came in short bursts, visible in the cold air. The leaves shook loose, scattering across the wood.

She knelt, careful but quick, his architect's steadiness guiding his movements. She pressed a hand to the deer's flank. "Heart's racing. Too fast." Her other hand brushed the tangled leaves. Her jaw tightened. Alder. Cedar. Maple. Fir. Yew. Oak. Birch. All seven. Twined together like the thicket.

Marley crouched, tears pricking her eyes at the animal's suffering. She stroked its muzzle gently, whispering soft reassurances it could not understand. The deer's eyes met hers—clouded, entranced, yet carrying something beneath the glaze, as though a message were trapped there.

"Why here?" she murmured. "Why bring this to my door?"

She rose and stepped off the porch, scanning the ground, noticing tracks. She followed them across the frosted grass, her lantern beam darting over prints. The hooves hadn't taken a straight path. They curved in long arcs, weaving tighter as they neared the house.

The path it walked—it's a spiral. Exactly like the one in the ledger. This deer walked the grove's shape. Marley felt her stomach twist. She looked back at the deer, still heaving, still half-dreaming. Its arrival wasn't random. It had been sent—or drawn—by something echoing the grove's memory.

She whispered into the animal's ear, "What are you showing me?"

The deer shuddered once, violently, then stilled, its breath slowing. Marley pressed her hand against its chest, willing strength into it, but the hum that answered was faint and fading.

Marley closed her eyes, grief washing over her. "Then the grove is out of balance."

She opened her eyes and looked into the deer's cloudy gaze, tears spilling down her cheeks. "And I don't think it's coincidence that Claire arrived when it began."

The animal shuddered again, leaves scattering across the boards. Marley's thought, "If the grove is trying to warn us, we can't ignore it. Whatever Claire is doing, wherever she's treading—it's unbalancing the natural memory."

The lantern flickered, the wind sharp against their faces. The deer's chest rose once more, then sank. Silence settled heavy.

Marley bowed her head against its neck, whispering, "We hear you. We'll answer."

The spiral had spoken through flesh and blood. The warning could not be denied.

DAMIEN'S LANTERN beam swept over the frosted grass again and again, tracing the hoofprints in widening arcs. The cold night air bit his lungs, but he ignored it, crouching low to measure the spacing. The deer had not stumbled in random circles. It had walked with eerie deliberation, carving the spiral into earth as though following instruction.

"Marley, the ledger wasn't just symbolic. The spiral they drew—this deer walked it exactly. Even the spacing matches."

His hands trembled as he flipped open his notebook. The vellum overlays he had sketched days ago slid out. He spread them on the grass, lantern pinned above, and set the compass at the spiral's center. The needle jerked wildly, then stilled, pointing not north but directly toward the ridge.

"Dammit," he muttered. "It's resonating. The spiral isn't just a drawing—it's a path the land remembers. And tonight, the deer carried it here."

On the porch, Marley stroked the deer's muzzle, her eyes swollen with grief. The weight of the creature's final breath pressed on her like judgment. She whispered aloud though only the night answered: "You chose my door. Why mine? What have I failed to keep?"

Her hands still smelled of cedar and birch leaves, sharp and sweet. She lifted one of the sprigs tangled in its antlers, its veins dark against the lantern glow. She could almost hear the hum in it, faint but insistent. *Not balance. Broken.*

Her shoulders shook. She wanted to weep for the creature itself—innocent, entranced, forced to carry the grove's message until its body gave out. But the grief sharpened into something harsher: accusation. The deer had died because the circle faltered. Because the Keeper of Seed and Flame had not yet learned how to hold all that was entrusted.

She pressed the sprig to her chest, voice raw. "I'm sorry."

Damien rose from the field, hurrying back up the steps. He crouched beside her, brushing hair from her damp cheeks. "Don't. This isn't your failure. The grove is reacting to disruption, not neglect. This isn't you—it's what Claire's been stirring."

Marley shook her head. "The grove doesn't care about excuses. It doesn't measure intent. It only knows balance or imbalance. And tonight—" She touched the deer's lifeless flank. "—it showed me what imbalance costs."

Damien's jaw tightened. He wanted to argue, to shield her from the guilt that clung like burrs. But he had seen the ledger, the erased names, the punishment doled out to those who tampered with what was sacred. The grove had always spoken through consequence.

He forced his voice steady. "Then we don't treat this as a punishment. We treat it as data. A warning delivered through symbol. If the spiral path is manifesting in animals, it means Claire's presence has fractured something precise. We find where the break is, and we mend it."

Marley looked at him through tears, desperate. "And if it isn't mending? What if it's unraveling?"

He met her gaze, fierce. "Then we hold it together until we learn how. That's what keepers do."

She broke then, leaning into his shoulder, the sobs she had held spilling at last. He wrapped his arms around her, lantern light trembling across their bodies. For long minutes, the only sound was her grief and the restless wind combing the ridge.

When her sobs quieted, he pressed the vellum into her hands. "See this."

She blinked through tears at the spiral diagram, at the careful notations around its curves. "The ledger's pattern," she whispered.

"Yes. And the deer followed it here, exactly. It's not just memory. It's geography. The spiral is etched into the land, into the creatures, maybe into us. That means if Claire's steps cross it wrong, the whole grid ripples."

Marley's hand clenched around the vellum. "She doesn't even know the weight of what she's pressing on. She's tugging at a thread and doesn't see it's holding the whole weave."

Damien's lips pressed thin. "Then we can't let her keep tugging. We have to confront her—soon."

Marley stared at the deer one last time. "Not tonight. Tonight I bury this warning."

They dug together at the edge of the grove, the lantern casting their shadows long and strange across the earth. Marley placed each of the seven sprigs atop the deer's chest, her hands shaking, before covering it with soil. She whispered as she worked, "Keeper hears. Keeper keeps."

When the last clod was patted down, the wind stilled briefly. The hush that followed felt almost like acknowledgment.

But Marley knew: acknowledgment was not absolution. The grove had spoken in blood and silence. Now it was their move.

LANTERN LIGHT SWAYED between them as Damien and Marley climbed the ridge, the earth still damp from where they had buried the deer. Neither spoke. The silence was heavy, deliberate, as though words might scatter the fragile thread of resolve pulling them upward.

When they reached the grove, the stones of the spiral clearing gleamed with dew. The air carried a strange tautness, alive with echo. Marley's compass—slung around her neck—tugged faintly, its needle shivering.

Damien set down the lantern on the central stone. "If the deer traced the spiral to us, then the spiral still exists in memory, not only in symbol."

Marley hugged her shawl closer, the staff strapped across her back. "And if Claire's intrusion twisted that memory, the spiral will show it. We'll walk it. We'll see where it falters."

She took Damien's hand, her palm cold in his. Together, they stepped to the spiral's beginning.

MARLEY LED WITH CAREFUL PACE, her feet aligning with the mossy path between stones. At first, the hum beneath the soil was steady, even reassuring. The air warmed faintly, the trees around them swaying in gentle rhythm.

"Balance here," Damien murmured, jotting a quick note on his pad even as he matched her steps.

They curved inward, the spiral tightening. Marley felt the ground breathe beneath her soles. She whispered, "It remembers us."

At the second curve, the air sharpened. The hum grew brittle, like glass under strain. Marley staggered slightly. Damien steadied her, his own brow furrowed.

"You feel that?" he asked.

She nodded, swallowing hard. "It's the first fracture."

Damien crouched, running his fingers through the soil. It was damp, darker than the rest, as though water had pooled unnaturally. "Not drainage. Disruption. Something pushed energy sideways here."

Marley closed her eyes. In the hum she felt intrusion, a footprint that didn't belong. *Claire's boots*, she thought bitterly. *Claire pressing where silence was meant to lie.*

THEY MOVED ON, following the spiral toward its heart. The further they walked, the stronger the resistance became. Where the spiral should have carried them in steady breath, it now staggered—warmth breaking into sudden chill, light fading into odd shadows.

Damien stopped, holding his compass flat. The needle spun once, then froze pointing south—not toward north, not toward the clearing's center, but outward, as though something beyond the grove pulled against the spiral's flow.

"That's not natural," he muttered.

Marley touched the spiral staff on her back. "It's like the grid is bleeding. The memory map is bent."

At the third curve, the trees themselves seemed to protest. A fir groaned, its trunk creaking though no wind stirred. The branches shook loose needles that fell like rain across their shoulders.

Marley knelt, pressing her palm to the earth. A jolt shot up her arm—an image of Claire bent over an herbal bundle, her camera glinting, her eyes hungry. Marley gasped, pulling back. "It's her. She stepped into the spiral. She marked it."

Damien's jaw hardened. "Then this isn't just disruption. It's trespass."

THEY PRESSED FORWARD, each step heavier. The spiral narrowed, carrying them toward its still point. The hum grew jagged, alternating between harmony and discord like a chord played with broken strings.

At the final stone, Marley stopped. The central clearing should have pulsed with balance, the resting heart of the spiral. Instead, the air was sharp, almost acrid. The soil smelled faintly of smoke.

Damien crouched, touching the ground. His fingers came away blackened, streaked with soot though no fire had burned here in years. He looked up at Marley, face pale. "It's been scarred. The spiral's heart is wounded."

Marley's throat closed. The image of the deer's glazed eyes returned. The animal had walked the spiral faithfully, but when it reached the heart—there had been no balance to hold it. No wonder it had collapsed.

She dropped to her knees, pressing both palms to the soil. "Keeper of Seed and Flame hears," she whispered, voice breaking. "I know you're unsteady. I know you're hurt."

The ground vibrated faintly, not steady hum but stutter. Marley bowed her head until her forehead touched the earth. "I'll mend you," she vowed. "I'll restore what was broken. But you must wait. You must not take more lives to prove your wound."

The vibration eased slightly, softening into silence. Not peace—only acknowledgment.

Damien touched her shoulder. "Marley, this is proof. Claire has bent the memory-map. We have to stop her before the spiral fractures completely."

Marley rose, her knees damp with soil, her palms streaked black. Her voice was raw but steady. "Then the grove has given us our charge. We'll confront her. We'll protect this balance, even if it costs us."

The staff on her back pulsed faintly, the spiral engraving warming. It had heard her vow. It would hold her to it.

THEY LEFT the spiral in silence, the lantern's flame guttering low. Behind them, the stones gleamed faintly, bearing witness. The spiral had shown them its wound. The deer had carried its warning. And now Marley and Damien knew: the battle for the grove's balance was no longer metaphor. It was flesh, soil, and memory.

And the price of failure would not be theirs alone.

18

THE BOTANIST'S PAST

Claire arrived at the bookshop before opening, a gray hood pulled tight against the ridge wind and a battered archival box tucked under her arm. Marley was unbolting the front door when she saw her reflection double in the glass—her own face tense, Claire's set like someone who had chosen a cliff and meant to jump.

"I need to speak with you," Claire said, as soon as Marley turned the key. "Privately. No cameras. No recordings." She lifted the box. "Just this."

Marley stepped aside and let her in. The bell above the door startled the quiet. Damien was already in the back with the kettle, measuring out leaves the way he measured light and distance, careful and exact. He looked up when Claire crossed the threshold, the lines at his eyes deepening.

"You don't come anywhere near the grove," he said, even before greetings could untangle. "Whatever this is—say it here."

Claire didn't flinch. "That's why I brought this." She set the box on the counter and opened the lid. Inside lay a stack of letters bound with faded ribbon, a leather notebook scraped bare of its gilt, and a folded cloth bag whose threads had paled to the color of fog. Claire worked carefully, as if the objects might cut. She slid the notebook forward and rested her palm on the cover. "My grandmother's."

Marley's stomach tightened. "Mirabel Colvin."

"Yes." Claire's mouth twitched into a smile that didn't reach her eyes. "The name you only say in whispers around here."

Damien came closer, the kettle forgotten. Marley watched his wariness take shape—shoulders squared, eyes cooling. The ledger lay under the counter, its stitched spine like a quiet spine in the room.

Claire opened the notebook. The first page held a neat hand, the ink browned with age. *On the preparation of tinctures derived from the unnamed fern of Brookwood; on the possibility of scaling for general use; on secrecy as impediment to medicine.* Beneath the header, a rough sketch: seven leaves in a circle and, below them, a rectangle—a label template—ruled in for dosage and warnings.

"Commercialization," Damien said flatly.

Claire didn't argue. "Ambition," she said, equally flat. "And a conviction that medicine hoarded is medicine lost." She turned another page. Lists of solvents, notes on drying times, tiny drawings of a flower Marley had come to know in her own garden—the undocumented bloom that had arrived unasked and fragrant with deja vu. In Mirabel's sketches, it was given no name, only initials—*S.P.*—and a ring around the letters as if to warn even herself what not to write.

"She believed the herb could do more than whisper to a few women in the woods," Claire said. "She believed it could steady fevers, ease lungs, slow bleeding. She believed secrecy was selfish. And for that, your Order erased her."

Marley didn't reach for the notebook. The words "ease lungs" and "slow bleeding" pressed too easily against the part of her that wanted medicine to be simple and good. She felt the tug; she did not move. "Your grandmother tried to bottle a sacred thing," she said. "The circle is a place, not a label. What's grown inside it breathes differently."

A flicker of anger crossed Claire's face and was gone. She folded the cloth bag open. Inside lay a handful of old glass vials, their corks darkened, their sides smudged with residue. She did not touch them. "She never sold these," Claire said. "She couldn't. They banished her before she could test more than a handful of times. The Council withheld rites. They made her name a curse and her work a ghost."

Damien reached in and lifted one vial by the cork. A smear at its base caught the light—green-brown, stubborn. He angled it toward the window. "Proof of intent," he said quietly. "And proof of why the Order did what it did."

Claire's shoulders sagged. When she spoke next, the edge had worn off her voice. "I'm not here to pretend she was a saint. She was impatient, arrogant, brilliant. She pushed past permission." Claire looked at Marley, and for the first time there was no calculation in her gaze, only hunger and grief braided into something almost clean. "But her name doesn't deserve to be ash. I'm asking to study the grove—not to harvest, not to steal. To understand what she touched. To restore her legacy to its full, complicated size. She made a wrong move for what she believed was the right reason. If we can name the wrongness precisely, maybe we can free the right reason."

Wind rattled the shop window. Behind the counter, the kettle ticked as it cooled. Marley felt the words catch in her, like a hook at the edge of a tender place. Claire's plea was dangerous because it wore a little truth. How many times had Marley herself wanted a cleaner story about medicine and help, about sharing what healed? How many times had she already felt the burden of being Keeper as cost?

"Say the words," Damien said, breaking the spell. "Say the part you omit: 'commercialize a sacred herb.' It matters where the money goes when the bottle leaves the woods."

Claire did not look away. "Mirabel Colvin attempted to commercialize a sacred herb," she said evenly. "And she was banished for it."

Damien nodded once, as though they'd finally named the ground on which they stood. "Intention matters more than redemption," he said. "You can't fix your grandmother's story by repeating her motive."

"I'm not repeating it," Claire said sharply, then forced the flare down. She spread her hands over the notebook, vulnerable. "I'm asking to observe. No plucking, no cutting, no digging. Let me place sensors, measure light, track dew. Let me write what I see. Give me a chance to do the opposite of a theft: a witnessing."

Marley let the silence expand until it had weight. She thought of the ledger's erasures, the quiet-session minutes Damien had found—*She would not bend her head to leave*—and of the deer that had died walking a memory into her porch boards. She thought of the fissure at the heart of the spiral, the soil black with the ghost of flame. The grove did not speak in arguments. It spoke in consequence.

"You'll have tea," Marley said finally, voice calm in a way that cost her. "Then you'll listen. After that, you'll hear the conditions of any study."

Claire's mouth parted in something like relief. Damien said nothing. He poured three cups and set them on the counter with the old care of a man who knew that heat could be hospitality and warning both.

While the tea cooled, Marley closed the shop door against the wind and let the room breathe. For the first time since Claire had stepped through the threshold, she felt the bookshop's old quiet return—the pared-down attention of paper and wood. When Marley finally spoke, it was with the steadiness that came from place as much as from vow.

"You'll hear the grove before you measure it," she said. "Or you won't step within the stones at all."

Claire wrapped her hands around the cup and nodded. "Then teach me how to listen."

Marley took a long breath. "You'll teach yourself. I'll show you where to stand."

Damien's cup went untouched. His eyes never left Claire's, as if waiting for the angle at which she'd look past the door and toward the vault.

THEY MET at the grove's western edge at dusk, where the forgotten path they'd cleared opened into the first stone. Marley had insisted on twilight; the hour of decisions seemed to unmask motives. Claire arrived with a small field kit slung at her hip: a light meter, a notebook, a watch. No camera. No vials. She held her hands out, empty-palmed, before she put them in her pockets. "As requested," she said.

Damien stood a pace behind Marley, the ledger's transcriptions in his coat and his compass in his fist. He had not slept well since the deer, the spiral of hoofprints imprinted on his eyelids every time he blinked. He watched Claire like a person listening for a hinge in a dark house.

Marley faced the stones. "You won't cross into the spiral," she said. "Not tonight. You'll stand at the mouth and you'll tell the grove your name and why you've come. Then you'll wait."

Claire exhaled. "You think it will answer."

"I know it will answer," Marley said. "I don't know how."

Claire looked smaller without the posture of authority she carried in town. She stepped to the edge where moss met stone. The air cooled subtly; even she felt it. "I'm Claire Whitcomb Colvin," she said—finally speaking the name she had avoided, the one that bound her to town rumor. "I'm here to witness what my grandmother wounded. I'm here to learn how not to harm. I ask for permission to see."

The clearing did not stir. No wind, no shaking of leaves. A long breath passed. Claire shifted and, despite her promise, reached instinctively for the light meter.

Marley's hand rose. "No instruments. Not until you get an answer."

Claire's jaw tensed. She lowered the meter, cheeks coloring. "And if the answer is nothing?"

"Then 'nothing' is your first lesson," Marley said. "Sit with it."

They waited. A robin's evening call stuttered into silence. Far up the ridge, an owl cleared its throat for the night shift. Claire's eyes flicked over the stones, the center, the thin seam of soil Marley had refused to call a crack. She wet her lips, fought the urge to fill the quiet with rationales. *It's a forest,* she wanted to say; *it's temperature gradients and hydrology.* But she had asked to be taught another grammar. She kept her mouth shut and listened to her own breathing until she could hear it slow.

The first response, when it came, was not light or sound. The compass in Damien's hand, steady for minutes, ticked once and rotated a fraction toward the western stones—the path of the directional markers they had uncovered. He glanced down, then at Marley. She nodded once, a small acknowledgment to the old device.

Then Claire felt it: a pressure under the soles of her boots, as if the floor of a great lung drew a careful inhale. The sensation moved through her ankles into her calves, a hush that made her spine rise. Not welcome, not refusal. Appraisal.

"It knows you're here," Marley said softly. "It hasn't decided if it wants you to be."

Claire, to her credit, did not argue with the idea of a place that decided. She closed her eyes. "I'm not my grandmother," she said into the quiet. "I loved her. I hated her choices. I'm here to make different ones."

The pressure eased. The taste of the air shifted—less resin, more damp loam. Damien's compass slid back to north. Marley let a breath out slowly. "It's not dismissal," she said. "It's not invitation."

"You're telling me the grove is Switzerland?" Claire blurted before she could swallow the joke. Marley's eyes sharpened; Damien's didn't move. "Sorry," Claire said quickly. "Nerves. I—Nerves."

"Hold the meter now," Marley said. "One reading at the edge. Log it. Write your description by hand. No photographs. If you need detail, draw."

Claire's relief was small and visible. She took a quick reading, scribbled numbers, then surprised herself by sketching—not the stones, but the way the ferns along the seam curled inward, as if leaning toward something they wanted to hear. When she finished, she waited again. The place did not punish her for busy-hands; it also did not reward.

"Next condition," Damien said, stepping forward at last. "Anything you publish uses Brookwood's consent. No naming species beyond common family, no geotags, no coordinates, no 'hidden valley' nonsense that draws the curious with shovels. The grove is not a headline."

Claire met his gaze. "I'm not here for a paper that trends."

"Good," he said. "Because you won't get one."

She nodded. "What can I get?"

"Maybe a map that refuses to be called a map," Marley said. "If you earn it."

Claire swallowed. "And how would I earn it?"

Marley touched the staff slung across her back, feeling its faint pulse answer the question. "You'll tend what you measure. You want the grove to speak? Pick up a rake. Clear the bramble you didn't plant. Carry water to a sapling. Sit through a night you'd rather sleep. If your notes don't smell like work when you hand them to me, we're done."

Claire's mouth opened, then closed. "Okay," she said. And something in her posture did change—the tilt of a person who has realized that belonging will not be given for eloquence, only for maintenance.

She worked for an hour as the light bled out. She untangled blackberry from alder roots, pried up the smallest of the fallen stones with her fingers, logged dew she could not count in numbers, only describe. When she tried to step a foot inside the spiral out of habit, the air resisted—not a shove, but the sensation of stepping into water at a colder temperature than expected. She retreated without a word. Marley watched that tiny act of restraint with more hope than any speech might have earned.

When the sky was fully sobered into night, Marley said, "Enough." Claire straightened, palms dirty, hair escaping its tie.

"Tomorrow?" Claire asked.

"We'll see," Marley said.

Damien added, "We'll also check the camera traps you set illegally along the ridge. You can help uninstall them."

Claire winced. "You found those."

"Of course," Damien said. "Intention matters more than redemption. Start proving yours."

THEY WALKED Claire back to town by the ridge road. The inn glowed ahead, Claire's room a rectangle of amber in the upper floor. At the steps, she turned, exhaustion making her honest.

"I want to tell you the neat version," she said. "That my grandmother was entirely wrong and I'm entirely right. That you can trust me because I've said the right things. But the truth is, I loved her. She taught me to listen to roots and to write down what I heard. She also taught me that speed wins grants. I've had both educations. I am trying to choose between them every day."

Marley heard the risk in the confession and accepted it at its cost. "Choosing isn't once," she said. "It's the work."

"Then let me keep choosing," Claire said. "Here."

Marley didn't promise. She nodded. "We'll meet again if the grove doesn't say no."

Claire's mouth twitched. "And how will I know if it has?"

"You'll hear it," Damien said. "In your sleep."

Claire's laugh was small and unhappy. "I already do." She touched the box she'd left with Marley earlier. "Keep those letters safe. They're the pieces of my grandmother that don't fit the legend. If you read long enough, you'll see she wrestled too." She started up the steps, then looked back. "I won't cross the stones without you."

"Hold that promise," Marley said.

When Claire disappeared inside, Damien and Marley stood a long while in the street. A moth battered itself against the inn's light as if convinced that heat could be translated into home. The smell of fried onions drifted from the kitchen below, ordinary and anchoring.

"She'll press again," Damien said softly.

"I know." Marley watched the window shade fall, leaving the room dark. "But tonight she pressed less. That's a start."

Damien slid his hand into hers. "The deer. The fissure. The staff. The ledger. We can't keep playing defense." His voice roughened. "We need to repair the grid faster than she can strain it."

Marley nodded, knowing he was right and that she would still refuse to use the staff as a shortcut. It had already shown her how quickly help could become harm. "We move with breath, not panic," she said. "We set boundaries that teach, not only punish. And when we confront her again, we do it with proof she can't argue down."

They crossed the square toward the shop. Inside, Marley placed Mirabel's notebook on the table beside the daughter's diary and the ledger. Three voices, braided by time, facing one another across a century. She opened to a passage mid-notebook, where Mirabel's script softened and crowded itself like someone writing in the margin of her own certainty:

If secrecy is cruelty, then exposure may be, too, when the thing exposed cannot live in light. How to choose? Perhaps consent is the only clear line, and I do not know how to wait for it.

Marley exhaled. She copied the last clause into her own journal—*I do not know how to wait for it*—and underlined it twice. She had an answer Mirabel never learned: *You wait because the place is alive.*

Damien spread a fresh sheet of vellum and penciled the spiral again, overlaying the seven trees, the directional stones, the seam they still refused to name a crack. "We bring the council this," he said. "We ask them to affirm the boundaries in public language. We ask Mrs. Keene to stand with us. We put it in the square where law can hear it."

"And we ask the circle to stand with us," Marley said quietly. "The living one we're remaking. Seven women. Seven candles. Not to perform, but to strengthen."

Damien's pencil paused. "And Claire?"

Marley gathered the letters, smoothed their brittle edges, and tied the ribbon snug. "We give her work. The unglamorous kind. If she keeps choosing it, the grove may let her closer. If she slips once—just once—into hunger, we sing her name into silence."

Damien looked at her, pain and pride tangled in his gaze. "You can do that?"

"I have to be able to," she said, the Keeper's vow cooling and hardening into something she could carry without breaking. "Love makes room for many legacies. It doesn't excuse the harm of one."

Outside, the ridge held its dark line against the sky. The lighthouse kept its quiet watch. The grove breathed. Marley laid her hand over the three books—ledger, daughter's diary, grandmother's notebook—and felt the hum through the wood of the table, faint as a pulse under a bandaged wrist. Unhealed, but alive.

"Tomorrow," she said. "We take the grid into town. We let the living hear it."

"And tonight," Damien said, turning down the lamp, "we sleep."

She smiled at the ordinary mercy of that word, blew out

the flame, and listened to the house settle. In the dark, the covenant did not loosen. Neither did the boundary.

Somewhere up the ridge, the spiral kept its shape through roots and stone. In town, a woman who wanted redemption lay awake and counted the cost of patience. In the bookshop, a Keeper placed a palm on old paper and told three restless ghosts what they most needed to hear:

"I will wait for consent. And I will keep what you could not keep."

19

GROVE DREAM #2 – THE BETRAYAL

The chant began the way wind begins—so soft she first mistook it for her own breath returning. Seven women formed the ring, branches lifted, flames steady as stars under a swollen, red-tinged moon. The grove shone with that strange interior light Marley now knew as consent: stones alive, moss bright, air thick with the old cadence of keepers calling balance into being.

Then the seam.

It was small at first, the kind of hesitation only someone listening with their ribs would hear: a single voice faltering, the seventh branch lowering a fraction. Marley's gaze found her—one of the seven, face blurred the way dreams guard what waking might weaponize. The woman's hand darted to the shallow stone pool, where seed rested at the bottom like a moonlet of green-gold. Fingers trembled. Not with reverence, Marley thought—hunger.

"No," Marley tried to say, but the dream would not grant her the power of sound.

The woman cupped the seed anyway, its glow bleeding through her knuckles, and backed away from the ring as if from a fire whose heat could yet be bargained with. The circle moved to close, but too late; the woman spun and ran, branches nicking her sleeves, the red moon painting her footprints in ash-colored light. She did not look back.

The song broke like a glass with a hairline crack suddenly asked to hold scalding water. Notes slid apart, then down. Flames guttered. The women's lifted branches lowered in a stunned, involuntary unison, and the pool shivered as if a wind had passed over it from below. Marley felt the ground at her feet stiffen and then seize, as though the earth had taken a deep breath and forgotten how to let it out.

The fissure opened.

It tore from the pool's rim along a line Marley had come to know in waking—a seam that ran toward the western stones, the very edge she and Damien had worked to clear. The split was clean and wrong, a mouth in soil flexing without sound. Light fell into it. The red moon grew dim as if someone had cupped it with a dirty hand. The remaining flames thinned to threads and then to nothing, smoke twisting into shapes that suggested letters but could not settle into words.

Marley reached toward the receding glow of the seed now vanishing in the dark between trees. The staff that had answered her hands in other dreams refused to manifest; she had only her body, and so she used it, dropping to her knees, pressing her palms to the crack as if the right pressure might reseal what choice had undone. The earth bucked once and held.

When she lifted her hands they were caked with damp soil. Dirt packed itself under her nails in clotted crescents. That detail snapped through the dream like a steel wire pulled taut. She looked up and found the circle's faces gone

—every one of them blurred now, not just the thief—leaving her alone in a grove whose breath no longer matched hers.

Something else broke then, not in ground or song but in her chest—an ache like a bruise under the sternum, as if a door there had been used as a shield and splintered in the saving. She felt it radiate outward, through arms and throat. Not panic. Injury.

From the trees came the faintest echo of the words she had once heard as a calling—*Keeper of Seed and Flame*—but the timbre was altered: not invitation now, but indictment, or plea. She could not decide which.

The fissure widened another inch.

Marley clawed again at the soil. It did not matter. The dream's law was already set: ring broken, seed removed, flame dimmed. She could only bear witness to the consequence.

The moon lowered, color leached from it entirely, and night became the kind of black that smothers silhouettes. She held the absence the way a mother holds a fevered child, close enough to be burned but closer anyway, as if proximity alone might constitute care.

The grove did not answer. The grove remembered.

When the hum finally returned, it was the rough rasp of a chest scraped by ash.

And then she woke—hands filthy, nails packed, chest aching as if she had spent a night hauling water from a burning house.

SHE SNAPPED the lamp on the instant she sat up. She moved the pad and pen from the nightstand toward herself, waiting until steadied breathing was enough to make the words legible.

She recorded it straight, without metaphor, trusting herself to supply none where none belonged: the thief, the seed, the ring broken, the fissure, the dimming, the ache. She checked the clock and wrote the time down—3:17 a.m.—then flipped to a blank page in the ledger transcript she'd been maintaining and wrote another word in block letters beneath it: *BETRAYAL.*

Jotting each phrase, she then flipped to the section of the old ledger she'd nearly memorized. "After the three erasures in 1912," she said, tapping, "you remember how their entries went brittle? I underlined a marginal note last time that felt like grief but read like instruction: *We do not write the place of the breach, lest the breach become a road.*" She slid the book closer to herself. "But here: a smudge. Someone pressed harder on a word they were trying to unsay." She angled the light. The ghost of the word rose: *seed.*

Marley pressed a knuckle against the ache in her sternum. "It wasn't theft like a child pockets a coin. It was extraction. Purposeful. Like a cutting taken too close to the heart."

She turned the lamp down a notch, softening the room. Thinking to herself that the circle never wrote the face. If they had, we wouldn't need to guess. It's almost cruel, the way history insists on protecting the person who did the harm more than the people left to hold it.

Marley's shoulders slumped. Thinking to herself "It's mercy. If the grove is a grid of memory, maybe their refusal to fix the betrayer's features is the one way they kept that betrayal from becoming ritual too. She shook her head. But I saw her run. Whoever she was, the ring broke at the precise moment she made herself a center.

She opened the window a crack. The night air edged in, rinsing the room. She took the compass from the dresser and set it on the bedspread. The needle spun once, then pointed—unhelpfully, painfully—east toward the ridge, toward the stones. I need to confirm there's a new displacement at the center, not just what we marked last week.

She closed her eyes. The ache tugged deeper, like the awareness of a splinter buried too far to reach without cutting. "It wants us there," she said out loud. "But the staff—" She stopped, blinking hard. The memory of nearly shattering the grid when she pushed too much, too soon, pulsed as a warning behind her eyes. "We go soft," she said. "Breath and hands. No staff."

Marley was accepting the hard truth because she'd asked to be Keeper and the work didn't include revision. If her desire is just a new version of the old—that hunger to take what grows only in circle and make it stand in a bottle—then the grove showed me the cost so I won't pretend I didn't know.

SHE DRESSED WITHOUT HURRY, the ritual of boots and coats and the choosing of a lantern restoring a little of the ordinary to a night that had asked too much. Before they left, Marley wrapped gauze around her nail beds—not to hide what the dream had carried into waking but to remind herself she was not a ghost in someone else's story. She was alive, in a body, and could choose how to move through pain.

They stepped into the predawn chill, the ridge ahead a black serif on the page of the sky. The town slept. The grove did not.

The clearing met them already awake, stones bright with dew that beaded like a script neither of them could read at a glance. Damien set the lantern low, light pooling flat so shadows wouldn't lie to them about depth. He placed the compass on the central stone. The needle swung, pointed past north, hesitated, then crept toward a bearing they recognized: the inward arc of the spiral they had walked a hundred times now with reverence and sometimes fear.

"Walk it?" he asked.

"Side by side," she said. "We'll stop wherever the breath catches."

They began at the outermost ring—feet careful on mossed stone, eyes tracking not just stones and trees but the small tells: a fern curled in rather than open, a ground spider webbing a seam as if to stitch. The first curve breathed evenly. The second held too long on the inhale. At the third, Marley pressed her palm to the soil and felt the proximity of a footprint that did not belong to deer or to ritual. A tread had paused here in reluctance or calculation —she could not tell.

"Boot," Damien said, crouching with the lantern and angling it. The compressed oval kissed the ground with the memory of a lug pattern he'd seen near the inn's back steps. He did not say the name. He didn't need to.

They continued, heads bowed as if in prayer. The grove's hum—once a comfort—ran rough as a throat scabbed from too much smoke. Marley breathed with it until they reached the final inward turn and stopped as one.

The center shocked her even though she had expected shock. The shallow pool they had cleaned weeks ago and invited to hold water again had darkened to a bruise. No ash lay in it, but the water carried an impossible shadow, as though it remembered being burned.

Damien dipped two fingers and lifted them to his nose. "Smells like wet iron," he said. His face hardened in a way that had nothing to do with anger and everything to do with allegiance. "No staff," he reminded himself aloud, as if speaking to the part that wanted to fix what ached with a single, decisive act.

Marley knelt. The ache in her chest became articulate, the way pains announce their shape when given a body's attention. It was not an arrow or a claw; it was the dull, radiating harm of something pulled away that had no business leaving. She placed her hands, open, on the stone rim. "I'm not here to force you to mend," she said to the place, the way one speaks to a child who has run so far the circles under her eyes have turned purple. "I'm here to admit we saw what you kept showing us."

The hum softened half a degree—the difference between a held breath and a breath given back.

Damien stood guard—watchful, not intrusive—murmuring what he observed into his notes in a cadence that had become as liturgical as any chant: "Center water: greyed. No scent of resin. Compass shift five degrees east on approach, returns to north when Marley speaks." He looked up. "Say the phrase."

She knew the one he meant. The old map had offered it at the center, the way some springs offer a cup. *Only in circle shall the breath of balance return.*

She spoke it—not as a spell but as a reminder, to the grove and to herself. "Only in circle shall the breath of balance return."

Something at the edge of the clearing answered—the faintest tremor in the birch, a needle-sigh from the fir. Not a fix. Not absolution. A listening.

Marley cupped water and drizzled it along the crack's lip where the fissure had first shown itself in dreams. She didn't pray. She didn't perform. She just offered the movement of hands that meant mending in every craft she'd ever learned: clean, place, wait. The ache under her sternum kept time, slowing the smallest fraction. She let tears fall—two, then three—not because she imagined them medicinal but because the body needs to mark harm with salt sometimes so the mind won't pretend it never happened.

They stayed until first light opened the trees like a curtain. Birds tried a few notes and then committed. The water in the stone was still darker than it should have been; the seam in the soil remained a seam. But the circle's breath, though shallow, no longer stuttered.

"Evidence," Damien said, not in triumph but in readiness. "We have what we need to draw the boundary in language a council can't ignore. And we have what you need to call the women." He didn't look at her when he said it, as if averting his eyes could keep the request from weighing more. "It won't return on the work of two."

Marley rose slowly. The world tilted, then steadied. She wiped her hands on her skirt and left the dirt there on purpose. "I'll ask them," she said. "Six to stand with me. Not to perform history, but to finish what history cracked. We'll bring the breath back with breath, not with spectacle."

Damien nodded and glanced toward the inn side of the ridge. A crow launched from cedar, arrowing into light. "And Claire?"

Marley lifted the empty bowl, watching the last beads of water skitter and cling. "She'll be asked to witness and to wait," she said. "If she steps into the spiral uninvited again, we sing her name into silence. Not to erase her, but to unhook the grid from her hunger."

They started down toward town, the compass steady, the lantern dim. Behind them, the clearing kept its dark blue of early morning a beat longer than the rest of the ridge, as if it were thinking. The ache in Marley's chest had not gone. She did not want it to—not yet. Some wounds are instructions. The pain, for now, was part of how she remembered to move with care.

At the bottom of the path the lighthouse winked pale in the newborn light. Sophie would be awake soon, asking for toast and not for theology. Marley smiled at the mercy of that. She had work that required no map at all: wash hands, make tea, write names, ask women, draw candles from their drawer and place them where breath and wick could meet. Small acts that teach the body what the mouth will soon promise aloud.

"Only in circle," she said again, mostly to herself.

Damien heard and took her hand because that was his part of the sentence. They walked on, their steps falling into a rhythm that would not yet be called procession but could be, if the grove agreed, in time.

20

REBUILDING THE CIRCLE

The moon hung heavy and whole, its light spilling silver across the ridge as though it, too, had come to watch. Marley stood at the grove's edge with the staff across her back, her shawl clasped at her throat. Her breath came steady, though her hands trembled, not with fear but with the recognition of consequence. Tonight, for the first time since the fissure tore open in her dream, there would be more than memory in the circle. There would be bodies, voices, lives choosing to stand together.

One by one, the women arrived. Mrs. Keene, oldest of the six, whose grandmother's name had appeared in the ledger beside Eliza Merrick's. Her hair was white as birch bark, her posture unbowed. She carried a bundle of dried lavender tied with twine.

Then came Mrs. Bennett, her blouse still dotted in flour from bakery work, her hands rough but gentle as she carried a clay bowl filled with spring water. She had once told Marley she dreamed in roots—seeing them beneath her fields as clearly as she saw sky.

Hazel followed, the owner of the metaphysical shop on

Main. When Marley asked her, she had not hesitated. She arrived with a candle wrapped in beeswax paper, her eyes wide with equal parts fear and purpose.

Tessa Kinney, local print shop owner and operator, stepped forward with a pouch of salt. Evelyn brought fresh-cut cedar branches, their scent sharp and steady. Last of all, Lorraine Gearhart, whose family name had been erased and whispered for generations, came with nothing in her hands but the courage of showing up.

Marley greeted each woman not with words but with the touch of palm to palm. No rehearsed liturgy, only the acknowledgment that hands, when joined, mean more than signatures. She led them into the grove where the stones curved inward, their moss glowing faintly under the full moon. The spiral waited.

They gathered at the center. Marley laid the staff across the stone rim of the shallow pool. Its spiral engraving caught the moonlight and held it, pulsing as if it had expected this night. She turned to the women, her voice steady though the weight in her chest throbbed with memory.

"Seven stood here once, and seven stand again. Tonight is not repetition. Tonight is repair. Each of us carries what was broken, but together we choose to breathe it whole."

She set the first candle in the soil. "Healing," she said. "For what was wounded and for what will be wounded still." Mrs. Keene bent and touched her lavender to the flame, the scent rising, binding itself to air.

The second candle, placed by Mrs. Bennett. "Balance," Marley named. Mrs. Bennett poured a trickle of water into the pool, its surface trembling as though in recognition.

The third candle, Hazel's. "Memory," Marley said. Hazel struck a match with shaking fingers, whispering the names she had found in the ledger's margins, names no one had spoken aloud in years.

The fourth, Tessa's. "Truth." She scattered salt around the stone rim, each grain catching moonlight like crystal, each word she spoke—*we will not lie to ourselves*—sounding like a vow.

The fifth, Evelyn's. "Silence." She laid the cedar branches in a cross, their scent a hush that pressed itself against every ear. "Silence," she whispered, "to protect what must be kept."

The sixth, Lorraine's. "Voice." She did not light the candle right away, holding it close to her chest first. "For every woman erased," she said, "for every story cut short. We name voice because silence without consent is harm." Then she struck the match, the flame catching quick and bright.

The seventh remained in Marley's hands. She set it in the center of the pool's rim, flame bending in the night air. "Trust," she said softly. "The hardest, the most fragile, the one we rebuild tonight."

The women closed the circle. Their seven flames cast light that danced across stone and soil. The grove exhaled, the hum beneath their feet growing steadier, fuller, as if it had been waiting for this exact number, this exact vow.

At the grove's edge, Damien stood with his notebook in hand, lantern lowered, his face carved with reverence and restraint. He had chosen silence, as they had agreed, bearing witness without the intrusion of voice. His presence steadied Marley more than she let show.

She raised her eyes to the moon. "Keeper of Seed and Flame hears," she said. "Keeper keeps. Keeper shares." Her words trembled into the clearing and did not echo back— they were absorbed, received.

The staff pulsed once, light threading its spiral. The fissure in the soil quivered, then stilled.

The circle held.

THE FLAMES GUTTERED in the slight night wind, then steadied as if some hand unseen cupped them. The seven women stood shoulder to shoulder, their eyes reflecting firelight and moonlight both. For a moment, silence itself felt like the most eloquent prayer. Then, as if on cue, Mrs. Keene began to speak.

"My grandmother Merrick" she said, her voice low but unwavering, "walked this grove when she was younger than most of you. She told me once that she never felt more herself than when she stood here, among these stones. She called it 'a breathing cathedral.'" Mrs. Keene's lavender bundle dropped ashes to the soil. "They silenced her when the banishment came. Tonight, I lift her voice again."

The grove stirred in answer—branches shifting though no wind moved the ridge. Marley felt the tremor underfoot, faint as a heartbeat, and knew the grove was listening.

Mrs. Bennett took her turn, placing her broad hands over the bowl of spring water she had carried. "Our family tilled fields, never asking why the soil gave more than it should. But I remember stories of my great-aunt. They said she would walk barefoot into the grove during droughts and return with her palms damp, as if the earth itself had wept into her hands." Mrs. Bennett's voice cracked. "She died before I was born, but my mother said the Council never forgave her for sharing the water with neighbors instead of keeping it hidden. I bring her back here, in water she never got to bless."

The pool shimmered faintly, its dark surface catching

moonlight in a ripple. Marley pressed her palms together, whispering thanks without speaking aloud.

Hazel, held her beeswax-wrapped candle higher. "I don't know what I'm supposed to say," she admitted. Hazel's eyes filled. "I want to believe my ancestors weren't just curious, but faithful. If they stole anything, I want to believe it was to keep it safe, not to sell it." She swallowed, looking at Marley. "Can I still honor them, even if they broke the circle?"

The question sliced the air. The other women shifted. Damien, at the grove's edge, stiffened but said nothing.

Marley stepped forward, laying her hand on Hazel's. "You don't honor betrayal. You honor the wound left behind by it. And you honor the possibility that the story was told wrong." She guided Hazel's hand to set the candle on the stone rim. "The grove knows what your great grandmother did. Tonight, it's your honesty that matters."

Hazel's tears fell onto the stone, sizzling faintly before soaking into moss. Marley heard a whisper then, thin and sibilant—*memory returns... memory returns...*—though she could not tell if it came from the trees or from her own chest.

Lorraine Gearhart stepped in with her pouch of salt. Her voice was blunt, more like a midwife's command than a confession. "The Gearharts were never brave enough to stand. My grandmother followed. She never led. But she bound wounds after the fire of 1920, when half the town's men came back from the ridge coughing black. They said she used ash and salt together, and the dying stopped. I don't know if she was Circle or not, but I know she carried their methods in her hands." She cast salt in four directions. "Truth: our line didn't fight for place, but we still healed. Let the grove see that as enough."

The hum beneath them grew steadier, as though approving her frankness.

Evelyn laid her cedar down in silence. The scent rose sharp and cleansing. She kept her eyes closed, lips barely moving. The quiet became dense, thick as smoke. Each woman stilled. Even Hazel's shuddered breathing fell calm. Marley felt the hush not only in her ears but in her bones, a pause that asked for reverence. Evelyn finally whispered: "Some things do not need repeating. Let the grove keep them safe."

Tessa waited until last. Her family's erasure was the most infamous; the Averill name had been spoken like a curse in town lore. She held her candle near her chest, eyes flashing with defiance. "They said my grandmother betrayed you all. They said she put coin above covenant. Maybe it's true. Maybe she made one desperate choice, and the men who wanted to control her called it betrayal. I don't know. But I am done with silence." She bent and struck her match. "My name is Tessa, and I am here to return the voice you took from my bloodline."

The flame leapt, brighter than the others for a breath before settling into its place. Marley saw the fissure in the soil quiver, then ease, as though the grove itself had exhaled.

For a long while, the circle held in silence, seven flames steady. But Marley felt it then: the test.

The trees leaned inward. Whispers rose, indistinct at first, then separating into threads: a hiss of warnings, accusations, half-remembered lines. She could almost make out words—*traitor... seed... silence her... trust broken...* The grove was not only listening. It was probing. Could they hold their unity under the weight of doubt? Could they rebuild when memory itself pressed them with fracture?

Mrs. Keene wavered first, looking toward Tessa with suspicion etched on her face. "If betrayal ran in blood—"

"No," Marley cut in sharply, voice ringing against the stones. She raised the staff, not as weapon but as anchor. "This circle is not inheritance of wound. It is inheritance of choice. Tonight, every woman here stands by her own vow, not her grandmother's shadow."

The whispers grew louder for a beat, swirling, then dimmed again to susurration. The test had not ended, but the grove had accepted her answer for now.

Marley steadied herself, the ache under her sternum returning. She knew the grove would not make rebuilding easy. It would probe them again and again, until trust was proved unbreakable. That was the cost of keeping balance in a place that remembered betrayal too well.

The women tightened their circle, eyes on the flames. Damien shifted at the edge, his silence a shield. Marley lifted her gaze to the moon, and whispered so only the grove could hear: "Test us. We will not break again."

The hum beneath her feet trembled in reply.

The grove shifted.

The whispers thickened, no longer indistinct murmurs but threads of discernible command. They wound through the branches like wind-driven ropes, tugging at each woman in turn. Marley felt the pull in her sternum sharpen—the ache she carried from betrayal now inflamed, as though the grove itself demanded proof that this gathering was not just performance, but promise made flesh.

The candles guttered and steadied, guttered and steadied. One by one, the flames seemed to lean toward their bearers. Each woman glanced at Marley, searching her face for instruction. But Marley knew the test could not be hers alone.

"Step forward," she said, voice low but clear. "Each of you. The grove calls not for words alone but for witness in your body. Embody what you lit."

Mrs. Keene moved first. Her lavender bundle crackled as she pressed it against her candle flame, reigniting the scent, filling the air with smoke sweet and piercing. She raised the bundle high, as though offering it to the moon. "Healing," she said, her voice stronger than her years. "For my grandmother who tended wounds unacknowledged. For every woman cut out of the ledger." She walked the circle slowly, waving the lavender smoke over each woman, and Marley felt the air ease, just slightly, as if the grove tasted the offering and did not spit it out.

Mrs. Bennett followed. She scooped water from her clay bowl and poured it carefully into the pool at the circle's center. The dark water quivered, then stilled. "Balance," she said. "Soil and sky, seed and flame, hidden and shared. May the grove know we will not hoard nor squander." The hum beneath their feet steadied for a beat, then shifted again, restless but listening.

Hazel stood trembling, her beeswax candle in hand. She lifted it to her chest. "Memory," she whispered. "Even the memory of betrayal belongs to us now. We do not run from it—we hold it, so it cannot sneak back in shadows." She shut her eyes, tears streaking her cheeks, but did not falter. When she reopened them, the flame burned steady, almost taller than before.

Lorraine Gearhart scattered her remaining salt in a line across the fissure, her movements sharp, deliberate. "Truth," she said, voice cutting through the grove's mutters. "The truth is we are afraid. The truth is we may fail again. But the greater truth is that fear will not stop us from standing here. This is the truth we offer." The ground itself seemed to still beneath her declaration, the hum pausing as if in recognition.

Evelyn, calm as ever, took her cedar boughs and laid them at the base of each candle. She said nothing at first, only let the silence she embodied expand until it filled the grove like water in a vessel. Finally, she spoke: "Silence, not as punishment, but as protection. Silence, to guard what words would wound." The whispers in the branches hissed louder, then fell into hush, pressed down by her offering.

Tessa's turn came. Every gaze swung toward her—hers was the name most tainted by rumor, the family marked by supposed betrayal. She lifted her candle with hands that did not tremble. "Voice," she said, her tone ringing. "Not the voice of greed, not the voice of secrecy, but the voice that names what others bury. Tonight I speak: my grandmother may have erred, but I will not be silent because of it. My voice is mine, and I give it to this circle." She held the candle high, and its flame burned the brightest of all. The fissure trembled, then narrowed by a hair's breadth.

Finally, Marley stepped forward. She placed her candle in the very center of the ring, where all their flames converged. "Trust," she said softly. The word trembled in her chest. "We cannot undo what was done. We cannot promise perfection. We can only trust that what we build together will be stronger than what can tear us apart." She lowered her hands, and the staff across the stone rim pulsed once with a glow that spread faintly into the soil.

The grove answered.

The whispers crescendoed, testing harder now, spitting old accusations—*traitor... thief... seed stolen... flame dimmed...* —but each woman stepped closer, shoulder to shoulder, closing ranks. They did not shout the whispers down. They let their offerings—smoke, water, salt, silence, voice, trust—speak instead.

Damien, at the grove's edge, wrote furiously, his pencil scratching across the page. He noted the compass's spin, the shift in the soil, the changes in the flame. But more than that, he bore witness with his silence, a sentinel who knew that his role tonight was not to intervene, but to anchor. His gaze never left Marley, his presence a wordless vow that he, too, was part of this circle, though without flame.

Then the moment came: the grove struck harder. The fissure split wider, a crack racing across the soil toward Tessa's feet, as if daring the circle to fracture where its weakest link might be. Tessa gasped, staggering back. But before she could retreat fully, Hazel caught her hand, holding her steady.

"Memory holds you," Hazel whispered. "You don't walk this line alone."

Tessa gripped her back, tears filling her eyes. The fissure halted, its edges crumbling but not widening further. The ground shivered, then began to knit itself—slow, tentative, but real.

The candles flared as one. Their flames leaned inward, merging at the center into a single column of fire that rose as high as their heads before settling back into seven distinct points. Marley's chest ached, but this time it was not wound—it was weight, holy and heavy, the gravity of covenant renewed.

The grove sighed, a long exhale through stone and branch. The whispers faded. The hum steadied, low and even, as if the land itself had decided—for now—that the circle held.

The women released one another's hands slowly, their

eyes wide, their breaths uneven. Mrs. Keene pressed her palm to her heart. Mrs. Bennett knelt by the pool, touching the water reverently. Tessa sank to the ground, shaking with the release of strain she had carried her whole life.

Marley looked to Damien. He nodded once, his silence more eloquent than any words. She knew he would record every detail, but more importantly, he would carry the memory in his bones, as sure as the ledger carried ink.

Marley turned back to the circle. "It isn't finished," she said, her voice rough but sure. "This was one night. One choice. We will be tested again. But tonight, the grove knows us. And we know each other."

The women bowed their heads, each touching their candle's flame briefly before extinguishing it. Only Marley left hers burning, in the pool's center, a lone flame reflected seven times in the dark water.

The grove's silence now felt different—less like absence, more like rest.

Marley laid her hand on the staff. It pulsed faintly, then stilled. She whispered so softly that only the grove could hear: "The circle breathes again."

The moon above broke free of a thin veil of cloud, bathing them all in light.

And in that light, the new circle stood—not perfect, not invulnerable, but alive.

21

THE MIDNIGHT BLOOM

The summer solstice had arrived like an unspoken promise, carrying with it a heat that lingered even after the sun dropped behind the ridge. Brookwood lay quiet in its valley, the town lanterns twinkling faintly, but the grove above was wide awake. Marley could feel it in the soles of her feet, each step along the familiar spiral path tingling as though the earth itself had prepared for her.

Damien followed a pace behind, his lantern low. He hadn't spoken much during the climb. It wasn't silence of reluctance but reverence, the way a man pauses before entering a cathedral. The compass dangled from his hand, the needle twitching in its usual erratic pattern. Tonight, he'd said softly, would be the test. If the grove meant to answer their months of patient tending, it would answer now.

When they reached the central clearing, Marley stopped short.

There, in the pool where fissure and shadow had once lingered, something stirred. At first she thought it was moonlight trapped in the water, a reflection sharper than it should be. But then it rose—a bloom, unfurling in silence, its petals luminous, pale silver-blue, as though woven from moonbeam and dew. The flower glowed faintly, its light enough to paint their faces and throw shadows across the stones.

Marley's breath caught. "Lunaflare," she whispered, the name rising from memory she hadn't known she carried. She dropped to her knees beside the pool, reaching toward it with a trembling hand.

Damien knelt beside her, his eyes wide. "It's real."

She nodded, the word too small for what pulsed inside her. "I've only ever heard whispers of it. A flower that blooms only under the longest night's balance, when the grove consents to show its heart."

The petals opened wider, releasing a faint shimmer into the air, not scent exactly but presence. Marley inhaled and felt her chest ease, the ache she had carried since the dream of betrayal softening into something gentler, like a bruise being stroked by light.

She pulled her healer's journal from her satchel—pages worn with months of entries, dreams, and sketches. With careful hands, she used a flat, cleaned blade to clip two petals, laying them between parchment sheets she had prepared with dried rosemary to preserve their glow. She whispered as she worked: "For memory. For those who will come after."

Damien placed the compass on the stone rim. They both leaned close, watching. For weeks, the needle had spun wildly at the grove's center, never resting, always trembling as though the earth beneath them could not decide its own north. But as the Lunaflare swayed faintly in the solstice breeze, the needle stilled. It pointed true, steady as iron, north aligned without wavering.

Damien let out a long breath, his shoulders lowering. "It's the first time. Weeks of chaos, and now…" He trailed off, shaking his head in awe. "The grove is still."

Marley pressed her palm against the soil. She could feel it: the hum had quieted, not into absence but into alignment. The grove breathed evenly again, no longer rasping, no longer aching.

The Lunaflare glowed brighter for a moment, then bent toward her as if acknowledging her hands, her role. Marley closed her eyes, tears slipping down her cheeks. "Thank you," she whispered. "We see you. We remember."

The flower shivered, and for an instant, Marley swore she heard Aurelia's voice—faint, like wind threading leaves —*keep the breath…*

Damien touched her arm gently, grounding her. "Write it down," he murmured.

She nodded, pulling the journal close, recording every detail: the solstice moon, the bloom's light, the compass's stillness, the whisper. Each stroke of ink felt like anchoring not just memory but covenant. She sealed the preserved petals between the pages and pressed the book to her chest.

Above them, the moon climbed higher, and the flower glowed on. The solstice had given them a gift—not just beauty, but proof that the grove still chose to bloom, to trust, to speak.

For the first time in months, Marley's heart felt light enough to match the glow before her.

THE FOLLOWING EVENING, the women gathered again. Marley had sent quiet notes to each, requesting their presence under the lingering moonlight of the solstice. No fanfare, no proclamation—just an invitation, scrawled in her careful hand: *The grove has answered. Come and see.*

They arrived one by one, lanterns bobbing along the path. Mrs. Keene first, leaning on her cane but walking with brisk purpose. Mrs. Bennett with earth still on her boots, smelling of fields turned by her hands. Hazel, clutching her candle stub like a talisman. Lorraine Gearhart with her salt pouch tied neatly at her waist. Evelyn silent but steady, a bundle of cedar pressed against her chest. And Tessa, eyes defiant but softened by the memory of the last circle they had held together.

Damien stood off to the side as always, lantern low, journal in hand. He offered nods of welcome, but his voice remained absent, faithful to the vow of witness.

Marley led them into the grove's heart. The pool gleamed faintly, and at its center the Lunaflare still bloomed. Its silver-blue petals shimmered as though woven of moonlight and dew, every curve of its form radiating quiet strength. The women halted in unison, gasps slipping from their lips.

"What in God's name..." Mrs. Bennett whispered, her voice caught between awe and fear.

"Not God's," Marley said softly. "The grove's."

Mrs. Keene stepped forward, eyes bright with a child's wonder despite her years. "My grandmother spoke of this," she murmured. "Said once, when she was young, she saw a flower glow under the moon. I thought it was only story."

Marley lifted her healer's journal and opened to the parchment where she had pressed the petals. Though dulled compared to the living bloom, they still held a faint sheen. "Its name is Lunaflare," she said. "The ledger never recorded it, but oral tradition carried whispers. It blooms on the solstice—when the grove consents to show us its heart."

The women drew closer. Marley held the journal out, and each laid her fingertips on the page, reverent, careful. As they did, a hush fell over the clearing—not silence alone, but something deeper, a smoothing of air, a settling of earth.

Marley felt it instantly: the bloom's presence extending beyond herself and Damien. The grove was not just showing them—it was testing whether unity could carry this gift.

"Close your eyes," Marley instructed. "Breathe."

They obeyed. For a long stretch, the grove itself seemed to breathe with them. The hum beneath the soil, once uneven, now pulsed in rhythm with their inhalations. Mrs. Keene's lined face softened. Mrs. Bennett's shoulders dropped. Hazel's trembling stilled. Lorraine unclenched her fists. Evelyn smiled faintly, her silence not heavy but light. Even Tessa, whose jaw was so often set in defiance, exhaled with a sound like relief.

Marley watched them, heart swelling. "Do you feel it?" she asked quietly.

"Yes," Hazel whispered, eyes still closed. "It's like...the ache in my chest isn't gone, but it doesn't rule me."

Mrs. Bennett nodded, her voice husky. "Balance. Like my fields after rain."

Lorraine's reply was blunt but full of awe. "Truth. There's no hiding in this light."

Tessa opened her eyes, meeting Marley's gaze. "Voice," she said simply. "It's as if the grove itself is listening. Not judging—just listening."

Marley placed her own hand over the journal. "The Lunaflare doesn't erase the wound. It eases the breath so we can bear it." She paused, letting the moment root. "But it only blooms if the circle is whole."

The words settled heavy. The women looked around the ring, each face illuminated by the faint silver glow. They knew what she meant: their unity was fragile, tested already by whispers, by bloodlines tainted with suspicion. The Lunaflare's bloom was proof of grace, but also of responsibility.

Evelyn broke the silence. "Then the test is not whether it blooms. It is whether we keep it blooming in memory after it fades."

Marley nodded. She stepped toward the pool and clipped another petal, laying it carefully on a fresh page of the journal. "Each of you will carry one, preserved. Not as possession, but as covenant. When doubt comes, when the town questions, when we question each other—you will have proof that the grove once trusted us enough to open."

She divided the preserved fragments she had pressed earlier, sealing them in parchment folded with rosemary and cedar. One by one, she placed them in each woman's hands.

Mrs. Keene wept openly, clutching hers to her chest. "My grandmother will rest easier in her grave tonight."

Mrs. Bennett closed her hand around hers like a seed she meant to plant. "I'll keep it with me in the fields."

Hazel's lips trembled. "I'll put it inside my students' storybook—where they keep the names of the past."

Lorraine slipped hers into her salt pouch. "Truth and bloom, side by side."

Evelyn said nothing, only tucked it into her cedar bundle. Her silence itself was a vow.

Tessa lifted hers high before tucking it into her coat. "Let them whisper. I'll show them light."

Marley's chest swelled with gratitude. She glanced at Damien, who wrote each reaction, each vow. His eyes met hers, warm with belief. For the first time, she saw not only witness in him but quiet certainty. He was not merely recording history. He was already a part of it.

The compass at his side lay steady, the needle pointing north without falter. He held it up for them all to see. "Weeks of chaos," he said softly, finally breaking his silence, "and tonight—stillness."

The women gasped anew. The sight of the compass, so long a symbol of disarray, now calm, seemed the final confirmation. They drew in closer, their circle tight, their breaths one.

Marley closed the journal with a firm hand. "We keep the petals. But more than that—we keep each other. The Lunaflare will wither by dawn, but if we honor what it gave, the circle will not."

The grove answered with a faint sigh through the branches, the sound almost like assent.

For a long while, they stood together in silence, flames forgotten, only the flower's glow binding them. And in that glow, Marley felt hope root deeper than it ever had.

They did not hurry the night. After the women had each received their small square of parchment—petal wrapped in rosemary and cedar—no one moved to leave. The Lunaflare's glow had settled into the clearing like a breath held without strain, and for once the grove asked nothing but attention. Even the compass at Damien's belt felt like a creature at rest.

Marley turned the healer's journal over in her hands, the leather warm from her palms. An impulse—clear and quiet as a bell struck far away—rose through her: *Give some of it back.* She looked at the living bloom in the pool, then at the spiral path, then at the faces around her. The ache she had learned to trust as instruction—not torment—stirred under her sternum and nodded.

"I want to test a question," she said softly.

Mrs. Keene lifted her chin. "Ask it."

"If the Lunaflare opens when the circle is whole," Marley said, "will the grove accept part of its light as offering? Not a theft. A return. Perhaps the spiral wants a marker, not in ink but in petal."

Lorraine's mouth pursed. "You're proposing to plant a petal."

"I am," Marley said. "Not at the center. Out in the path. Where we walk our vows."

Evelyn's gaze moved from bloom to spiral to Marley. "Ask first," she murmured. "Out loud. So the refusal, if it comes, has air to travel in."

Marley nodded. She stepped to the pool, bowed her head, and spoke to the water that held the Lunaflare like a small moon: "We cut none of you to own you. We ask to carry a fragment back into the path as witness. If the answer is no, we will hear it."

For a heartbeat nothing changed. Then the bloom swayed toward her of its own accord—a tilt so slight it might have been breeze, except that no leaf in the clearing stirred. Marley felt her throat loosen, her hands steady. Consent could be this simple, she thought; it could look like permission that needed neither explanation nor excuse.

She chose the smallest petal still attached at the bloom's outer edge and clipped it with the cleaned blade, a movement careful enough to feel like prayer. The petal's glow cooled as it left the flower, not fading so much as learning how to be carried.

"Where?" Mrs. Bennett asked, eyes on the spiral. "Outer ring, where we enter? Or where the breath caught us last—second curve?"

Marley glanced to Damien. He had already unfolded a small vellum overlay, his pencil poised. "If you plant at the outermost ring," he said gently, "the town might see first—curiosity before understanding. If you plant at the second curve where the fracture once hummed, you mark a place already tender. But if we choose the third curve, just before the inward turn—" He tapped the page. "—we choose the moment before commitment. We sanctify the choice."

Tessa's voice, usually flint, softened. "Make the place of choosing the place of light."

Marley smiled, small and grateful. "The third curve."

They moved as one, seven women and Damien with the lantern, along the mossed path. The Lunaflare's glow followed them in the corner of their sight—less a beam than a memory of light stitched into air. The third curve lay where the birch leaned inward and a fern's fronds had always seemed to listen. The soil there was dark and forgiving, the hum beneath it steady.

Marley knelt. "We will not make a hole with steel alone," she said. "We'll open it with what we are."

They made a small liturgy of the work without calling it one. Mrs. Bennett cupped spring water in her palm and let a few drops soften the soil. Lorraine pinched salt and sprinkled a circle no wider than Marley's palm, whispering: "Truth binds." Mrs. Keene brushed a little lavender smoke across the ground. Evelyn held cedar over the spot, her silence a shelter. Hazel spoke three names aloud—women lost to the ledger—and pressed her fingertips to the earth. Tessa leaned in and said, simply, "My voice consents."

Only then did Marley lay the petal on the dampened soil. It did not sit like a scrap, flat and dead. It curved slightly, as if remembering flower-ness, and its faint light warmed the dirt beneath. Marley widened the circle with her thumb, pressed the petal gently down, then drew soil over it—a thin cover, no more than the thickness of a leaf. She did not pack it hard. She let the ground decide how close it wanted to hold the gift.

"Breathe," she said.

Eight breaths rose and fell. The grove answered with a low tremor that reminded Marley of a cat's purr—vibration more than sound. Damien lifted the compass. The needle twitched toward the center, hesitated, then—slow as a decided mind—ticked back to north and held.

Hazel clutched Marley's sleeve. "Look," she whispered.

From the freshly covered spot, a thread of light—no thicker than a hair, no brighter than frost in starlight—ran outward and then inward at once, like a root seeking both water and kin. It reached toward the nearest stone, brushed it, and the stone's moss brightened a shade. Another thread reached toward the pool, not a straight line but a soft curve that mirrored the spiral itself. The two threads met halfway and stilled, as though a circuit had been closed.

Damien's breath left him in a sound halfway between awe and relief. He sketched quickly, hand sure, eyes wet. "It's mapping," he murmured. "Not for us to take, but for us to recognize."

Marley pressed her palm to the soil again. The ache under her sternum shifted—no longer wound alone, but weight properly placed. She closed her eyes, and a picture slid behind her lids: not a single bloom in a single summer, but seven small flare-points planted along the spiral, each at its own curve, each answering a candle they had lit—healing, balance, memory, truth, silence, voice, trust. Not all at once, not as spectacle, but over seasons: solstice, equinox, between. The grove whispering a calendar into the land that their bodies could learn by walking.

"Future blooms," she said under her breath, more to the soil than to the women. "A teaching, if we keep our vow."

Mrs. Keene's hand, light as a leaf, rested on Marley's shoulder. "It wanted you to see that."

"Us," Marley corrected gently. "It wanted *us* to see. I was only the hand."

They remained at the third curve until the faint light-thread ebbed back into the ground. Nothing remained to prove the moment except the steadiness of the compass and the easy rhythm of their breaths. That was enough. If the grove meant permanence, it rarely used show.

Back at the pool, the Lunaflare's bloom had tipped farther toward the water. Its glow was smaller now; dawn tugged at the edges of the night like a seamstress ready to hem. Marley knew the flower would close soon, and perhaps not open in their lifetime again. She did not feel robbed by that thought. She felt entrusted.

"Two more minutes," Damien said softly, not as order but as courtesy to the night.

Marley opened her journal and wrote while she could still see without lantern: *Planted one Lunaflare petal at the third curve of the spiral. Soil received. Threads of light connected stone and pool—temporary visible, likely persistent below. Compass still. Breath easy. Consent spoken by all present.* She listed the names, not because paper needed them, but because the women did: Mrs. Keene, Mrs. Bennett, Hazel, Lorraine, Evelyn, Tessa. She drew a small circle beside each, the way her aunt had once taught her to draw space around a name as if to give it room.

"Add mine," Damien said.

She looked up, surprised.

"I stood without words," he said. "But I chose this, too."

She smiled and made a seventh circle within the column of witness, not under the candles but beside them. *Damien.* It looked right there—its own keeping.

Mrs. Bennett exhaled. "What does the spiral ask now?"

"To be walked," Marley said. "In the morning, in the afternoon, in the beginning of night. Not as pilgrimage only, but as maintenance—clearing bramble, carrying water, noticing where the breath catches. The bloom has given us stillness once. Our work is to practice stillness until we don't need a miracle to find it."

Tessa's laugh was low, almost disbelieving. "Work postures don't trend as well as miracles."

Evelyn's look was kind and severe at once. "We're not trending," she said. "We're tending."

A sound answered her—real and unmistakable this time: a bell-tone so low it bordered on touch, as if someone had struck a metal bowl hidden in the roots. The trees held the sound for a breath before releasing it. All eight of them closed their eyes like people in a church who didn't know they had wanted prayer until the note found them.

Hazel shivered. "What was that?"

"Approval," Mrs. Keene said. "And a reminder."

Lorraine pointed to the horizon, where a line of gray separated darkness from dawn. "And that."

The Lunaflare drew itself smaller, its petals folding, glow condensed to a pearl at its heart. Marley fought the urge to clip again. Desire wasn't the measure. Consent was. The bloom had given, and the grove had returned stillness.

Greed would be to keep taking from a mouth that had already fed them. She bowed, a gesture she had learned mattered as much to herself as to any living thing. "Rest," she whispered to the flower. "We'll carry you without cutting more."

Damien, still silent, took three photographs. He had asked the circle weeks ago if he could capture certain moments for archive; tonight their nods had been unanimous. The shutter's soft click marked time without dominating it. He lowered the camera, eyes shining like a man who'd just watched an attic window open in a house he'd thought was sealed.

They doused their lanterns in order, one by one, until only the paling sky lit the clearing. The compass remained still, the needle holding north with a stubborn grace. Marley felt the staff on the stone rim pulse once more—a heartbeat mirroring hers—and then settle.

As they turned to go, Tessa paused at the third curve, laid her palm flat where they had planted the petal, and spoke without drama: "I'll be back here tomorrow. I'll bring a rake."

Hazel nodded. "I'll bring my students next week. We'll read their names where children can hear them."

Mrs. Bennett grinned. "I'll bring water when the day runs dry."

Lorraine patted her pouch. "And truth when our stories get fancy."

Evelyn lifted her cedar, then lowered it again. "And silence when we'd rather explain."

Mrs. Keene held her square of parchment to the dawn. "And healing when memory aches."

Marley said nothing. She didn't need to. Trust had already spoken. It hummed under her feet, ran through the wood of the staff, rested in Damien's steadying hand at her back.

They walked down together, seven women and a witness, as birds began to test the morning with hesitant notes that grew confident in company. The town lay below, its roofs soft with the first light. Somewhere a porch door squeaked. Somewhere a child would wake and speak a new word.

At the base of the ridge, Damien slowed. "The bloom will fade," he said, voice husky with the long night finally claiming it. "The compass will waver again. People will argue. They'll mock. They'll threaten a fence."

"I know," Marley said.

He looked at her, then at the path they had cleared and the light just touching the grass. "But you planted something that isn't just flower."

"We planted a way back," she said. "Even if we forget for a while, the spiral won't."

He slipped the compass into her palm. It lay there warm from his hand, needle unwavering. "Hold this until noon," he said, smiling tiredly. "I want you to feel what stillness does to your pocket."

She tucked it into her shawl. "I already do."

They reached the lighthouse road. Mrs. Keene hugged Marley hard, Mrs. Bennett squeezed her shoulder, Hazel pressed her cheek to Marley's in a gesture that surprised them both. Lorraine gave an awkward pat, which meant more than elaborate words could have. Evelyn bowed slightly. Tessa, almost shy, bumped Marley's fist.

When they had gone, Marley and Damien stood a moment longer. The ridge behind them breathed easy. In her mind's eye, Marley saw a ring of small, future lights at each curve, not bright like spectacle but steady like habit.

Children learning the spiral by feet. Elders resting along it and remembering out loud. A calendar you walked, not one you hung on a wall.

"Write it down before sleep steals it," Damien said, nodding at the journal.

"I will," she said. But first she closed her eyes and whispered—so the grove would overhear, so the town might, one day, overhear, too: "We remember. We root. We rise."

The Lunaflare's glow, far above, went out with the last star. The compass in her pocket held true. And the petal beneath the third curve began its quiet, invisible labor—threading light where words would never be enough.

22

ANCESTRAL VOICES SPEAK

The grove smelled of cedar and damp earth, the air thick with the residue of the Lunaflare's bloom. Summer had ripened on the ridge, but beneath the canopy the air was cooler, cloaked in shadows that lengthened even when the sun was high. Marley knelt at the spiral's third curve, where they had planted the petal days earlier. Her journal rested on her lap, its pages trembling with the faint breeze. She closed her eyes, slowing her breathing until the pulse of the grove seemed to settle into her chest.

She had begun this meditation as a discipline—fifteen minutes at dawn, fifteen at dusk. Yet tonight, as twilight thickened and fireflies blinked into the clearing, the discipline felt less like practice and more like summons.

"Keep the breath..."

The voice was faint, a thread of sound woven into silence. Marley's eyes flew open, but no one stood near her. Damien had settled further down the path, sketching the stones and tracing their alignments. The women were absent tonight; this was her time alone with the spiral.

Her palms pressed to the soil. The hum beneath her skin shifted. She closed her eyes again.

"Keep the breath..."

It came clearer this time, a woman's voice—not singular, but layered, as if spoken by many mouths in unison.

Then another: "Ink the root..."

Marley shivered. Her aunt's timbre laced through the words, though her aunt had been dead for years. And beneath it she could swear she heard Aurelia Ward herself, the matriarch whose journals had haunted her steps since she arrived in Brookwood.

"Silence is not forgetting..."

The phrase fell heavy into her ears, more command than comfort.

Her breath hitched. "Who are you?" she whispered.

The fireflies thickened, circling her, until it seemed she sat in the center of a constellation. Their light pulsed in rhythm, and for a moment she thought she saw faces inside the glow: a stern mouth, a soft brow, eyes watching her not with judgment but with the patient curiosity of teachers.

She felt heat spread across her palms where they touched soil, the way her dreams often bled into waking. Her aunt's face surfaced in her mind—not as memory alone but as presence.

"You are Keeper," the whisper insisted, layered again, many voices threading into one. "Seed and Flame. Breath and Root."

Marley's heart thudded. She pressed her forehead to the soil, tears wetting moss. "I am not enough," she murmured, voice shaking. "I will break like they did before me."

The fireflies swirled tighter, pulsing. "You are not alone," the voices replied. "Circle keeps."

A hand touched her shoulder. She startled, eyes flying

open. It was Damien, crouching beside her, his face etched with concern.

"Marley," he said softly, "you're glowing."

She blinked, bewildered. "What?"

He gestured around her. The fireflies formed a halo, clustering so close their light cast her shadow across the stones. Her hair shimmered in the glow, and her skin looked lit from within, like embers.

"Didn't you hear them?" she asked, voice urgent.

"Hear who?"

"The voices—my aunt, Aurelia, others. They spoke to me. They told me—" She broke off, chest heaving.

Damien shook his head slowly. "I heard nothing. But I see everything." His gaze softened, awe settling in his features. "Marley, if the grove ever doubted, it doesn't now. You are the next Keeper. I believe it."

She looked down at her hands. Soil streaked her palms, but beneath it, faint lines of light still glimmered, as if inked by the grove itself. The whispers still hummed faintly in her chest.

She closed her journal with trembling fingers. "Then we'll need to believe it together," she said.

The fireflies pulsed once more, then scattered into the night. The grove exhaled, leaving only silence. But silence, Marley now understood, was not forgetting. It was remembering without words.

THE AIR still shimmered faintly where the fireflies had been, their glow leaving threads of afterimage across Marley's vision. She sat back on her heels, her palms damp with soil, her chest fluttering as if she had run a long distance. The whispers—her aunt's cadence, Aurelia's authority, the layered resonance of women she couldn't yet name—still thrummed in her sternum. *Keeper of Seed and Flame. Breath and Root.* The titles didn't feel like honorifics. They felt like burdens carved into her skin.

Damien's hand lingered lightly at her shoulder. He had not moved since crouching beside her. His eyes kept flicking from her face to her hands, to the soil where faint light still clung like dew. His silence wasn't reluctance; it was absorption, the way an archivist stares at a relic knowing it must be remembered with fidelity.

Finally, he unhooked his journal from his belt, balanced it on his knee, and began to write. His pencil scraped with urgency, not the careful strokes of a curator but the hurried markings of a man afraid the vision might evaporate before it reached the page.

"You don't have to—" Marley began, but he cut her off with a glance so steady it silenced her.

"I do," he said simply. "You heard. I saw. Between us, the grove will not be forgotten."

She swallowed, nodding, and folded her arms across her knees. The soil's coolness had seeped into her bones, calming but heavy. Her aunt's voice—*Keep the breath*—echoed again, like the start of a sentence left unfinished. Marley's throat tightened. "Damien, what if I can't carry it? What if their command is too large for me?"

He didn't pause in his writing. "Then it isn't meant for you alone. A Keeper doesn't mean solitary." He underlined a word, glanced at her, then bent back to the page. "They wouldn't have spoken with witnesses present if they meant for you to hide."

She closed her eyes, heart thudding. "They said silence is not forgetting. Maybe that's their warning—that even if I never speak these words, the grove itself will remember.

And maybe the remembering will burn me from the inside out."

Damien finished his line, then set the pencil down, palm flattening the page. "Or maybe silence is the way the grove keeps its secrets safe. You don't have to shout to prove you heard. You don't even have to tell the town. You just have to breathe with it."

Her throat loosened at his words. He had always known how to anchor her—not with romance alone, but with the patience of a man who trusted earth's slow processes. He looked at her now not as partner, not even as historian, but as co-keeper. She leaned into that gaze until her fear steadied into resolve.

"I want to try again," she whispered.

Damien's brows rose. "So soon?"

"The voices weren't finished," she said. Her fingers brushed the soil again. "They gave fragments—breath, root, silence. I need to know if they'll speak more, if I listen deeper."

He studied her for a moment, then nodded once, resolute. "Then we test it together. I'll record what happens. You step back into it. But this time—we'll mark the compass, the time, every change in the grove."

He rose and moved to the central stone rim. Pulling the compass free, he set it on the rock, its needle steady since the Lunaflare's bloom. He noted the position, the minute hand on his watch, the temperature of the air by feel. Each line went into his journal with meticulous care. Then he returned, kneeling a pace away from her.

"Close your eyes," he said softly. "Let me be your witness."

Marley breathed deep, letting the night air fill her chest. She felt the hum again, low and patient, threading up from soil into her bones. The fireflies had scattered, but as she settled her breath into the grove's rhythm, a few blinked back, hovering above her shoulders like sparks waiting for tinder.

Her palms spread wider into the soil. Her forehead dipped toward moss. The ache behind her ribs deepened into vibration, as if the grove had slipped into her chest cavity to drum there.

The first whisper came, clearer than before: "Keep the breath... it binds circle to seed."

She trembled. *Bind circle to seed.* The words expanded inside her, meaning just beyond her grasp.

Another voice, lower, Aurelia's timbre: "Ink the root... it holds what speech forgets."

She felt the earth shift faintly under her fingers, as if roots coiled tighter. Ink? Roots as parchment? Or was the soil itself the ledger they had been searching for, always beneath their feet?

Then her aunt's voice, gentler but firm: "Silence is not forgetting... it is choosing what memory protects."

Her eyes welled. Protecting memory through silence— was that why so many of the Order's women had allowed themselves to be erased? They hadn't been defeated; they had been deliberate.

The voices layered then, overlapping, many at once: "Keep the breath... ink the root... silence is not forgetting... Keeper, hear..."

Her body swayed, and Damien reached to steady her shoulder without breaking her trance. His hand's warmth kept her tethered even as the voices swelled.

The fireflies surged around her again, their light brighter, clustering so thick Damien gasped under his breath. In his journal he scribbled furiously: *Light surrounding Marley. Fireflies increase tenfold. Compass needle vibrating faintly but steady north. Subject's body emitting low glow, especially hands.*

Marley's breath came ragged. "I hear you," she whispered aloud. "I hear."

The voices faded, not into absence but into a sigh that threaded the trees. The fireflies loosened, scattering into the clearing. Marley's glow dimmed, her body slumping forward until Damien caught her by both arms and eased her upright.

She blinked at him, tears streaking her cheeks. "They gave more. Breath binds circle to seed. Root ink is memory. Silence protects." She gasped, clutching his sleeve. "They're teaching us, Damien. They're handing me the vows piece by piece."

He smoothed her hair back, eyes fierce with awe. "I saw it all. I heard nothing, but I swear, Marley, you shone like ember. If I ever doubted..." He shook his head. "You are Keeper. The grove has claimed you."

She pressed her palms to her chest. The ache there no longer felt like wound but like covenant etched into bone. She whispered through tears, "Then I will not refuse them."

Damien closed his journal with reverence, pressing it against his heart. "And I will not let them be forgotten."

Above them, the grove stood hushed, the kind of silence that held meaning rather than emptiness. It was not forgetting. It was keeping.

THE CLEARING still quivered with residue from Marley's second trance—fireflies drifting like embers after a fire, soil warm beneath their palms, Damien's journal heavy with fresh ink. They might have left then, satisfied that the grove had spoken more than either of them dared hope. But Marley's chest burned still, an ache that was not exhaustion but insistence.

"They aren't finished," she whispered.

Damien froze, half-packing away his compass. "Marley—"

"No," she said, her voice steady despite the tremor in her limbs. "I feel them pressing. If I stop here, I'll only carry fragments. They want more. A full invocation."

He studied her, lips tight with worry, then exhaled sharply through his nose. "Then we do it once more—but with safeguards. You don't go under alone. I'll hold to you, even if I can't hear. If the grove means to give more, it will show us both."

Marley nodded. She lowered herself back onto the moss, palms spread, journal set aside. Damien crouched beside her, one hand resting lightly on her shoulder, the other holding the compass flat on his palm.

"Breathe slow," he said, his voice gentler than any command. "Match mine."

Together they inhaled, exhaled, until their rhythms synchronized. The grove answered with its own pulse, low and steady, beneath them. The fireflies thickened again, but this time Damien noted a change immediately—each glow didn't merely hover; it lingered, tracing shapes in the air like letters written in slow fire. He scribbled quickly in his margin: *Patterns forming—glyph-like—uncertain origin.*

Marley's voice came soft, nearly inaudible: "I call."

And the reply: not one voice, but many, woven into a choir that filled the grove like wind through hollow trunks.

"Keeper... Keeper of Seed and Flame... Keeper of Breath and Root... hear."

Damien's eyes widened. He couldn't hear words, but he

felt the vibration in the soil travel up through his boots, into his bones. Marley shuddered under his hand, her palms glowing faintly again.

"Circle unbroken... silence shelters... ink remembers... breath binds..."

Marley gasped, repeating the words aloud as though her mouth were merely conduit. Damien scrawled them in his journal, each phrase underlined, his heart hammering.

Then the air changed. The fireflies spiraled upward, clustering above Marley's head in a perfect ring. They pulsed in rhythm, seven beats, then held still. Damien stared, awe-struck. This was no simple glow; this was design.

Marley's voice deepened, layered with tones not her own. "Seven keep... seven vow... seven return."

The compass in Damien's hand quivered. The needle spun wildly for a heartbeat, then stilled again, pointing not north but toward the spiral's center. He nearly dropped it, scribbling notes with frantic haste. *Compass pulled inward— unprecedented.*

The soil beneath Marley's fingers warmed further, almost hot, and a faint crackling filled the air, like kindling catching flame. She cried out, but not in pain—in release. The invocation poured through her lips:

"Breath to bind, root to ink, silence to keep, flame to guard, seed to grow, trust to hold, circle to return—"

The words thundered, shaking the clearing though no storm touched the ridge. Damien clutched her shoulder tighter, grounding her as the firefly-ring widened until it encompassed them both. For the first time, he saw what she felt: the grove itself luminous, every tree edge lined in silver, the stones humming with resonance, the soil glowing with veins of light like roots turned inside out.

The compass needle wavered once more, then snapped inward to the center, where the Lunaflare had bloomed.

Marley's eyes flew open, pupils dilated, irises shimmering with reflected light. "Do you see?" she whispered hoarsely.

Damien, throat tight, managed a nod. "Yes. I see."

The invocation slowed, the voices softening, their final chord dissolving into the night like smoke thinning in the wind. The fireflies scattered, the glow receding until only a few lingered near the stones. The compass fell silent in his hand, needle steady again, pointing true north.

Marley collapsed forward, her palms still pressed into moss, tears streaking her face. Damien eased her upright, his chest heaving with the force of what they had witnessed. He tucked her against him, but her gaze was fixed on the center of the spiral, where the soil pulsed faintly once, then stilled.

"They gave it whole," she whispered. "The vows. Seven strands. They wanted us both to see."

Damien stroked her hair back, awe and fear intermingled in his voice. "You're not only Keeper. You're voice. And I —" He shook his head. "I may never hear them, but I'll be the record they cannot erase."

Her hand found his, their fingers intertwining, the soil still warm beneath them. She exhaled, slow, deliberate, and the grove seemed to breathe with her—quiet, but alive.

"Then we'll keep it together," she said. "Breath, root, silence, flame, seed, trust, circle. They gave us the whole. And we'll hold it."

The night lay hushed, not empty but full—the kind of silence that meant remembering. And for the first time, Damien felt it too.

23

THE TOWN'S DIVIDED OPINION

By morning the story had split and flowered across Brookwood the way rumor always does—fast, tangled, carrying seed no one remembered planting. It began as a handful of half-heard reports: lanterns up on the ridge, women seen climbing after midnight, a low bell-tone drifting down to porches like a far-off buoy calling boats home. By noon, the café blackboard bore chalk scrawls about "moonlit gatherings." By evening, someone had taped a printout by the post office boxes: **KEEP THE HILLSIDE PUBLIC** in bold, with **IS IT A CULT?** penciled beneath by an anonymous hand.

Marley stood behind the bookshop counter and watched the town read itself. The bell chimed; patrons pretended to browse and then asked the question they wanted to ask most.

"I heard you're leading rituals up there." The woman in the straw hat made "rituals" sound like a stain.

Marley shrugged with a gentleness she'd practiced. "We're caring for a neglected place."

Another customer leaned in, lowering his voice as if

reverence were contagious. "My grandmother used to speak about the circle. Said she stopped after the council cracked down. If you're bringing it back, thank you."

By late afternoon the shop had grown warm, the kind of heat that makes paper smell like loaves just out of an old oven. Marley stacked new arrivals—field guides, memoirs, a novel about a lighthouse keeper learning the language of tides—and tried not to flinch each time her name surfaced across the room like a fish in shallows. She had chosen silence as vow, not as evasion. *Silence is not forgetting,* the voices had told her. But silence in town cut a different shape —into which people poured whatever they wished.

Mrs. Keene arrived at dusk with a basket of shortbread and a look in her eye that meant war dressed as hospitality. "They're holding a listening session," she said without preamble. "Tomorrow night at the Grange. Councilwoman Nora Benning requested it. She's already talking about a moratorium on the ridge path while they 'assess safety and community impact.' In other words: a fence with a lock."

Marley poured tea to steady her hands. "I won't argue at a microphone."

"You may not need to," Mrs. Keene said, glancing toward the back where Damien was printing photographs in the makeshift darkroom they'd set up. "He can. And I will."

The bell chimed again. A pair of college students breezed in, a camera dangling between them. "Is this where the witches meet?" one blurted, half-mocking, half-thrilled.

Mrs. Keene turned so slowly that the tea in her cup didn't ripple. "If you mean the women who carried this town through fires and famines while men made speeches, yes," she said. "We do meet. But we don't pose."

The students flushed. They mumbled apologies and bought a field guide they would likely never open. After they left, Mrs. Keene softened. "It won't be all mockery," she told Marley. "People remember more than they admit."

Damien emerged a few minutes later, sleeves rolled, the tang of developer on his hands. He laid three photographs on the counter: the Lunaflare blooming like a caught moon; the compass frozen steady; a distant shot at dawn where the spiral path held a faint vein of light at the third curve, impossible but there.

"Proof without revelation," he said. "Images that show the grove alive without giving away what the grove wants to keep." He looked at Marley. "I'll speak tomorrow. You hold your silence. It'll matter that way."

She nodded, grateful for the shape his words made in the air. "What will you say?"

"That the grove is a living archive," he said, answering so quickly she knew he'd been forming the sentence all day. "Not a playground, not a cult site. An archive of this town's soul."

Marley lowered her head. The phrase settled into her like a seed finding loam. Her aunt's voice rose in memory: *Ink the root...* Damien was doing exactly that, with light instead of pen.

That night, the lighthouse flashed a measured cadence over the bay while Brookwood read aloud its own past in kitchens and on porches. A hairstylist whispered about an aunt who had used "circle smoke" to ease a newborn's breath. A church deacon muttered that the devil loved candles. A fisherman told his son about the time the hillside went quiet during a storm, as if listening for a lost name. A councilwoman rehearsed a phrase in her bathroom mirror —*we must ensure public safety*—and liked the way it made her jaw look decisive.

Marley slept briefly, and when she slept, she dreamed

nothing. It was a mercy. On waking, she found the compass on the windowsill precisely where Damien had left it, the needle at rest as if it, too, knew that arguments had a magnetic field and would try to pull them off true north. She slid the instrument into her pocket, not as prop, not as talisman, but as reminder: when asked to answer with heat, choose steadiness.

Morning carried the smell of cut grass and salt. She walked the spiral at dawn, the planted petal invisible but working, a secret labor underfoot. *Keep the breath,* she whispered. The grove hummed acknowledgment, and the day began.

THE GRANGE HALL had three kinds of light: fluorescent strips humming like summer flies; late sunlight slanting in dusty beams; and the glow from cell phones, faces bent toward glass like parishioners receiving communion. The metal chairs clanged and scraped as people claimed rows by habit —left side for families who'd been in Brookwood long enough to have stories, right side for newcomers who'd come for the scenery and stayed for the argument.

A paper sign at the door read **TOWN FORUM: HILL-SIDE USE AND ACCESS.** Below, someone had inked **THIS MEANS THE GROVE** and someone else had added **IT HAS A NAME** in firmer hand.

Marley stood near the back with Mrs. Keene, Mrs. Bennett, Hazel, Lorraine, Evelyn, and Tessa—a circle unbroken, in daytime clothing. Damien set up along the side aisle, photographs clipped to a portable line he'd brought, notebook ready. He had shaved, but left the day's stubble—the small, accidental armor of a man who knew he would need it.

Councilwoman Nora Benning called the room to order with a gavel too large for the job. She was tidy, composed, hair pinned in a hard curve that did not admit compromise. "Our purpose tonight is simple," she said. "The hillside is public land. Recent reports of gatherings—ritual or otherwise—raise questions of safety, equity of access, and community standards." She looked directly toward Marley, then past her, the way a person glances around a mirror to avoid seeing herself. "We will consider a temporary closure while we study the matter."

Murmurs swelled: *studying* sounded reasonable until one remembered that closures often went on studying until everyone forgot the door had ever been open.

The first speakers framed the debate in old ruts. A shopkeeper worried about "branding" and tourist expectations—"Are we a quaint seaside town or a witchy curiosity?" A father fretted about teenagers with candles starting a fire. A church elder warned of "imported mysticism." A biology teacher countered, practical: "It's a sensitive ecosystem. Controlled access could improve it, not harm it."

Then Mrs. Keene rose, leaned her cane against the chair, and used her full height like a bell tower. "My grandmother called it a breathing cathedral," she said, the phrase landing like a household object reclaimed. "Public land means the public cares for it, not locks it and forgets. When a place breathes, you don't put a bag over its head and call that safety."

Scattered applause. Nora Benning made a note without looking up.

Mrs. Bennett followed. "I live by weather," she said. "The ridge has been wrong and now it's righting itself. If you close access, you close the hands that are keeping it steady." She held up a callused palm, the best credential in town.

Hazel, voice shaking but sure: "I teach your children. They deserve to learn our history from more than gossip. Let us design guided visits. Let them hear the names we used to hide."

From the other side, a young mother asked, "Who decides the rites? Who decides truth? If a circle gathers to pray in a church, there are rules. If a circle gathers in trees, who sets the rules? The loudest? The oldest?" Her not-unfair questions sat like a stone in the aisle; people stepped around them but kept glancing back.

Tessa stood then, chin lifted. "You all know what they said about my bloodline," she began. The room shifted—some eyes dropped, some sharpened. "Those rumors were used to take our voice. I'm here to ask you not to use your fear to take the hillside, too." She held up a square of parchment. "A petal from a flower none of you has seen. I carry it because the grove trusted us once. If you fence it, you break that trust again."

Councilwoman Benning lifted a hand. "We're not arguing mythology tonight—"

"We're arguing memory," Tessa snapped, and somehow her anger carried more dignity than outrage. "That's not the same."

Nora pressed her lips into a shape that meant reining the room back in. "You'll have time to speak," she said, though the room had already decided who mattered and who didn't. "Last, we'll hear from Mr. Damien Hawthorne, curator and historian, who requested time for a short presentation."

Marley felt the air in her chest tighten and then loosen. This was the hinge. She squeezed the compass in her pocket once, then let it go. Damien stood, smoothed the page on his clipboard as though it were the sole wrinkled thing in the hall, and took his place at the front.

He did not bring a lectern between himself and the town. He did not clear his throat. He simply began.

"I GREW up believing archives were rooms," Damien said, his voice carrying further than it had a right to, filling the metal bones of the Grange the way cello notes fill a church. "Temperature controlled. Dust filtered. Doors locked not to keep people out, but to keep objects safe from air and hands." He held up a black-and-white photograph of the ridge from 1938—trees scalloped, a human chain hauling buckets during a brush fire. "I was wrong. An archive can be a landscape that remembers us better than we remember ourselves."

He pinched a clothespin free and replaced the old photo with one he'd taken days ago: the Lunaflare, glowing out of darkness like a secret made kind. Gasps. A few scoffs. He'd expected both.

"This flower bloomed on the solstice," he said, calm. "It exists in oral history but not the written ledger. We didn't plant it. We didn't harvest it. We watched. We recorded. We let it close."

Murmur, a wave running the hall: **let it close** as ethic, not abdication.

He clipped up the next image: the compass frozen true. "For weeks, the needle spun at the grove's center. On the night the flower opened, it stilled. I don't offer this as mira-cle. I offer it as evidence that the place is responsive—that our choices register in it. That the hillside is not inert resource but living record."

Councilwoman Benning folded her hands. "And yet what we see are pictures. A picture can be staged."

"It can," he allowed. "Which is why I'm not asking you to believe a photograph. I'm asking you to admit what you already know about this town. The ridge has always been a library without shelves. Our grandparents read it. We forgot how." He let his gaze settle without accusation on the church elder, the shopkeeper, the father, the young mother. "Closing the path would be like nailing shut the archive and calling it preservation."

He took the compass from his pocket and set it on the table in front of him. The needle held, as if even the bickering behind it could not shake its little piece of north. "You want safety? So do we. I propose a stewarded access plan. Guided hours. Work days. No-forage rules. A sign that says what the grove has already said to us: *Silence is not forgetting.*"

He turned then to Marley and did the bravest thing—he didn't ask her to speak. He held his silence beside hers like two pillars holding the same roof.

From the back, Mrs. Keene's cane thumped once, a small thunderclap. Mrs. Bennett's hands folded in approval. Hazel dabbed her eyes. Lorraine gave one decisive nod. Evelyn looked down—prayer, anyone else might have guessed— but those who knew her understood it as consent. Tessa stood without rising, a paradox that made perfect sense.

Councilwoman Benning lifted her gavel, lowered it to the table without striking. "Mr. Hale," she said, and though she clearly disliked the pivot she felt forced to take, she took it, which is all one can ask of a public servant, "you're asking us to maintain something we haven't defined. The word 'archive' implies authority, catalogue, accession, deaccession. Who decides what belongs? Who decides who belongs?"

Damien didn't avert his gaze. "Not I. Not you alone. We establish a council of stewards—historians, elders, educators, naturalists. We start with a 90-day plan. I'll draft it—pro bono. We'll measure outcomes. We'll invite the public to witness the work." His smile was slight but real. "And we will be quiet when quiet is what the grove requires."

From the second row, the young mother raised her hand again. "If my teenager wants to walk up there with a girlfriend and not do anything 'ritual,' does he get to?"

"During open hours, yes," Damien said. "Because it's public. And because the grove belongs to teenagers who aren't us yet."

Laughter, relieved and real. Tension shifted.

An older man with tar on his sleeves stood. "I fought that brush fire in '82," he said. "We needed every hand. If these folks are offering hands instead of fences, I'll bring my rake."

A pastor stood next. "I don't agree with rites in trees," he said plainly. "I won't pretend otherwise. But I believe stewardship is holy. If the plan honors boundaries and doesn't make a spectacle, my congregation can volunteer for trail repairs. Love your neighbor includes the land."

The hall, which had begun as a verdict, became a workshop. This was not sudden harmony; it was the cautious music of a small town remembering it could disagree in the same room without choosing exile. Councilwoman Benning conferred briefly with the clerk, then rapped the gavel just once.

"The motion to close the hillside is tabled for thirty days," she said. "Mr. Hale will submit a draft steward plan within two weeks. We'll hold a second forum at the end of that period." She glanced toward Marley—still silent, still standing. "No unauthorized harvesting, no fires, no night gatherings during the interim." She paused, then added, "And no cameras placed without permission." Someone in the corner—Claire had not come, but her shadow had—shifted back into anonymity.

The crowd exhaled. The chairs scraped. People who had drafted speeches for war shook hands instead. A few scowled out the door and would scowl at dinner. A few offered Marley bread rolls wrapped in napkins, the only language some knew for blessing.

Damien took down his photographs and slid the compass into his pocket. When he reached Marley, he didn't ask how she felt. He inclined his head the smallest degree, the way one bows to a living thing that has every right to be angry with humans and is not, tonight.

"Living archive," she said, testing the words he'd given the town.

"Living keeper," he returned, as if the phrase belonged to her more truly than any title a council could bestow.

They stepped out into evening. The ridge line was a black serif against molten sky; the lighthouse counted heartbeats out at the point. On Main Street, the café sign squeaked as someone flipped it to CLOSED. The town hummed, re-shelving its opinions, labeling its feelings in pencil, erasing, relabeling.

Marley slipped her hand into Damien's. He did not squeeze. He simply kept pace. Above them, the hillside held its breath, then released it. The archive was open still. And for one more night, that was enough.

24

———

THE CEREMONY OF SEVEN

The full moon rose blunt and bright, a coin pressed to the night's dark palm. On the ridge, the grove gathered light into itself the way a lung gathers air —quietly, steadily, without show. Marley led the climb with the staff across her back, a soft sheen threading the spiral carved into its wood. Behind her came Mrs. Keene, Mrs. Bennett, Hazel, Lorraine, Evelyn, and Tessa—seven women moving with the slow intent of people who had learned that haste is sometimes a kind of disrespect. Damien followed at a distance with a lantern, a notebook, and the compass, keeping to his promise to witness without directing.

They had agreed to meet at moonrise, after dinner plates were dried and stacked, after porch lights flicked off up and down Brookwood's streets. The town had not closed the hillside; the council had tabled the vote. For thirty days, the ridge would be what it had always been: public, which in this town still meant shared, with luck. Tonight, the grove belonged to no one and to everyone. Tonight, the circle would ask permission again.

They stepped into the spiral clearing, and the stones

received them, moss luminecent under silver. The Lunaflare had long since closed, but the air retained a faint sweetness at the center—a scent like memory rinsed in moonlight. The compass Damien set on the central stone held true north without tremor.

Marley lifted the staff from her shoulders and rested it along the shallow pool's rim. She didn't speak right away. The grove had taught her that silence before an invocation isn't emptiness; it's making space. When she did lift her voice, it carried without strain.

"We won't reenact what cannot be repeated," she said. "We'll answer what the grove asked us, in the language it gave: keep the breath, ink the root, remember without shouting. Tonight we enact a modern rite, not to impress or perform, but to align." She looked at each woman in turn. "You bring seven gifts. Not relics. Symbols we can use, not just display: herb, stone, letter, tear, memory, silence, and light."

Mrs. Keene stepped forward first. "Herb," she said, placing a small bundle of lavender she had dried on her kitchen rack. It smelled of summer and linen, and of nights when a child slept better because a grandmother had crushed a sprig between her palms. "Anna Brant taught me to rub this and breathe when a room went too loud," Mrs. Keene added, laying the herb at the southern stone.

Lorraine Gearhart followed with a river stone, flat and gray, worn by years. "Stone," she said simply, setting it to the west where the directional sigils had once hid beneath bramble. "Truth is heavy. It belongs to the hand." Her knuckles brushed the rock as if confirming weight by touch.

Hazel unfolded an envelope carefully sealed with wax. "Letter," she whispered, cheeks flushing in the moonlight. "It's addressed to those the ledger erased, and to those who erased them, too." She placed it at the east where dawn would find it first. "My students will copy it by hand," she added, voice stronger, "so the names travel."

Tessa stood, already crying. She laughed at herself, wiping at tears that kept coming anyway. "Tear," she said, cupping one against her palm and then letting it fall into the pool. It rippled and was gone. "So the pain that haunted my family gets to be water now, not rumor."

Evelyn cradled a stack of small index cards bound by twine. On the top one were names written in neat, precise script—Aurelia, Joan, Eliza, Mirabel, others. "Memory," she said. "Written, not to fix in place, but to remind us what moves through us." She placed the bundle at the north.

Then she reached for her cedar, held it above the pool, and did what she, and only she, could do with authority. "Silence," Evelyn said, and did not speak again. The hush that followed wasn't awkward. It was shaped.

Finally Marley lifted the beeswax pillar she had carried tucked in her shawl. "Light," she said, striking a match. She waited for the flame to steady, then set the candle on the stone rim. Seven offerings, seven stations.

Damien watched the women as if committing each posture to an archive beyond paper. He noted the direction of the breeze, the sound the birch leaves made rubbing against each other, the way the moss at the base of the central stone looked as if someone had brushed it with a wet hand. He leaned to the compass—steady. He did not lift his camera. The circle had asked for privacy during the rite, and he honored the boundary he had helped write.

Marley took her place at the center. She could feel the familiar ache behind her sternum—the place where dreams had struck her body like bells—and she did not fear it now. It wasn't a wound tonight. It was a tuning fork, already vibrating in time with the ground beneath her boots. She closed her eyes and listened until the grove's hum resolved into the key she needed.

"Keeper is never one," she said, opening them again. "Keeper is the circle agreed." Her voice was not louder; it was clearer, like water poured from a high place.

They joined hands without cue. The circle tightened, not to keep anything out but to keep each other from drifting. At the edge of the clearing, Damien drew one slow breath, then another, letting his exhale fall in time with theirs. In his palm, the compass warmed the skin as if it, too, remembered heat.

The wind sifted through branches. Far off, the lighthouse turned its careful eye. The town below had tucked itself into rooms, into beds, into opinions. Here, above it, a place old as names waited for the word that would name it again, not to capture, but to honor.

"Begin," Marley said.

Mrs. Keene moved first. She lifted the lavender bundle to her lips, breathed through it, then crushed a sprig between thumb and forefinger. The oil released, sharp and sweet, made the air feel suddenly useful, like a cloth warmed on a radiator and laid on a fevered brow. "Herb to soothe and to call back," she murmured. She kissed the sprig as if it were a grandchild's crown and waved the scent over the circle. Marley felt the grove's hum pick up half a degree, the difference between a held breath and one returned to circulation.

Lorraine knelt at the western marker. "Stone to ground," she said. She rubbed the river rock with her palm until it shone. "Truth is not what we shout about each other. Truth is what we can set a pot on and not worry it will tip." She placed the stone, then pressed her hand to it, and the moss beneath whitened briefly—some natural trick of pressure and light—and then darkened again. The grove's low note lengthened.

Hazel stood at the east. Her hands shook as she broke the seal on the letter. "I wrote this with a pencil," she said, almost apologizing. "Ink felt too permanent for a voice finding its shape." She read: "*To those named and unnamed: a child in my class asked today why some names sound like prayers and some like warnings. I told them the warning belongs not to the name, but to the story the powerful told about that name. I pledge to teach the story you would have told, if you could have stayed to tell it.*" She folded the page and set it on the stone. The breeze lifted a corner, thought better of it, and laid it down. The grove's chord gathered harmony.

Tessa wiped her face and laughed again, this time without embarrassment. "Tear to wash," she said simply, and bent to the pool. "This one's for the rumor that made me hate my own blood for a decade." She let it fall. The surface quivered, then smoothed, a small mirror agreeing to reflect again. The hum underfoot softened, fuller, as if water had found a channel once blocked.

Evelyn held up the bundle of names. She untied the twine and spread the cards like a fan. "Memory to order," she said, but the word *order* didn't mean hierarchy tonight. It meant arrangement that allows breath. "We will not stack you in glass cases. We will carry you like recipes." She placed the cards at the north, then lifted her cedar and did what only she could do: she closed her eyes and made silence. The hush lay over them like a blanket, warming without smothering, heavy without harm. Even the night insects slowed their speech.

Marley felt the moment arrive, like a note she'd been

hearing approach since she first set foot in the circle months ago. She lifted both hands, palms open, the beeswax candle steady on the rim. "Light to witness," she said. "Not to perform, not to sell, not to trap. Light to see and to be seen by what remembers us."

She did not recite an ancient script. She spoke the invocation the grove had taught her in pieces and then whole, the way a child learns a song from her mother's humming and later realizes she knows every word:

"Breath to bind, root to ink, silence to keep, flame to guard, seed to grow, trust to hold, circle to return."

The wind stilled. It was not theatrical; it was precise, as if a hand had pinched the wick of the night's draft and said gently, *hush.* The leaves shivered once and then waited. Even the lighthouse's rotation seemed to thicken into slower time, though Marley knew that was all her. The grove's hum steadied into a tone so pure she tasted it on her tongue.

Then the bell.

It didn't clang or toll. It sounded the way a bowl sings when a wet finger slides along its rim—low, resonant, the kind of vibration you feel in ribs and teeth before your ear gives it a name. The trees did not move, but the sound moved through them, from pine to birch to fir, each trunk becoming an instrument for a single sustained note. It spread along the spiral path and down the slope in a ribbon that no human could have woven by hand. Damien pressed the heel of his hand to his sternum and felt the tone there, steadying, undeniable.

He did not write. He stood very still and let the sound inscribe itself where it wanted to. The compass on the stone turned a fraction—not spinning, not confused—aligning inward to the circle's center the way a face turns toward a voice that has just said its name.

Marley felt the ache beneath her breastbone loosen and settle. She understood something she had not known she craved: affirmation that wasn't flattery. The grove did not say *well done*. It said, *we heard*. That was enough.

"Keeper is never one," she said again, but this time she didn't mean to instruct the others. She meant to instruct herself, a woman who had spent years mistaking solitude for strength. "Keeper is the circle agreed."

Mrs. Keene circled back to the south and tucked a lavender sprig into the seam of a stone, not to decorate it, but to remind herself where breath enters and exits the ground. Lorraine returned to the west and pressed the rock with the heel of her hand, as if stamping a passport at a border she had no intention of closing again. Hazel laid a second sheet beside her letter, blank, for future writing. Tessa released another tear before laughing at her own abundance. Evelyn picked up the cedar, held it shoulder-high, and offered silence like bread.

Marley raised the candle. Wax had begun to puddle at its base, hot and honey-scented. She let three drops fall into the pool. They hardened instantly, small moons. "Light is not scarce," she said, almost to herself. "We don't have to hoard."

The note in the trees deepened, then faded, not into absence but into the kind of quiet that makes room for ordinary noises to come back without sounding profane: a night bird clearing its throat, a fox settling, someone's lantern shifting on its hook. If music is proof of order, silence is the proof that order can rest.

Damien took one photograph—the tips of their hands just as they released, the candle reflected in the pool, the lavender tucked into stone. It was an image that would mean nothing to a skeptic and everything to the ones who had stood here, which was the point. He slid the camera away and took out the compass once more—steady again on north, as if nothing had happened and everything had.

Marley lowered the staff to the stone rim and felt it pulse once. Not the urgent thrum of warning she'd felt in other nights, but a benign acknowledgment, like a master handing a tool to an apprentice who has finally learned to hold it without white-knuckling. She did not try to do more than that. An invocation accepted is its own completion.

"We'll leave the gifts," she said. "But we won't come back tomorrow expecting the same tone." She smiled lightly, and the others smiled with her because they understood. "Habit is holy when it stays listening. Otherwise, it becomes a costume."

They stood with the kind of fatigue that feels like health returning—limbs warm, minds unclenched, nothing dramatic burning in the chest. The full moon watched without judgment. The grove waited as if content.

THEY DID NOT SCATTER down the ridge as if fleeing a scene. They lingered, and in lingering, let the rite become part of their muscles. Mrs. Keene and Lorraine collected their bags; Hazel slid the blank page under her letter; Tessa breathed long, proud breaths through a nose still wet with tears; Evelyn replaced her cedar in its cloth wrap, bound with a single loop that would slip free at a tug. Marley lifted the candle from the stone—still lit, still steady—and looked to each woman in turn.

"We'll walk the spiral once more," she said. "Not to wring a second miracle. To press our footprints into what the grove has given."

They made a slow procession, not in lockstep, not

dramatic—just people moving with attention. At the third curve—the place of choosing—they paused without speaking. The petal planted there weeks ago lay invisible, working the way ground works: thread by patient thread, below sight. A moth crossed their path and disappeared into the birch. Somewhere farther down the slope a night animal barked once, annoyed at nothing anyone could name.

On the outer ring, Marley stopped. The wind held its breath again for a heartbeat, then resumed as if pleased to have been asked. She looked over the town, where porch lights clipped neat squares out of dark. Somewhere a TV droned; somewhere a baby fussed and then subsided; somewhere two people spoke in a kitchen with their foreheads touching, not needing to be heard by anyone but the walls.

"Tomorrow," Mrs. Bennett said finally, "I'll bring the girls from the farm. We'll teach them how to lay cedar leaves like bookmarks, so they'll find their way back to the same page."

Hazel nodded. "I'll bring a class schedule up the ridge. We can mark times when the spiral is for walking and times when it's for working and times when it's just for listening." She glanced at Marley. "No cameras. Just pencils."

Lorraine snorted softly. "And rakes," she said. "I'll organize those who want to help repair the western path. People love a job as long as it's obvious when they've done it."

Evelyn tilted her head, hearing something the others didn't, or did and couldn't name. "We'll teach them the difference between silence that hides and silence that guards," she said. "It will take repetition."

Tessa held up her square of parchment with the preserved petal Marley had given her days before. "And I'll meet gossip with invitation. If they call it cult, I'll say, *come see the herb and stone and letter and tear*, and I'll keep my voice level until their tone changes or they walk away."

Mrs. Keene planted her cane in the moss and looked at Marley with a bright, bright gaze. "You'll lead the invocation again one day," she said. "But not every time. We all need to hear our own mouths make the promises."

Marley nodded, a warmth rising that wasn't only from the candle. "Keeper is the circle agreed," she said softly. The sentence fit her tongue without effort now.

Damien hung back until the women turned toward the path down. Only then did he step beside Marley. "The tone," he said. "I felt it in my bones."

"I know," she said. "I saw you still. That mattered."

He set the compass on his palm and held it out to her. The needle held true. "It's foolish, I know, to assign meaning to a needle's pause," he said, smiling at his own mixed loyalties. "But I need such foolishness. It keeps me from thinking my work is the only work."

She took the instrument and slid it into the pocket over her heart. "You called the grove an archive," she said. "Tonight, it catalogued us. Not for ownership. For remembering."

He looked at her then with a tenderness that wasn't soft; it had edge, a curator's clarity. "You're not only Keeper to me," he said quietly. "You're home."

The word landed in her like a stone set on a hearth—a weight that stabilized the room. She did not answer with language. She squeezed his hand until the message had nowhere left to go but marrow.

They began the descent. The seven women walked ahead, their lanterns describing small moving constellations between trunks. The path was clearer for their footsteps, the brush already pushed gently back by their attention. The ridge breathed in and out, in and out. Halfway down, they heard the bell again—fainter, more like memory than sound —and it occurred to Marley that perhaps the tone would repeat every time the circle kept its promise, not because they demanded proof, but because the grove loved to answer with music when silence had already done its work.

At the edge of town, they parted the way townspeople always do—without ceremony, because the ceremony had already happened where it mattered. Mrs. Keene turned toward a house that smelled like cinnamon and old paper. Mrs. Bennett angled toward fields that breathed dark loam. Hazel headed for the small apartment over the schoolhouse where lesson plans waited. Lorraine cut toward the lane that led to her clinic, where she would open the door at dawn to an ankle and a shoulder and a fear. Evelyn went without a word toward the cottage whose windows glowed softness instead of glare. Tessa walked straight down Main as if power were a posture anyone could practice with enough repetitions. Damien and Marley took the lighthouse road.

They did not talk about the councilwoman or the draft stewardship plan due in two weeks. They had already decided what they needed to: they would write down every-thing they could that did not belong to the grove's silence and they would keep everything else where it lived best— between hands, in breath, underfoot.

On the porch of the lighthouse cottage, Marley set the candle in a dish. The flame shrank and then steadied, the way a person does when the work turns from public to private. Damien went inside for a moment and returned with a sheet of vellum and a soft pencil. He laid the paper flat and drew a circle. Without measuring, he placed seven small marks along its edge. He wrote beneath them: *herb, stone, letter, tear, memory, silence, light.* He did not assign names. He didn't need to.

"Hang it where you'll see it when you grab your coat," he said. "So you'll remember that keeping isn't episodic."

Marley nodded and lifted the paper to the doorway where breeze could move past it without taking it. She stood a long time watching the candle flame reflect on the glass, small and stubborn.

In bed, she did not dream. Silence performed its best work—re-stitching a person to herself. At some hour the gulls began their rude hymns; at some hour the lighthouse clicked; at some hour a child somewhere in town woke from a nightmare and discovered it had resolved into thirst, easily tended.

At dawn, they climbed again, not for spectacle, not for another tone, but to pick up trash the wind had blown into the understory and to rake a section of path that had muddled with heavy feet. The grove greeted them with something like indifference, which is to say, with the trust that comes when a place no longer has to defend itself against those who claim to love it. The lavender tucked in the stone still breathed. The stone still held. The letter lay dry and whole. The pool showed no sign of tears—water keeps secrets kindly. The cards at the north ruffled but remained. The cedar waited in its cloth. The candle's wax moons floated at the edge.

Marley stood at the center and closed her eyes. The ache under her sternum did not flare; it warmed. The phrase rose again, unchanged now because it no longer needed to speak louder than doubt.

"Breath to bind, root to ink, silence to keep, flame to guard, seed to grow, trust to hold, circle to return."

She smiled because the words were not a spell. They were a description of something already true.

Damien, from the edge, wrote one line only: *Wind still, bells remembered, circle intact.*

The day opened. They walked the spiral as caretakers do —rake, gather, pause, listen. And when they went down into town, the ridge did not keep them with a miracle, which felt like the greatest blessing of all. The grove could sing without proving, and they could keep without being seen. The ceremony had worked because it had not tried to be anything but what the place required: seven gifts given and received, a bell tone honest enough to live in bone, and the wind stilling just long enough to teach them what moving rightly could sound like.

25

———

DAMIEN'S CHOICE

The letter came in a cream envelope with the return address stamped in clean serif type: Northeast Institute for Cultural Memory. Damien knew the name well. He had written for their journal, lectured in their auditoriums, and once walked through their archives with a mixture of awe and hunger. Their collections reached across centuries, and their exhibitions were the sort of polished stories that made donors open checkbooks and schoolchildren lean forward. He slit the envelope carefully, the way one handles an artifact.

Inside, the letter unfolded with professional weight. They wanted him to curate a traveling exhibition on **"Living Archives: How Communities Carry Memory."** It would tour Boston, Chicago, Seattle, and London. The stipend was generous; the prestige unquestionable. The timeline, however, was firm: ten months of preparation, six months of travel. They expected relocation—Brookwood could not be his base if he took the job.

Damien sat at his desk where the wood still smelled faintly of salt and lamp oil. The sea whispered through the cracked window. He read the letter twice, then once more, each time feeling his pulse shift. Ten years ago, he would have accepted without hesitation. Five years ago, he might have fought to balance it with his personal life. Now, with the grove's hum still lodged in his chest from the Ceremony of Seven, the words on the page felt less like invitation and more like a test of allegiance.

He reached for the compass resting near the lamp. Its brass casing warmed quickly in his palm. The needle, steady since the Lunaflare bloom, pointed north without quiver. He remembered the night it had spun so wildly that Marley had pressed her hand over his and said, *"It's listening to you. Not to direction."*

The sound of footsteps interrupted his reverie. Sophie padded into the room, her hair still damp from an evening shower, the hem of her nightgown trailing. She was carrying her sketchpad, the one she'd been filling with drawings of the grove—spirals, flowers, trees bending as if bowing.

"Dad," she said softly, "can I stay up a little? I want to finish this page."

Damien gestured her over. She perched on the edge of the desk, her pencil tapping lightly against the corner. "Look," she said, flipping the sketchpad around. She had drawn the Lunaflare bloom from memory, its petals glowing with faint pencil shading, surrounded by fireflies rendered in quick flicks of graphite.

"It's beautiful," Damien said, and he meant it. The flower's glow had etched itself into him, but seeing it through his daughter's hand was another kind of permanence.

Sophie tilted her head. "Are you worried?" she asked, glancing at the letter still lying open. "You look like when you're deciding whether to put something in the exhibit or keep it in storage."

Her words made him laugh gently, though the truth pricked. "Something like that," he admitted.

She leaned closer, her voice dropping as if sharing a secret with the sea. "If it's about leaving, I don't want to. The grove talks to me. Not with words, but...you know." She tapped her chest. "Here."

Damien looked at her, and the ache he felt was a father's ache: pride so fierce it hurt, and fear just as sharp. His daughter had inherited more than his eye for detail. She had inherited the pulse of the place, the same pull that kept Marley walking the spiral even when town gossip turned sharp.

He kissed the crown of her head. "Go on," he said. "Finish your page. Then bed."

When she slipped back down the hall, Damien turned once more to the letter. He let the institute's offer sit like a stone in his palm. Legacy, it whispered. Recognition. But another voice, quieter and stronger, asked: *Legacy for whom?*

He carried the letter to the porch where the lantern light brushed the waves into silver. Marley was already there, wrapped in a shawl, her gaze turned toward the ridge. She didn't turn as he joined her. "The grove hummed tonight," she said. "Like it was full after supper."

Damien laid the letter on the table between them. "They want me," he said. "To leave."

Only then did she turn, eyes searching his. "And do you?"

He didn't answer. Not yet. The sea filled the silence, and the lighthouse swept its slow blessing across water and wood. Damien felt both pull and weight, as if the night itself were asking him to declare allegiance not to a place, but to a promise.

THE NEXT MORNING, Damien walked into town carrying the letter folded in his pocket. He moved through Brookwood as though he were already seeing it from a distance, the way one does before a departure—cataloguing details: the worn grooves in the café's wooden counter, the chalk doodles children had scrawled near the post office, the gull feather caught in a crack of the boardwalk. Each small mark whispered: *You belong to this, too.*

At the café, Mrs. Keene waved him over. "You look like you've been cornered by an ancestor," she said, sliding him a cup of black coffee.

He smiled wearily. "Something like that. The Institute wants me for an exhibition. Travel, relocation."

Mrs. Keene raised an eyebrow. "They'd love to own your eye. But what about your hands? Who would the grove trust to photograph its moods if not you?"

He stirred his coffee, watching the ripple spiral. "It's prestige. A chance to put Brookwood's story in front of thousands."

"And to miss the story being written here," Mrs. Keene countered. "Prestige is just applause from people who don't know your name well enough to call you for soup when you're sick."

Her words landed with the weight of lived truth. He thought of Marley, of Sophie, of the compass steady on the stone rim.

Later that day, he climbed the ridge alone. The grove greeted him not with sound but with presence—a stillness so thick it pressed against his chest. He walked the spiral, letter still folded in his pocket, and stopped at the center. He took the compass out and set it on the stone. The needle quivered once, then stilled.

"You've got no opinion about this, do you?" Damien murmured. "Archive doesn't travel. Archive is here."

He pulled the letter free, unfolded it, and read it aloud—not to decide, but to let the grove hear. When he finished, a gust swept through the clearing, lifting the page from his hand. He caught it just before it flew. The grove had made its point.

By evening, he returned to the lighthouse. Marley was waiting with two mugs of chamomile. She studied his face. "You went up," she said.

"I read the letter to the stones."

Her eyes softened. "And what did they answer?"

"That legacy isn't only in glass cases. It's in how we keep places alive."

He told her about Mrs. Keene's words, about Sophie's sketch, about the compass steadying as if reminding him north was already known. Finally, he said, "I don't want to leave. But I don't want you to feel bound to me if staying means less than what you deserve."

Marley set her mug down. "I chose the circle. I chose the vow. And I chose you. None cancel the others. But I won't ask you to stay. You have to want it."

He took her hand, rough from books and soil. "I do. I want it. I've just been trained to measure worth by distance, by scale. But maybe worth is smaller. More rooted."

"Seed instead of spectacle," Marley said.

He laughed softly. "Exactly."

The sea kept time. The lighthouse swept its arc. And the folded letter lay forgotten on the table as if already a relic, a document from another life he had just declined.

.   .   .

THE FOLLOWING MORNING, Damien took Sophie to the spiral path. The dew was thick, clinging to boots and hems. She carried her sketchpad again, clutching it like a compass of her own.

"Why here?" she asked as they reached the outer ring.

"Because I want you to see where I decided."

They walked in silence, father and daughter, the spiral tightening around them until they reached the center. Damien took the folded letter from his pocket and placed it on the central stone. He set the compass beside it.

"This," he said, "was the offer. To travel, to curate, to be important in places far from here."

Sophie frowned. "And?"

"And I told the grove. And the grove answered." He smiled. "It told me home is not a place. It's a promise."

She tilted her head. "What promise?"

He knelt so their eyes met. "The promise I'm keeping—with you, and with Marley. That we'll tend this place, even when it doesn't sing. That we'll stay, even when leaving looks shinier."

Sophie reached out and touched the compass. The needle held steady, pointing true. "Then we'll keep it together," she said.

Later, back at home, Damien told Marley the words fully. He laid the letter down, smoothed it flat, and looked at her across the kitchen table.

"My work is here," he said. "My home is not a place. It's a promise I'm keeping—with you."

Marley's breath caught, not because she doubted, but because she knew the cost of what he had turned down. She rose, circled the table, and placed her hands on his shoulders. "Then we keep together," she whispered.

That night, they lit a small lantern and carried it to the porch. The flame burned without wavering, steady as the compass needle, steady as the vow between them. The sea stretched out dark and endless, but Damien no longer felt pulled by distance. He felt rooted, exactly where he needed to be.

The Institute's letter remained on the table for a week before Marley finally slid it into a box of mementos. Not as temptation, but as reminder: choices are also archives. And this one would always mark the night Damien turned from acclaim to presence, from prestige to promise.

The grove hummed that evening as if in approval, though it owed them no such affirmation. Still, they felt it— the resonance of a decision made not for legacy alone, but for love rooted deep.

26

MARLEY'S HIDDEN MEMORY

The dream began with earth beneath her fingernails. Not the ordinary grit of Brookwood soil, but a darker, richer loam that pulsed faintly as if it were alive. Marley knelt in a ring of women, all clad in robes dyed green from crushed leaves. Their hands moved in rhythm, each gesture a petition. The air was heavy with smoke from herbs smoldering in shallow clay bowls— sage, cedar, and something unfamiliar that carried a sweet bite, like citrus wrapped in resin.

She looked down at her hands and realized they were younger—slimmer, unlined, quick. Her sleeves bore stitched patterns she recognized only faintly from Aurelia Ward's journal sketches. She wasn't watching from the outside; she was living inside the memory, and the body she wore wasn't borrowed—it was her own, across time.

Aurelia stood beside her, the Grove's first guardian, her presence as steady as an oak trunk. She bent low and whispered, "Plant secrets with petals, truth beneath trees. Every seed carries a vow. Every vow roots itself deeper than memory."

Marley's hands trembled as she received a pouch of dried herbs from Aurelia. She dug a hollow at the base of a sapling—its bark smooth, its leaves small, trembling like the skin of a newborn animal. Into the hollow she pressed the herbs, each crumble releasing scent. As she covered them, her lips moved without conscious thought, whispering words that rose like smoke:

"By root and rain, by flame and seed, I bind silence to keep, memory to breathe. Let truth grow taller than lies, let this circle stand when flesh has turned to dust. Keeper I am, Keeper I vow."

Her voice echoed with others around the circle. She looked up and saw seven faces in the moonlight, each intent, each illumined. They laid their herbs, they whispered their vows, and together they leaned into the tree as though lending it their spines.

The sapling quivered. Its roots pulsed beneath her palms. Aurelia placed a hand on Marley's shoulder. "Apprentice, you carry what comes after me. You'll bear the whisper, even when voices fade."

Marley's throat ached as if her own name had been pronounced across centuries. She pressed both palms to the soil, leaving an imprint that glowed briefly before fading into the earth. When she lifted her hands, a thin ceramic token lay between her palms, wet with soil, inscribed with the spiral. She knew she had shaped it, fired it, marked it as part of the vow. On its underside were letters—not hers, not yet: *M.T.*

The world blurred, and she woke with a gasp.

Her chest tightened. Some part of her already recognized the tree's outline—its trunk, its trembling leaves, its position within the spiral's hidden arc. She felt as if the grove had been waiting for her to claim it.

By the time she dressed and stepped into morning light, the vow still rang in her ears, and she knew what she had to do: return to the grove and find the tree that remembered her across lifetimes.

THEY CLIMBED the ridge as the sun lifted over Brookwood, gilding the dew into jewels. Marley walked with unusual urgency, her boots crunching on gravel, her shawl slipping loose around her shoulders. Damien followed close, carrying his satchel with the compass, his notebook, and a small trowel.

"Describe it," he urged as they neared the grove.

Marley closed her eyes briefly. "Smooth bark. Leaves that flutter even when the air is still. It was a sapling then, small enough to tremble beneath my hand. By now..." She opened her eyes, scanning the trees, heart pounding. "By now, it should be mighty."

They stepped into the spiral clearing. The Lunaflare's scent still lingered faintly, though the petals had long since been preserved. Marley let her feet guide her beyond the central ring, toward the grove's northern edge where light filtered through birch and pine. Her pulse quickened when she saw it: a tree taller than the rest, bark pale and unscarred despite its age, its leaves trembling even in the morning's hush.

"That's it," she whispered.

Damien studied it with the critical eye of a historian. "It doesn't match the others—different species, slightly displaced from the spiral but still aligned." He lowered his voice. "It could be what you saw."

Marley approached, her palms sweating. She pressed one hand to the bark. A shiver ran up her arm, into her chest. For a moment, she felt the circle of women around her again, Aurelia's hand heavy on her shoulder, vows whispered like smoke.

"It remembers me," she said, eyes wet.

She dropped to her knees, brushing leaves aside, fingers clawing at the soil. Damien knelt too, using the trowel to clear away earth at the base. The soil was thick but gave way easily, as though it wanted them to dig. Minutes passed, sweat streaking their foreheads, until Marley's hand struck something hard.

She froze. Together they cleared the earth until a small ceramic token emerged, its spiral still etched, faint but intact. She lifted it with trembling hands.

"M.T.," she whispered, turning it over. The letters were shallow, worn, but unmistakable. "My initials. Mine. From then. From now."

Damien stared, his skepticism collapsing under the weight of evidence. "It can't be coincidence," he said hoarsely. "This was buried before you were born."

Marley cradled the token as though it were alive. A vibration hummed through her palms, faint but certain. She heard the vow again in her bones: *Keeper I am, Keeper I vow.*

Her breath shook. "I've carried this promise across lifetimes."

Damien reached for her shoulder, grounding her. "And now you've found proof."

Tears streamed freely down her cheeks. "It means the grove has been waiting for me. Not just as heir. As return."

THEY SAT at the base of the tree until sunlight dappled the clearing. Marley traced the spiral on the token again and again, each stroke deepening her sense of recognition. She placed her palm against the bark and whispered, "I am here."

The grove answered—not with words, not with fireflies or bells, but with a deep stillness that wrapped around them. Damien felt it too. He glanced at the compass; its needle had shifted, not north, not inward, but aligning directly toward the tree itself.

"Do you see?" Marley breathed.

"I see." His voice cracked. "This is more than memory. It's lineage. You are Aurelia's apprentice, across time."

Marley laid the token at the base of the tree, then hesitated. "Part of me wants to keep it, proof in my hand. But the vow was to bury it. To let it root."

Damien nodded slowly. "If it's a vow, breaking it might fracture what you've reclaimed."

She pressed the token back into the earth gently, covering it with soil. Her fingers lingered, patting the ground smooth as though tucking in a child.

When she withdrew her hands, the air shifted. A gust ran through the grove, and every tree bent slightly inward, branches whispering. Damien swore he heard syllables, though he couldn't shape them. Marley knew: *Keeper returned. Vow remembered.*

She rose, brushing dirt from her knees, her face glowing with awe. "The grove has bound me twice now—once then, once today. There's no mistaking it."

Damien clasped her hand. "Then we walk forward as keepers, together. Your vow isn't just memory anymore. It's present."

As they descended the ridge, Marley felt lighter, yet more rooted than ever. The grove had shown her who she had been, and in doing so, confirmed who she must be now. Her legacy was no longer an abstract inheritance—it was a circle of vows planted across centuries, still alive beneath the trembling leaves of a tree that had waited patiently for her return.

The wind whispered through branches, and for the first time, Marley didn't flinch at the sound. She whispered back, certain the grove would carry her words into its roots:

"I remember. I root. I rise."

27

THE BOTANIST'S REDEMPTION

The knock came at twilight, when the sea and sky were the same color of gray and the lighthouse beam had only just begun its slow rotation. Marley was in the bookshop, closing out the register, while Damien prepared supper upstairs. The sound was soft but deliberate, and when Marley opened the door, Claire Whitcomb stood there—wind-tousled, travel-worn, and strangely subdued.

Her usual sharpness, the eagerness that had once pricked Marley's nerves, was absent. She carried no camera, no notebook, no measuring tape slung across her shoulder. Instead, in her hands, she clutched a sealed envelope, its edges worn as if carried through many miles of hesitation.

"May I come in?" Claire asked, her voice careful, cautious, stripped of its earlier bravado.

Marley studied her, searching for the telltale glint of ambition, the kind of hunger that had always made her wary. But what she saw was something else—fatigue, perhaps grief. She stepped aside. "Come."

Inside, the shop smelled of herbs and cedar oil. Claire

looked around as if the place were both sanctuary and tribunal. She did not sit until Marley gestured to a chair by the fire. For a long moment, Claire simply held the envelope in her lap. Finally, she placed it on the table between them.

"It's my grandmother's," she said. "Mirabel Colvin. Before she died, she wrote this. I was too afraid to bring it until now."

Marley reached for the envelope but did not open it yet. She felt the weight of it, as though paper could carry centuries. "Why now?" she asked.

Claire exhaled, hands tightening together. "Because I've been wrong. I thought if I studied enough, proved enough, I could restore her name by force. But the grove doesn't yield to force. It's... it's memory woven with mercy. And I've been neither merciful nor patient." She swallowed, her eyes bright. "I came not to claim, but to confess."

Marley let silence stretch. She had learned that silence could be sharper than accusation. Claire met her gaze and did not flinch.

"I know you don't trust me," Claire continued. "You shouldn't. I photographed what wasn't mine. I demanded access without offering reverence. But when I read this letter —" She tapped the envelope lightly. "—I realized her exile wasn't only punishment. It was grief. She regretted what she'd tried to do. She wrote of the Circle she betrayed. She wanted forgiveness."

Marley's throat tightened. Forgiveness was a word that tasted both bitter and sweet. She traced the edge of the envelope with her finger but still didn't break the seal.

"You said you came not to claim," Marley said softly. "Then what do you ask?"

Claire leaned forward, the firelight etching hollows beneath her eyes. "I ask only that you let me show this letter to you. That you decide if it belongs in the ledger, or if it belongs in the fire. And if I publish anything, it will be only with your consent, in your words, and for memory, not acclaim."

Marley listened, weighing tone against intention. For the first time, she believed Claire's urgency wasn't ambition but atonement. Still, trust could not be handed over like a coin. It had to be planted, tended, watched.

At that moment Damien entered, wiping his hands on a dish towel. He froze at the sight of Claire, then moved instinctively closer to Marley. "What's this?" he asked, his voice low, protective.

Claire stood, hands trembling but visible. "I've come to return something," she said simply.

Marley held up the envelope. "Her grandmother's letter."

Damien's jaw worked. He looked at Marley first, then at Claire. Finally, he nodded once, though his body remained taut with suspicion.

"Let's open it," Marley said. Her hands shook slightly as she broke the seal.

Inside was a folded sheaf of cream stationery, written in ink that had browned with time. The script was steady, elegant, unmistakably old-fashioned. Marley read aloud, her voice breaking on the second line:

To the women of the Circle I betrayed—though I am unworthy of your hearing.

The fire cracked. Outside, the lighthouse swept its rhythm across the bay. Marley read on, carrying the words of the dead into the room.

·   ·   ·

THE LETTER WAS LONG, more testament than apology. Mirabel wrote of the moment she had tried to profit from a sacred herb, believing her research would "elevate" the Circle in the eyes of outsiders. She admitted that her motives were poisoned by pride. When the Circle cast her out, she raged for years—but in time, she understood that exile had been mercy, a chance to recognize the weight of what she had endangered.

I wished to turn living vows into commerce, the letter confessed. *And so I broke the vow myself. Yet the grove did not strike me down. It simply turned its face away. That absence was worse than any punishment. I would have chosen fire over silence. But the silence was my inheritance, and I accept it.*

At the end, Mirabel wrote: *To whoever tends the grove after me, know that my bloodline carries regret, not defiance. Do not punish my granddaughter for my sin. Let her serve memory, if she serves humbly. And if not, let her be forgotten with me.*

When Marley's voice fell silent, the room seemed to contract around them. Damien sat with arms crossed, his eyes on Claire. She sat motionless, tears glinting on her cheeks.

"She wrote that near the end," Claire whispered. "I found it in her desk after the funeral. For months I couldn't bear it. I kept thinking—I can undo this, I can prove we're not all traitors. But every time I pushed, the grove resisted. I think it was her silence echoing."

Marley placed the folded letter back on the table. Her heart ached—not only for Mirabel's regret, but for Claire, who had carried both ambition and shame like twin burdens.

Damien spoke at last. "Words on paper don't undo damage. The Circle was broken for decades because of what your grandmother did. You can't publish your way into redemption."

"I know," Claire said quickly. "I know. That's why I'm asking Marley. Only Marley. If she says no, then it dies with me. I won't force it. I won't repeat the mistake."

Marley studied her closely. For once, Claire's gaze wasn't calculating—it was pleading. And not just for herself. For her bloodline.

"What do you want from me?" Marley asked quietly.

Claire's answer was simple. "Permission to honor, not to claim."

Marley felt the weight of decision press against her ribs. She looked at Damien. His expression was stone, protective, skeptical. Then she looked at the letter again, its ink trembling slightly in the firelight.

"The grove teaches us that silence is not forgetting," Marley said. "Perhaps this letter belongs in silence, but not in ashes. Perhaps it can rest, not erased but remembered for what it teaches."

Claire bowed her head. Relief mingled with sorrow in her features. "Then that is enough."

Marley rose, crossed to the shelf where she kept the Lunaflare petals preserved between glass pages of her journal. She opened the case, lifted one delicate petal shimmering faintly in the firelight, and returned to the table.

She held it out to Claire. "Take this. Use it to heal—not to claim."

Claire's breath caught. She accepted the petal as though it might shatter. Her hands shook. "Thank you," she whispered. "I won't fail this gift."

. . .

THEY WALKED TOGETHER to the grove that night, not to conduct ritual, but to lay the letter to rest. The moon rode high, silvering the spiral path. Marley carried the letter pressed against her chest, while Claire held the Lunaflare petal cupped in both palms as though it were flame. Damien walked beside them, watchful, steady, neither granting nor denying trust—only bearing witness.

At the central clearing, Marley knelt and dug a shallow hollow at the base of the trembling-leaf tree, the one where she had unearthed her vow token. She laid the letter gently inside, covering it with soil. "Silence, not forgetting," she murmured.

Claire stepped forward, tears streaking her face. She bent low and placed the Lunaflare petal atop the freshly turned soil. For a moment, the petal glowed faintly, then faded into the earth as if accepted. Claire pressed her palms together. "For healing," she whispered.

A hush fell. The trees bent inward slightly, branches whispering in a sound like breath. Marley felt the grove acknowledging—not absolving, but acknowledging. Damien's hand tightened around hers. Claire wept quietly, her shoulders shaking.

When they rose, Marley turned to her. "Your grandmother's name remains marked by exile. That cannot change. But her apology is now rooted. And your choice—this choice—will be remembered."

Claire nodded, wiping her cheeks. "I don't ask for more. Only to serve memory with honesty."

They descended the ridge together, the lighthouse sweeping its beam across the bay. At the bookshop door, Claire paused. "I'll leave Brookwood tomorrow," she said. "I'll take nothing but what you've given me. When the time comes, if you choose to let the world see, I'll be here. Until then, I'll keep silence."

Marley placed a hand over her heart. "Then the grove may yet redeem your line."

Damien said nothing, but as Claire disappeared into the night, he exhaled a long breath. Marley knew he still doubted—but doubt could coexist with grace.

That night, as they lay beneath the sound of waves and the steady heartbeat of the lighthouse, Marley whispered, "Healing, not claiming."

Damien answered softly, "And silence, not forgetting."

And in the grove, the soil cradled both letter and petal, binding regret into memory, and memory into seed.

28

THE GROVE RECLAIMS ITSELF

It began without warning.

One morning, when mist still clung low to the hillside and gulls skimmed the water with ragged cries, Marley stepped into the grove and froze. The air was saturated, lush in a way she had never felt. Overnight, green had exploded.

The winter-browned grasses that had lined the spiral were now interwoven with sprigs of mint, wild chamomile, and small bursts of lavender—plants that had no business blooming this time of year. Ferns, too, unfurled in thick clusters, their fronds damp and shining as though they had been washed by spring rain, though no storm had passed.

Marley's breath caught. "It's happening," she whispered.

Damien, a step behind her, lifted his camera instinctively. His finger hovered over the shutter, then hesitated. He lowered the lens slightly, caught between archivist and worshipper.

"Take it," Marley urged softly. "The grove wants remembering."

Click. The sound was sharp against the hush. Another

click, then another, as Damien began to capture the miracle: sprays of goldenrod bending against pale birch, anemones blooming in clumps where only moss had been, a sudden burst of bluebells ringing silently at the base of the spiral stones.

The air vibrated with scent. Rosemary mingled with rose, pine with unexpected jasmine. Marley closed her eyes and let it wash over her. It was not chaos but harmony— each note clear, each bloom purposeful.

And then she heard it: the faint trickle of water.

Her eyes flew open. She turned toward the grove's center. Where once had been only compact earth and Lunaflare petals now bubbled a clear spring, water seeping gently from beneath the soil as though the grove had pierced its own skin to bleed renewal.

"Oh," Marley breathed. She dropped to her knees, hand hovering just above the pool's surface. The water was cold, crystalline, carrying with it the smell of stone and time. She touched it at last, and a shiver ran up her arm.

Damien crouched beside her, his camera clicking. "It's in Aurelia's journal," he murmured. His voice trembled with reverence. "The shallow pool. She called it 'the mirror of breath.' Said the Circle gathered there to see their vows reflected."

The pool widened as they watched, no flood or violence, just slow insistence. Pebbles shifted. Fern roots adjusted. The spiral path seemed to bend subtly toward the spring, as if recognizing its center had returned.

Marley scooped a handful of water and let it slip between her fingers. "It's alive again," she whispered. "The grove reclaims itself."

Damien finally lowered the camera. His eyes were wet, though not with grief. "I've photographed ruins rising from excavation, archives pieced together from dust. But this—this is a living archive."

She leaned against him, still staring at the pool. "Then capture it. Not as evidence. As prayer."

And so he raised the lens once more, and the grove answered with bloom and water, holding them both in its resurgence.

By MIDDAY, word of the bloom had reached town. Mrs. Keene climbed the ridge first, followed by a trickle of towns-folk who could not resist whispers of sudden color in the heart of Brookwood's most haunted hillside. Marley feared intrusion, feared the press of doubt against fragile newness —but when they entered the grove, the hush deepened instead of breaking.

No one spoke loudly. Children bent low, touching petals as if they might burn. Elders pressed hands to their hearts. Even skeptics who had muttered at the café found them-selves silenced by the scent, the spring, the impossible blos-soms unfurling in unison.

Mrs. Keene turned to Marley. "I was a fool to doubt." Tears streaked her weathered face. "It's not legend. It's here."

Marley squeezed her hand. "It's more than here. It's remembering us."

Damien moved among them like both host and witness, capturing expressions as carefully as he captured blooms. His photographs became portraits of awe—wrinkled faces lit as though by candlelight, children's eyes wide with wonder, families huddled close as if afraid the grove might vanish again.

When he lowered the camera, Damien knelt by the spring. He dipped his hand, then filled a small vial from his satchel. "For record," he murmured. But when Marley raised a brow, he added quickly, "And for reverence."

That evening, after the visitors had left and twilight spread its silver cloak, Marley returned alone. She carried the preserved Lunaflare journal and the compass. The grove's glow was softer now, but still pulsing. The compass needle pointed directly at the pool.

She knelt at its edge. "What do you want from me?" she whispered. "Why now?"

The water rippled though no breeze touched it. Fireflies gathered again, hovering above the pool like a crown. In their light, Marley glimpsed her reflection, but layered—her face, Aurelia's, the Circle women, countless others. Keeper upon Keeper, all breathing through her.

She pressed her hand flat against the soil. "I'll hold it. Not as mine. As ours."

The fireflies blinked once, twice, then scattered, leaving her heart trembling with the weight of the grove's reply.

THE FOLLOWING MORNING, Damien returned with his tripod and began the careful work of documenting the transformation. He set exposures long enough to catch the way light refracted on the water, the way petals seemed to glow even without direct sun. Marley sat nearby, journaling each bloom with names both botanical and ancestral.

As she wrote, a pattern emerged: seven clusters, each distinct yet circling the spring. Herbs in one quadrant, flowering shrubs in another, ferns in another still. It was as though the grove itself had reformed the Circle—not of women this time, but of flora, each bloom a vow embodied.

"Seven again," she murmured.

Damien looked up from the lens. "Always seven."

They decided together to let the pool remain untouched, unbottled beyond Damien's single vial, unfiltered by human hand. The townsfolk would be invited back under guidance, not as spectators but as witnesses.

At dusk, they brought Sophie to see. The child stood at the water's edge, her eyes wide. "It's breathing," she whispered.

Marley felt tears rise. She placed a hand on her daughter's shoulder. "Yes. And so are we."

Damien lifted his camera one final time, but this photograph he did not check afterward. He simply let the click stand, a sound like benediction.

That night, as lantern light flickered across the lighthouse walls, Marley and Damien sat with the photographs spread between them. Images of blossoms, of water, of faces awed into silence. Damien touched one where the pool shone like glass. "This isn't just history. It's covenant."

Marley leaned close, her voice steady. "The grove has reclaimed itself. And now it claims us, too."

The spring gurgled faintly in the distance, and the grove stood in bloom—unseasonal, undeniable, unforgettable. Nature itself had spoken, and their only task now was to listen, to tend, to keep.

29

LOVE ROOTED DEEP

The grove had already begun its evening hush when the circle gathered beneath the trembling-leaf tree. Twilight draped the ridge in blue shadow, and the new spring gurgled faintly in the distance, as if whispering its blessing to what was about to unfold. Marley stood with Damien at the center, not before a minister or altar, but before the living cathedral of branches and stone that had tested them, broken them, and bound them together.

There were no pews, no aisle. Only moss soft beneath their feet and the spiral clearing that had become their covenant ground. The new keepers—six women drawn from families once entwined with the Order—stood in a half-circle. Each held a sprig of rose, its petals releasing a faint sweetness into the dusk. They were not there as attendants but as witnesses, guardians, extensions of the vow Marley and Damien now came to speak.

Damien's daughter, Sophie, nestled against Mrs. Keene's side, clutching her own tiny rose stem. She gazed wide-eyed at her father, the fear she had once carried toward the grove softened into reverence.

Marley drew in a breath and let her hand slip into Damien's. His palm was warm, his grip steady. For so long, she had feared holding too tightly to love, certain it could be taken, consumed, or tested until it broke. But tonight, beneath the canopy of leaves that had remembered her vows across lifetimes, she felt no fear. Only release.

Damien began. He reached into his pocket and withdrew a compass, the same one Marley had been gifted when the town first began whispering about their engagement tea. He held it in both hands, then placed it between them.

"This," he said, his voice carrying into the quiet, "has pointed in every direction but true north since the day we stepped into this grove. It spun at your dreams, at the circle's whispers, at the Lunaflare's bloom. I thought it was broken. But I see now it was only waiting for us to set direction together. My vow is to follow where you walk, to steady when you falter, and to record not only what history shows, but what love reveals."

Marley's throat tightened. She touched the compass lightly, its cool brass warming beneath her fingers. Then she reached into the small pouch tied at her waist and withdrew a single seed—smooth, dark, no bigger than her fingertip.

"This is from the Lunaflare," she said softly. "It carries light even when buried, promise even when unseen. My vow is to plant what we are together, not in fear of losing, but in hope of sharing. To let roots deepen even when storms bend us. To grow a love that does not end with me, or with you, but flows forward like this spring into soil that needs it."

The seed lay against the compass in her palm, the two symbols touching. The witnesses lifted their roses, and Mrs.

Keene began to circle them slowly, scattering petals across moss. The air filled with scent, then with smoke as another of the keepers lit a bundle of dried rose stems, the fragrance spiraling upward in a thin column.

The circle of women did not speak. Their silence was deliberate, a blessing of stillness rather than word. They closed their eyes, each bowing slightly, as though the grove itself had hushed them.

Marley's heart swelled. For once, she did not cling to the fear of absence. She saw her late relative, Aurelia, all the women of the ledger, and even Mirabel Colvin's regret folded into the soil. Every vow, every loss, every flame and fracture—they were not hers alone to bear.

Damien squeezed her hand. "We don't need rings," he said quietly, only for her. "We have roots."

Marley nodded, tears wetting her cheeks. She looked into his eyes and saw not only the man who had grieved, who had doubted, who had feared for his child, but the man who had chosen to stay, again and again.

"Everything sacred," she whispered, "is shared now."

The grove answered with a sigh of wind, branches leaning inward, the spring bubbling louder as though to mark the vow.

And so, beneath the central tree, compass and seed bound in their palms, they sealed what had been growing long before either dared to name it: love rooted deep.

The silence held.

It was not the fragile quiet of hesitation, but the kind of silence that thickens into substance—where every heartbeat, every breath, becomes part of the liturgy. Marley felt it press around her shoulders like a cloak, steady and weighty.

She did not shrink beneath it. For the first time in her life, she recognized silence not as absence but as presence multiplied.

The six women of the circle raised their roses higher, the blossoms trembling in the dim light. Each petal seemed to catch what little moonlight had managed to pierce the canopy, glowing faintly pink and red, hues of life itself. Mrs. Keene moved again, sprinkling more petals in a widening arc, until the ground beneath Marley and Damien was thick with them, like a carpet. The air grew heady with their perfume.

Sophie slipped free from Mrs. Keene's hand and padded forward, her small rose stem held like a torch. She looked at her father, then at Marley, her gaze solemn and unafraid. Without prompting, she placed the rose across the compass and seed. Her gesture was awkward but sure, and when she stepped back, Marley felt tears burning her eyes.

"Blessing doesn't come from words," Mrs. Keene said softly, her voice breaking the silence without shattering it. "It comes from witness. We've seen. We've held space. That is enough."

One by one, the women moved closer. They circled Marley and Damien, weaving a pattern with smoke and steps, each pausing to touch their joined hands briefly, as if sealing the vow with human warmth. Each woman left something small behind: a sprig of thyme, a smooth river stone, a folded scrap of cloth with initials inked faintly. Their offerings joined the compass and seed, building a small altar born of memory and present love.

Damien looked around, wonder softening his features. "This isn't just our vow," he whispered to Marley. "It's theirs too."

Marley nodded, her throat tight. "And theirs before

them." She thought of Aurelia's apprentice vow, of her own hands digging into soil across lifetimes. How many ceremonies had layered upon one another here, each one carried into silence, never erased? This was not hers to own. It had never been hers to own.

The smoke of roses thickened, rising like incense. For a moment, Marley thought she heard voices beneath it—low hums, perhaps memory, perhaps imagination. Damien's camera hung forgotten at his side. He didn't dare raise it. He seemed to understand instinctively that to document would be to diminish. Some vows could not be captured, only lived.

Marley's gaze drifted to the spring visible beyond the spiral. Its water glimmered faintly, reflecting the rose smoke like liquid glass. She remembered the ledger's phrase: *Only in circle shall the breath of balance return.* Tonight, balance had indeed returned—not in perfection, but in participation. Every life gathered here bent toward a shared center.

Mrs. Keene raised her hands, palms outward. The others mirrored her. Marley and Damien followed, their compass-seed altar cradled between them. The air pulsed.

"Keeper of Seed and Flame," the women intoned together, their voices finally breaking silence in unison. Marley startled. She had not told them of her dream—of the title whispered beneath the blood moon. Yet here it was, alive on their tongues, spoken without rehearsal, as if it had been seeded into them.

Marley's knees buckled. Damien steadied her instantly, his hand gripping hers tighter. Tears blurred her vision, but she managed to lift her chin. "I do not hold it alone," she whispered. "Not anymore."

The grove answered. A gust swept through the trees, scattering rose petals upward instead of down. They rose in a spiral, carried on unseen current, then drifted across the pool until the surface rippled with pink. Fireflies emerged from the underbrush, tiny lanterns floating among smoke and blossoms.

Marley felt herself opening, surrendering—not to burden, not to isolation, but to union. Her legacy was no longer hers alone to guard. It belonged to every hand raised tonight, every witness, every keeper past and present. Even the grove itself seemed to breathe with them, its roots carrying the vow deeper than soil.

She looked at Damien through the blur of tears and light. "I'm not afraid anymore," she said.

His eyes shone with quiet certainty. "Because it's shared."

The silence that followed was different now—lighter, more buoyant, like soil loosened for planting. Marley closed her eyes, leaning into it, into him, into the circle that had remade her vow.

She no longer feared losing. Love rooted deep was not a fragile flower—it was a tree whose roots had always reached beyond her, holding her steady whether she knew it or not.

And with that realization, Marley surrendered completely.

The hush after Marley's surrender seemed infinite, stretched thin between earth and sky. Then, without prompting, the first of the keepers stepped forward. Mrs. Keene, her rose stem now stripped bare of petals, knelt and pressed the thorny stem gently into the soil beside the compass and seed. Her voice was steady, though low.

"I embody Healing," she said. "For what has been torn, for what has been lost, for what aches unseen. May the grove remember that mending is not weakness, but strength."

The air seemed to bend around her words, the smoke curling tighter before loosening again.

Next came Chelsea, the librarian's granddaughter, her dark braid loose across her shoulders. She set down a river stone, smooth and unassuming, placing it carefully beside Mrs. Keene's thorny stem.

"I embody Balance," she whispered. "For every tilt of flame, a root. For every silence, a voice. For every loss, a return. May the grove hold the scales even when we do not."

The stone gave off a faint warmth when Marley's gaze lingered, as though Balance itself had been acknowledged.

The third keeper, Leona, who had always spoken little and listened much, unfolded a small square of paper. She placed it atop the altar of offerings. Ink bled faintly in the dim light.

"I embody Memory," she said. "This is a letter from my grandmother, written but never delivered. Her regrets live here, but so does her love. May the grove remember us truthfully, not perfectly."

Marley's chest constricted. Memory was the thread that had always bound her here, the whispers, the dreams, the ledger. To hear it claimed aloud steadied her in ways she hadn't expected.

One by one, the others followed.

"I embody Truth," Vickie declared. "Even when it cuts. Even when it stains."

Another, who had barely spoken during gatherings, stood in silence for a long time. Then she cupped her hands around her mouth and exhaled nothing but a long, steady breath.

"I embody Silence," she said. "Because silence, too, is part of vow. May it be kept holy."

Finally, the youngest of them, Sophie, stepped forward. She carried a lantern lit with beeswax flame. She set it down beside the compass and seed, its glow reflecting across their joined faces.

"I embody Light," she said simply. "That which guides, that which warms, that which exposes."

Now the altar was complete: thorn stem, stone, letter, drop of blood, silence, flame. Around it sat the compass and seed—direction and promise—offered by Damien and Marley together.

Marley trembled. Not from fear, but from the magnitude of belonging. For years she had carried the sense that her legacy was a solitary weight. Tonight she saw clearly that it was communal, woven into others who had stepped forward not because they were asked, but because they chose.

Damien brushed his thumb over her hand. "This is covenant," he whispered.

The grove itself seemed to agree.

The wind shifted, rising not in a gust but in a slow, resonant swell. Branches swayed, not chaotically but in rhythm, as if answering some inaudible chant. The rose smoke spiraled upward in a column, unwavering. The spring burbled louder, water spilling gently into the spiral path, trickling in rivulets that caught moonlight like silver threads.

Then it happened.

The tree above them, the trembling-leaf that had witnessed vows across centuries, shed its leaves in a single motion. But they did not fall with autumn's death. They glowed faintly, each leaf shimmering like the Lunaflare petals. They drifted downward not in chaos but in spiral, mirroring the path carved in stone.

The women gasped. Sophie clapped her hands once, then stilled, her eyes wide. Damien did not lift his camera. No lens could contain this.

The leaves settled gently on heads, shoulders, palms. One landed on Marley's cheek, warm against her skin as though it had been lit by inner flame. She pressed it to her lips, tasting earth and light at once.

"It has sealed us," Mrs. Keene whispered.

Marley nodded. She felt it too—the grove had accepted, affirmed, inscribed their vow not just in memory but in living witness. The leaves glowed for a few moments longer, then dimmed into ordinary green again. But they remained scattered across them, proof enough that the grove had spoken.

Marley turned to Damien, her heart unclenching fully. "We are rooted," she said.

He smiled, tears glistening in his eyes. "And we are shared."

The circle closed around them, the seven keepers standing shoulder to shoulder with Marley and Damien at the center. There were no more words. There didn't need to be. The grove's sign was enough.

When the spring finally quieted and the rose smoke thinned, they descended the ridge together, the compass and seed still pressed between Marley and Damien's palms.

Behind them, the trembling-leaf tree stood bare yet radiant, its vow renewed, its memory anchored. The grove had reclaimed itself weeks ago. Tonight, it had claimed them in return.

And no one present would ever forget.

30

LEGACY IN BLOOM

The morning the papers were signed, Marley stood on the courthouse steps with a satchel tucked beneath her arm and the steady hum of voices around her. The Brookwood Healing Trust was no longer dream, no longer whispered plan—it was legal entity, born of ink, witness, and will. A foundation rooted not in property rights but in shared covenant.

The mayor herself had signed, though reluctantly, and three council members who once muttered about "cult sites" now stood among the first donors. Their signatures had been pressed by tide of public support, by photographs Damien captured of the grove's luminous bloom, by testimonies from the seven women who had stood in silence with Marley beneath the trembling-leaf tree.

The Trust's charter had three guiding principles: preservation of ecological balance, education through guided retreat, and protection of Brookwood's ancestral memory. Marley had spent long nights drafting it, Damien editing by her side. Mrs. Keene contributed phrasing drawn from the ledger, Clara from old family archives. The wording was precise: the grove was not to be owned, but held in steward-ship—"a living archive of soil, breath, and flame."

As Marley stepped away from the courthouse, townsfolk gathered. Some clapped, others simply bowed their heads. She felt their energy press toward her like sunlight breaking fog. It was not adoration—it was acknowledgment.

Damien reached for her hand. "It's done," he said.

"No," Marley whispered. "It's just begun."

THE FIRST RETREAT was planned for the solstice. Invitations went out to families of the Circle, to local teachers, to scholars who had once dismissed oral lore as folklore. Marley insisted the gathering not be spectacle but instruction. "The grove is not theater," she told the planning committee. "It is classroom, sanctuary, and healer's table all at once."

On the morning of the solstice, they climbed the ridge in silence. Dozens of townsfolk trailed behind Marley, Damien, and Sophie. Children carried pouches of seeds. Elders leaned on walking sticks carved with old sigils. A historian from Portland clutched her notebook like a talis-man, while a botanist from the university carried vials but kept her head bowed.

The grove met them in full bloom. Herbs spilled across the spiral like ink strokes. The spring reflected morning light in gold. The trembling-leaf tree shivered though no wind stirred.

Marley gathered them at the spiral's edge. She spoke not as Keeper, not as heir of Aurelia or apprentice of dream, but as neighbor, daughter, woman who had learned that legacy was only whole when shared.

"We come here not to watch, but to join," she said. "The

soil remembers us when we plant, the trees remember us when we breathe, the water remembers us when we cup our hands. Today we remember the grove—and each other."

She knelt and pressed her palm to the soil. Damien followed. Then the others bent low, until the circle of bodies mirrored the circle of stones. For a moment, no one spoke, and the silence of vow returned, not heavy but full.

Then Marley stood, lifted a pouch of seeds, and tipped it into her palm. Small, ordinary specks against her skin. She held them up. "Every child here will plant one," she said. "So the grove will carry your name in root."

The children's eyes widened. They shuffled forward, each receiving seeds into small hands. Damien passed them gently, his camera slung behind him, forgotten. Marley watched as tiny fingers dug holes, pressed earth, patted soil with care. The spiral path filled with new promise.

When the last child stepped back, Marley scattered the remaining seeds at the center. She pressed her lips close to the soil and whispered:

"We remember. We root. We rise."

The words sank into earth, carried by roots and water, by breath and silence.

And the grove answered.

THE PLANTING WAS ONLY the beginning.

When the last seed had been pressed into soil, a stillness fell over the grove. It was not unlike the hush that had lingered after Marley and Damien's vow, but this was broader, woven of many threads. Children huddled together, brushing dirt from their fingers; elders leaned on canes or stones, their eyes misted not just with age but with recognition.

It was Mrs. Keene who broke the silence. She stooped down, laid her palm against the soil where a child's seed had just been planted, and whispered, "My grandmother walked this path. She told me stories I never believed. I believe them now."

A murmur spread through the gathered. One by one, others bent low, pressing their memories into the ground.

"I was married beneath this ridge," another woman said. "We thought the grove cursed then. Now I see it was waiting."

"My father used to tell me the trees whispered when storms came," a man added, his rough hands cupping a fistful of soil. "I thought it was nonsense. But when my son dreamed of fire last winter, I heard it too."

The children, shy at first, began mimicking the elders. One boy, freckles bright against his skin, whispered, "I found a feather here once, white as snow. I kept it. Maybe it was yours, Grove." His sister giggled, then knelt to add, "I told my doll the trees could hear me. Maybe I was right."

Their words, halting, playful, solemn, became a litany. The grove received them without distinction—child or elder, skeptic or believer, grief or joy. Every memory poured into soil until the ground itself seemed to pulse with inheritance.

Marley stood at the center, her journal pressed to her chest, breath trembling. She had imagined preservation: charts, maps, guided paths. What she witnessed now was not preservation but expansion. The Trust was already larger than her vision. It was becoming a vessel for stories that would otherwise fade, roots woven with human breath.

Damien stepped beside her, his camera still slung, but unused. He had not taken a single photograph since the planting.

"You're not recording?" she asked softly.

He shook his head. "Some things are meant to live only in memory. If I took it, I'd risk stealing it."

She looked at him, then back at the circle of voices. "Then we'll write them. Together."

She opened the journal and knelt. Each time someone spoke, she recorded their words—not polished, not cleaned, but raw and alive. *I found a feather. My grandmother walked this path. The trees whispered when storms came.* Each line a root, extending the circle beyond stone and spiral.

When the children saw her writing, they crowded close. One tugged her sleeve. "Can I draw it?" he asked.

Marley smiled and tore a page free. "Yes. Show the grove how you see it."

Soon, little hands scrawled flowers, trees, spirals, suns. The journal filled with sketches and shaky words: *seed, rose, light.* The elders added initials, family names, dates. Mrs. Keene pressed a petal between pages. The Trust was no longer just legal charter or idea. It was alive in ink and soil, preserved in voices that had carried through centuries.

As twilight deepened, fireflies appeared, swirling like punctuation around the gathering. Children chased them, shrieking with laughter, while elders sat back on their heels, content. The spring bubbled steadily, reflecting a sky strewn with stars.

Marley closed the journal and held it to her chest. She felt its weight, not as burden, but as heartbeat. "It's larger than me," she whispered to Damien.

He nodded, his hand finding hers. "That's the point. It always was."

Her gaze swept the grove—petals, smoke, laughter, silence. For the first time since stepping into Brookwood's mysteries, Marley did not fear what came next. The Trust had already grown roots deeper than she could measure.

It belonged to them all now.

THE SEEDS HAD BEEN PRESSED into soil, children's laughter echoing across the spiral path, when the grove gave its reply.

At first, it was subtle—a shift in the air, as though every leaf had inhaled at once. The trembling-leaf tree stood motionless, though no breeze stirred, its branches drawn taut as if listening. Then the spring at the grove's heart surged, spilling with sudden clarity. The water ran bright as glass, carrying flecks of light not reflected from sky but born from within.

Marley felt it before she saw it. A low vibration thrummed beneath her knees, rising through her body, as though the earth itself had laid a hand on her spine. She pressed her palms into moss. The hum deepened, and she whispered into soil the words she had claimed:

"We remember. We root. We rise."

The children fell silent. One by one, their gazes turned upward.

Above the spiral, light unfurled. Not flame, not firefly, but a veil of luminescence rippling like dawn's first edge. It hovered above them, pale green and silver, casting soft glow on each upturned face. The petals the women had scattered earlier lifted from the soil, rising into that light. They circled once, twice, then scattered gently across the children's hair and shoulders.

Gasps broke the hush. Mrs. Keene fell to her knees. Damien gripped Marley's hand so tightly she thought their bones might fuse.

"The grove accepts," he whispered, his voice breaking.

Marley's heart pounded. She felt her chest expand with something larger than breath, larger than her own name. It was not possession, nor was it burden—it was belonging. The words returned to her, not from her lips but from the air itself.

We remember. We root. We rise.

The children echoed it instinctively, their voices rising high and clear. "We remember! We root! We rise!" Their chant wove into the humming earth until the line between voice and soil vanished.

Then the final sign came.

Where the seeds had been planted, small shoots broke the surface—too soon, impossibly soon. Green tendrils stretched toward the luminescence. Not every seed, but enough: seven shoots, one for each child who had pressed soil with solemn care. Their leaves trembled though no wind touched them.

The crowd gasped again, some weeping openly. Marley rose slowly, tears streaking her face. She extended her hand above the seedlings but did not touch. "Grow," she whispered. "Grow with us."

The light above pulsed once more, then thinned into firefly glow, scattering into trees until only starlight remained. The grove exhaled. The spring stilled. Silence returned, full and whole.

No one moved for several breaths. Then Mrs. Keene stood and spoke the truth aloud: "It has sealed us."

Damien finally lifted his camera. Not for the miracle—that could never be captured—but for the faces. He photographed the children, dirt still beneath their nails, eyes wide with wonder. He photographed the elders, bent shoulders softened with awe. And he photographed Marley, standing at the spiral's heart, her journal clutched against her chest, her hair crowned with petals.

When his eyes met hers, he lowered the camera again. Some things could never belong to film. Some things lived only in circle.

Marley turned to the children, her voice steady though her body trembled. "The grove has given its trust," she said. "Not to me. Not to Damien. To you. To us. To all who remember, who root, who rise."

The chant returned, soft at first, then strong as the circle picked it up: "We remember. We root. We rise."

The words became more than mantra—they became covenant.

LATER, when the people dispersed down the ridge, Marley lingered. Damien and Sophie stayed beside her. The grove was quiet again, but not empty. Its silence pulsed like a living heartbeat, the new seedlings glowing faintly in moonlight.

Marley knelt, pressing her hand over the soil. She whispered one final time, only for the earth: "Legacy is not mine to hold. It is ours to grow."

The soil was warm beneath her touch.

And she knew, with certainty that settled into marrow, that the grove's story—her story—would not end here. It had only begun to bloom.

EPILOGUE: THE GROVE'S LEGACY

The first autumn after the Trust was founded arrived softer than most. The hillsides of Brookwood did not flame with fire or thunder with storms; instead, the season unfurled slowly, as though time itself had taken Marley's whisper—*We remember. We root. We rise.*—and decided to linger in each syllable.

The grove, once cloaked in secrecy and bramble, now welcomed steady streams of visitors. Children in field trip clusters, elders leaning on the arms of younger kin, historians with notebooks, botanists with sketchpads—all moved along the spiral path that Marley and Damien had once entered in hesitation.

But no one entered alone. That was the first rule the Trust had inscribed: *The grove is circle, not line. It must always be walked together.*

Marley often stood at the entrance, her hands tucked into her shawl, listening to the mingling voices. Some visitors prayed, some sang, some murmured fragments of memory. Others said nothing, only walked. She welcomed each, for the grove did not demand words, only presence.

Damien captured moments—not the grand visions of glowing leaves or impossible blooms, but the quiet ones: a child dropping a pebble into the spring, two strangers holding hands while kneeling in the soil, an elder tracing sigils onto bark. His photographs, displayed at the town hall, had become silent ambassadors. They reminded Brookwood that the grove was not spectacle but mirror: it reflected what people brought to it.

At home, Sophie's laughter filled their evenings. No longer plagued by whispers that frightened her, she spoke of the grove as if it were an old friend. She drew its spiral in chalk on the lighthouse stones, pressed petals into her schoolbooks, and asked her father endless questions about Aurelia Ward.

"Will the grove remember me too?" she asked one night, curling into Marley's lap.

"It already does," Marley answered, pressing a kiss to her hair. "Every seed you planted carries your breath."

The question haunted Marley nonetheless. The Trust was secure on paper, yes. The townsfolk had rallied, yes. But legacy was not measured in signatures or charters—it was carried in children's questions, in whether future generations would feel what she felt when she pressed her palms to moss. Would they still kneel? Would they still listen?

One evening, after leading a small circle of healers through guided meditation, Marley lingered long after the others had gone. She placed the compass on the ground, then the seed she and Damien had exchanged in their vow. She whispered her question into soil:

"What if they forget?"

The silence did not reply in words. Instead, a single Lunaflare petal drifted into her lap, though the season for its bloom had long passed. Marley wept quietly, relief flooding her. The grove had already written memory deeper than time.

THE FIRST SIGN that the Trust had taken root in Brookwood was not in charters or ledgers but in the schoolhouse.

Miss Talbot, the town's primary teacher, began walking her students up the hillside once a week. At first it was only science—observing plants, sketching leaves, comparing bark. But soon she folded in story. She read aloud from the ledger Marley had transcribed, told of Aurelia Ward's circle, of women who once stitched secrets into petals and whispered truths beneath branches.

The children absorbed it not as history but as belonging. They pressed their palms to stones and asked questions that adults rarely dared: *Do the trees know our names? If we sing, will the ground remember?*

Parents, at first skeptical, began to join. By winter, families were bringing picnics to the spiral path, choosing to share meals where once they had feared shadows. The phrase "meet me at the grove" entered common speech, no longer coded or whispered, but ordinary as "meet me at the café."

IN THE EVENINGS, the café itself hummed with change. Conversations that once orbited gossip or politics now circled back to soil and memory. People traded herbs gathered in the spiral, seeds passed hand to hand, stories once left unspoken. A carpenter designed benches for the grove. A stonemason offered to carve sigils on waymarkers so no one would lose the path.

At the council hall, debates softened. The councilwoman who had once threatened to close the hillside now stood among its defenders. "It is not cult," she declared at a town meeting. "It is culture. Ours." The chamber applauded, and even those who had muttered of superstition found themselves carried by the tide.

The Trust's meetings grew crowded. Farmers, shopkeepers, historians, children—all claimed a voice. The bylaws expanded to include seasonal festivals, youth apprenticeships, and elder councils. Marley often sat silent, marveling as the structure outgrew her hand. This was no longer her vision. It was theirs.

DAMIEN WATCHED it all with a photographer's eye, but also with something softer. He saw his daughter come home with dirt beneath her nails and stories on her lips, stories of Aurelia as if she had walked beside her. He saw Marley's shoulders ease when others took up the work she once thought she must carry alone.

One night, he stood with Marley on the lighthouse balcony. The town glowed below them, the grove a darker silhouette against the hills.

"It's strange," Damien said. "Every mystery we uncovered felt like it wanted to stay hidden. And now, here we are—ending not with secrecy, but with inheritance."

Marley leaned her head against his shoulder. "Maybe that was the grove's test all along. To see if we could turn mystery into memory without breaking it."

He thought of his late wife, of her sketches of spirals, her notes about "a breathing cathedral." He thought of the ledger entries, the exiled names, the fractures healed through circle. "She would have loved this," he murmured.

Marley's hand tightened in his. "Then she does. The grove remembers her too."

By spring, Brookwood was no longer the same town. The grove's spiral echoed in its school lessons, its art, its prayers, its laughter. The compass of the Trust pointed steady, no longer spinning.

Marley realized then that the mystery had not ended. It had become legacy. And legacy was not a conclusion—it was a root that kept growing, deeper and wider, long after the story's last page.

It began on an ordinary evening, the kind no one expected history to choose.

The town had gathered for the midsummer festival, a new tradition seeded by the Trust. Lanterns hung from branches, tables spread with bread and berries, fiddles tuning against the backdrop of cicadas. Children darted through the spiral path, their laughter echoing into twilight. Elders sat together, telling old stories now woven with new certainty.

Marley moved among them, greeting each with warmth. She carried the healer's journal pressed close, its pages swollen with years of entries: petals, initials, whispered memories caught in ink. Damien followed at her side, his camera resting but his eyes alive. Sophie tugged at her father's sleeve, urging him to hurry—"The moon's almost here!"

As the last rays of sun dimmed, the grove shifted.

The air cooled, though no breeze stirred. The lantern flames steadied, every wick burning without flicker. Then, from the heart of the spiral, a glow unfurled. It began at the spring, the same that had bubbled since Aurelia's time. The water shimmered pale gold, as though moonlight had seeped upward through stone.

Gasps rippled through the crowd. Children crowded forward, their eyes wide. Mrs. Keene clutched Marley's arm, her voice trembling. "It remembers."

From the water's surface, a bloom rose.

Not a Lunaflare—though its glow was kin to that rare flower—but something broader, wilder. Its petals unfurled in layers, each catching the moonlight differently: silver at the edge, green at the core, flecked with gold at its heart. It rose higher than a child's head, yet delicate as breath. The air filled with fragrance—not sweet, not cloying, but clean, like rain after drought.

The bloom pulsed once, and a sound followed.

It was not a bell, though it rang. Not a song, though it carried melody. It was resonance, low and deep, rolling through soil, through trunks, through bone. People pressed hands to their chests, startled to feel their own hearts beat in time with it.

Marley fell to her knees, tears blurring her sight. She heard the words again, not from her lips, but from the grove itself:

We remember. We root. We rise.

The crowd took up the phrase without hesitation. Children shouted it. Elders whispered it. The voices rose together, woven with the resonance until the grove itself became choir.

Damien caught Marley's gaze, his eyes fierce with awe. He lifted Sophie into his arms, and she shouted the words too, her small voice carrying like an arrow into night.

The bloom opened further, scattering seeds into the air.

Not heavy, not falling, but drifting like stars loosed from their moorings. The seeds landed on shoulders, on palms, on soil. Wherever they touched, tiny green shoots appeared, glowing faintly before settling into steady growth.

The spiral path lit with these seedlings, each new stem bending toward the heart of the grove as if bowing.

"It is sealing us," Marley whispered, her voice breaking. "It is giving itself to all of us."

No one contradicted her. They could all feel it: the circle completed, not by secrecy, but by inheritance. What had once hidden now flourished in plain sight, not diminished but multiplied.

THE BLOOM REMAINED UNTIL DAWN. When the first light touched its petals, it folded gently back into the spring, leaving only ripples behind. The seedlings remained, scattered across the grove like living lanterns, their glow faint but steady.

That morning, the townsfolk did not leave in haste. They lingered, kneeling to touch the new shoots, whispering blessings. Children tried to count them all; elders argued about which tree or stone they had sprouted beside. No one claimed ownership. All understood: the grove belonged to itself, and by its grace, to them.

Damien captured one photograph as the bloom dissolved, but only one. The rest he left untouched, a secret between soil and witness.

Marley closed her journal, pressing her palm over its cover. She no longer feared forgetting. The grove had made its promise, not to her alone, but to the circle, to the town, to every child yet to kneel here.

As they descended the hillside, she whispered once more: "We remember. We root. We rise."

And this time, the words did not echo—they answered.

So the Brookwood Mysteries ended, not in unraveling or silence, but in bloom. The town carried its inheritance into every dawn thereafter, each voice part of the circle, each memory pressed into soil. The grove lived, and because of it, so did they.

The End

AFTERWORD

A Reflective Legacy

The Brookwood Mysteries began, as so many stories do, with silence.

It was the silence of a bookshop whose shelves held more than novels—the silence of Clara's vow, of words written in margins, of echoes that could only be heard when someone dared to listen. Marley stepped into that silence not as an intruder but as an inheritor, though she did not yet know it. *The Bookshop Secret* showed her—and us—that history breathes through the most ordinary doors, waiting for hands brave enough to turn the lock.

From there, the path wound into resonance. *The Bridge of Echoes* carried voices across time, testing whether past promises could be trusted in the present. Each echo reminded Brookwood that memory is never idle—it insists, it demands, it shapes. Marley and Damien began to realize that listening was not passive but covenant: if they carried the echoes, they must also answer them.

The Lighthouse Prophecy shifted the gaze outward, to signals cast against darkness. It asked: what do we guard, and what do we guide? In that season, the town learned that prophecy is less prediction than mirror. The light did not foretell what must be—it illuminated what already was: a community standing on the threshold of its own forgotten story.

The Winter Bell gave voice to stillness. A bell that should have rung but didn't, a vow that had been broken, a bride whose absence echoed for decades. Silence again—but this time charged, asking whether absence could be as loud as sound. Marley and Damien discovered that love and loss, entwined, toll not as ending but as call.

And now, *The Hidden Grove* has revealed itself as culmination, not simply continuation. The stones, the spirals, the ledger, the seed—all mysteries unfolded into memory, and memory unfolded into inheritance. What began as secrecy became community. What began as whispers became vows. What began as one woman's step into a bookshop became an entire town's covenant with its own roots.

Brookwood's Legacy

The mysteries were never puzzles to solve, never riddles to conquer. They were invitations—to listen, to remember, to rise. At every turn, Brookwood asked its people a single question: *Will you keep what was entrusted to you, not as possession, but as promise?*

Marley answered yes. Damien answered yes. The townsfolk, hesitant, divided, afraid—they too answered yes.

And so the series does not close on a solved case or a quiet denouement. It closes on a circle, still widening. Children's hands pressing seeds into soil. Elders whispering names into bark. A grove alive with bloom and resonance.

The mysteries of Brookwood will always remain, not

locked in secrecy but alive in inheritance. And so, the circle holds:

We remember. We root. We rise.

Brookwood Mysteries
Book 1 - The Bookshop Secret
Book 2 - The Bridge of Echoes
Book 3 - The Lighthouse Prophecy
Book 4 - The Winter Bell
Book 5 - The Hidden Grove

ABOUT THE AUTHOR

Jordan Jace is a Pacific Northwest author whose mysteries and heartwarming tales are set against stunning landscapes. With a deep connection to the PNW region's natural beauty, Jace infuses each story with the magic of misty mountains, lush forests, and tranquil coastlines. Jace believes that joy can be found in the smallest moments and the most unexpected places. When not writing, Jace is exploring the world, seeking inspiration in every corner for the next unforgettable story. Discover more at visionsinprint.com